Praise for

THE JASMINE THRONE

"*The Jasmine Throne* pulls you under, sweeping you away on a current of gorgeous prose and intricately imagined magic and politics. It left me breathless."

—Andrea Stewart, author of *The Bone Shard Daughter*

"Raises the bar for what epic fantasy should be. Tasha Suri has created a beautiful, ferocious world alongside an intimate study of the characters who will burn it all down."

—Chloe Gong, author of *These Violent Delights*

"Tasha Suri writes the female characters I didn't realize I was aching to see in fantasy, to devastating effect. *The Jasmine Throne* is a fiercely and unapologetically feminist tale of endurance and revolution set against a gorgeous, unique magical world."

—S. A. Chakraborty, author of *The City of Brass*

"Suri astounds with the spellbinding epic fantasy that launches her Burning Kingdoms trilogy....A fierce, heart-wrenching exploration of the value and danger of love in a world of politics and power....This is a blade-sharp, triumphant start to what promises to be an exciting series."

—*Publishers Weekly* (starred review)

"*The Jasmine Throne* is an intimate, complex, magical study of empire and the people caught in its bloody teeth. It's about resistance and power, histories both personal and political, and the heroes who must become monsters to survive. I loved it."

—Alix E. Harrow, author of *The Once and Future Witches*

"This powerful series opener will undoubtedly reshape the landscape of epic fantasy for years to come."

—*Booklist* (starred review)

"Gripping and harrowing from the very start."

—R. F. Kuang, author of *The Poppy War*

"This is a powerful and intense opening to an epic trilogy.... Lush, evocative, richly characterized, emotionally dense, with a scope that at first seems intimate and turns out to be much, much larger. Suri's skill—never minor—here seems to have taken a step or three up: there are few epic fantasies I have enjoyed, or admired, as greatly."

—Tor.com, Liz Bourke

"A riveting and gorgeously written tale set in an intricate, expansive world. [The characters] will live in my imagination for a long time to come."

—Genevieve Gornichec, author of *The Witch's Heart*

"Like the magic in this tale of reclaiming power, *The Jasmine Throne* will work its way under your skin with Suri's compelling characters and gorgeous, effortless prose."

—Sam Hawke, author of *City of Lies*

"A masterpiece. *The Jasmine Throne* is the powerful, female-centric series I've hungered for—with deftly-woven prose and a pair of glorious women destined to wreck your heart."

—Heather Walter, author of *Malice*

"Lush and stunning.... Inspired by Indian epics, this sapphic fantasy will rip your heart out."

—*BuzzFeed*

"*The Jasmine Throne* more than lives up to the hype with its rich and expansive world, compelling characters, cool magic system and Suri's excellent writing, which holds it all together."

—*BookPage* (starred review)

By Tasha Suri

THE BURNING KINGDOMS

The Jasmine Throne

The Oleander Sword

THE BOOKS OF AMBHA

Empire of Sand

Realm of Ash

THE
OLEANDER
SWORD

BOOK TWO OF
THE BURNING KINGDOMS

TASHA SURI

orbitbooks.net

Copyright © 2022 by Natasha Suri
Excerpt from *The City of Dusk* copyright © 2022 by T. S. Sim

Cover design by Lauren Panepinto
Cover illustration by Micah Epstein
Cover copyright © 2022 by Hachette Book Group, Inc.
Map by Tim Paul
Author photograph by Shekhar Bhatia

Orbit
Hachette Book Group
1290 Avenue of the Americas
New York, NY 10104
orbitbooks.net

First Edition: August 2022
Simultaneously published in Great Britain by Orbit

Orbit is an imprint of Hachette Book Group.
The Orbit name and logo are trademarks of Little, Brown Book Group Limited.

The publisher is not responsible for websites (or their content) that are not owned by the publisher.

The Hachette Speakers Bureau provides a wide range of authors for speaking events. To find out more, go to www.hachettespeakersbureau.com or call (866) 376-6591.

Library of Congress Cataloging-in-Publication Data
Names: Suri, Tasha, author.
Title: The oleander sword / Tasha Suri.
Description: First edition. | New York : Orbit, 2022. | Series: The burning kingdoms ; book 2
Identifiers: LCCN 2021060522 | ISBN 9780316538565 (trade paperback) | ISBN 9780316472661 (hardcover ; library edition) | ISBN 9780316538534 (ebook) | ISBN 9780316538541 (ebook other)
Subjects: LCGFT: Novels.
Classification: LCC PR6119.U75 O44 2022 | DDC 823/.92—dc23/eng/20211217
LC record available at https://lccn.loc.gov/2021060522

ISBNs: 9780316538565 (trade paperback), 9780316472661 (hardcover, library edition), 9780316538534 (ebook)

Printed in the United States of America

LSC-C

Printing 1, 2022

For my family

PROLOGUE

KARTIK

"Have you ever seen a girl of greater purity, my prince?"

Those words were not meant for Kartik, but he heard them all the same. High Priest Hemanth stood with his head bowed close to the young prince's ear. His voice was pitched low, but his words still carried. That could not be helped. The High Priest's voice was rich and unmistakable—a vast thing, neither loud nor soft, but *pervasive*. It was a voice made for mantras, for song, for guidance. For pouring faith, like wine, into the cup of a waiting heart.

The two of them, priest and prince, were standing in the gardens of the imperial temple, birds trilling in the trees above them, and the wind swaying the branches. All of that noise was just loud enough to mask Kartik's presence: his small, surprised stutter of breath, and the motion of his broom, scraping up a cloud of dust from the marble path.

He stepped back, into the shadows of the temple wall, his broom clutched tight in his hands. He hardly dared to breathe.

The High Priest spoke again. Gentle. Coaxing. His hand upon the young prince's shoulder. The words reached Kartik's ears like leaves falling onto steady waters: a soft collapse followed by a ripple of motion that ran right through him.

"Will you protect her? Will you guide her, so that she may keep her goodness?"

That was how priests often asked questions, Kartik had learned. Questions mildly phrased that demanded answers clawed from the marrow of a man's bones, the deepest blood of his heart. And sure enough, the young prince nodded slowly and said, "Yes. Of course I will. What kind of brother would I be, if I didn't save her from tarnish?"

Kartik waited for them to leave. Finished his chores in a kind of numb, ecstatic haze. His hands were steady, but his vision was a blur of lights and color. He walked across the temple floor, seeing everything with new eyes: the sandstone of the walls, carved with flowers; the gossamer curtains that filled every door and alcove, billowing in the wind. On every surface he saw the High Priest's words echoed back at him, rewritten, remade, calling him.

Have you ever seen a girl of greater purity?

Kartik should not have heard those words; should not have carried them with him in the aftermath, inked indelibly into his own skull, as shining and constant as prayer song. But he had a mind made for knowledge, or so he had always been told. When he had been only a boy, and a disciple in a lowly Saketan temple to the faceless mother, his ability to recite hundreds of mantras and prayers from memory—and the Book of Mothers in its entirety—had drawn High Priest Hemanth's attention, and led the High Priest to pluck Kartik from his old life. His mind had led him here: to Harsinghar, and its jasmine-veiled palace, and the imperial temple where he now served.

To the temple garden where a boy in training for his faith may stumble, unwitting, on the second prince walking alongside the High Priest, speaking of the imperial princess herself, and feel a truth reverberate through him that he did not yet fully understand.

She was here, at this very moment. In the temple hall, the young princess was kneeling before the statue of Divyanshi. All five mothers of flame—every single noblewoman who had willingly burned, giving her life to break the power of the yaksa and bring an end to the Age of Flowers—were depicted in the prayer hall. Four of them were arrayed in a crescent, their figures carved from gold: Ahamara, with her long hair loose around her, coiling like flame; Nanvishi, a star of fire blooming from her forehead, her palms outspread; Suhana with a broken bow in her hands and her face upraised; and Meenakshi, face lowered in prayer, hands clasped.

Divyanshi stood at their center, her statue taller than the rest, grandly wrought, with silver flowers trailing her arms. She stared forward, proud and beautiful, her golden face serene. The princess, kneeling at her feet, was entirely in her shadow.

The princess pushed a garland of flowers toward the statues of the mothers. The garland was deftly made, each blossom pierced through the heart with pristine white thread and gathered close to the next. Jasmine, a mingling of yellow and white, caught between weighty pink roses. He had seen those roses left as offerings so often that he recognized them as the ones the emperor's wife grew in her own private garden.

Even in the vicinity of the temple, people gossiped. As if they did not know how their voices wafted in through windows. *A beauty*, they called her. *One day she'll break hearts. The emperor will want to watch her closely.*

But he didn't listen to gossip. He listened to truths and secrets. Kept them, and learned from them.

He listened now, as she bowed her head and whispered to the mothers. She could not see him, where he stood in the shadow, his broom still in hand. But he could see her. Hear her, and know.

It was then—when he was only a boy—that he began to see the shape of the future in a way even the High Priest did not. And though the High Priest's question had not been for him, in his heart he answered it.

No. He had never seen a girl of greater purity. Never, in all his life.

MALINI

A rider returned from Ahiranya on the day Malini first glimpsed the sea.

An army on the move had a particular, unpleasant stench: of horse-flesh and elephant dung, sweating men and the tang of iron under hot sunlight. Malini had hoped, over weeks of travel, that she would grow accustomed to it. But she had not. Every time the wind blew, and the thin curtains surrounding her chariot billowed back and forth, Malini smelled it all anew.

The breeze that carried the ocean with it cut through the smell like a shining knife. It was a sharp scent, bitter with salt. She stood taller in her chariot when she felt it touch her cheek—reached to draw her curtain aside and let the wind reach her unimpeded by cloth.

Without the fabric clouding her vision, she could see the army that surrounded her: warriors from Srugna, with maces hefted over their shoulders; Saketan liegemen with liegemarks emblazoned on their sashes, and whips coiled at their waists; Alorans with chakrams at their wrists, riding alongside Dwarali archers on their white stallions with blood-red saddles; and her own Parijati forces, ringed around her, dressed in imperial white and gold with their sabers bare, the steel gleaming beneath the sun. This was her army, the combined forces of the city-states of the empire, that would help her unseat her brother and seize the throne. *Her* throne, by right of blood and of prophecy.

And over their heads, she could see the thinnest trace of blue.

The sea.

She had known she would see it eventually. Before Aditya had rejected his birthright one time too many—before Malini had been named empress—the handful of lords who had stood in staunch support of Aditya had made plans for their forces to meet and follow the path to Dwarali, keeping to a route along the coast wherever possible, land that was under the purview of those less loyal to Chandra. They had intended to make their way to the Lal Qila: a fort on the edge of the empire, built to withstand attacks from the nomadic Babure and Jagatay who lived beyond the empire's borders. A fort, they hoped, that was strong enough to keep Chandra at bay too.

Malini had seen no reason to alter plans long in the making; plans that *she* had helped to form, with carefully placed suggestions and cajoling letters, in her time as a princess of Parijatdvipa under Chandra's thumb. But still, there had been something viscerally satisfying about watching her army grow, as foot soldiers and elephant cavalry had joined them along the journey; as new lords had welcomed her arrival on their lands, swearing loyalty and opening their villages and havelis to Malini's men, feeding them and arming them, and sending their own heirs and warriors to join the growing procession heading to the distant Lal Qila.

Even facing lords who were more reluctant to ally with her had been its own kind of pleasure. To watch them stand proudly against her and then crumble when faced with her army, her allies, the steadiness of her smile? That had done more than any flattery or veneration ever could to blunt the edge of the constant hunger in her: the writhing, burning craving that would only be sated by Chandra's death.

So many distant plans were finally blooming to life before her eyes—and not in Aditya's service, but in her own. After the hard, endless work that had gone into the making of them, her plans now moved like a force of nature, like waves that swelled and grew, each one feeding into her rise to power. It was *exhilarating*.

As she gazed at the sea, she mused that if she had been a woman of greater faith, she would have considered her glimpse of it a sign: that her army was itself a vast and unstoppable sea. That nothing could stand in the way of her fate. But she had more of a pragmatic nature.

She took a more practical interpretation of the sight, instead. When she had gazed at maps of the empire and charted the route with her eyes and her fingertips, she had known her army would touch the coast when they were a mere week from Dwarali's borders. Now they were here—breathing in a greenness of salt, a cold breeze that moved through the army and made a few men pause, raising their sweat-slick faces to capture that coolness on their skin. They would reach Dwarali soon, and the Lal Qila soon after that. The next step in her rise to the throne had almost begun.

Next to her, Lata let out a noise of quiet awe.

"Have you seen the sea before?" Malini asked. She could feel Lata craning her head to catch a glimpse of it over Malini's shoulder. Obligingly, Malini leaned back to allow it.

"In scripture," said Lata. "Illustration in books. Art. But not in person. And...and you, my lady?"

"You know I have not," Malini replied. She waited a moment longer, then let the curtain fall back into place. "There are plenty of rivers and lakes in Parijat, but the imperial mahal is as distant from the coast as it's possible to be."

"A shame," Lata said, "that we cannot stop and admire it."

"The men will need to rest eventually," said Malini. "No doubt we'll have our chance then. Perhaps we can even go swimming." She could *feel* Lata's look, at that. "I'm sure they will all turn their backs respectfully if I ask them to."

"You're making a joke," Lata said dubiously.

"Clearly not a very good one," Malini said. "Of course we'll do no such thing."

But she would have liked to. She thought, with wistful grief, of Alori and Narina. Her heart sisters would have loved the sea. Narina would have walked in the water ankle-deep only, holding her skirt up with both hands. She had always been far too careful of her clothing to do more. Alori would have waded in deep, slipping into the water like a fish. Alor was full of as many rivers as Parijat, and her brothers had all taught her to swim as well as they could.

I miss you, she thought, speaking to nothing in the quiet of her heart. *I will always miss you.*

Unbidden, the thought of Priya rose in her mind, as it so often did. What would Priya think of the sea? She could not imagine Priya out there. In her mind's eye, all she could see was Priya as she'd been in the forest, waist-deep in water, hair sleek, loose, and soft in Malini's hands. The feel of Priya's mouth against her own.

She tucked the thought carefully away, like a treasure.

That night when Malini's tent was erected, there was no time to admire the coastline, and in truth Malini had not expected there would be. She was relieved, almost, that there was not. It would not have been the same without her heart sisters. Better to leave it as a dream.

The most senior—and loyal—of Parijatdvipa's highborn joined her for the evening meal. Wine was brought out in carafes of beaten metal, and tea for those who did not imbibe: small cups, rich in milk and sugar and cardamom. The food was simple but far more lavish than what was being fed to the rest of the men: fresh parathas, dhal thick with ghee, and rice heaped with onions fried a deep, lustrous gold.

There were special dishes, occasionally, to please the palates of different highborn: sharply spiced sabzis for the lords of Srugna had been brought out today; these were a particular favorite of Lord Prakash, who was one of the oldest lords in attendance and made no bones about being set in his ways and his tastes.

Malini listened attentively as Lord Mahesh, the man she had named as the general of her army, informed her of the progression of their journey. She maintained her posture, her calm, and touched barely anything—not even the wine, though the sip she had brought to her lips had left heat in her blood. Lata was seated in the corner of the tent. Watching. She was Malini's only female companion; the men all thought her present for the sake of propriety.

It was a curiously difficult business, to uphold the image of propriety and prophecy and goddess-chosen empress. *Especially* when you were eating. She had seen her own father deep in his cups, staining his clothing—but then, her father had been an emperor, and Malini was—not. So she ate only sparingly, knowing she would have a proper meal later, when the night was cold and deep, and she and Lata could share food intended for common soldiers: a little pickled mango or onion practically stoppered in oil for a long journey, and a paratha gone dry, unsoftened by a golden sheen of ghee; a quick gulp of lukewarm tea, spiced so heavy-handedly that it burned almost unpleasantly on the way down.

"Prince Rao is absent again, I see," said Lord Mahesh.

He did not speak loudly enough for the other highborn to hear him.

"He has his responsibilities," Malini replied.

"We all do," Mahesh said. "One of them—a most vital one—is this. A moment of bonding. Of discussion. We must be united, Empress. Moments such as this are what make us whole." He gestured at the men around them, wreathed in soft lantern light.

It was amusing to hear Mahesh speak of bonding and unity, when Malini was herself so conscious of how different she was from the men around her. How carefully she had to hold herself apart, and how distant she felt from them. They were of use to her, and she liked them for that, of course. But they were not Alori or Narina or Lata. Not Priya. She did not know how to love them, truly love them, and had no desire to.

"Lord Mahesh," Malini said. "You know, as I do, where Prince Rao goes."

A shared look. Without breaking eye contact, Mahesh refilled his cup of wine.

"Do not mistake me, Empress. I am glad he is able to counsel and comfort Prince Aditya. I would be glad if the prince allowed others to do the same."

Mahesh was a powerful figure in Parijat, with many highborn Parijati allies, due to the ancient standing of his family—his ancestor had been there when Divyanshi, and the mothers of flame that followed her, burned.

Ever since, they had been a family known for its military prowess and its religiosity.

And Mahesh had always been loyal to Aditya, not Chandra; had unwaveringly supported the idea of Aditya taking back the throne he had abandoned. His refusal to agree with Chandra's form of faith had won Malini followers she would not otherwise have had.

She had chosen him as her general for all those reasons. His presence at her side was an advantage.

But his affection for her brother was a . . .

Well. Not exactly an irritant. But a potential problem in the making, for all he had been unfailingly respectful of her. Respect did little good if she could not grasp control of his loyalty and bind it to her permanently.

"You sought him out again?" Malini asked.

"He refused my company. As he refuses everyone's."

Everyone's but Rao's went unsaid. And Malini's, of course.

"My brother feels adrift," she said. "He seeks to focus upon his relationship with the nameless, and find a new path for himself. When he finds his way, he will surely welcome the comfort of old friends and allies."

"Perhaps you can speak to him, Empress."

"I do," said Malini. "And I shall." *If he refuses to listen*, she thought grimly, *then that is his own business.*

A rustle of cloth. A guard drew back the tent flap.

Yogesh, one of the military administrators who managed her army's supplies, entered and bowed low. He was dressed plainly, in a turban and sash-bound tunic, but even if she had not known him by sight, the single chakram on his wrist and the dagger neatly tucked into his turban wrapping would have marked him as an administrator from Alor, and accordingly loyal to Rao—and through Rao, to her.

"My sincere apologies for the interruption, Empress. My lords." The light of the oil lanterns flickered over his face as he tilted his head in Malini's direction. "But an urgent messenger has arrived for the empress."

Her heart gave a sudden thump.

She had many, many riders in her service. An empress needed even more eyes and ears than a princess, and Malini had ensured that she would have spies and messengers across the breadth of the empire. Not a day passed without word from allies arriving or departing, carried by men on horseback.

But among all these riders, she had used only one of Rao's loyal men. And that man had been tasked with one particular journey.

An urgent message could have been anything, absolutely anything; and yet, the presence of Yogesh and no other administrator, and the meaningful look on his face, made hope grasp her insides.

"Well then," she said, and rose.

Mahesh gave her a grave look, half rising himself.

She waved a hand.

"Enjoy your meal. There's no need to stop for my sake."

"Empress," Yogesh said, ducking his head in respect. "The messenger is in Prince Rao's company. I can ask for him to be sent to you immediately—"

"No need," she replied. "Take me to them." Better to have this conversation with Rao present; she'd learned that messengers did not respond well to being spoken to directly by a prophecy-blessed empress, and she could not see Rao alone in her tent, even with Lata and guards for company.

The tent the military administrators shared was full of books and ledgers carried from site to site, expertly wrapped in scented cloths that kept the paper from rotting in the heat or rain and repelled the various insects they encountered. As she entered there was a scramble of bowing, papers dropped. She ignored the commotion, seeking out the messenger.

She saw Rao first; dressed up in his princely finery, with his brace of daggers and his chakrams, speaking to a broad-shouldered, very nervous-looking Aloran man.

When they saw her, Rao bowed; the rider scrambled to press his face to the earth.

"Rise," Malini said to both of them, and they did, though the rider kept his face lowered.

"What news?" she asked Rao.

"Ahiranya has new rulers," said Rao. "The regent is dead."

Lady Bhumika? she thought. *Priya?* She had hoped. Hoped—

"Tell me what happened," she said.

The man looked too awestruck to talk, so Rao said, gently and firmly, "Tell the empress."

Priests, he told her, ruled now in Ahiranya. No, not priests—temple elders, like the days of old. Or people who claimed to be temple elders. Two women were among them. "Some say the High Elder was once the regent's wife," the rider said.

"Who told you so?" Rao asked.

"People talk," he replied. "Merchants and—people in the city. People on the road."

"You did not see them directly?"

"No." He hesitated. "But..."

"Go on," said Rao.

Everyone knew, he said, that the temple elders were truly what they claimed to be, because since their rise to power the forest around Ahiranya had grown stranger than it ever had been. He'd heard tales of trees turning and twisting as if they were alive, *watching* people pass them by. Emperor Chandra had apparently sent a small group of scouts, then another, to test Ahiranya's borders. A fruitseller, who regularly traveled in and out of Ahiranya, had found a dozen imperial soldiers dead, speared on thorns as thick as a man's arm. The rest were simply never found.

The rider himself had never seen any violence. Only Ahiranyi living their lives as they normally did. The merchants he'd seen—a reluctant handful at most, who went out of desperation and necessity rather than desire—had traveled through Ahiranya unharmed. And the rider had gone unharmed himself, of course. But he had seen new soldiers on the streets—not the regent's men in Parijati white and gold, but groups of men and women in plain, mismatched armor, carrying sickles and bows instead of traditional Parijati sabers.

Malini could feel Rao watching her. He knew something of her relationship to Ahiranya, if not everything. No one, not even Rao, was owed everything. But he knew she had been saved by the Ahiranyi; knew she had a bond with them.

"Thank you," she said to the rider. "Go with Yogesh, and you'll be rewarded."

Coin, and a warm bed to sleep in and food; and she would make sure he was watched, to see if his information was handed to anyone else.

When she returned to her tent, she called Lata to her side. "I'll need you to scribe for me," she said.

As Lata sought out ink and paper and lit a candle, Malini began to search for the right words; the politically expedient words—something to affirm her support for Ahiranya, something that would tell Lady Bhumika and Priya, and anyone they had allied with, that she had not forgotten what she had promised them, once she had her throne.

The best emphasis she could give her words, of course, was action. Once this letter was done, she would send others to her allies in Srugna and the estates that bordered Ahiranya, encouraging them to maintain strong trade ties with the new temple elders. The forest might have grown strange—stranger even than when she had known it—but the rider had made no suggestion that it was dangerous to anyone but Chandra's men. Surely, then, the forest and all its strength lay in Lady Bhumika's control, and Priya's. And Priya, at least, she trusted. She could not entirely help herself.

She wanted to tell Priya that she had not forgotten her.

But forgetting or not forgetting Priya was not a political concern. It was a thing of her heart: the husk of a flower she wore on a chain around the throat. It was the memory, preserved green and shining in her mind, of the two of them lying by a waterfall, gazing at one another, water glinting on Priya's dark hair, her smiling mouth.

She should have banished the thought. But she did not. Instead, she decided she would ask Rao for his rider again. She would send a discreet message.

One for the elders of Ahiranya. And one . . . not.

She told Lata what to write, and Lata did so. This letter, exquisitely formal and written in Lata's careful, elegant script, would pass under the eyes of a military administrator, and the lords who served her.

But the letter for Priya would not. And she wanted to write it with her own hand.

"I can write this message for you too, my lady," Lata said, when Malini took up ink and paper.

"This one will not be seen by the lords tomorrow," Malini said.

Lata was silent, but her silence was pointed. It made Malini laugh faintly. She raised her head.

"I know there are no true secrets," she said. "But there will be nothing to trouble them in this, should it fall into their hands. And even an empress may send a kindly letter now and again, to an old ally."

If anything, Lata's face grew graver. She had spent a great deal of time with Malini on this journey. She knew more of Malini's heart than anyone, though Malini had not spoken of it.

"There is a saying, among the craftsmen and women of Parijat who turn bronze and gold and stone into effigies of the mothers," Lata said. "They say, when a statue is first wrought, it shines so brightly, any man may look upon it and see a mother divine. But all things tarnish, when the rain falls upon them."

"Poetic," Malini murmured.

"Empress," Lata said, in a quieter voice. "You have a golden tale surrounding you. Do not allow it to weather so soon."

Malini thought again of the men kneeling before her. The sun beating overhead. Their voices chanting. Empress Malini. Mother Malini.

"It will tarnish one way or another," said Malini. "And I need to start telling new stories to replace it. Make sure the letter is given to Rao's rider when I am done. And give him coin enough to encourage his discretion."

Lata argued no more.

Malini should not write it, she knew.

But she wanted to.

I have looked upon the ocean, she wrote. *And it made me recall the tale of a river. And of a fish, searching for a new world on its bank.*

And I remember a tale of garlands. And ill stars. And two people who found their way to one another.

Tell me, do you remember it too?

2

PRIYA

Every root and every inch of green in Ahiranya's soil sang to her. She heard the song all the time—sleeping, waking. Felt its weight as if she were the limb of a much larger beast, a giant thing slumbering in Ahiranya's trees, its earth.

She closed her eyes, the sun touching warm fingertips against her face through the thick canopies of the trees. Slivers of cool shadow broke the heat into fragments. She didn't need to open her eyes to find her way. The song guided her. The soil yielded to her footsteps, rippling like water. *This way*, it hummed. *This is where you will find what you're searching for.*

"If you don't look where you're going, you're going to walk straight into a tree," said Sima.

Priya opened her eyes and turned to give Sima a glare.

"I *won't*," she said. "I would never."

"Oh, maybe not, but it'd be very funny if you did," Sima replied. "Aren't you meant to be exuding holiness and authority? It'll be very hard to do that if you're felled by a branch."

"*Sima.*"

Sima grinned at her.

"It might be best to keep your eyes open just in case."

Priya was, in fact, meant to be maintaining a certain image. Even though she'd known today would be messy work, she had dressed in the plain whites of a temple elder. For practicality she had donned a salwar kameez rather than the traditional long tunic, but the loose cloth was bleached white as bone, and her hair was bound back in a high braided knot with beads of sacred wood darted through its length, here and there, in the same style the temple elders had once worn.

It was Kritika, of all people, who had encouraged her to take up the style. Soon after pilgrims began to arrive in waves at the Hirana's base, pleading for guidance from their new elders, Kritika had taken Priya aside and advised her to dress as the elders had once dressed. *There will be worshippers who remember the elders, as I do*, she'd said. *And for the rest...you must serve as a symbol, Elder Priya. And you must guide them.*

Priya was uneasy with the idea of being a symbol. She was uneasy with Kritika too, and with all the ex-rebels who had once served her brother. But she'd chosen this path: chosen the rebels who now called themselves mask-keepers, and the title of elder. She was far too stubborn to do anything but embrace this life with her arms flung wide. And if the right clothes made worshippers weep tears of reverence, and feel *hope* again, and trust that Priya and Bhumika would rule them wisely? Well, then. Priya would wear white. And she would do her very best to act like the person she was meant to be.

Priya offered Sima only the subtlest and most ladylike of the extensive collection of rude gestures she knew—which made Sima laugh under her breath—then straightened up and squared her shoulders, and kept her eyes open as she strode forward with what she hoped was a confident kind of grace.

Around Priya and Sima, other figures walked between the trees: a few once-born ex-rebels, with traces of magic coiling through their blood and scythes in their hands; a handful of soldiers, carrying sabers; and six of the men and women who had once been servants in the regent's mahal, but now served the two temple elders of Ahiranya in a different capacity. For months, they had been training with Jeevan in the mahal's practice yard, heaving around maces and beating fake soldiers made of wood and straw with hand sickles. Sima had even been given some training in archery, and she carried a bow and a quiver of arrows with her now. She only looked mildly nervous, but some of the other servants were nearly gray with fear. That was understandable.

They were hunting imperial soldiers, after all.

Ganam, one of the ex-rebels, made his way toward her. He wore the same mask he'd worn when he had been a fighter against Parijatdvipan rule: a wooden oval, large enough to conceal his entire face, with crude holes for eyes and a hollow for the mouth. She shouldn't have been able to see the questioning look he was giving her, but she could read the tilt of his head well enough.

Priya shook her head. Not here. Not yet.

Then she turned her attention back to the soil. She felt through it—felt the imperial soldiers ahead of her.

Some were already impaled on stakes of thorn. Bhumika had set up that trap. She had a gift for things grown slow and strange.

And Priya, well—

She had a useful wellspring of anger.

"Now," she said. And they crossed the last wall of trees—and found the soldiers before them.

The fight was quick and bloody.

Priya tried to use her magic to subdue most of them, but one man, disarmed of his sword, wormed his way beyond her vines and tried to grapple her. She had the pleasure of punching him in the face.

He went for the knife at his belt. Tried to gut her.

This is why, she thought—blood simmering, her pulse pounding in her ears. *This is why you're killing them. Breaking them. This.*

The soil pulled his feet deeper. Deeper. His hands were still free. That was no matter. Priya could still attack him with her vines; still see him suffocated, dragged under.

There was a whistle and a thud. An arrow had gone through his throat. She looked behind her and saw Sima, gray-faced, clutching her bow.

"Messy," Ganam remarked. "But the job's done." He straightened, squaring his shoulders. "Elder Priya," he said. "What now?"

They went home.

Priya drew a dark shawl around her shoulders to conceal her attire, then dived into the city's depths with her companions surrounding her.

Invisible in a crowd of soldiers and mask-keepers, she was free to take in the sights around her without having to worry that she'd be recognized and bowed to, worshipped or feared in a way that made her teeth itch with discomfort.

Hiranaprastha's streets were busy around them, noisy and heaving with people. There were food stalls here and there, and groups of children playing, and people squatting in the shade, watching the crowds drift by. Under the blue sky, the city was all churned mud and brightly painted stalls and shops. Empty lanterns hung from verandas, wavering in the mild wind. At night, those lanterns would be filled with candles, and the city would glow like a constellation.

For months, Hiranaprastha had been a shadow of itself—broken by both violence and fire. But the buildings had slowly been fixed or simply put back to use by necessity since then. Priya caught a glimpse of a house with a partially broken wall as they moved through the streets. Someone had strung a curtain of wooden beads and colored glass across the gap. Sunlight through the glass shone green, blue, pink.

Priya turned toward Sima. Brushed their shoulders together to catch Sima's attention. In return, Sima offered her a tentative smile. Her face still had an ashy pallor, but she was starting to look more like herself now that they were nearing the mahal.

"How are you feeling now?" Priya asked.

"Oh, just fine," Sima said. It was such a blatant lie that Priya almost laughed.

She didn't, though. She didn't want to hurt Sima's feelings. She wanted to comfort her.

"It's all right if you feel—conflicted," Priya said. "About killing someone. Or if you're still a little afraid. It *was* frightening."

Sima looked down at her own hand and laughed awkwardly.

"I think maybe I was a little afraid," she admitted. "And I was trying so hard to be brave, too."

Priya knocked her shoulder against Sima's again—as close as she could get to a hug without embarrassing her in front of their companions.

"You did really well," she said. "Trust me."

"Does it ever get easier, the fear?" Sima asked. "Do you start going into fights and just find a way to ignore all of, you know...?" She waved a hand around vaguely. "Or does being powerful the way you are stop you being afraid?"

Priya didn't know how to explain that her relationship with fear had been complicated long before she became thrice-born.

"It helps," Priya admitted. "But you've got nothing to be afraid of, Sima. You've got me."

Ahead of them, Ganam was using his bulk to cut a swathe through the crowd, carving their group a path back toward the mahal. Priya could see it in the distance, looming above the low buildings of Hiranaprastha. Only the Hirana stood taller than it—an ancient mountain with the temple proper at its zenith.

People took little notice of them as they walked, though a few gave them nods of respect. In Hiranaprastha, the patrols that worked for the temple elders had become just as unremarkable a sight as the regent's soldiers had once been. Simply part of the fabric of city life, with all its rhythms and routines and dangers.

"I don't always want to hide behind you, Pri," Sima said ruefully. "Maybe I want to be able to look after you too. Have you considered that?"

"Sima, you literally shot a man through the throat for me," Priya said. "Do you have any idea how impressive that is? I don't mean that you're weak or—or anything like that! I just mean..."

"I know what you mean," said Sima.

"We protect each other."

"I know," Sima said again, her smile softening into something more real. There was almost color in her cheeks again. "I really am getting better with a bow. Jeevan's going to be so pleased."

"Absolutely," Priya agreed. "He'll have you teaching the little ones before you know it."

Sima gave a theatrical shudder. "Don't threaten me with that," she said.

They strode up to the main entrance of the mahal.

"You all did well," Priya said, once they were inside. Took off her shawl and wiped what remained of the dried sweat and blood of battle from her face, her neck. "Does anyone know who is on the next patrol? They'll want to check that no more imperial soldiers are hiding somewhere."

"I'll ask Kritika who volunteered," Ganam said. "I told her I'd join her on the Hirana anyway."

"Then I'll talk to Jeevan," Priya said. The mask-keepers were Kritika's people, just as the ex-soldiers were Jeevan's, and the balance of power was always... *interesting*, at best. Priya was desperately glad that Bhumika was so good at soothing the tensions between all the fragmented groups that made up Ahiranya's new, ragtag government. She had no head for that kind of emotional, tiresome work.

"*I'll* talk to Jeevan," said Sima. "You need to go and wash and change. Aren't you meant to be receiving people on the Hirana this evening? You can't go like that. You'll scare people."

Priya was meant to be on the Hirana later, it was true. Welcoming worshippers and helping the rot-riven. Placing her hands on them, and freezing the rot within them, so it would progress no further. So they would live.

And then, tomorrow, she would be out on patrol again.

"Thank you," Priya said. She gave Sima a grin and turned, intending to hurry back to her own room, where she could change. But instead, she found her feet leading her toward the orchard.

Time to herself was so rare now. And though she didn't exactly have complaints, she couldn't resist the urge to take a moment alone. Just a moment, when she could walk under trees and pluck a ripe fruit from a low-hanging branch, and purge the memory of imperial soldiers and imperial steel with the comfort of being alone in a familiar place.

She had barely stepped into the orchard when she heard a voice calling her name.

"Priya!"

She looked up.

"Rukh," she greeted him, squinting against the sunlight. He was seated on a high branch—leaning forward so he could see her and waving one arm to catch her attention. "What are you doing up there?"

"Nothing," he said. "Want me to throw you a fig?"

"Yes," she said. He chucked one down, and she caught it one-handed. Bit straight into it. Between bites, she said, "You're hiding, aren't you?"

"'Hiding' is a strong word," Rukh said. "I said hello, didn't I? If I were hiding, I would have kept quiet."

"I know you're not hiding from *me*. You're meant to be in training."

"Do you want anything else?" Rukh asked helpfully. "I can climb a different tree if you like. Any tree."

"Jeevan is going to skin you."

"He would never," said Rukh. "He's too nice. He'll just make me run around the practice yard."

Nice wasn't a word Priya would have applied to Jeevan, who was solemn and harsh-faced and unsmiling and seemed to spend all his time hovering around Bhumika or herding his trainees around like cats. But she didn't argue. "Ganam's back."

Rukh's expression visibly brightened.

"Where is he?"

"He's going up the Hirana."

"I'm going to go see him," Rukh said decisively. "Maybe he can train me later. Then Jeevan won't be disappointed."

Rukh and Ganam had been rebels together, once. Rukh had vowed to serve Bhumika and had been saved from death by Priya—that kind of bond stuck. But he and Ganam had grown something special in their shared time in the mahal, and Priya was glad of it. Often, she found the two of them together—Ganam patiently demonstrating the use of a sickle to Rukh, who'd copy him, frowning, all focus.

"Jeevan will still be disappointed, but do what you like," Priya said with a sigh.

Rukh jumped down. He straightened up. Once, he'd been so thin and so small—but even the short time he'd spent in the Hirana had added flesh to his bones and softened his face. He was stronger, taller, his curling hair thick enough now to almost conceal the fronds of leaves growing from his scalp. "Do you want to come?"

She shook her head. "I've had a busy morning."

"Are you going to see Elder Bhumika?" Rukh asked.

"I wasn't planning to," she said. "Do you know how our little grandma is doing?"

"Padma doesn't look like an old lady anymore," Rukh said in his most disapproving voice. "Well. Mostly. She's not crying as much, I think. Khalida said Jeevan got her a wooden bracelet to bite on to help her gums stop hurting."

"Sweet of him," said Priya. Then: "Is there a reason I should see Bhumika?"

Rukh—who'd gained a disturbing interest in knowing absolutely everything—said, "She's got a letter for you in her study. Something from the empress."

A beat of silence. Priya swallowed, her heart racing. Finally, she said, "I'm not even going to ask how you know that."

"I was helping Khalida look after Padma. We went to bring her to Lady Bhumika, and I saw it then," he said anyway. "Do you know what the letter's about?"

"Go and find Ganam, you beast," Priya said. "I won't tell Jeevan I saw you unless he asks."

She turned, walking sedately until Rukh—who yelled his thanks with a laugh—had scampered off behind her.

She didn't quite start running, but it was a close thing.

She read the official letter from the empress to the elders of Ahiranya first. It was lying plainly on Bhumika's desk. Bhumika's study was barred to outsiders, but Priya, of course, had a key. Maybe Bhumika had known Priya would wander in at some point and rifle through her papers, and had decided to make Priya's life easier. She often made such small, thoughtful gestures. Sometimes Priya would return to her room and find sachets of herbs to perfume her clothes, or a meal wrapped in cloth, and she knew it was Bhumika trying to take care of her, even as their responsibilities kept them so often apart, like two ghosts haunting the same space, never quite crossing paths.

Next to the official missive, propped pointedly against a pile of books, lay a letter plainly addressed to Priya. It had no official seal of the empress on it—no sign it was from Malini at all. But Priya knew.

That Malini had gone one step further and *written* to her, had put down some of what bound them permanently in ink, was—well. It made Priya feel soft and tender, and stunned by Malini's foolishness.

She opened the letter. Pressed it flat. That writing—it had to be Malini's. It was too graceful to be anyone else's.

She wrote of garlands. Of Mani Ara, and her river. And other tales of yaksa and mortals.

"I didn't tell her these," Priya whispered. Which meant that at some point, Malini had read the Birch Bark Mantras. Had she learned the tales for Priya's sake?

Priya couldn't write back. She knew it. Whatever subtle means Malini had used to deliver this to her—and spirits, she hoped they had been subtle, for Malini's sake—there was no way Priya should write to her in return.

But somehow she found herself sitting at Bhumika's desk. Grasping a clean sheet of paper. Writing down words.

I miss you, she began.

MALINI

Malini's appointed room in the Lal Qila was intimate—a circular chamber with narrow windows that opened to the sky, and a low fire burning to maintain heat. The floor was a familiar marble, but swathed in a grand carpet that would have rotted in Parijat's greater heat: a hand-sewn expanse of knotted goat's wool, depicting the moon and stars, and prey animals running across snow. She stared and stared, tracing the patterns with her eyes, sinking into meditative calm, as she waited for Lord Mahesh to bring her his daughter.

She heard a door creak open.

Lord Mahesh entered, and bowed. A girl entered with him. She was a slip of a thing, with an unremarkable face and long hair, a shawl draped over her shoulders to ward of Dwarali's cold, and shadows of exhaustion around her eyes. Her journey to Dwarali must have been grueling. Malini wondered if Mahesh had even allowed the girl a moment to rest before dragging her into Malini's presence.

"My daughter, Deepa," Lord Mahesh said, urging the girl forward with a hand at her back. Deepa stumbled. Bowed hastily. "As I told you, she is a biddable girl, and only a few years your junior. I am sure she will be an able addition to your court."

It was laughable to mention Malini's court when she had none to speak of. Oh, she had her highborn lords and princes, and she had Lata. But she had no court of *women*: no heart sisters to share her secrets with. No elder women or grandmothers to counsel her, and no daughters of allies to foster ties with. That had to change.

"Thank you, Lord Mahesh," Malini said. "You may leave her with us. I'll be sure to make her welcome." Her mouth tilted into a smile. "I know Prince Rao has been searching for you."

"Empress," Mahesh said, bowing his head. Then he turned and departed.

Deepa was still staring at her own feet. The crackle of the fire filled the silence. Lata stood by the hearth and met Malini's eyes briefly, a question in her own gaze. *What are you going to do with her?* Lata's eyes said. *What use is this girl to you?*

"What are your skills, Lady Deepa?" Malini asked. Deepa's head darted up.

"Skills, Empress?"

"Yes," Malini said patiently. "What do you bring to my service?"

Deepa lowered her eyes again, clearly embarrassed. *Look at me,* Malini wanted to stay. *Show me your strength. Do not be timid for my sake.*

"I like to read," Deepa admitted softly after a moment. "To study. I am not a good musician or—I don't tell very good jokes. But I can work. And I like numbers. If... if you need anyone for such work."

Numbers and scholarship. Those were not the skills taught to a daughter intended for marriage.

"Good," Malini said, as if she did not have a dozen military officials to hand, and more arriving daily, to do such work. "You can assist Lata, then."

"I am Empress Malini's sage," said Lata then, nodding in acknowledgment. "I will be glad of your help, Lady Deepa."

Deepa stammered out thanks and said, "Anything you or—or the empress needs of me, I am honored to do."

"I am glad to hear, Lady Deepa," Malini said. And then she smiled at the girl. Deepa flushed, clutching her shawl more tightly. "I'm sure you'll find yourself happy here."

She dismissed Deepa. The door closed softly behind her, leaving Lata and Malini alone in the warmth of the room.

"He brought his daughter to spy on you, my lady," Lata said after a moment.

"Of course he has," Malini said easily. "And soon all the highborn lords and princes who have sworn loyalty to me will try and do the same. How else will they win my favor?" She shrugged. "I have nothing to fear from spies," said Malini. "Not spies I am aware of, at least. And I have the measure of Lady Deepa."

A plain girl. Or more specifically, a girl who had been told she was plain. Not the oldest daughter or the most marriageable, but the one her father thought clever enough not to offend an empress.

"She's nervous and frightened, but if she was truthful, then she has a good mind and she'll do anything you ask without complaint. Don't tell me an assistant wouldn't be useful to you, Lata."

"As you say," Lata replied, which was her polite way of saying she disagreed but did not think it worth arguing over the matter.

Malini looked into the flames and thought of Alori and Narina again. The grief worked its way through her, rising like a wave from her heart to pour through her limbs, then ebb once more.

It would be so much easier if you were here, she thought with a pang. *I always knew I could trust you.*

But they were gone. Her heart sisters would never return. She would never have a court full of women who had grown up alongside her, who were written into her soul as she was in theirs. She would have to settle for one with women ambitious enough to see the benefits of allying with her, and clever enough to recognize that betraying her would be the height of foolishness.

She did not have that yet, she admitted to herself. Lata, of course, she could rely upon. But Lady Deepa had not yet proved her worth.

If she wanted better allies—allies with strength and cunning—she would have to seek them out herself.

"I'm going to talk to our host," Malini said, rising to her feet.

"Lord Khalil is patrolling with his men," Lata said promptly.

Malini shook her head. "Not him," she said. "Hand me my shawl, Lata. There's no need to accompany me. I'll soon have plenty of chaperones to guard me."

From the Lal Qila the world beyond the subcontinent was visible like a half-forgotten memory: great mountains, so high they seemed to vanish into pale nothingness; snow, whiter than bone, blanketing mountains green with life. The Lal Qila itself was all deep red stone, tall and imposing, an edifice that seemed to have an ancient life and grandeur all of its own.

Lady Raziya stood at the edge of the ramparts, swathed in a thick blue shawl. Around her stood a semicircle of women armed with bows: female Dwarali archers who traveled with her everywhere. Malini had not lied when she had told Lata she would have chaperones to spare.

When Malini's army had first arrived at the Lal Qila, Lady Raziya—Lord Khalil's wife, and the mistress of the Lal Qila—had greeted Malini's army at the gates on horseback. She had looked like a seasoned general waiting for battle, her face turned toward the full mass of Malini's forces unflinching, her saber gleaming at her hip. Even now, clad in a delicately embroidered salwar kameez with a dupatta laid demurely over her hair, she had the look of a soldier about her. As Malini approached, she turned, and her women turned with her as one, faces alert and spines straight.

"Empress," said Raziya. She smiled, her eyes crinkling. The faces of the women around her did not change.

"Lady Raziya," Malini greeted her. "I hoped I would find you here. May I join you?"

"Of course." The guardswomen moved aside, allowing Malini to stand beside Raziya. "How did you know where to find me, Empress? I would have come to you if you had summoned me."

"People talk." Well. *Maidservants* talked, if they were coaxed appropriately, with a smile from an empress, or a coin from a sage in return for details on the daily routine of the mistress of the Lal Qila. "And I know you would have come, Lady Raziya. But I wanted to see the views here myself." As she spoke, her breath formed small clouds before her. "They're beautiful."

Raziya gave her a sidelong look, assessing and amused.

"Step back," she said crisply, and her guardswomen vanished like ghosts, moving to stand some distance away, their backs turned. Only then did Raziya turn to look Malini directly in the eyes.

"Although I would like to remark upon the beauty of Dwarali to you, and ease you into a discussion of favors," Raziya said, "I find I must take advantage of our privacy to be frank: My husband has intimated that he will follow you into the battle, and all that comes after. That he will follow you until Chandra is defeated."

"He's told me much the same," Malini said.

"I have no wish to remain where he is not," said Raziya. "If you allow me to accompany you, I would be grateful. My sons and daughters are old enough to hold the Lal Qila in our stead."

Malini gazed off into the distance for a long moment, watching the clouds drift slowly by. Raziya's request certainly made things a great deal easier. Malini had corresponded with Raziya enough that she felt as if she had the measure of her: Incisive and thoughtful, Raziya had a huge amount of influence over her husband's political choices.

And Malini already wanted Raziya on her side, in her court. She also knew Raziya was not the kind of woman to act from adoration for her husband alone—and surely she could not think that Malini would believe such of her.

"Is it love alone that compels you?" Malini asked.

Raziya laughed.

"A certain amount of sentimentality drives me," she said. "But no, not love alone. I am ambitious for my family, Empress. I have no shame in it. And it strikes me that in the court of an empress, a woman may rise very far. I am a seasoned leader, Empress. I know politics, and do not fear war. Take me with you, and you will have no regrets. Of that, I can assure you."

"It sounds like I could gain a great deal from having you at my side," said Malini. "Tell me, Lady Raziya. What does a woman of your power and position seek from my service? What can an empress offer you to bind your loyalty?"

"It would be a terrible thing," Lady Raziya said mildly, "for my husband to contemplate turning against the sultan. The sultan is your ally, and rules Dwarali ably. The lord of the Lal Qila is no more than his obedient servant. As the wife of the lord of the Lal Qila, I cannot ask my empress to give my husband a throne. I know some things cannot even be dreamt of without cost."

And yet you dream them regardless, Malini thought. *You have so much and you want more still.*

She could understand that hunger. Admire it, even.

"I am sure Lord Khalil would not reject a gift freely given," Malini said evenly. "When I win the empire in my grasp, Lady Raziya, I will show him my gratitude." How she would take the throne from the sultan, she did not yet know. But it could be done, and would be. Malini kept her promises. "But I wonder: Why dream of power for him, and not for yourself?"

"Empress," Lady Raziya said. "I love my husband. What greater love is there than wanting to lay the world in your beloved's hands?"

It was deep, dark night when an Aloran messenger arrived with a message from Ahiranya. It was worn from travel, dust-stained, and had clearly passed through many hands. It did not have Malini's name on it, but she knew at once that it held Priya's words. Priya's voice.

I miss you, the letter said. Artless words. She could feel Priya in them, and it made her heart bloom with helpless fondness.

Such grand stories you know now! Where did you discover them? Did you seek them out?

I don't know if I will ever have your answer. Maybe it's enough to wonder. Maybe that's what you want, for me to think of you.

There is so much I wish I could tell you. But I have no head for poetry, though I've met it from time to time.

I will say only this.

I made you a promise once. Say my name, and though it makes me a fool—and I know it does—I'll find my way. I'll come.

4

CHANDRA

The first bloom had sprouted in his mother's garden. After the first trees were felled—after fires burned day in and out, painting the sky black with smoke—he had sifted through the ash and found it:

A flower of fire. Proof of the rightness of his rule. An assurance that the bone-deep certainty that had carried him this far was entirely correct.

He was the rightful ruler of Parijatdvipa. And his cause was just.

But his mother's garden had not been enough. As his sister defeated his army in Dwarali, Chandra tended carefully to his flowers. Fields were cleared, and pyres planted with women tied to them, and set alight.

His sister murdered his men at the border of Alor.

He built more pyres and watched his flowers bloom.

He sent men to Ahiranya. The two soldiers who returned came to the imperial mahal with hollow expressions and horrified eyes. They spoke of thorns as large as swords that could run a body through, and vines that could choke the life out of a man. They told him temple elders ruled in Ahiranya. *Monsters*, they said. *Monsters with the faces of women*.

Chandra gathered ash from his fields. Flowers needed soil, and *his* flowers of flame needed the gristle and bone-dust that had made them.

He stood in a room of carefully stored fires, each preserved in its own carved chest of stone on a bed of ashes, and told himself grimly, *My sister must die first*.

When she is dead and gone, I'll show the Ahiranyi their place.

Now, he stood in the heart of the imperial temple. He could smell the pyres even from here, the smoke wafting in through the windows, settling a patina of gray on the flowers that lay at the feet of the mothers, wrought in gold.

In an alcove, veiled by a partition curtain, were two more statues. Mothers Alori and Narina, who had burned before Chandra's eyes. He had visited it today and laid flowers at their feet. Jasmine, for his sister, who had worn it so often in her hair. His sister, who should have burned with them.

It comforted him, being here. Calmed him. He had come to the imperial temple often as a boy—walked through its gardens, his heart and his bones aching with fury at the injustice of the world. To be born a prince of an imperfect empire—to be born second, and never able to change it for the better—had galled him.

His brother Aditya had been a beloved crown prince. Born first, and born perfect: a friendly, smiling creature, good at making allies and fighting with sabers, playing with dice and drinking himself sick. These were the qualities valuable in the heir to Parijatdvipa. Drunkness and frivolous charm. It was no wonder, then, that Chandra had not been admired as his brother had been.

Ill-tempered, Chandra had been called, by his father's court. *Arrogant. Unwilling to bend.*

For a time, he had believed it—had *hated* himself for being unworthy of his blood and his status and power. Whenever his father had offered Aditya praise, or a seat alongside his advisors, and dismissed Chandra without a word or a thought, Chandra had burned with that hate. And still, he had done all in his power to try to improve the world, and received nothing in return for it. When he had punished his sister for ill-bred behavior, she had fled from him in bitter disobedience. When he had reminded his brother's friends of their place with his words and his fists, Aditya had shoved him so hard he had fallen to the dirt. Chandra had been punished by the sages who educated him after that. *This is not how a prince treats his allies*, they'd said, as they had taken a rod to his palms.

They are not my allies, Chandra had thought, remembering the way those boys with their flawed Saketan and Aloran blood had laughed and talked with Aditya, as if he were their equal. There was an insurmountable chasm between their actions and the reality that they were lesser, by blood and by nature, than a mother-blessed imperial prince of Parijatdvipa.

When his brother had come later, with salve for his hands, and tried to speak to him, Chandra had turned him away. Aditya was not his ally either. Aditya, who allowed others to debase him.

Chandra's only comfort had been the High Priest.

You have strength your brother does not. Faith, a righteous heart, obedience to the will of the mothers—these have a value beyond all else. He still remembered the words. Remembered walking around the temple with the priest's hand at his back. A soothing weight.

You will be a great man one day, Prince Chandra. Wait and see. I see the light of the mothers in you.

And Chandra had learned to recognize his own worth.

Aditya—smiling, perfect Aditya—had no room in his nature for the unyielding, fierce weight of true devotion to the mothers of flame. Aditya was shallow and empty. He had never felt the same writhing anger that Chandra felt constantly in his own heart. It was that anger that made Chandra strong. Chandra's so-called ill temper and arrogance were fire and pride, honor and vision. His brother was pitiful and weak and saw only goodness in a world that was rotten to the core. But Chandra—Chandra had the mettle to be merciless.

Chandra was better than him in all the ways that mattered. He always had been.

"Emperor." The voice came from behind him. He turned, and saw the High Priest approaching. Hemanth was a slight, white-haired figure with gentle eyes beneath his ash-marked brow, and an air of serenity about him. His mien of calm never failed to calm Chandra in turn.

"Priest," Chandra said in return. "You asked to meet with me."

"Your wedding approaches." The priest's tone was neutral. "Have you considered quenching the fires before your bride's arrival?"

"My bride should understand," said Chandra. "My fires are burning to save her father, after all. My priests, trained for war, carry it as gifts to his door. Won't she be glad to know that more will come? That her father's reign is secure?"

"I do not believe all women consider practicalities on their wedding days," the High Priest said. A faint smile touched his mouth. "Or so I have been told."

"Some women," said Chandra, "do not understand the price of leadership. She'll learn."

A breeze wafted through the temple again, scattering garland petals at the feet of the mothers, making the oil lamps flicker. Chandra closed his eyes and tried to force thoughts of the war away. His sister, seizing Alor's and Srugna's support. His sister cutting a swathe through Chandra's allies. His sister in Saketa, turning her avaricious eyes on the High Prince, the one ally who had remained true to Chandra through all the hard months since his sister had taken up a false title and ruined herself all the more.

"Emperor," the High Priest said. "There is one more thing we must discuss."

Chandra opened his eyes.

The High Priest's expression was grave.

"You have striven valiantly to save Parijatdvipa from itself," he said. "From foolish men, led by greed and pride. From your brother, who turned his face away from his blood-given faith. From the collapse and decay that comes to all nations that forget their vows and their purity. But I fear that your quest demands a price you do not wish to pay."

"Speak," Chandra said.

"Princess Malini," said Hemanth. "She must burn."

"I promise you she'll die," Chandra replied, feeling that pang of fury again—that desperate hunger to see his sister dead.

If there is anything of you that hears me, mothers, he prayed with love and fury, *then let her die. Let her die in pain and suffering, knowing she is a disgrace to her name. Let her die by my hand. I will push her into the flames myself. I will watch the skin shrivel from her bones, and I will dedicate the flower that blooms from that death to your names.*

"She must *burn*," Hemanth said, with careful emphasis that pressed upon Chandra's anger like a finger to a bruise. "And she must do so as the mothers of flame did: for all our sakes, willingly and selflessly."

"Not all my women burn willingly," Chandra said. And even the ones who had risen to his pyres with glad hearts, sure in their faith, happy to follow in the footsteps of the mothers, had regretted it when the fire began to eat through their flesh. "And still, their deaths bless us all."

"A willing death of a daughter of Divyanshi's line would be a different magic entirely," Hemanth said. "I know you recognize this, Emperor."

The chiding note in his voice galled. If anyone else had spoken to Chandra that way—as if Chandra were a mere child—they would have died seconds later, gutted on the end of his sword.

But Hemanth was different. Hemanth had always been different.

"You believed once that her burning would cleanse her," Hemanth said, pressing onward. "Free her. That it would, in turn, give you the strength to change Parijatdvipa for the better. Has that belief altered?"

He thought of Malini's bare neck, bloodied under his hands. His sister baring her teeth at him like an animal. Ruined beyond repair by her own will, her own choices, even though he had offered her a path to immortality, a meaningful death.

I will never burn for you, his sister had vowed.

"I have my weapons," he said. "I have my marital alliance. I have pyres that will give me gifts, *mother*-blessed gifts, no matter how the women who die for them may scream and claim to refuse me. I have my soldiers, and priestly warriors, and I have you." He looked at Hemanth, suddenly clutched by a desperate fear. "I will not beg her to burn," he said raggedly. "I cannot do it. She cannot—I cannot *think* of her without wanting the world to wither to dust, you understand? I will not give her the satisfaction of my pleading, when I know she will refuse to do what is right. I will save Parijatdvipa by my methods. By my own glory and strength." His hands stung from the bite of his own nails against his palms. He stretched them open and said, "You told me yourself, many years ago. The mothers destined *me* for greatness. The crown fell into *my* hands, because Parijatdvipa is rightfully mine. To rule, *and* to save. Will you stand with me? Will you guide me, priest, as you always have?"

The High Priest's gaze had softened. He touched a hand to Chandra's cheek, and Chandra's shoulders finally released their tension. He sagged. Small with relief.

The High Priest had always been more father to him than his own. Always. At least this, he could rely on.

"Chandra," Hemanth said quietly. "Emperor. You are more than a son to me. If this is the path you wish to take, I will follow you upon it. And I will be glad to be beside you, and proud indeed, when you change the world for the better. When you save us all."

MALINI

Priya,

Of course I sought out grand tales.

I do not like my own ignorance. And those tales were the ones that made you. Surely, you learned them as a child. Surely they were as much the milk that shaped you, as tales of the mothers were for me.

Don't you realize I want to know everything about you? That even now, when I should have forgotten you, all I desire is to know your heart better than my own?

Malini's army made it all the way to the edge of Saketa before the monsoon rains barred their path. No one with any sense battled when the deluge of rainfall swept across the empire and churned the soil to a sea of mud, so her army made camp and waited for the skies to clear.

In the respite from battle, Malini listened to the rain beating against the walls of her tent and wrote letters to Priya that she would never send.

If she were wise, she would burn her own words. If she were wiser still, she would not have written them at all.

But this was her indulgence. She wrote and wrote and preserved the letters carefully in the lining of a jewelry box, unpicking the lining at night so she could read them all over again.

And surely there were worse indulgences than wanting to love someone. To be *known*.

Sometimes I think of my army as a wave. I never placed my feet in the sea when I had the chance, but now I think of my army as the waters that carry me. And my throne—my throne is the inevitable shore.

We have fought Chandra across the empire. In Dwarali. In Alor. He has no gift for keeping allies. He wants people to bow and scrape and beg for his scraps, but why would they, when I have offered them so much more? So his armies crumble, and I stride onward, and bind myself to allies with vows and deals and promises.

I have so many debts, Priya. Debts to my men. Debts to you.

I never forget my debt to you.

Her men huddled in tents and drank wine and played games of chance by lamplight. And her women gathered with her and played their own games. One of the women from Dwarali—Sahar, a broad-shouldered archer with a particularly filthy sense of humor—suggested the singing game, a mischievous light in her eyes. "One bawdy song begins, then the next starts on the syllable that the last ends with, and so on, until there are no more songs, or the players are too drunk to remember them," she said, and cracked a grin at Malini's expression. "Empress, what good is a game if it doesn't allow its player to speak a little filth?"

"I like strategy games," Deepa offered faintly, looking mildly horrified. Raziya poured her a particularly large glass of liquor and slid it over sympathetically.

"I promise you, all the young lords and soldiers will be playing the same game in their own tents," Raziya said, sharing a brief, amused look with Sahar. "And their songs are much less refined than ours shall be."

"As long as I am not required to join in with them, they can do as they like," Malini said dryly.

"But you will play with us, hm?" Raziya said, raising an eyebrow.

Malini could not bring herself to refuse.

It was difficult to remember songs over wine—and more difficult still to find common ground between the songs from Dwarali and the bawdy songs from Parijat. Lata turned out to be the best of them. When Malini woke in the morning, she found herself laughing, at odd moments, at the memory of Lata passionately reciting a full range of rude verses about mothers-in-law from across the empire.

In the daylight hours, as the rains crept on, Malini tried to soothe her aching head and focus on writing letters that brought her very little joy but were nonetheless necessary to achieving her goals.

Experience had taught her that the most successful battles were the ones won by words. Phrases, carefully chosen, could be like a knife: threatening, promising, wounding. She had learned from Lord Narayan, one of the loyal Saketan nobility who had accompanied her from Srugna, that the rot had spread through Saketa. "The rot," he'd said carefully, "is not simply an Ahiranyi problem, as it was once was. The High Prince is a man driven by fear, Empress. Fear of the loss of his throne. Fear his people will starve. But his fears are...not unfounded."

So she set the blade of her words carefully to the High Prince's weaknesses. She wrote to him with the offer of crops from Alor and Srugna to feed his people. The restoration of the loyalty of the low princes who had abandoned him to serve her. New trade with Dwarali. Food and prosperity and a future.

I cannot betray the rightful emperor, his scribe had written in return. *The only hope Saketa and my people have lies upon a righteous path. A path carved long ago, for all of us, by the mothers. I will not stray from it.*

Weeks passed, as her messengers traveled to and fro from the High Prince's fort in pouring rain; as her pile of unsent letters to Priya grew, the language blooming wilder and stranger with honesty. *I miss you,* she wrote to Priya, and to herself. *But not as you miss me, I think. I miss you because I let myself care for you. For a brief time, I let you into my heart. And I find now that I am empress, now that the world lies at my feet, my heart is a closed door. I am meant to be someone beyond mortal feeling—someone shaped by fire and prophecy into more than flesh and bone and want.*

What I was with you, I can never be again.

To the High Prince she replied, *I am the mother's chosen, prophesized by the nameless god. Following me is a choice blessed by the mothers and the nameless god alike.*

Trust me, and all will be well.

On the day the rains cleared, Malini finally received the response she had been waiting for:

He would surrender to her. He would return land to the low princes who had turned on him.

He would trust in the will of the mothers, and in her.

More often than not Malini woke up exhausted, dreams tangled in her skull, Narina's and Alori's voices fading in her ears like distant storm winds. But today she opened her eyes long before the dawn chorus of birdsong to the unfamiliar feeling of hope blooming open in her chest.

Today—if she was lucky, and clever, and all her politicking worked as she had intended—she would take Saketa from her brother's grasp. His last ally would finally yield into her hands.

Malini met the day by bathing from a cold bucket bath. She kneeled to have her hair oiled and combed and plaited to the now familiar sounds of her army awakening: the clatter of pots. The grumbling, low voices of men. The crackle and spit of vats over fires, as the camp cooks prepared the morning meal. As her maid Swati knotted ivory flowers into a crown at her head, as she tucked the pleats of her own sari to knife sharpness, she waited for the familiar rhythmic thump of dozens of booted feet against the hard soil. When she finally heard the soldiers on night duty pass her tent on their final patrol, she released a slow breath and said to her maid, "Prepare the tea and bring the map, Swati."

The women began to arrive, the guard beyond Malini's tent announcing them as they entered: Raziya and her attendant women; then Deepa, with apologies from Lata. "She'll be here soon, Empress," she said. "She was working late into the night—preparing for your meeting with the High Prince. I—I saw her with the Prince from Alor earlier—"

"Thank you, Lady Deepa," Malini said, before the girl could continue.

There was a large table installed in her tent—large enough for the map of Parijatdvipa to be unrolled in its entirety. The map was made of a thick cloth, the borders of each city-state and the farmland and villages that surrounded them embroidered in weighty darts of thick silk. It was an old piece of work, one gifted to Malini by the Sultan of Dwarali himself. The maze fort of Saketa—the High Prince's ancient home—was drawn in swirls like a multi-petaled flower, its thorns held within its bloom. Malini considered it, and considered too how close her goal now was.

Once she had the High Prince's surrender, she would be able to turn her army toward Parijat with no risk of an enemy army at her back. The Saketan low princes and lords who had chosen to serve her would have their loyalty rewarded with new wealth, and with the lands they had lost to the High Prince when they had refused to accept Chandra as their emperor. Her army would have a taste of victory, and Saketan gold, and the promise of a clear and shining path toward Chandra and his army—and the throne.

Once the High Prince was dealt with, she could finally destroy her brother.

The tent curtain rustled once more.

"My lady," one of her guards said, a crescent of his helmed face visible through the gap between curtain and tent. "Prince Rao and your sage are here."

"Let them in," Malini said.

Lata swept in first. Lata's hair was bound back in its usual tight knot of braids, woven into a corona around her head. But she wore a rich sari of fine silk, its dark fabric patterned with deep blue lotus flowers.

She had protested when Malini had first gifted the clothing to her. "This isn't the way of sages," she'd said. But Malini had insisted. "You're a reflection of me. Consider it a responsibility of your new role."

"I am only a sage, still," Lata had said levelly.

"As my advisor, you know that isn't true," Malini had replied, and that had been the end of that.

A moment after Lata, Rao entered and made a brief, courteous greeting. His turban was neat, his sash properly tied, his brace of knives glittering and well-oiled at his belt. But Malini had a strong sense that he had not slept. It was something about the way he held himself: shoulders too tight, eyes pinched and shadowed, his head craned forward as if he couldn't manage its weight.

"Drink some tea," she told him, and he managed a wan smile. "And you too, Lata. I know you haven't rested."

"I had to consider every aspect of your intended pact with the High Prince, Empress," Lata said, even as she obediently took up a cup. "I'll sleep once the work is done." A slight, sidelong glance at Rao. "We both will."

"We have bad news," Rao said. "But not entirely unexpected." He took his tea; drank fast, as if he didn't even taste it. "Our food supplies are decreasing fast."

Malini bit back a curse. Rao was right. She had known this was a possibility. The army was vast, and had to be fed, and supplies from loyal city-states arrived at best unevenly. Her men had begun taking food from Saketan villages and fields by awful necessity. But more often than not, the villages they passed were starving, the fields... wrong.

"Do we have enough food to see us to Parijat?"

It was Lata who answered.

"It's possible," she said. "But we will have to be—careful. And we will have to move on Parijat as swiftly as we can."

Malini left her tent to join the morning war council with her women arrayed around her. She wore her own saber, a gleaming scar of a blade, lightweight enough for her to carry comfortably upon her hip. Lady Raziya and two of her favorite guards, Manvi and Sahar, carried heavier bows at their backs, their gait proud. Together, they walked beneath tasseled parasols held up by attentive Parijati guards, the soldiers going silent or bowing their heads as they passed.

Malini had seen her father walk as she did now, many times, through the halls of the imperial mahal with his sword at his side and his advisors around him, servants and soldiers alike falling into worshipful stillness at the sight. There was satisfaction in following in his footsteps, at least in this.

An emperor's power lay in the wisdom, loyalty, and clout of his closest confidants—in maintaining ties with highborn men from across the empire. A princess's power was demonstrated through her adornment: the weight and shine of her jewels, the flowers in her hair, the beauty of her attendants.

And an empress's power? Well. There had been no empresses before Malini. So she had carved out the rules and requirements of empresshood herself, and hoped that throwing together the authority of one role and the visage of another would be enough.

The war council took place in a vast, circular tent. Near her own seat stood Lord Mahesh, his expression severe. There was no sign of Rao. He had left her, as he often did, long before the war council took place, on his own business.

When Malini entered the space, the men bowed. She arranged herself on the makeshift dais of gold brocade cushions that stood in place of her throne; straightened her spine, and raised her head.

Before Lord Mahesh could rise to his own feet and delve into the minutiae of the negotiation with Saketa's High Prince that lay ahead of them, another lord stood abruptly. He was from Srugna, but Malini was only vaguely familiar with his face, which was not young but still relatively lineless, and twisted in defiant anger.

"I speak for Srugna," he announced.

Malini let her gaze linger, momentarily, on the old, familiar lords who sat behind him. By the uneasy—but unsurprised—looks on their faces, he did *not* speak for Srugna. But he was not acting entirely out of turn either. Lord Prakash, seated behind him, watched with shrewd, thoughtful eyes. Waiting to see what she would do in the face of a challenge to her power, no doubt.

Malini said nothing. She let her gaze fix on the lord once more, as he clenched and unclenched his hands, waiting for her to respond. As if he had the right to her ear. He had already erred, by standing out of turn, by demanding to be heard, by showing her and her council disrespect. Let him continue to lay the wood for his own pyre, if he liked.

Everything about him was clean and polished, the fabric of his tunic new and cut in the latest court style set by the king of Srugna himself, with a narrow sash and angular darts of bright fabric at the shoulder. His skin was pale brown. She glanced at his collar and at his wrists, but no lighter strip of skin was visible.

He was new. Fresh to the war for Parijatdvipa, and full of his own self-importance. Even the highborn who zealously protected their skin had turned sun-brown at the face and hands, after long enough traveling in the open.

The Srugani had sent supplies a mere half month ago. This man must have come with them. Who knew what poison had been poured into his ear, in the Srugani court, before he had come to join Malini, fresh coin and fresh soldiers at his command?

It would be interesting to find out.

"We cannot afford to be generous to the High Prince," the Srugani lord said, when Malini merely stared at him. "If you insist on forgiving a traitor, Empress, Srugna may insist on retreating from a foolish war."

The Srugani lords shifted anxiously. Lord Prakash was the only one who did not squirm. He watched intently, unmoving. But his brow was furrowed.

This threat, then, had not been expected. By him, at least. She was glad he had not condoned it, even if he had not done her the favor of silencing his fellow lord.

To her left, Lord Mahesh was clearing his throat, demanding attention. "You are unfamiliar with war, I think, Lord Rohit. When I have spoken of strategy, you may express your... concerns. But you should not threaten us." His tone was courteous, but there was a warning in his eyes that the Srugani lord would have been a fool to miss.

"We should not be here," the lord burst out. A fool after all. "We should be in Parijat, dragging that dog from his throne. We did not come here to sacrifice our men and our coin to the squabbles between the High Prince and his low kin."

The Saketan princes stood abruptly, one sea of buzzing, angry movement.

"The High Prince is a traitor," one said sharply. "Allied with that dog. We fought for the empress in Dwarali. We fought in Alor. And in return, he seized our lands, our ancestral villages, our taxes. But we would rather win than face unnecessary strife. You think *Srugna* has a right to demand blood from Saketa's highborn?"

"Rohit," one of the Srugani lords murmured, trying to quell him—far too late, in Malini's opinion.

"You would be starving without Srugna," Lord Rohit retorted. "You needed the food from my estates. A significant portion of my crop, taken—and what has Srugna had in return? What? We deserve—"

"You jumped-up fool, you deserve nothing!"

"*Enough*," Malini said.

The men fell silent. Good. At least she had power enough still for that.

"We cannot enter Parijat with the threat of Saketa at our backs," she said, calm and even. Let the truth speak for her. It was implacable, inescapable, and they were—nearly all of them—seasoned warriors. Let them recognize it for themselves. "We cannot leave our allies without peace on their own lands."

She did not say: *We bargained for the loyalty of these low princes, when we fought Chandra's forces in Dwarali, as he threw wave after wave of soldiers against the walls of the Lal Qila, breaking them like waves upon the rocks.* She did not say: *If I break my word, my bond, our efforts to see Chandra deposed will come to nothing.*

This Lord Rohit was owed no explanation from her.

So instead, she said, "Perhaps the Srugani lords wish to inform this lord how he has erred."

"I," began Lord Rohit. His words died as Prakash laid a heavy hand on his shoulder, urging him back down to his seat. The Srugani contingent were gray-faced, jaws tight with embarrassment and anger. Whatever they had hoped to achieve by sending forward Lord Rohit with his bluster and righteous rage, they had not achieved it.

"Empress," said Lord Prakash. He bowed his head. "Lord Rohit meant no harm. If you will show forgiveness..."

The Srugani lord's speech faded as Aditya entered the room.

Malini's eldest brother was dressed, as always, like a priest of the nameless, in a pale blue dhoti, his long dark hair uncovered and tied neatly behind his back. But in place of the traditional shawl over a bare torso, he wore a tight tunic, padded with fabric and panels of metal. Clothing for battle.

This was the only concession he had given to the world he had been unwillingly dragged back into. He would not seek to take Chandra's place upon the throne; would not be the imperial crown prince he had once been, before a vision from the nameless god had led him to a life in the priesthood. But he could not be simply a priest any longer. The saber at his belt, strange against the pale worship blue of his dhoti, clinked as he bowed to Malini, then kneeled at her right.

Malini kept her eyes fixed on the Srugani. Waited, with stony patience, until Lord Prakash remembered himself.

"Our most sincere apologies." Whatever speech he'd intended to make was reduced to one phrase. He bowed again, and at an unsubtle kick to his knee, Lord Rohit scrambled to his feet and bowed also, before lowering himself once more.

In her position, Chandra would have had Lord Rohit's tongue torn from his throat, or arranged him a slow and brutal execution. Her brother had never taken kindly to slights to his pride.

But Malini did not have the luxury of such careless cruelty, and her anger burned colder and slower than Chandra's ever had. She nodded instead, allowing it, and thought, *When this is done, and Parijatdvipa is mine, I will remember you.*

"Lord Mahesh," Malini said. "Please continue."

After a moment, Mahesh began to speak, and laid out the task ahead of them.

As Malini approached her chariot, her army parted around her. Half her forces, arrayed in their armor, kept their eyes on her. She kept her gaze forward and her head high. She could not look afraid.

This was not meant to be a battle. It felt like one. She felt the battle in the pounding of her heart as she climbed into her chariot; in the way her senses sharpened, knife-keen. She heard the creak of the metal beneath her feet, the quiet shudder of her chariot's canopy in the wind. The clatter of hooves as her armed riders surrounded her: a sea of cavalry, carrying Parijatdvipan banners, painfully white under the beating sun.

Lady Raziya rose up onto the chariot beside her, bow in hand. Her guardswomen, on horseback, arranged themselves smoothly into a sickle formation around the chariot.

To their right, Malini's general rose onto his own chariot. Lord Mahesh met her eyes. He gave her a grave nod.

She grasped the rail of the chariot. Her charioteer had his ear turned toward her. Waiting.

"Signal the men," she said to Lord Mahesh.

The chariot shuddered forward. The clatter of armor and hooves filled the air as her army moved across flat, dusty terrain, under a gleaming blue sky, toward the High Prince's fort.

It loomed before them. Small at first, on the horizon, then larger and larger still as they drew closer to its walls.

There was a greeting party awaiting them. A handful of Saketan soldiers. No more than that.

"The High Prince knew we were coming," Malini murmured to Raziya. "Why has he not arranged an appropriate welcome?"

The High Prince was not the first highborn ruler who had been unwilling to bow to Malini. But when they had negotiated their surrender, they had all acknowledged her with ceremony. A proper coterie of warriors and their finest horses. Courtiers. Gifts.

Before her was... almost nothing.

Unease seeped through her.

"I don't know, Empress," Raziya said, sounding similarly wary. She looked to her women. Raised her hand in signal. One of them drew closer.

"Warn the others to be watchful," Raziya ordered.

Malini turned toward Lord Mahesh.

"The High Prince's negligence concerns me. Something is wrong," Malini said sharply, pitching her voice to carry over the churning noise of wheels and hooves. He turned his head, meeting her gaze.

"It is wise to be cautious," Mahesh said. But he did not sound the conch at his belt and call for the attention of his commanders. His chariot continued rolling forward, dust rising in clouds beneath its spoked wheels. "But the High Prince has always been a strange man. I knew him, in our shared youth, and I can assure you he has never cared for pomp or ritual. He will surrender. We must simply wait."

He has not surrendered yet.

If she ordered Mahesh to halt their forces, would he? Could he? She knew an army had its own momentum and could not be easily stopped in its tracks. She turned her head forward, gazing over the expanse of men before her. Beneath her, her chariot shuddered to a slow stop as they neared the edge of the city. She thought of all the High Prince's messages—the fear she had read in them, the anxiety knotted through it all. How she wished she had crossed paths with him at least once during her years in the imperial mahal and taken the measure of him herself. Ink, it seemed, was not enough to weigh the heart of a man.

They waited. Silence growing, wind rippling through the flags of Parijatdvipa that hung from chariots.

The gates of the fort slowly yawned open.

No army emerged. Only one man. The sight was so strange that Malini's own men froze, unmoving, as the gates drew shut once more, barring them from the city.

He was unmistakably a priest. Ash-marked, his expression mild, he crossed the dusty ground that lay before the gates of Saketa. As he walked, a cloud of that same golden dust rose around him, haloing him like motes of light.

Malini's guards did not move.

Finally, a single commander on horseback made his way forward to greet the priest. The ground was silent for one breath, then two.

The commander rode back to Malini and said, "Empress. He wishes to speak with you. On the High Prince's behalf."

"Bring him to me," said Malini.

A susurration ran through the men, sudden as a rippling breeze, as the priest was brought before her chariot.

He bowed in one graceful motion, then raised his head. He was an old man, gaunt and sun-wizened. But his eyes were fierce.

"You will not be allowed to enter the city, Princess Malini," the priest said, by way of greeting. His mouth widened into a smile. "And the High Prince will not be leaving his throne to greet you here."

Ah. So this was a trap.

But what kind of trap? The High Prince was well defended in his city. The fort of Saketa was famed for its complexity, its multiple walls that wound and twisted, covered with watchtowers. It was said that if someone had been able to view the fort from the sky, its structure would resemble a blooming, hundred-petaled lotus. Malini had examined its likeness on her map mere hours ago. To siege the city would be nigh on impossible. To starve out the people within it would cost Malini more than she could afford to give.

If the High Prince had invited her into his palace—if he had surrounded her and her advisors there—then perhaps she would understand the nature of the vise she had been caught within. But this. This, she could not comprehend.

"If the High Prince will not negotiate with me, I can only offer him war," Malini replied.

The priest inclined his head.

"I am a priest, but I am also a warrior," the priest said. His eyes were flint. "Emperor Chandra has not waited idly for the betrayal of his blood siblings, Princess Malini. The priesthood has grown. There are those who pray by fire and kneeling, by flowers and funerary rites. And then there are men like me, who have learned a different kind of prayer."

"Will you raise a sword to me, priest?" Malini asked. She did not allow herself to feel fear or even anger. She had faced worse. And if Chandra had given holy men sabers, and sent them to war with her— well, what did that matter? They would be either poor at faith and politics, or poor at war, and either suited her well enough.

"I am here to serve the High Prince on Emperor Chandra's behalf," the priest said. "I have come, as have my brethren, for the sake of Parijatdvipa. Because I understand sacrifice. But you do not, Princess Malini." There was a sudden, strange urgency in his voice. Distantly, she heard the low wail of a conch being sounded. One of the commanders had seen something.

Another wail.

Something was glinting on the walls of the fort. Archers.

Warning. Danger. *Danger.*

The priest's voice rose higher as the highborn lords muttered and turned their heads, slow to mark the danger; as soldiers drew their shields; as Malini straightened, tense in her carriage, unwilling to show weakness, forcing herself to trust in the defenses surrounding. Next to her, Raziya calmly reached for her bow, nocking an arrow as if she was contemplating shooting the priest square through the eye.

"The mothers of flame blessed their sons," he cried out, words tumbling over themselves. "When the mothers chose to die by fire, their deaths—their sacrifice—were a blessing, an act that summoned magical flame to the swords of their followers."

"We have all read the Book of Mothers," Mahesh said impatiently. He was gripping his saber hard. "Men, restrain the priest—*carefully.*"

"If you understood the nature of sacrifice, Princess Malini," the priest said swiftly, as soldiers surrounded him, "you would do your part, as so many other women have. Willingly and gladly. For your emperor brother's sake."

"Other women," she repeated flatly, as her heart thudded, as a sickening jolt of understanding ran through her.

He stared back at her. The fervent light of his smile had faded, leaching from his mouth to fill his eyes, which were painfully wide and fixed upon her.

"The weapons that shall be turned upon you and all the emperor's enemies are carried in their ashes," he announced with pride. "They burned to save the world. As the mothers burned. You can do no less. Know your place, Princess Malini. And see what women braver than you have wrought."

He raised a hand.

Malini looked up as the gate of the fort opened once more—flung wide to release riders on horseback holding blades that glowed, tendrils of smoke rising around them.

Looked up, and saw the fire begin to rain from the sky.

Her army had faced fire arrows before. They were a weapon of war, and the commander of each branch of the army sprawled across the field before her—horse cavalry, elephant, foot soldier—knew how to respond to such tactics. Even staffs or swords covered in flame could be fought.

But this fire was—wrong.

It bloomed. Winged like birds. Soaring. Jumping from one body to the next, sentient and graceful. As one body fell, it shifted to the next, seeking fuel.

Alive. It was *alive*.

The air filled with the smell of smoke, of burning bodies.

She could see only the barest glimpse of Mahesh, still upright in his chariot, gripping on tightly as his horse careened forward, trampling through the press of foot soldiers ahead of her. Before her and around her, men ran back and forth without direction, some of them burning, the air filled with an awful char and screaming. Malini thought of a line from the Book of Mothers, a line that spoke of holy fire, sentient and twisting and writhing, *its many forked tongues, its wings of flame, did turn hands upon the yaksa, and reduce them to ash, and did not rest, until everything lay dead in its path—*

Malini looked sharply back at the camp. She heard distant cries. Half her army remained behind. *Someone* in the camp would surely have noticed by now what was happening. They would send more men, and swiftly.

She could not allow that. Not against this. They needed to retreat. They needed to *think*.

The chariot jolted. The horse was panicking, rearing up no matter how her charioteer tried to soothe it, his own hands trembling. It jolted again, and once more. Malini was thrown roughly from her feet and against the side of the chariot. She looked at Raziya and saw the woman on her knees, clutching her own skull. Her hand was bloodied.

"*Raziya,*" she yelled, alarmed.

The woman's head shot up. Eyes sharp, still.

"It's no more than a cut," she said crisply. "Get up."

She grasped Raziya hard by the arm. "Down," she ordered, as loud and sharp as she could. "We'll be safer on foot."

Raziya hooked her bow at her back and nodded grimly, grasping Malini in return. The two of them leapt.

Overhead, fire shot through the air. A Dwarali woman's horse was struck by it—Malini heard the awful noise of a dying animal, and the crash as another distant chariot overturned. Raziya stumbled back, dragged aside by one of her women's hands, swearing as a soldier ran past her, racing away from the battle in utter panic. And then Malini saw the horse leashed to her chariot fall, and the charioteer slump, an arrow through his throat. She saw her own chariot tip toward her, with all its wood and metal, its great spoked wheels, the sheer weight of it. Raziya was out of range, Malini was almost sure. But Malini was not.

The chariot was going to crush to her to death.

Pressure, against her body. Her feet going out from under her. She had no time to even be afraid, as a soldier shoved her bodily forward, propelling her away from the chariot.

She heard a terrible noise. The crunch of bones. She heard his breath punch out of him with the smallest sound, more surprise than agony. And then he went still.

His body was beneath the chariot. Only his head and one out-stretched arm exposed. He was dressed in Parijati white and gold. He was one of her own soldiers. Numbly, even as the sound of screaming and fire filled her ears, she removed his helm. His eyes were open, his mouth parted. The hair bound in a high bun, away from his face, was knotted.

A priest's hair. A priest's face.

Another priest, she thought with a kind of hysterical surprise. By the mothers, had *all* priests of the mothers taken up armor and blades? Why had one chosen to try and kill her, and another chosen to die for her?

"Empress." Raziya barked. Her voice was ragged, frayed in a way Malini had never heard before. "Empress Malini. We must move. Come on now."

She would. Just not yet. Not yet.

She found herself leaning closer to the priest. Turning his out-stretched arm over. It was partially bare, the sleeve of his tunic ripped. She saw marks on his arm—Saketan script, blurred ink in skin—

A hand gripped her by the shoulder, hauling her up. The guards-women had surrounded her, and two soldiers had joined them, sabers drawn protectively. Their horses were gone. She tried not to think what had become of the poor creatures. Raziya looked down at her, face bloodied and pale, her gaze focused on Malini, so fierce that it forced Malini to focus on her in return.

"Empress, we must go," said Raziya. "Right now."

"Return to the camp, Lady Raziya," Malini heard herself saying. She hardly knew her own voice. It was raw, scraped thin as if she had been screaming. "I must call for our retreat." Why had Mahesh not called for them to do so already? Why were her men still trying to *fight*? "A conch. I need a conch."

"Empress," one of the soldiers choked out. "If. If you fall..."

"Empress, what can you do here?" a Dwarali woman demanded. "That is—that is the *mothers' fire*—"

She ignored those voices. With some difficulty, she raised her eyes, looking upon the immediate dangers surrounding her: the dying horses, the dead man beside her, the soldiers and guardswomen watching her wide-eyed. The fire, leaping from body to body, like a thing with mind and hunger and a mortal's cruelty. She watched, with a kind of glassy numbness, as a man was swallowed whole by flame. As he fell to his knees, and then what remained of him fell further still, the fire leaving him as swiftly as it had arrived.

Raziya was gripping her shoulder. Calling her name, louder and louder.

"If you will not get me a conch," Malini said deliberately to the peo-ple around her, "then I will get one."

She would have to move between panicked horses and panicked men in armor, but there in the distance she could see a charioteer with a conch at his hip, frozen on his war chariot, staring at fire as it fell. The commander he must have been carrying was likely long gone—lost in the crush.

"Watch for my safety," she said to Raziya's guardswomen. She stood, and Raziya's grip tightened momentarily before releasing. "Empress," she said. But Malini did not want to be stopped or cajoled. She strode forward, fast, then faster. And then she was running, her hair streaming around her, her saber clanking against her hip, a useless weight.

"You heard the empress." Raziya's voice, distant now, but steely. "*Defend her.*"

She ducked as an arc of flame rippled close enough for her to feel the heat against her cheek; tripped over a wounded man before finding her footing and crossing the ground. One of the High Prince's men was ahead of her, on horseback. Out of the corner of her eye, she saw an arrow go into his chest. Saw him fall. Saw the shadows of one guardswoman, and another, circle around her. She kept on running.

The chariot was ahead of her. Malini, shaking with anger and determination, grasped its edge and dragged herself inside. "Your conch," she demanded, holding her hand out to the charioteer. He fumbled for it and placed it into her hands. "Turn back," she commanded. "Lady Raziya needs our assistance, and then we must return to camp."

"E-Empress." His lips were almost bloodless. Hands trembling. "That was—mothers' fire—"

"Turn. Back," she said deliberately.

"The horse," he managed to say. "It may—"

"You have your command. *Go.*"

With a crack of his whip the chariot lurched forward, then to the side. Back over the ground she'd run over. She saw Lady Raziya with ash upon her cheeks. One of the guardswomen lay dead on the ground in front of her. The chariot juddered, and Malini clutched the conch more tightly. Swallowed her own breath. No more careful position in battle, swaddled by soldiers and cavalry and shields. She was deep in the fray, the wind scouring her face, dust a harsh salt on her lips.

"Stop," she commanded the charioteer, and he managed to tame his horse long enough to allow Lady Raziya to scramble on.

"Sahar," Raziya said sharply. "Manvi, both of you, come with us."

"We'll follow, my lady," Manvi said urgently, frantically urging the chariot forward with her hands—as if she could move its bulk to safety by sheer will alone. Sahar said, "*Go*, my lady."

An arrow embedded itself in the ground to Raziya's right. The horse reared.

"Steady," Malini called out, as the charioteer held the reins—as if her order had any kind of power to change the course of what was happening around her. Raziya went down to her knees, holding the chariot's edge, swearing again. And Malini ground her feet into the base of the chariot. And prayed she would not fall.

She tilted her head back. Brought the conch to her lips.

Three sharp, wailing calls punctured the air:

Retreat. Retreat. Retreat.

6

PRIYA

I wish they wouldn't bow to me, Priya thought. Even in her own head, she sounded embarrassed.

The waiting crowd of villagers, huddled together at the edge of the forest and already bending forward into genuflections of respect, was large. Priya tried to keep her face impassive. She straightened her shoulders and held up her chin, trying to look proud, ready. But it was difficult, perched as she was in an unveiled palanquin, her legs crossed beneath her, her back straight, as if she were some noble lady instead of—well. Herself.

She hated the palanquin. Alighting from it always felt like an embarrassing affair. There were always eyes on her, and cheers. Sometimes fresh petals were scattered on the path before her. Today, there was an older woman with a basin at the ready, who offered to bathe Priya's feet as a gesture of respect. Priya rejected the offer with as much as grace as she could muster, which wasn't much.

Spirits, she hated politics. Hated smiling sweetly, and pretending she wasn't sweating through her fine, pale sari. She adjusted one of the wood and gold enameled cuffs on her upper arms, resisting the urge to fidget with the seam of her blouse. It was getting tight. She'd developed new muscle in the last months, ever since she'd started training in earnest alongside her sister's guards. She'd have to let the seam out, or get one of the maids to unpick and resew it for her.

Ganam's ungainly jump down from his own palanquin blessedly

distracted the crowd's attention from Priya. He straightened up awkwardly, offering the villagers a stilted greeting. This was his first time
accompanying her, and as soon as he'd found out about the palanquins,
he'd desperately tried to avoid riding in one.

"You want those poor men to carry a big ox like me?" he'd asked,
when it had been brought to him at the mahal's entrance. He'd gestured at the guards waiting by the palanquin—all of them smaller than
him by far. "Why torture them when I can walk?"

"Because we have to present a certain image," Priya had said. "We
need to look grand."

Ganam's expression had been skeptical.

"I think," he'd said slowly, "that packing my body into that little
palanquin won't make me look grand. People will laugh."

"They wouldn't dare," Priya said. And then, with a sidelong glance
at some of the watching guards, she'd raised her voice and said, "But if
you refuse the palanquin, I suppose we can both walk—"

"Absolutely not." The voice had come from one of the latticed windows above them. Through the bands of wood, Priya had seen her sister's face, narrow-eyed, staring down at them. "Priya, you're taking the
palanquin." A pause. "Both of you."

Ganam had grimaced, even as Priya had smiled in return, all teeth.

Sometimes—often—she forgot that she wasn't meant to like him.

"Well, Elder Bhumika has spoken," Priya had said cheerfully.
"Cheer up, Ganam. Maybe if you keep on accompanying me, someone
will build you a bigger palanquin."

Now, Ganam moved to stand beside her. He let her lead, allowing her to greet the chiefs of the village and accept the sparse garlands
they offered, and the cups of sweetened milk, covered in a thin filigree
of saffron. He let Priya nod and smile and pretend at grandness. And
when she said, "Will you show us to the fields?"—Ganam heaved a
small sigh of relief and followed behind her.

Niceties were excruciating. But work—and the rot—they both
understood.

The field they were led to was half marsh, and laden with deep,
green water rippling with algal plant life, insect larvae, and small,

strange, darting fish, glimmers of onyx and silver in the dark. The croak of frogs sounded in the air. The water smelled stagnant: both bloody and sweet as sugar, a honeyed and unnatural scent.

One of the village elders told them, with some anxiety, that the field had long served them well. Their village sat not far from it, the houses perched on stilts to keep them clear from the regular floods. There were families that had cared for this land and its waters for generations. The insect larvae were a delicacy, and exquisite when fried in oil and dipped in sweet tamarind. In other circumstances, the elders would have offered the finest of them to Priya and Ganam, as respected guests.

But of course, nothing from the marsh could be eaten right now. Nothing could safely be touched, for that matter. One of the village girls who regularly set her nets in the water had returned home with a rash on her arm. Overnight, it had burst into small white flowers. The rot was in the marsh: in the plants, in the green algae on the water.

That was why Priya had come, of course. To put it right.

Well. To *try* to put it right.

"Has anyone else become infected?" Priya asked one of the village leaders. He shook his head.

"No, elder," he said—and Priya, mindful as ever of her grandness, bit down on her tongue to avoid laughing at the absurdity of a man at least thirty years her senior calling her *elder*. "We've been careful. We have other fields."

The *for now* went unsaid.

The rot spread. That was its nature.

"I'll see to her after, then," Priya replied, and the leader murmured his thanks, his gratitude for her benevolence. The words prickled over her skin in a hot itch of embarrassment. But she nodded regardless, and smiled, and said, "If you could step back..."

"Of course, of course," the leader said hastily, and as one the villagers stepped back and out of harm's way.

Ganam and Priya stepped forward, out on the marshy ground.

"It's a big tract of land," muttered Ganam. "And a lot of water."

As they walked, Priya stared down. The algae on the water's surface moved: a visceral pulse that spoke of lungs breathing and muscles contracting. The stench of it was unpleasant, metallic. It was drawing in flies.

"It is," she agreed.

"Have you ever...?"

"Nothing so large as this." She'd put right the odd tree. A small copse, once, at great cost. No more.

A pause. Then Ganam said, "Are you sure about this?"

A deep breath. "Well, I have to try somewhere," she told him. "And you're here."

"What should I do?"

"Just watch for now," Priya said, because in truth she wasn't sure if there was anything he *could* do. She'd succeed or fail on her own.

She took another steadying lungful of air and kneeled down. The mud immediately seeped through her sari. Maybe that would convince Bhumika that high-status clothing did Priya no good. A nice brown tunic and dhoti, like the guards wore, would be more suitable—easier to clean, too.

Focus.

She closed her eyes. Breathed. Deep, winding breaths. Mouth closed tight, she felt the hum of her own inhalations against her teeth, a subtle reverberation. Put some voice in it, and it would feel like a song.

The rot hummed with her—every deep, fleshy strand of it, knotted into the soil and the water, the green and the blue. It moved with her magic.

As it should. She was a temple elder, after all. Elder Priya, thrice-born. She had traveled three times through the holy deathless waters and survived. She had the gifts of the ancient yaksa in her. And whenever she closed her eyes—closed them as they were closed now—she felt the whole of Ahiranya like a winged insect, beating its body against the cupped palm of her hand. This field—rot or no rot—was no less hers.

She stretched out her magic. Breathed. Breathed. Just so.

Reached for the rot.

This was no different from fixing the rot in a mortal body. No different, she reminded herself, as the skeins of the sickness tangled and lashed and writhed around her. She could do this.

She sank deeper.

Distantly, she could hear voices. Ganam's hand on her shoulder, five points of warmth, beams of light around the sun of a palm. Was he trying to call her back? Was the urgency in his voice?

Priya.

The roots of the rot wound around her. They had hollowed themselves a place in the earth, just as they hollowed a place inside the bodies of rot-riven mortals. She could not erase the rot in this field without murdering it entirely. But she had stopped its growth in human skin. She could stop it here.

She reached deeper.

Priya. Priya! Oh spirit's sake, fuck—

Sapling. My sapling.

A hand on her jaw. Tight grip. Wood-grain-whorled fingertips. Nails of thorn.

Priya.

Sapling.

She rose to the surface of herself with the reflexive panic of a body on the verge of drowning. She lashed out: felt the soil churn and crack around her, sundered open. She heard a muffled shriek, and the thud of a dozen footsteps as the villagers watching from the edge of the field flinched back, caught between freezing and fleeing.

"Priya." She recognized Ganam's voice. Hoarse. Careful. "Are you back with us?"

Her eyes opened. Her vision cleared, like smeared glass rubbed clean. There was a blunt, winding rope, a noose of root, tangled around Ganam's throat. It was...fairly tight.

Priya swallowed. Forced the noose to release. It slithered to the ground, back into the soil. The wet earth closed over it.

"Yes," she said, voice thin and hoarse. "I am now."

After a short rest and a cup of something sweet to soothe away the new tremor in Priya's fingers—tea, this time—Priya attended to the village girl with the flowering arm. She placed her fingertips against the girl's skin and broke the power of the rot in her. She told the girl and her family that the rot would spread no further.

"She'll live, then?" the mother asked, voice small and tight with hope.

"She will," Priya confirmed gently, and the woman broke down into tears.

Untouched by a thrice-born's hands, the rot was a death sentence. The girl would always carry this small mark of magic on her—would always need to conceal it with long blouses, and pluck away the petals with her fingers, so only the buds riddled her skin's smoothness—but she would not die. That, at least, was something Priya could do.

There was nothing to be done for the field. Ganam used his own small once-born magic to help her build a barrier of trees around it, enclosing it from the surrounding fields and the village itself. Deep-rooted trees that ate moisture were best, so Priya poured her strength into forcing banyan after banyan from the soil. When it was done, she sat down on the exposed roots of one tree and chugged a carafe of water, exhausted, while Ganam explained to the village leaders that they would return if the rot escaped its carapace; that they could not fix it. That they were sorry, but even the temple elders of Ahiranya, newly empowered and ensconced, could only do so much.

"Thank you," she said, when he came back.

"I don't think I was tactful enough," he muttered.

"You were fine," Priya said. True or not, what was done was done. She stood. "Come on. Let's walk back."

"What about the palanquins?"

"We've already failed." She kept her voice light, dismissive, even as the shame of it curdled into a hard knot of determination in her chest. "We don't need to pretend to be grand anymore."

As if sensing her mood, the guards didn't try to force them back into the palanquins. They all walked together instead, through the forest. Insects whirred in the air, so thick between the trees they formed clouds that undulated like dark gauze. The ground crunched underfoot. Ahead of the others, Priya and Ganam had no stick for beating the path to scare off snakes, as was customary. But there was no need for one: Ganam was applying his once-born magic to the carpet of leaves and twining flowers before them, shaking it in warning.

It was a trick Priya had suggested to all of the once-born as a good method for refining their magic. The once-born—the rebels who'd fought and killed, brutally, for the independence of Ahiranya—had seized on the exercise as a way to hone their control.

Ganam was one of the best. He moved the vegetation before them in elegant waves, a ripple that grew and spread like the aftershocks of a stone meeting still water. So it was no surprise to Priya when he opened his mouth and said, "If you had help, maybe you'd be able to do it. Maybe it'd be easier."

Priya was damnably tired. The mud on her knees had dried, crusted over into twin crescents of soil. She didn't want to have this conversation again.

"Bhumika doesn't have time to help with things like this," she said.

The once-born had magic. But it was nothing like the depth of power that lay in Bhumika and Priya. Only the thrice-born could stop the rot in its tracks. Only they could do what Priya had tried—had *hoped*—to do.

Only they had a hope of curing the rot.

"You and she don't have to be the only thrice-born," he said.

"I know," Priya said. "I really do know. But we don't want—neither of us..." She stopped. "It's dangerous."

She wouldn't have dragged him along on these journeys if she didn't think that one day he'd pass through the waters. But her words came out of her clumsy.

"No man or woman who fought at Ashok's side is unaware of that," he said. He didn't sound angry, but they'd had this argument often enough that she didn't need to look at him to know that a spark of mingled grief and fury had lit in his eyes. She felt the same thing—always—at the mention of her dead brother's name. "But we're not afraid to die for the sake of Ahiranya."

"Maybe right now Ahiranya needs you to live for it," Priya said as gently as she could. "We can't afford to lose anyone."

Ganam said nothing. After a moment, Priya shook her head.

"I don't want to argue," she said. "Let's just get back."

There would be plenty of time to argue in the future.

"It sounds like it could have been a lot worse," Sima said later.

They were sitting with their backs to a tree in the orchard. It was night, velvet and dark, and they had a carafe of wine between them.

"Probably. I just can't think of how right now."

Priya didn't usually become maudlin when she drank wine, but it had been a trying day. She had been rambling on for some time—tracing the rim of the bottle restlessly, constantly, with her thumb.

"If I sat all day in a room and did nothing but tend to rot sufferers, I'd still barely make a difference. I'd be like—like one ladle in a bucket the size of the world. You understand?"

"Never try to become a poet, Pri," Sima said. She'd spent the day tending to the running of the mahal and was about as tired as Priya, but mellowed by liquor. She smiled a little.

"I was a poet to her," Priya said quietly, letting the confession slip free. "I . . . I wrote to her, you know."

"How is your empress?"

"Who knows." Priya shrugged. She suddenly felt a little exposed. Her face was warm. "But we're not talking about that."

"You're the one that mentioned her."

"Look, she's—she's not important. What matters is this, okay? I can't fix a field," said Priya. "Not of rot sufferers, I don't mean field like I meant ladle, but—oh, I should never have turned poet at you, you're right. Look, the plain truth of it is this: There's so much work to do, and I can't do it alone." The words exposed a hollow ache in her chest—a sheer knot of anxiety that she couldn't ignore any longer. "We need more elders. More thrice-born."

Sima exhaled.

"That's hard, Pri." Silence. Then she raised her head and looked at Priya. "What would you say," she said slowly, "if I wanted to be more than I am? If I wanted to travel through the deathless waters like the mask-keepers? Like you?"

Priya stared down at her hands.

"I don't think it's what you really want."

"Why not?"

"You're not like they are." From the corner of her eye, she saw Sima's shoulders tense, saw her visibly bristle. Quickly, Priya said, "Not like— Sima, not in a bad way."

"In what way, then?"

"Let me take a drink," Priya said. "Then I'll explain."

They sat in taut silence as Priya swigged the bottle, taking three or four methodical mouthfuls. Her lips burned. Her throat felt fiery.

"The kind of strength you need to pass through the waters and survive—it's a hard kind. A scarring kind. The kind of scars that sit inside your soul, under the skin." She closed her eyes. "I don't. I don't want that for you. I don't think you really want that for yourself, either. You're too smart for that."

"It's pretty scarring to learn weapons too, you know," Sima observed. "And the fear never really goes away. The guilt, either. What's the difference, getting a weapon that lives in your blood instead of your hands?"

"It's different," Priya said. "Believe me."

"I've known hardship," Sima offered. "And I'm willing to know more if it's for something worthwhile. Protecting the home we've built, the family we've made here...that feels worth it."

"You don't know the price," Priya said. "And I..." Her voice cracked a little. Something flickered through her—the image of a knife, a flower. Wood, bones. "They've already done it. Paid some of it. They can't go back. But it's not a price I'd ever want a friend to pay."

A pause.

"What happens," Sima asked finally, "when you enter the waters? What is it like?"

Priya laughed and shook her head. Drank another mouthful of liquor. She bit her lip lightly, flesh-sour and liquor-sweet.

"I'm not even sure I know," she said. "I'm not even sure I remember."

But there was one thing she was sure of, from her time in the field of rot; from her sleepless nights after Ashok's death; from the whispers that flickered through her, sometimes, in a voice as sweet and rich as a flowering rose.

Oh, sapling.

The waters remembered her.

7

MALINI

Malini arrived back to the camp with her lungs full of smoke and her body crawling with sense memory: the smell of burning flesh and hair and cloth. The sweetness of ghee and perfume mingling with the char of living women burning. Alori and Narina, on fire before her, the scent of them and the sound of their screams filling her and hollowing her. She nearly fell from the war chariot—would have, if Raziya had not caught her.

Strong hands. Living flesh. At least this woman lived.

"Empress," Raziya said, holding up Malini so firmly that her hands would surely leave bruises. "The soldiers are watching. Remember yourself."

They were the words of an elder to a younger woman who had failed herself. *Don't let them see you weak,* that voice said, and the strength of it gave Malini the push to remember herself and the person she had to be.

Malini forced herself to nod and straighten, throwing her shoulders back, holding her head high. Guards were running toward her. The battle had not lasted long. The High Prince's riders had drawn back into the walls of the maze fort swiftly, taking their fire with them— coiling, she'd heard soldiers say frantically, back onto swords and arrows, ready to be used again.

She could see the forces of her army milling about, at loose ends, now that the threat was gone. Whispers of the words *mothers' fire* drifted into her ears. Seeped like poison into her blood.

She stepped down from the chariot. "Take me to Lord Mahesh," she said to the nearest guard.

"Yes, Empress," he said, and turned, clearing a path before her, his companions moving to guide her.

She expected Raziya to follow. But there was nothing but silence behind her, and when she turned, she saw that Raziya had lowered herself to the floor of the chariot, pale, clutching her skull. Malini began to walk to her—and was stopped by a hand on her arm.

"I'll take her to Lord Khalil, Empress," a male Dwarali archer said. His eyes were bloodshot from smoke. "She'll be seen to. I vow it."

"Don't take her to her husband," Malini said. "Take her to a physician."

"Empress," he said again, and bowed. Then he walked to Raziya and climbed into the chariot with her.

Malini watched for one heartbeat, then sucked in a breath and forced herself to turn away.

This was a political crisis in the making. There was no time to indulge her own finer feelings—to allow herself to worry, or wait, or feel the clawing voice at the back of her skull that howled *fire, fire, fire, fire*. Like ghosts, her heart sisters flickered before her eyes. So she thought instead of what must be done, here and now, to shore up her defenses. She thought of what actions she could take, in order to see her continue on her journey toward the throne. She pressed the thoughts into her own skin like a mask, like something that could stop her from flying apart.

She found herself in Lord Mahesh's own tent.

She wanted to tell him to summon Rao for her. To find Lata, and her military officials, and any Parijatdvipan lords who could be swiftly gathered up. She needed Lord Khalil, and Lord Narayan, and beady-eyed Lord Prakash. She needed to draw her council around herself and plan and strategize and weigh up resources and count the dead. She needed to carve a path *forward*.

One look at Lord Mahesh's grimly furious face as he shouldered through the tent's curtain told her that none of that would be possible. Not yet.

"Empress," he said, voice rough with smoke. "We must speak alone."

"We *are* alone, Lord Mahesh," she said.

His gaze flicked to the guards.

"Leave us," she announced, waving a hand at her guards. They hesitated for a moment, but Malini gestured once more, and said evenly, "Lord Mahesh will ensure I am safe. Go. Stand beyond the door."

It was only when they were gone—taking up posts outside the tent as ordered, of that Malini had no doubt—that Malini allowed herself to inspect Mahesh more closely. His face was cut—a long line of blood snaked across his cheek. His clothing was torn. Ash had stained the Parijati white of his tunic a dull gray.

Mahesh stared back at her, his eyes narrowed, red from the miasma of smoke.

Lord Mahesh had served her ably since his appointment. But now she looked at him and thought of how he had not sounded the conch on the battlefield—how she had, in all her helpless panic, been forced to risk her own life to do it.

As if hearing her thoughts, he spoke.

"You should not have sounded retreat, Empress," he said. "That was a grave error."

"My men were in danger," Malini said levelly. "It was a massacre of our forces. They were burning. I was not going to allow it to continue. As my general, *you* should not have allowed it to continue."

"I should have and would have," he said. "I would have let hundreds die, if need be. That is the nature of war, Empress—those men should have died gladly. You should have trusted my judgment."

"I was not trained in the military arts alongside my brothers, Lord Mahesh, but I know a strategy that results in nothing but wasteful death when I hear one," she replied sharply. "You know I sought to end the war for Saketa with minimal bloodshed. Why then, would you choose a strategy—*without my say-so*—that would see my army burn?"

"A battle is not simply a balance of lives," he gritted out, looking more furious by the minute. "Empress, a battle is a tale written in blood. And this is the tale that men shall tell about your retreat before

the High Prince's fort: that Emperor Chandra sent a priest of the mothers, who brought with him blessed fire of the mothers. Fire that once
destroyed the yaksa—fire that now proclaims the emperor's mother-
blessed right to the throne, and condemns you as a usurper. They will
say the traitor empress saw the fire of the mothers, and knowing she
was a false claimant to the throne, tainted in the eyes of the mothers
she claimed to serve, she *fled*." A beat, as he allowed the words to sink
in. "Do you understand, Empress?"

"What a leap to make, on limited evidence," Malini said tightly.
"I do not believe people will make such an assumption, Lord Mahesh.
And if they did, they would be entirely wrong to do so."

"They will think it, Empress. I am sure of that."

How can you be sure? Malini thought. But she did not ask. As soon
as the question came to her, she knew its answer.

He thought it. That was why. Her own general had gazed upon that
fire and felt his faith in her crumble.

"That was *not* the fire of the mothers of flame," Malini said, with
far more conviction than she felt.

"It was no natural fire," Mahesh replied, his voice quieter now,
steadier. "What else could it have been but their flames? That is what the
people will say, and believe. They will say the mothers did not choose
you for the throne after all. They will say you are not the rightful ruler."

Righteousness, rightfulness—oh, how she hated those words. Their
sole purpose seemed to be to keep her in her place: a life with narrow
walls and standards of purity that pressed her thin, erased her to nothing but her blood and her good bones and the worth of a pleasing face.
A life where she would never contemplate ruling; a life where she would
obediently bare her neck for a knife, or gladly embrace the pyre.

"I am the rightful ruler of Parijatdvipa," Malini said. "And that fire
was not the flame of the mothers. Must I continue to repeat it, Lord
Mahesh?" Perhaps if she said these words often enough, with enough
assurance, they would wear a groove into reality and become unassail-
able truth. "And as the rightful ruler, I had no desire to waste the lives
of those who serve me. I could not have allowed more men to—to burn
for the sake of obeying laws that Chandra himself does not respect."

The word *burn* brought a harshness to her voice—broke the even calm she had so carefully maintained, all through this exchange. His eyes sharpened at the sound of it.

"Empress," he said. "Malini."

Oh no, she thought. Familiarity did not bode well.

"I understand if the sight reopened—old wounds," he said delicately.

"I have led men to many battles, Lord Mahesh," Malini said, still cursing herself internally. She knew the price of weakness. She *knew*. "I am not fragile."

"But fire, of course . . . it would be understandable . . ."

"You were there, Lord Mahesh, when I burned down a monastery," she replied, with a voice like iron. "I set it alight with my own arrow. Fire does not frighten me."

It did, of course. Even today she had nightmares. Perhaps she always would.

"You should rest," Mahesh said, as if he had not heard her. "There will be time enough to discuss what must be done. For now, you must recover from this ordeal."

As if she could allow herself the luxury of rest. There would not be *time enough*, as he claimed. The urgency of the work ahead of her made it difficult to look at him without anything but incredulous anger.

"You acted as you did in error, Empress, but we may still be able to right it. We can move forward on this when the camp is more—peaceful."

As if to underscore his words, there was another crash from beyond the tent's walls, and indecipherable shouting.

"I would rather summon the other lords now," she said, controlled. "I would rather discuss how we must proceed."

"And I," he said, with more steel, "think it would be better for you to recover. That is my advice. Respectfully. Empress."

Silence fell.

This was defiance. Oh, Lord Mahesh could speak of respect all he liked. But he knew his worth to her.

She thought of standing taller. Thought of saying to him, *I am your empress, and you will obey me.* She thought of all the things her father would have done in her position, or her brothers, or any emperor, any faceless man garbed in power.

You would never have spoken to me so, she thought, her blood a deep river of anger that swelled and moved inside her, threatening to flood the plains of her heart, *if I were either of my brothers. And yet I am a better leader than both of them, in every way.*

"Perhaps you're right," she said, and let herself sag a little, shoulders rounding as if exhaustion had overcome her. "I will rest, Lord Mahesh. And then—later—we will discuss what must be done."

Her own tent, like everywhere else in the camp, smelled of burning. But the scent was fainter here. Swati had swept the floor and perfumed the air. She had arranged bowls of water to trap the smoke.

They were all waiting for her: Deepa and Lata, and to Malini's surprise and relief, Raziya. Her head was wrapped with cloth, her hair bound to one side. Sahar, still bloodied and ash-stained, stood at the entrance of the tent, acting as another guard. Lata strode over the very second Malini entered the tent. "My lady," she said, gaze flickering anxiously over Malini's face, her clothes. "Are you hurt? What happened out there? Why did you go to Lord Mahesh without me? Shall I summon Rao? He's seeing to his men, but I can ask—"

"No." Malini shook her head. "Everyone I need is here."

"I've arranged you bathing water," Swati said softly. "Refresh yourself, my lady. You'll feel much better."

"Are you well, Lady Raziya?" Malini asked. "You should be resting."

There was a pointed hum of agreement from the tent entrance.

"You should have waited for me," Raziya said. Her hands were clenched in her lap. It took a moment for Malini to realize that the flinty look upon her face was anger. "I was indisposed," she said stiffly. "But, Empress, you should have waited for me. Or if not for me, then Lata or Lady Deepa."

"My father would not have allowed me there," Deepa blurted out. Then flushed. A look passed between Lata and Malini. Nothing was said.

Malini moved behind a privacy screen and unraveled her sari. Let it fall into a heap behind her, knowing she would never willingly wear it again. After a perfunctory wash with a cloth and bucket, her hands shaking despite herself, she dressed again in clean clothing.

She unbraided her hair as she walked back into the main tent. Ran a comb through it in long, thoughtless motions, waiting for her heartbeat to settle. Swati made a soft noise. "Let me, my lady," she said, and took up the task, swiftly drawing Malini's hair into a new braid.

Another of Raziya's archers entered the tent. "There's a war council being held," she said, voice urgent. "Right now."

"The empress will be ready in a moment," said Raziya. "Tell the men—"

"No, my lady," the guardswoman said. "You don't understand. The council has started. And they are not... they have *chosen* not to summon the empress." She swallowed, and said weakly, "It was one of our lord's men who told me, my lady, on Lord Khalil's behalf."

Silence.

Raziya said, "We may attend regardless, of course, Empress." Her voice was cold, all the fury in it suppressed. "We will ensure you have an appropriate retinue with you. All of us will be at your side." Deepa squirmed a little at that, but Raziya continued calmly, "Nothing will be amiss."

They all looked at Malini. Waiting for her response.

"No," she said. She would not go to them unprepared. She would not go with shaking hands and fire flickering behind her eyelids. That wasn't how wars were won. "How do you celebrate battles being won, in Dwarali?"

"With drinking," Raziya said.

"And battles not yet won?"

"Battles *lost*, Empress?" A raised eyebrow. "I do not know. We don't lose battles in Dwarali. And if we do, we don't survive."

"It is lucky, then, that Parijatdvipa is a vast empire full of many paths—and that we women know something of rising anew from the flames of ruin," Malini said. "Swati," she said. "Arrange for wine to be brought. We are all going to remain here, in this tent, and celebrate our continued survival."

"And sherbet," Sahar muttered. "Wine's no good for those with bleeding heads."

Raziya gave her a narrow-eyed look. Malini said, swiftly—with a pang of annoyance at herself, for her own oversight—that sherbet would be ideal.

Wine and sherbet were poured. Malini told them what had happened outside the High Prince's fort, and watched as Lata's face grew tighter, and her eyes more calculating, as she considered the implications of what had passed. She observed the way Deepa shrank further in on herself, like a small prey creature seeking to conceal itself from danger.

"Deepa," Malini said, finally. Deepa startled visibly, then settled back onto her cushion. "If you wish to see your father, you may go. He must be worried for your well-being."

"I—I don't need to see him, Empress. My apologies."

"Will he not want to see you? Ensure your health?" Malini enquired.

Deepa shook her head. "No, Empress."

"Then I must, in his place. *Are* you well?" Malini asked. "It was frightening for Raziya and me to face fire on the battlefield; but it is frightening, too, not to know what may be coming for you."

"I am well, Empress," Deepa said. "Thank you for your concern."

Malini allowed a moment to pass, as more smoke-filled air wafted in through the tent curtain; as Deepa clasped her hands tighter, under the watchful eyes of Malini's inner court.

"Did you want to serve me, Deepa?" Malini asked softly. "I am afraid I have not asked you since war began in earnest."

"I..." Deepa hesitated.

"Was it your father's will or your own, to serve me?" Malini pressed.

Deepa lowered her gaze. "My father asked it of me," she said. "But I was happy to come."

Malini nodded, slowly. "Of course you were," she agreed. "You are an obedient daughter. Your first loyalty is to your father. You love him. And he controls your fate: your marriage, or lack. Your status. All of us understand this," Malini went on. "And I understand—and forgive you—for watching me for his sake, and your own."

Deepa lifted her gaze. Eyes a little wider. A little wild.

"Empress," she blurted out. "I have said nothing—nothing—" She stopped, and seemed to steel herself. Then said, "I am the third of five daughters. Not the prettiest. Or the most charming. My father—he only wished to give me an opportunity to rise."

Malini was silent for a moment. Then: "What did you tell him about me, Deepa?"

"Nothing, Empress. Nothing."

"Be honest with me now," Malini said. Low and chiding. "Don't let your panic mislead you. You're intelligent. Educated. Lata speaks highly of your mind. Tell me what you have told your father. Tell me what *I* am in your eyes."

Deepa hesitated. "I . . . Empress. You are. Dedicated to winning this war. And you. You work tirelessly. You are always—as you are," she said haltingly, gesturing jerkily to Malini. "You are. Brave and—and poised. A true heir to Divyanshi. I have told my father this."

"And what else?" When Deepa remained quiet, Malini leaned forward. The other women watched, tense and silent. "Compliments and flattery are all well and good, Deepa. But I know they are not all you say. I am asking you for the truth."

Deepa was intelligent, and thoughtful. Malini could practically see the thoughts flitting through the younger woman's mind—tightening her jaw, making her mouth part on words she couldn't quite say, then close again.

Finally, Deepa came to a decision. Her gaze hardened.

"You speak of the mothers," she said. "And you—Empress, you speak of being mother-blessed. But you do not pray. Or. Or speak *to* the mothers." Her confidence grew, her voice wavering less as she continued. "You are not gentle or kind. You try to be but . . . there's a coldness in you, Empress. You do not forget those who slight you." Alarm rose in her face as she said swiftly, "But I did not tell my father so."

"Why not? Do you think it insults me?" When Deepa only looked more panicked, Malini smiled, letting her voice gentle with it. "I wanted your honesty. And I thank you for it. And in return, I have some honesty for you.

"Your father has lost his faith in me. And your father holds great sway among certain factions of my allies." Malini's decision to make him her general had only strengthened his power. "I would like to know what he does. What he says, or does not say. Watch him for me. Tell me what you learn, and you will be rewarded with more power in my court than you could ever achieve as an unfavored daughter in your father's household."

"My...my family," Deepa said haltingly. "My sisters. My mother. I need to know they will be. Safe."

"If you were your father's son, and I your emperor, you could ask me for assurances that you would be recognized as the head of your family," Malini said. "If you chose the empire's future over your father's ambitions and errors, you could ask me to vow that your sisters would be protected and given a future unbound from your father's fate."

Deepa swallowed. "I am not a son," she said.

"And I am not an emperor. So what will you do, Lady Deepa?"

She looked away. She looked at Lata and Raziya and Sahar; at Swati, watching quietly. Slowly, the panic seemed to bleed from her face.

"My father bid me to serve you, and I did not say no. I did not even try to refuse." She met Malini's eyes again. "I wanted more. Is it selfish, to want even more than this, Empress?"

Are you leading me astray? her eyes asked.

"It is not selfish to serve your empire," Malini said steadily. "And it is not selfish to protect your family from your father's errors. And he has erred, Deepa. You have in your hands the power to right his wrongs. Will you do so?"

Deepa swallowed. "I have always wanted more," she confessed. "Always wanted—purpose."

"I know," Malini said, looking at Deepa with all her focus, all the charm she could force into her own voice and eyes and body. Let Deepa know she was seen. Let Deepa know she was valued. It was true enough, surely, to grasp her loyalty and chain it fast. "I know."

"I want the assurances you spoke of," Deepa said. "I...I want to know I will be rewarded. And my family shall be safe. And in return... Empress, I will tell you everything of my father. And I will be your loyal servant, as I have always been."

Malini smiled.

*   *   *

Later—much later—she sat with no company but Lata, and thought of how else she might protect herself from men who had stopped seeing her as a living god.

"When this began," she said quietly, watching Lata raise her head, attentive. "I believed I would have the empire in my grasp by now."

Or that I would be dead.

Sometimes she thought she would spend the rest of her life like this, on broken roads surrounded by armed men, always negotiating webs of politics and power with allies who bowed and bristled and measured her worth to them as she measured theirs in turn. She would always be one step away from success or from ruin. She would never see Chandra dead.

Could something be achieved by sheer force of want alone?

Lata sat on the ground, cross-legged, back straight. She sat in the pose of a sage at debate, ready to help Malini unravel the thorny knot blooming in her own skull.

Malini calculated a new path forward.

"Bring me Yogesh," she said, lighting the oil wick lantern by her papers, collecting her writing instruments close; ink, a thick sheaf of paper. "Try not to draw any attention to yourself, Lata."

Lata nodded and left without another word.

Malini thought of the power of a tale—the way it could splinter into shards and cut the throat of its own maker. The tale of a crown prince turned priest, a firstborn son, still held more sway than the myth she'd wound around herself from prophecy and fire and her own sheer ambition.

She needed a weapon no one else had. She needed—she wanted—someone she could trust. Someone who had loved her even after a knife to the throat; who had held Malini's face in her own two hands, warm and alive, and said, *I know you. I know this face, and it is mine.*

She had dreamt of writing to Priya again so many times. She *had* written to Priya so many times.

*I am always thinking of you. I think of you in battle. I think of you
in the dark of night. When my mind is silent or full, you wait there
for me.*

It galls me that I want you as much as this. That my heart so thoroughly belongs to you. The power you have over me, Priya. Why does it refuse to fade?

I think of the way the earth would yield to your hands, flowering for you. I think of what you could do for me, if I put you to use. And I should put you to use. *Somewhere, you must wonder why I haven't.*

I think of how you could have made a weapon of anything.

Do you think of me, in the quiet? I wonder—

No more. She could not think of it any longer.

She wrote a different letter. Not for Priya, or at least, not for Priya alone. She wrote as empress, with all the weight of her status behind her words, and none of her heart.

She hoped Priya would understand anyway. She hoped Priya would come. For the sake of the alliance between the empire and Ahiranya. And for the sake of what still lay between them, or at least lay inside Malini, turning forever to the memory of Priya like a thing of the earth seeking light.

8

RAO

Rao had arrived at the war council late, and had been greeted by chaos—shouting, yelling, Lord Mahesh leading and claiming the empress was too overwrought to attend. Rao should have spoken for Malini—had wanted to. But he had met Lord Khalil's eyes; seen the lift of an eloquent eyebrow and the faintest shake of a head. And Rao had kept his calm and his silence, even as his frustration grew.

Malini had to have a plan. Malini always had plans.

He had kept his calm as he saw to his men and made an accounting of the injured and the dead. Had *continued* to be calm when one of his own Aloran military officials begged to speak to him, and told him that Yogesh had been ordered to carry a message for the empress, and was already gone.

And yet here he was, in Malini's tent, trying desperately to keep a level head in the face of her quiet amusement. As if his worry *entertained* her.

Maybe it did.

"You sent a message to Ahiranya," Rao pressed on. "An imperial missive, placed in a military official's hand."

"You've found spies of your own, Rao," she murmured. "That's good."

"My men are just loyal," he said. "What did you say? What orders did you send?"

"You don't know?"

"I didn't read your letter."

"Out of loyalty, or because you lacked the opportunity?"

A pause, a breath of silence that he filled by shaking his head and closing his eyes.

"I thought as much," she said. Oh, she definitely sounded amused. "You're not quite that moralistic. If you were, you'd never get anything done." *And I'd have no use for you* was unsaid but heavily implied. "Though you've grown overly fond of lecturing me."

"I don't lecture," he said. "My job is to advise, and that's exactly what I do, when I'm actually afforded the chance to do so."

"Advise me, then."

"The Ahiranyi are still viewed with great suspicion."

"I am well aware of that," she replied.

"Then I have to ask why you're reaching out to them," he said. "Especially now, when you have . . ." He paused, and said more quietly, "After the fires—and the war council—you have enough problems to contend with here."

"How *did* Mahesh's war council proceed without me?" She raised an eyebrow at him. "I'm curious. Did anyone outright say that Aditya should have the throne, or did they only imply it?"

"If you want me to be your eyes and ears, then it would be helpful if you could be honest with me in turn," Rao said, in what was absolutely not an irritated tone of voice.

"I have spies enough," said Malini. "And until I am able to attend my own war councils without fear that my own men may seek to protect me from the war *I* am leading, you will have to forgive me for holding some truths close to the chest."

You don't have to lie to me, he thought, and did not say. It sounded too pitiful even in his own head to be spoken. *Don't you understand what you are to me?*

Like all royals of Alor, his true name had always been a secret—a prophecy waiting to be spoken. His true name had been the guiding star of his faith and fate, dragging him onward. Leading him, inevitably, to kneel before her in the sun-drenched dirt on a road toward Dwarali, where he had revealed it to her and given her the right to her throne.

When she is crowned in jasmine, in needle-flower, in smoke and in fire, he will kneel before her and name her. He will give the princess of Parijat her fate. He will say: Name who shall sit upon the throne, Princess. Name the flower of empire. Name the head that shall reign beneath a crown of poison. Name the hand that lit the pyre.

He will name her thus, and she will know.

Didn't she understand that his fate was still tied to her own? That the nameless god had made him like this, and he could not change his nature, his purpose? He had named her empress, and she...

She did not trust him.

He swallowed back hurt.

"You can't always assume that people are going to turn on you. That they need to be managed and—and manipulated." Rao was turned away from her, knowing his face was still painfully open—that she would see right through him, if he allowed her to. "You're going to have to trust them."

Silence.

"Rao," she said after a moment. He looked at her again. The amusement had drained from her face. What was left was tired, and shaken, and world-weary. "I've trusted all through this war," said Malini. "I trusted those men when we traveled to Dwarali. When we forged new alliances there. When we faced battle after battle. I trusted they would fight and die to see me on the throne. I trusted that I would not find a knife placed against my throat in my sleep. That is plenty of trust, Rao. Any more trust, and I'll be making my own noose."

"I just don't believe the Ahiranyi will be as much help as you hope they will be," Rao said. "I worry that this error will cost you."

"We will see," Malini said, voice unreadable. "But there's no worth in sending a messenger to stop a messenger. My message will reach Ahiranya, and Ahiranya's temple council will respond, and I will deal with the consequences if and when they turn up at my door. That is all."

Rao knew a dismissal when he heard one. He bowed.

"And Rao?"

He paused.

"Next time put your morals aside," she said. "You could have chased after Yogesh, if you'd tried. I cannot coddle you. I cannot treat you as my friend, and I don't ask for friendship in return. I ask for the cunning and canny advisor I know you have the capacity to be. Do you understand?"

"Yes, Empress," he choked out.

He bowed again, and swiftly left the tent before he could yell at her.

By the nameless, did she want him to be a traitor? Was that what she wanted?

She wants you to be more like her, a voice in his head said. It was his own, but calm, reasonable, devoid of the strength of feeling currently coursing through him.

She wants you do to everything you're capable of to achieve her ends.

Somehow, without meaning to, he did not walk back to his own sleeping tent. Did not seek out the military officials who served the Aloran branch of the army, who always had need of him for something. Did nothing, in fact, that would make him useful.

Instead, his feet led him to Aditya.

Even in the thick of battle, Aditya's tent was a tranquil pool, a place of peace carved out on the edges of war. It was untouched. The smoke-darkness roiling around them barely seemed to brush its edges.

One of the guards gave him a nod of respect.

"Shall I announce you, my lord? Arrange refreshments?"

"No need," said Rao, and entered.

Aditya had clearly been praying. There was a water basin on the ground before him, its surface black and utterly still, as reflective as glass and as dark as night. His head was lowered over it. When he raised it, his eyes were as dark as the water, his expression unfathomable. It took a moment for humanity to return to his face—for his eyes to light up with recognition, and his shoulders to soften, the tension leaching away from them. "Rao," he said softly. "Come in."

He was sitting cross-legged on a floor mat, in nothing but his plainest blue priestly shawl and dhoti. The tent was dim, unlit, though Rao could see Aditya reaching automatically for an oil lamp, preparing to set it alight. His steady hands struck a spark, lit the cotton wick.

Light illuminated his face: his elegant bones, his dark eyes, his serious brows.

Rao relaxed at the sight of him. He could not help it.

"You look surprised to see me," said Rao.

"You're not the usual visitor I receive at this hour," said Aditya. "But you are the most welcome. Besides, the guards usually announce you."

Rao shook his head.

"I told them not to," he said. "I wanted it to be just us. I . . ."

Rao collapsed. It was a controlled fall, as collapses went—his knees jarring the ground, his breath leaving him. He'd been waiting to break. He wouldn't have another chance.

"Rao," Aditya said, alarmed. He moved to kneel by Rao's side. Aditya's hands clasped Rao's shoulders, and he said, "Are you well? Breathe with me. Here."

A hand pressed to Rao's chest. Rising, falling. After a moment, Rao breathed with the motion of it. He felt sick with relief, and sick with fear both.

"There," Aditya murmured. "There. Breathe with me. You're well."

"Surely you've smelled the smoke," Rao managed to say.

Aditya nodded, almost imperceptibly. But Rao caught the gesture. As his face moved, the light painted it. There were deep shadows under his eyes.

"Has my sister burned the city?" Aditya asked. He said it with resignation, as if he expected it of her.

"No," Rao said. "No."

How could he even begin to explain it?

He tried. He told Aditya, haltingly, about what he'd seen during the siege. The men, uneasy, waiting for word, as negotiations took place. The sudden sight of swords and arrows wreathed with flame.

The fire. The strangeness of it. The attempt against Malini's life.

Aditya nodded, expression grave. He knew, even better than Rao, the significance of magical fire.

"It was a game Chandra and I used to play, you know," Aditya said finally. "When we were small boys. When we were still training with blunted weapons. The two of us, flinging ourselves into battle with our swords, imagining they were burning with magical fire. That we were mother-blessed."

A smile flitted across his face—lit his mouth and his eyes—then faded away as swiftly as it had come.

"We were very young then. And I left him soon enough, for my own training and my own lessons."

"I remember," Rao said. He'd arrived at the imperial mahal himself as a boy; been raised alongside Aditya as his companion, to foster ties between Alor and Parijat. He remembered how relieved he had been, to become Crown Prince Aditya's companion, not Prince Chandra's. Aditya had welcomed him with a smile; had spent days showing him around the imperial mahal, and had let Rao borrow his favorite horse, his favorite books. *We're going to be friends all our lives*, he'd said, when Rao had expressed reluctance to take what was rightfully Aditya's from him. *Surely friends should share everything?*

Chandra had not even looked at him when he arrived. Had refused to talk with him or eat with him for months, and curled his lip in disdain at any effort on Rao's part to make friends. Once, during a practice battle under the watching eyes of their sages, Chandra had beaten Rao around the skull with his training saber. One blow so vicious it left him unconscious. He was trapped in the sickroom for a week before he recovered.

It was only then that Rao learned Chandra disdained him for being a follower of the nameless. *My brother spends too much time with the High Priest*, Aditya had said absently, fussing with Rao's bandages like a mother. *But don't worry. He'll calm as he grows older. All the sages tell Father so.*

"No matter what anyone says—no matter what my sister may believe, Rao—Chandra is not inherently evil," Aditya said now. There was something raw in his voice—almost an entreaty. "He's been misled. He's chosen to walk a terrible path. I left my apparent fate once, and embraced another. Maybe Chandra can one day do the same."

Aditya's hand was still against his chest—a light, meaningless weight. Rao shifted away from him, and the hand lowered.

Rao thought of Alori. Her hair caught in the wind. Her eyes fixed on distant birds. The way her cheek had dimpled when she smiled. He thought of her and all the anger he had refused to feel rushed through him, alchemized into grief.

He squeezed his eyes shut, holding back tears. He wasn't going to cry.

"Malini isn't alone in believing he's beyond saving," said Rao, voice tight. "He murdered my sister. Alori never had a choice to walk a different path. I don't see why Chandra should be allowed to, when he stole that from her."

"Men do terrible things," Aditya replied. That plea again in his voice. "That does not mean they have no capacity for good."

"Our men are *burning* because of him," Rao said.

"They are not my men," said Aditya. "They're Malini's. The burden of that must lie on her, just as it lies on Chandra. And if I look in my heart every day and forgive my sister..." Rao opened his eyes, just in time to see the expression of quiet anguish that crossed Aditya's face, before it settled into calm once more. "Rao. I must forgive my brother too."

They could have been Aditya's men. They could have been. If Aditya had not refused his birthright over and over again.

If Rao had not kneeled before Malini and prophesied her rise and Aditya's fall.

If Aditya had found a way to forgive Malini and Chandra, had he found a way to forgive himself too? Had he forgiven Rao for his part in Malini's rise?

"Why are you here?" Aditya asked, finally. With a start, Rao realized he had been silent for some time, staring blankly at Aditya, wanting to do—something. Wring Aditya by the throat, perhaps, or shake him. Or hold his face and say *I wish you could be more than this. I wish you would grieve as I grieve, and hate as I hate, and be the person you were when you and Prem and I were boys. I wish, I wish.*

"If you've come for comfort," Aditya said, "or prayer, then I've failed you utterly, Rao. I'm sorry."

There were many things Rao could have said.

I came to tell you what happened.

I came to ask for your help.

I came to tell you that Malini is fighting to make those men obey her, and I fear this will break her control of them, and you...Aditya, I don't know why she allows you to live, when you're a threat to her, and I hate myself for even thinking it, but as long as you're here—

A tumult of thought. Too much, and none of it useful.

He told a truth instead, if not *the* truth.

"I came to see you," Rao said. "Because you're my friend. And I needed to see that you are well. And. Now I have."

"I'm unchanged," Aditya said gently. "As always."

Low murmurs sounded beyond the tent. This time a guard peered in, announcing the presence of a military official, who entered and bowed low.

"Prince Aditya. Prince Rao." He lifted his head and said, "Prince Aditya, Lord Mahesh has requested your presence."

"For what purpose?" Aditya asked.

The official's gaze darted to Rao, then away.

"He and a few lords from Parijat wish to—speak with you. They earnestly hope you will attend them."

Another meeting that Malini had not been invited to. Rao would have to make sure she heard of it, if one of the attending officials had not already passed the information to Lata.

Aditya shook his head. "I have meditation to engage in," he said, as if this were a far more vital task.

"Prince Aditya, please," the official said, pleading. "What must I tell them?"

"Lord Mahesh will know my reasoning," Aditya said calmly. "We have spoken of it often enough."

"My prince, please."

"I will come if my sister summons me," Aditya said. There was new iron, under the mildness of his voice. "Has she?"

Rao considered him carefully. There was a sharpness to Aditya's gaze.

"The empress will not be present," the official said reluctantly.

"Ah, it grows late," Rao said, clicking his tongue. "Who knows where the empress has got to! She's a busy woman, isn't she? No matter." He rose to his feet. "Do tell Lord Mahesh I can find her for him."

"Th-there's no need, my lord," the official stammered.

"No, no, it's no trouble," Rao said, smiling. "As Prince Aditya has said, he cannot accompany you. You should go and give Lord Mahesh his apologies."

The official did not protest, but he left radiating anxiety and disapproval.

Rao turned to Aditya.

"I wish I could have stayed longer," he said frankly. Through all his frustration with Aditya—and yes, his anger—that was entirely true. But he had responsibilities, and unlike Aditya, he couldn't turn from them.

Rao turned to the entrance.

"Rao," said Aditya. Rao's thoughts careened to a halt.

"Yes?"

"I would like you to assess my guards," he said. "You have my permission to make changes to the roster. A few of your own men would be—ideal."

Despite Aditya's enforced peace, the world kept on creeping in. In smoke, in fire. In men.

"Not all visitors are as welcome as you are," Aditya said.

"I'll arrange my own men," Rao said carefully. "And next time, Aditya…"

"Yes?"

"I'll bring you some wine," he said, keeping his voice light. This was his friend. Never mind anything else. That remained true.

Aditya nodded once, in graceful thanks. And Rao left him behind.

9

BHUMIKA

Bhumika woke as the sky began to lighten, black softening to a dark hue of blue. She dressed in a plain white sari and bound beads of wood through her hair. The mahal was almost quiet, almost peaceful—but in the distance she could hear the hum of voices, and knew that worshippers were already gathering at the base of the Hirana, waiting to climb the mountain and make their offerings.

Her crown mask lay swaddled in white cloth at her bedside. She unwrapped it with care, pushing back layers of fabric to bare the oval of wood. The hollowed sockets for eyes stared back at her. She cupped the shape of the mask in her palm, feeling the weight of it, the smoothness of the grain.

The mask-keepers wore their own wooden masks in honor of this one: the crown mask of the High Elder, leader of the temple elders who ruled Ahiranya's faith and now ruled Ahiranya itself. It was carved from sacred wood and imbued with yaksa-born magic. The power in it was so strong that touching it would make skin blister and burn. Pressed to flesh long enough, it could eat its way down to the bone.

But Bhumika was thrice-born, with the deathless waters running through her veins. She had nothing to fear. She could not be hurt by sacred wood. The crown mask filled her flesh with warmth that made her blood sing, and when she raised it up, pressing it to her own face, it settled against her skin, pouring its gifts through her.

She felt Ahiranya around her—felt the rolling expanse of it, all the green, every thorn she had raised from the earth, every trap she had set, every flowering thing that watched the roads and pathways through the city for her with her own eyes, waiting for imperial soldiers to dare darken Ahiranya's borders again. *Come*, she thought, *and my sister and I will deal with you again.*

Come if you like. Ahiranya is waiting for you.

She walked to the Hirana with a handful of mask-keepers. The worshippers, waiting at the base, parted around her with a sigh. She held her masked face high and set her feet against the first steps. The stone knew her, welcomed her. As she walked, the Hirana carried her like a gentle wave. Up, up to the entrance. Into the corridors of the temple.

For many of the years the regent had ruled Ahiranya, the temple had been a ruin: fire-damaged, marked with the ash and flame that had killed so many of Bhumika's temple siblings and her elders. The statues of the yaksa in the shrine rooms had been destroyed. The paintings and carvings on the walls had faded or been carefully obliterated. But Bhumika was High Elder now, and her regent husband was dead.

She entered one of the shrine rooms and was struck again, anew, by how much had changed. Now, the floor was swathed in a large mat of pale rose. There were lanterns hung upon the ceiling—delicate glass things that filled the room with soft, welcoming light. The walls were no longer stained and empty, but marked with dozens of alcoves, each filled with a statue of a yaksa.

The yaksa had once been innumerable. Once, every village, every family had their own shrine and their own effigies, their own tales of the Age of Flowers.

Artisans, carefully chosen by Bhumika herself, had tried to craft likenesses of as many of them as possible. Bhumika was surrounded by eyes of flowers and hands shaped like the fronds of drooping leaves; skin patterned like seeds or bark whorl; bodies, carved in frozen motion, that writhed like vines.

She reached for her mask, prying it from her face. The cool air touched her skin, and the scent of incense filled her nose, her throat. She breathed it in.

She heard the light motion of footsteps behind her.

"Are you ready to meet the worshippers, Elder Bhumika?" a mask-keeper asked.

Was she? She bowed in worship to the yaksa to give herself a moment's reprieve. The effigies stared back at her—inhuman and beautiful, painted gold and green and blood-rich red, their eyes gleaming in the lantern light. The worshippers would bow at her feet, as she bowed now, and make offerings for the yaksa. They would weep, or smile, and ask her for miracles, or thank her for existing—as if her rise were miracle enough for them.

It filled her with disquiet. She could not help it.

All they want are the blessings of the yaksa, she reminded herself sternly. *All they want is to see me, and believe that Ahiranya has a greater fate lying before it.*

This desire—this dream—was part of the fragile weft keeping Ahiranya whole. Whatever Ahiranya had suffered, its people had gained this: their faith returned. Their mantras and myths given life. Temple elders, and deathless waters, and *hope*.

"I'm ready," she said. "I'll greet them in the triveni. Guide them there."

There was a murmur of agreement, and the mask-keeper vanished.

Bhumika searched in her heart for the things she understood to be the bones of faith: the quiet, lingering hope of a tale of yaksa. The gleaming rush of power that her own magic filled her with. And memories, of kneeling with her temple siblings, and feeling like part of a greater whole. As if, in worship, there could be a future.

Her faith, like her temple siblings, was at best a ghost—a shadowy thing that fluttered in her head and heart, half-remembered. She held the wisps of it tightly, forcing herself to feel it.

If her brother were alive, he'd laugh at her. He'd always believed in great dreams, in an Ahiranya that could never be. Now Bhumika had no choice but to do the same.

In the mornings, Padma liked to attempt to toddle at top speed while screaming at the top of her lungs. Unfortunately, she could not yet walk without clinging on tightly to the nearest surface, so her efforts were in vain and often ended in tears and bruised knees.

Because she could not wreak the havoc she desired unaided on her chubby year-old legs, Bhumika often facilitated her efforts, holding Padma carefully beneath the arms, steadying her shaky steps on the ground. Bhumika didn't run, of course—she didn't need to. "My legs are much longer than your own," she said to Padma, as her daughter careened on the spot in Bhumika's arms. "But I am happy to help you run," she went on with false solemnity, as Padma burbled and tried to fling herself headfirst onto the marble floor. "Practice hard enough, and I'm sure you'll outrun us all one day."

After leaving the Hirana, Bhumika had immediately changed into a more familiar, colorful sari and wrapped her mask away. Then she had gone to find her child.

That morning, Padma had been with one of the older maids, who handed her over gratefully. "She's a handful, elder," the woman had said.

"I know," Bhumika had replied, trying not to sound too proud.

Bhumika had never thought she'd be the kind of woman who would play with a child like this. As the wife of the governor of Ahiranya, she had known she would be required to uphold a certain image. Holding children was all well and good, but running with them, chasing them like a maidservant? That would have been unacceptable for a woman of her status.

But she was not the governor's wife any longer.

She was free.

Around them, light poured into the mahal: through the open windows, framed by flowers, and the cracks in the walls and the roof that had not yet been repaired, and perhaps never would be. Bhumika could feel every curling vine and trembling petal, a low-level awareness that hummed in her blood. But she ignored it for now, as she spoke to Padma, and laughed with her, and occasionally offered the mahal dwellers who walked by her a nod of acknowledgment.

Jeevan found her, eventually.

"My lady," he said, bowing appropriately. His face was set in its usual forbidding lines: angular and tense, his mouth firm. Then he looked at Padma—who was flailing extremely enthusiastically—and his expression softened into a smile. "May I?" He asked.

Bhumika nodded, and he kneeled down and offered Padma his hands. Bhumika released her daughter and she teetered forward, grasping onto him with an ear-piercing shriek of what Bhumika could only assume was happiness. He held Padma steady, his eyes on her, and said, "Lord Chetan is waiting for you."

Chetan was a highborn Ahiranyi. He'd tried to seek her out at the festival of the dark of the moon, full of concerns and questions, and she had diplomatically put him off. Now, here he was again. Apparently.

"Is he," Bhumika said neutrally. "I didn't request him."

"He claimed you had planned to meet."

"No." Bhumika pursed her lips. "Khalida has a record of all my arranged meetings."

"I haven't seen Khalida this morning, my lady."

Sometimes she missed the ease with which the household had run before—*before*. But now all her servants were also her advisors and her soldiers. All her soldiers were her allies. She did not have the structure and support of an empire to back her rule, as her husband had. Just as her mahal was half broken, held together by luck and magic, so was her government.

"I'll find her," Bhumika said. She kneeled down, and Jeevan nudged Padma until she was clinging to her mother's hands instead.

"Have one of the girls serve him refreshments."

"My lady," he said, and bowed once more before striding away.

Bhumika walked into her own chambers and found Khalida waiting. Khalida looked sweaty, harangued.

"The roof came down on one of the rice stores," Khalida said grimly.

"Is anyone injured?"

Khalida shook her head.

"Have any stocks been lost?"

"Some," Khalida said shortly, which meant that a handful of servants were still working their way through the wreckage and making an accounting of the damage. Bhumika winced internally. They could not afford to lose any supplies.

A hand tugged at her sari.

"Up," Padma demanded.

"You're a terror," Bhumika said, with utter fondness, and swept her daughter up into her arms. She kissed Padma's face and over and over again until Padma shrieked and kicked her little legs furiously.

"My lady," Khalida said impatiently. "Hand her to me and go."

Bhumika did, with one further kiss. It felt good to briefly relish this: the smell of her daughter's hair, the soft riot of her curls; the sheer, joyous fury with which she greeted the world.

Khalida thought Bhumika overindulged her child. That was fine. That was a mother's prerogative. Let her daughter be a terror, at least for a time.

Some believed they could ready a child for the cruelties of the world with punishment and unkindness, callousing the heart before the world could set its knives upon it. But Bhumika was raised a temple child—taught to excise her softness and weakness, and to face the world with her teeth bared. And still, every loss she had experienced had hurt her. Still, she carried the scars of her own choices, and the choices made by others.

She wanted a different path for her daughter. Perhaps all lives became brimful of pain, eventually. Well, then. Let her daughter's start painlessly, in joy. Let her have at least that.

"My apologies for the delay," Bhumika said, sweeping into the room. "I was tending to my daughter."

Chetan nodded stiffly. He was seated by a low table, under a latticed window, in the only relatively unscathed receiving room of the mahal. A gouge in the wall had been carefully concealed behind silk curtains. There were perfumed flowers in bowls, at intervals across the room, and a single maid holding a plate of delicacies. She remained by the door, eyes lowered demurely, as Bhumika crossed the room and kneeled down across the table from the highborn lord.

"How old is she now?" Chetan asked.

Quintessential small talk, but not without purpose. It allowed Bhumika the opportunity to smile, and wave over the girl to pour out tea and offer pastries. Chetan accepted the tea, but declined the rest.

"She has passed her first year," said Bhumika. "You have children of your own, don't you?"

"I do," Chetan agreed. "Two boys. The eldest will soon be fourteen."

"My congratulations," Bhumika said. "It is a fine thing to have your heir near adulthood."

For a moment, his gaze warmed. Then, as he visibly remembered himself, it shuttered. He leaned back. In a severe voice he said, "If we may begin, Lady Bhumika, I have serious concerns, many serious concerns, and they have not been properly addressed by you or your courtiers."

Since her "courtiers" were cooks and maids, not all of whom could read, and a handful of rebels who couldn't be convinced to put down their masks or their knives and engage in anything resembling diplomacy, that was no surprise.

"I welcome the guidance of Ahiranya's highborn," Bhumika said. "I have taken advisors from all the great families. I hold audiences with them regularly, as you must be aware, Lord Chetan." And what a dull business that was: listening to the concerns of each and every highborn representative, the complaints as their income from their pleasure houses dwindled faster and faster with each day. As the war between the would-be empress and the sitting emperor dragged on. Every audience more laden with fear as time passed, every suggestion for new sources of profit more wild. But Bhumika could not make money appear out of thin air. She could not make the highborn wealthier when there was no money to be had. She could barely stop Ahiranya's people from starving. "I would have your advice too, of course. You have views on the governance of Ahiranya?"

"I do. My views are straightforward, elder: The highborn of our country were better served under Emperor Chandra." His gaze bored into her. "Many of us would rejoin the empire if we could."

"How did Emperor Chandra better serve the needs of my fellow highborn?" Bhumika asked immediately. "No, do not scowl at me, Lord Chetan—I am asking. Tell me."

"Elder Bhumika, you and your temple council are well aware that we struggle for food. For grain, for rice, for meat."

"Ahiranya has struggled for many years. And my council and I are ensuring that the rot does not spread to further fields. We will have crops enough," Bhumika replied.

"Trade is dwindling," he retorted immediately. "The merchants beyond our borders are frightened of us." *Of you*, he did not say. *Of the power in you.*

But she heard it. Oh, she heard it.

"Empress Malini's allies trade with us," Bhumika pointed out. And what a relief it had been, when the first Srugani merchants had arrived—just as Empress Malini had promised they would, in her official message to the temple elders of Ahiranya. *I keep my vows*, she'd written. Bhumika hoped that would continue to hold true. "And even were that to change, Ahiranya must of course learn to rely upon our own strength. These are...unpredictable times, Lord Chetan. We have a duty to strive for self-reliance."

His mouth thinned. "If I may be so bold," he said.

She inclined her head in permission.

"We have so long relied on support from the empire," he said. "I— and many of my fellows—are not convinced our country *can* survive alone. If the elder would consider other forms of diplomacy..."

Bhumika sipped her tea. Set the cup down gently.

"No one would wed me now, Lord Chetan," she said. "My fellow elders would not be a suitable prospect, either."

"I did not mean—"

"Did you not? Forgive me. I am not sure what other avenues of diplomacy are available to us," she said evenly. "I could, of course, plead for mercy for Ahiranya and lay down my life. But Emperor Chandra would still visit punishment upon us. I do not mean to be combative, of course, Lord Chetan," Bhumika went on, allowing her voice to soften. "But the emperor is not a kind man or a forgiving one. We are lucky that he has been so thoroughly distracted by rebellion and upheaval in his own empire, or Ahiranya's borders would be swarming with even more Parijatdvipan soldiers than they already are. As it is, my sister and I have dealt with enough of them to know that the emperor does not view Ahiranya as a friend."

"And what became of those men?" Chetan asked. "Those Parijat-dvipan soldiers? *I* have not seen them, and I promise you my guards patrol my estate diligently."

Bhumika thought of giving him a demonstration of power. But no. She was trying to maintain a fine balance. She needed him intimidated but not alienated. Loyal, despite all his misgivings. She took another sip of her tea. "I skewered them through. I am efficient, Lord Chetan. If you have seen no imperial soldiers, it is because my sister and I left none alive. I see no way he would *not* inflict punishment on all of us for that, elder and highborn alike."

Chetan said nothing.

"My lord, your line is ancient," she went on. "Your ancestry is almost as illustrious as my own. Since your early youth, when you rose to the head of your family, you have spent a significant portion of your coin on funding rebellion. Many of the mask-keepers who serve upon the temple council were aided by you." *And you did not think on how we would survive then*, she thought with a savageness she did not allow to touch her face, her voice. *You merely played at rebellion. You liked the sweetness of the idea, and never considered the bitterness that reality would bring.*

"We cannot reclaim the glory we had under the empire," she said, to soothe his feelings. There had been no real glory, of course. But the empire had assured the highborn of wealth and security, and now that that promise was gone, they were faced with a shadow of the same real-ities all Ahiranyi faced—of hunger and of instability, of an unkind world. It was a shock to them. But they would have to adjust to it. "What we have now is hard won, and we will struggle to hold it. Per-haps you think we would be safer and happier under Emperor Chan-dra. Or perhaps you think there are highborn better suited to the task of ruling Ahiranya, who could step into the place of the council—"

"Lady Bhumika—"

She raised a hand to stop him.

"It does not matter," she said. "I don't seek to see into your heart. I have the utmost respect for your suffering. I think of what my uncle would have faced, had he lived through what befell the city, and I . . ." A pause. "I mourn for what you've lost," she said, to remind him of what *she* had lost. "But you need the strength of the temple council. The magic within me and my fellows. If you wish to hold on to what wealth and privilege remains to you, you will remain steadfast in your loyalty to me and mine, and an independent Ahiranya. Or everything you love will fall."

"As you say," he managed.

"I would, of course, accept children of our highborn as temple children," she told him. "I would never deny my fellow highborn their right to rule alongside the elders, in whatever capacity you choose. But it is a dangerous path, as you know. Better, I think, if we work as allies. Come to the next audience, Lord Chetan. Advise me. Steer our country. Or send me your youngest child, if you wish. There are many choices before you. But Chandra is not one of them."

She paused long enough to let the words settle. Long enough for his jaw to tighten, and his eyes to lower, as her words rattled through him and settled into his bones. "Now," she said, gesturing over the maid. Compassion stitched into the shape of her mouth and her creased brow, so he would know they were allies still. "Have more tea, Lord Chetan. And try these mathiya. I promise you they're very good."

It was night when Bhumika climbed the Hirana again. Pitch dark, nothing but the stars and a faintly silver half moon to guide her. But the Hirana welcomed her like an old friend. In the daylight, with an audience, it had moved like water. Now, with the worshippers long gone, the stone merely molded to her feet. This rising was a slow, gentle thing. She gazed up as she walked—at the fissures in the rock, and the figures carved upon it. Yaksa stared down at her, their eerie faces glowing under moonlight.

Priya was already there. Sitting on the plinth at the center of the triveni. Around her, the triveni was open to the night—the stars shining on her through the open disc above the plinth, the lights of the city shining up from the velvet dark below.

"Tell me how it went," Bhumika said, by way of greeting.

"Oh, it was fine."

Bhumika pursed her lips. Something had gone wrong, then, but she'd have no answers from Priya now. Not without an argument she wasn't in the mood to have.

"Why don't you walk with me?" Bhumika asked instead.

Priya slid from the plinth and joined her.

Priya was so often gone, patrolling to deal with imperial soldiers or gather their bodies, traveling across Ahiranya with one of the mask-keepers or with Sima or one of Jeevan's men, managing rot in the fields and orchards, or stopping the rot's progress in sickened mortal bodies. But she and Bhumika were never truly apart.

They met in the sangam. Beneath skeins of stars, on strange rivers, they spoke to each other. Shared truths and tales. They were temple elders, and flesh could no longer limit them.

But every time Bhumika saw Priya in person, she was struck by how *worn* Priya looked: her skin unevenly sun-darkened, her body in restless motion, her eyes tired but always searching, always rising to track the movement of birds on the horizon or swaying leaves on distant trees.

Like Bhumika, Priya could feel the pulse and lifeblood of Ahiranya: every vein of green, every blade of grass, every insect burrowing under the soil. Unlike Bhumika, she seemed to lack any ability—or desire—to ignore it.

Even now, with Bhumika maintaining a slow and even pace as they circled the triveni, Priya was restless—moving to the edge and back again, seeking magic in the stone around her. The Hirana responded to her eagerly.

"Maybe I should ask Billu for some of his hashish," Priya said, carving grooves into the triveni with her heels. The stone shuddered under the press of her foot, pulsing in time with each swift, thoughtful blink of her eyelids. "Maybe it would make me feel calmer."

"You could just grow your own," Bhumika pointed out dryly.

Priya wrinkled her nose.

"Too much effort."

Bhumika rolled her eyes. "It would be no effort and you know it. I don't know why you insist on saying things you don't mean."

"Next time let me bring some wine with me and I'll keep quiet."

"I can smell the wine on you already," Bhumika said dryly. "Besides, you need to be able to concentrate, Pri."

"Oh, you know me," Priya said. She smiled, a kind of reflexive twitch of her lips, as she looked at the edges of Ahiranya in the distance. "I never let my focus falter."

"I met with Lord Chetan today," Bhumika said instead of lecturing, and told Priya everything.

"I can't believe you of all people told a highborn that we need to be self-reliant," Priya said with a grin. "I don't care for politics, particularly..."

"As I'm well aware," Bhumika said.

"...but you've always been very, very clear that Ahiranya can't survive alone. And now you've changed your mind?"

"My mind hasn't changed." Bhumika looked over the lip of the triveni—off, off at the horizon as Priya had done. "I would never have chosen this path. But since we're here, we must make the best of it. And for all the empress's promises—and generosity—we cannot rely on Parijatdvipa to trade with us when Parijatdvipa is ripping itself apart."

There was a certain expression Priya wore sometimes. It came over her most often in the dark of an evening, or in the lulls in conversation about the Parijatdvipan empire: its politics, its city-states, its ugly and grinding war. She wore it now.

"Priya," Bhumika murmured.

Priya blinked. The look flitted away, swift as a bird in flight.

"We have to discuss the mask-keepers," said Bhumika.

"Ganam spoke to me about it again."

It. The deathless waters. The power waiting for them there, if they were willing to risk death.

The power Bhumika and Priya had.

"Of course he did."

"They're getting restless." A pause. The ground shifted, as Priya rocked back on her heels. "Maybe it's time it happens. We can't say no forever."

"We do need help," Bhumika said, eventually. "We can't continue to be the only two thrice-born in the world."

"Well, we have a good division of labor," Priya said with a shrug. "I deal with the fields and the sick, and those gangs out in the villages, and you deal with the highborn and the politics."

"There are a lot of fields," Bhumika said mildly. "And a lot of people."

"There are," Priya agreed. Then she huffed out a sigh; long and slow and achingly tired. "There are."

"I don't know if you want the mask-keepers to pass through the waters or not," Bhumika said. "You argue in their favor and against them."

"I'm not arguing. I'm just pointing things out."

"Maybe I want your view," Bhumika said, a little irritation bleeding into her voice. "Maybe I need the advice of my fellow elder."

"Ah, Bhumika," Priya said. "Do you really want me to advise you? We'll only disagree."

"If I can take advice from people like Lord Chetan, I think I can stay calm with you."

"I don't know about that. I can be very annoying when I want to be."

"Priya."

"See?"

Instead of pressing forward into the inevitable argument, Bhumika said, "I received another emissary from Srugna."

"Did you?"

"Mm." This time, the Srugani king had sent one of his minor wives—a shrewd, beautiful woman with fashionably blackened teeth and kohl thick around her eyes, who had shared a fine meal with Bhumika and cooed over her daughter, then laid out the desires of her husband and his council. "They're willing to pay us handsomely to have their own fields cleared or saved."

"Well then, I suppose I'm going to have to learn how to do that," Priya said. She sounded tense. "The rot's spreading farther and farther every day," she muttered. "It won't be the Srugani alone who need help soon, I expect."

"And that could afford us an opportunity. But it isn't one we can take advantage of with you alone to do the work. You understand?"

"I wish," said Priya, "that I could cure it. That I...Ah, Bhumika, I wish I weren't so slow."

"You're not slow," Bhumika said. "You're trying to attempt the impossible."

Priya's forehead wrinkled as she frowned.

"You don't know that."

"I know it would be easier if you had help, and I have no time to spare." And nothing like Priya's skill with the delicate work of untangling the rot. "I have grown to know Kritika a little better. But you're more familiar with the other mask-keepers. What do you think of them?"

"I think they want a better Ahiranya," Priya said. "Or at the very least, they want Ahiranya to survive, and they want it to be led by its own people. They're always happy to help me with my work. But I don't know if that makes them trustworthy." A pause. "They're *not* trustworthy."

"You seem to be fast friends with Ganam."

"That doesn't mean I don't know what he is," Priya said. "Spirits, Bhumika, you really think I'd trust anyone."

"I don't," Bhumika said. "But you have put your faith in some... interesting people."

Priya laughed. "I guess I have. And look where it's got us. Ruling our own country."

Instead of responding, Bhumika paused and pondered, rifling through possibilities.

Allowing the mask-keepers—the *rebels*, as they always would be named, in the privacy of Bhumika's mind—to have the same sheer power that Bhumika and Priya now possessed seemed foolhardy at best. But Bhumika had ruminated over the problem; turned it over in her head, time and time again, and she could see no alternative. She could not refuse them without civil war. And ah, soil and sky, she and Priya desperately needed their burden lightened.

"If you really want my view," Priya said slowly, watching Bhumika's face, "then I think now that they've become once-born, it's all inevitable. I remember what it was like. Craving the waters. They're going to feel that want rolling through them day and night until they get the chance. And that lot have never been afraid of death."

"No indeed," Bhumika murmured. "Fine. I'll talk to Kritika. We'll do what's needful."

"Do you ever wonder," Priya said, "what it would be like if more of us had survived? If we weren't the only temple children left?"

"No." *Yes. Often. Always.* "I don't allow myself to dwell on it," Bhumika lied.

"Do you think it would have been easier? All of this."

Priya did not remember their siblings as Bhumika did.

"I think we would not be here," said Bhumika. "I think our lives would have been very different. I can't imagine it, and I don't wish to."

"Sima's told me she'd like to pass through the waters," Priya said then, cutting through the jumbled weight of Bhumika's own thoughts. "And there are others—Billu, definitely—who'd like to try, too. And don't tell me maidservants and cooks aren't fit for it, Bhumika. *I'm* an ex-maidservant."

"You were a temple child first. Besides, Priya—don't you want better for them than this? Would you have chosen this for yourself, if there had been another path?"

Priya went silent at that.

"Tell me," Priya said eventually, voice softer, "how Padma's been. Does she still yell all the time?"

"Yes. Because she's still a baby," Bhumika said in her driest tone. "Come and see her in the morning, if you like. She misses you."

Bhumika was finally considering whether it was time to prepare for bed, when there was a sharp rap on her chamber doors. Khalida opened them. Jeevan strode in.

"Lady Bhumika," Jeevan said, with a neat bow. "There's a messenger waiting for you urgently." A pause. He straightened up. "From Empress Malini."

Bhumika's heart gave a thud.

"I'll be there immediately," she said.

This time, she headed to the receiving room with appropriate haste.

A thin man waited for her. He looked as if he had stumbled from his horse and come to her directly, and smelled like it too—but his bow was polite, his voice respectful when he said, "Elder. I have been sent with a message from the empress herself. A missive written in her own hand."

Bhumika took the letter from him.

"Thank you," she said, with as much grace as she could muster. "If you follow my maid, she'll see to it that you have some sustenance and a comfortable place to rest."

The messenger bowed again, murmuring his thanks. And Bhumika began to read.

It was a short message. Her hand trembled, just slightly, as she creased it shut once more.

"Jeevan," she said, turning to the door where her commander waited, gaze alert. "Please. Summon Priya. I need her."

KUNAL

Kunal did not like Parijat. It was a cold city. Cold marble. Cold people. Its flowers far too pale, too fragile, its food too sweet and milk-rich. So he was glad, as Varsha was, when a priest from Saketa guided them around the imperial mahal and kindly asked after their father in Saketa, and the temples of the faceless mother on local estates—a source of shame they had both been told not to speak of in Parijat.

"I began my training in a temple of the faceless mother," the priest Kartik confided in them with a smile. "I believe those who serve the faceless mother have a great deal to teach the priests of the mothers who reside in Parijat itself. But do not tell anyone I said so," he said in a confiding tone, eyes warm. "It shall be our secret, as fellow Saketans."

Varsha giggled a little, covering her mouth with her hand. Even Kunal was comforted by the priest's consideration.

"Perhaps you will be able to guide me in the future, priest," his sister said timidly. "I am inclined to worship."

"My apologies, princess," the priest said, slowing to allow her to match his pace. With a pang of embarrassment, Kunal did the same. "The High Priest summoned me to assist you and your brother in settling comfortably into the mahal. But my temple lies near the Veri river, and I must return to it."

He was, he explained, the one who trained the priestly warriors who now served in the mahal and had also been sent trooping to Saketa with casks of mothers' fire. Fire harvested from the deaths that filled the mahal constantly with the ugliest perfume of smoke. Charred flesh.

"Any priest you've met who can wield a weapon is under my purview," he added. "You need only tell them you are a friend of Kartik, and they will treat you with respect."

The priest even honored them with a meal from home—bursting with spice and flavor, pleasantly sour—that they devoured more swiftly than was probably sensible. The next day he departed.

And Varsha prepared for her marriage.

The wedding was inevitable. It had been inevitable for a long time: long before Kunal's father had called him into his chambers and served them both cold sherbet and said, "The emperor seeks a closer alliance. You will accompany your sister to Parijat." A pause. "Keep her safe, Kunal."

A queen, but not Emperor Chandra's *only* queen, for all that his father and his father before him had only taken a single wife. It had been explained to Kunal, by his father and by the priests that served in the High Prince's private temple to the mothers, that the emperor needed a Parijati bride.

But the emperor also needed an alliance, now that so many highborn had turned traitor and allied with his sister. And Saketa...Well.

Saketa needed food.

"I never thought I would marry the emperor himself," Varsha said in a small voice. Gifts were arranged around her. Gold-embroidered saris. Jewels. Vases of flowers. Silk ribbons, and parasols, and slippers bejeweled with diamonds. "Will I be happy, do you think?"

Kunal thought of the day he had first met the emperor. The way the emperor had taken him to a private garden. A place so beautifully manicured it should be a haven; and at its heart, the remains of a woman still burned. The way the emperor had smiled, ever so casually, and said, "This is what will save your country and my own. A sacrifice taken by a true emperor. Is anything more righteous?"

He remembered his father's eyes, more tired by the day, as his low princes defected to the service of the false empress.

"Our country is dying," his father had told him. "We need Emperor Chandra's support if we wish to survive. I will pay any price. Even her."

"Yes," Kunal said. He tried to smile at her. "I think you will be."

* * *

On the morning of the wedding, Kunal was summoned to the emperor's chambers.

He bowed low as the emperor dressed. As the emperor told his servants what food to be arranged, and how guests should be seated, and what traditional games would be allowed. In the same offhand manner, he told Kunal that no more men could be sent to Saketa, and no more weapons. But Saketa would be required to stand against the false empress with its full force of power.

"Either my sister and the traitors who support her will be destroyed, or their forces will be depleted," Chandra said genially. "She will not be able to turn on Parijat with your father burning her people alive."

The tailor laid more cloth across the bed: a white jacket embroidered in seed pearls so closely sewn together that they resembled armor. A long, red achkan for luck.

"And my father?" Kunal managed. "And his men? The people in the fort?"

"Your father has my assurance that I will support your rise to High Prince," said the emperor. "Your sister will be the mother of my children."

Not, a voice of cold reason whispered in Kunal's mind, *the mother of his heir. Note what he does not say.*

"Your people," the emperor went on, holding out his wrist so that his servant could adjust the heavy torcs of gold adorning them, "will not starve. The rot will be handled. Your food supplies will be secure." He gave Kunal an indifferent smile. "Remember that, and be glad of my benevolence."

Kunal bowed his head and proclaimed he was glad indeed.

He watched his sister walk around the ceremonial wedding fire, garbed in resplendent red, and thought, *My country is dying.*

He watched her bow for the garland, and thought, *Our father is dying.*

He watched her as she lowered her head for the wedding garland, and thought, *My sister will die.*

And there is nothing I can do.

11

PRIYA

Priya read the letter three times. She could feel Bhumika's gaze on her. But she didn't look up. Even after she had stopped reading, Priya traced the words with her eyes—each loop and each whorl, the steady boldness of writing in Malini's own hand.

"What do you make of it?" Bhumika asked, when Priya was silent for another second too long.

"I think she's in some danger," Priya said finally. "Enough that she risked—this."

"*The traitor emperor possesses a weapon of fire. A green-sabered warrior in a highborn's court,*" Bhumika quoted from the letter. "The empress knows the Birch Bark Mantras very well."

"She does," Priya said quietly. "She uses it like your poets do. Telling one story to tell another. But you know that, don't you? You've read every word she's sent me."

"I've read every word the self-proclaimed empress of Parijatdvipa has sent my fellow elder of Ahiranya, yes," Bhumika said with exaggerated patience. "If you want private correspondence, Priya, then perhaps you'll decide to seek the affections of a less powerful woman. You don't need to be annoyed with me over it."

"I'm not annoyed about it," Priya lied.

"I'm sure," Bhumika said. "Do you have any more insight into the choice of 'green-sabered warrior' than I do?"

The tale Malini had referenced was obscure enough that it was likely very few people from beyond Ahiranya would know it. Even in Ahiranya, it would not be well known. It was a small fable—the story of a warrior who claimed his sword of green wood was yaksa-blessed, that it contained a yaksa's great powers. With his lie, he entered the service of a highborn—and brought about the death of his lord in battle. It was a warning.

"A false weapon," Priya murmured. "A false flame that is not blessed. That will bring ruin." She hesitated, then said, "Have you heard anything about fire? Anything that happened to Mali—to the empress's army?"

The war had felt distant to them, so far. They had only faced limited attacks from the emperor's forces, easily quelled by the forest and their magic, and Jeevan's carefully arranged patrols of soldiers. The emperor's focus was clearly on his sister, and as long as she concentrated her efforts on places that were not Ahiranya, the emperor would do the same.

"I don't have spies in the *empress's* army, as much as I'd like to," Bhumika said dryly. She'd definitely caught Priya's slip. "But the messenger she sent to us shared a little with the maid who brought him his dinner and offered him sympathy for having to travel so far so swiftly. The empress was intending to treat with the High Prince of Saketa. But when she arrived, the High Prince's men attacked her own with fire. The messenger implied it was—unusual flame. But he was reluctant to say more."

"I'm sure he was," Priya muttered. Bhumika's best maidservants were very good at prying information out of people, but there was a limit to what could be accomplished discreetly. "Do you think it's fire like their mothers of flame once used upon the yaksa?"

"I think the Parijatdvipans may believe it is, even if the empress doesn't," Bhumika said steadily. "I can imagine that has some—implications."

The pause between her words was heavy with meaning.

"You're going to have to tell me what all the implications are."

A sigh. "Priya."

"What? I'm just being honest. Or I can pretend I have a mind as clever as yours. Would you like me to lie?"

"The Parijati worship the mothers and their fire," Bhumika said. "A person who controls that fire is, surely, the rightful ruler of the empire. And if it is not Empress Malini, then she will not cling to that title of *empress* for long." Bhumika's gaze flickered between the letter still clutched tenderly in Priya's hands, and Priya's face. "You're going to have to try to think as I do," Bhumika went on. "If you do as she wishes."

And there it was. The request Malini had made. Between tales from the Birch Bark Mantras, and remarks about weather and travel, and wishes for Ahiranya's health, and the health of its elders and highborn—there was the real reason for her letter.

"I don't know what to do," Priya admitted. "She's asked for an elder. That doesn't mean..." Priya paused. Swallowed, and said, "What do you think I should do?"

"Think like me," Bhumika said. "Just for a moment."

Priya tried.

"Why does she want an elder at all?" Priya asked, finally.

"She doesn't want an elder," said Bhumika. "She wants you."

You don't know that, Priya thought. But of course Bhumika did. Just as Priya knew. It was Priya she had written to; Priya she had remembered, even when she stopped being a princess and took up a greater crown.

"I don't see how I could help her," Priya said.

"Can't you? With your gifts?"

"The gifts that the elders had before us were no good against the mothers' fire, long ago."

"If the fire is false, our gifts—your gifts—will suffice," said Bhumika.

"I'm needed here."

"So many excuses," murmured Bhumika. "It's almost as if you don't want to go. Is that so?"

Priya swallowed. "This is home. And I have so much to do. The people—the rot—"

"I can manage the rot."

"And run a country at the same time?"

"We just discussed how the mask-keepers want to pass through the waters," Bhumika said. "They want to become twice- and thrice-born. They will be able to help with the rot. And with governance, if they must. And you'll come home and continue your work eventually." She gave Priya a steady look. "We need the empress to take her throne. Nothing is possible if she does not. Perhaps she recognizes that she requires your strength for that. One ancient magic, false or not, against another. Perhaps she just wants you beside her." A sigh. "It doesn't matter. I'll make do. Ahiranya will make do. What choice is there, really, Priya?"

There's always a choice, Priya thought. What could Malini do, from across the breadth of an empire? And she had not ordered them. Not threatened. The letter had been very clear on that.

And yet. And yet.

There were always words, words under words, with Malini.

Malini never lied. But her truths were deep waters.

I ask you, with courtesy, as my allies—

"We'll still have the sangam," said Bhumika. "We'll maintain our evening discussions."

"I can't believe that you think I should go," said Priya. "I thought you'd try and convince me not to."

Bhumika shook her head. Her mouth was thin, troubled. "I always knew you would seek her out."

"Not while Ahiranya still needs me," Priya retorted hotly. "Not while you still need me. Not when we have a handful of once-born you don't really trust, and the chance you're going to lose half of them to drowning. Bhumika, I can't."

"Many of our alliances only exist because of your Empress Malini. If we lose her goodwill..." Bhumika shrugged delicately.

Priya nodded, saying nothing for a moment.

"We cannot afford for her to fail. Or to die," Bhumika said into the silence.

"You told me once that if she turned on us, I should remove her."

"That would be a death on our terms, for our purposes," Bhumika said. "Any other kind of death would ruin us."

Malini failing. It was hard to imagine. Ever since the news had made its way back to Ahiranya that it was the princess, not the prince, who sought to take Emperor Chandra's throne—in whispers and rumors carried by merchants and traders, swirling through to markets ahead of the arrival of an official imperial missive, signed with a flourish by Malini's own hand—Priya had believed that Malini would win. She was too clever to lose. Too willing to pay any price. Even in her own skull, Priya couldn't lie to herself: Malini would do what was necessary to ensure her own success, even if it cost her Priya.

She'd burned priests, people said. And Priya had thought of Malini's face after they'd kissed in the forest—the fierceness in her eyes—and thought, *She would. She would.*

How desperate was Malini, to have summoned one of them at all? *Was* she desperate? Her letter had been all diplomacy. There were no creases from tense fingers; no salt from tear marks.

But there had been the tale from the Birch Bark Mantras. There had been all her words before. Her *Priya, I think of you—*

Priya swore and pressed her hand to her face.

"Ah, spirits. Does it have to be me? Wouldn't you like to go on a trip, Bhumika?"

"I'm sure I'd do very well in the empress's court," Bhumika said. "But you know it has to be you."

"I don't know how to talk to kings and princes."

"You've spoken to at least one prince before," Bhumika pointed out. "And an empress. Though I suppose you did more than speak with her—"

"Bhumika."

"Am I not allowed to make the occasional joke?" Bhumika said, smiling a little when Priya scrunched her face in response. Then her expression turned grave again. "You'll manage. They're just highborn."

"You're better suited for dealing with them," Priya said to her. "We both know you are."

"It's you she wants," Bhumika said quietly. "She may not have asked for you by name—wisely enough—but you know it to be true. And even if that were not the case, I cannot go."

Bhumika didn't have to say it: Ahiranya could survive for a while without Priya; without her hands on its soil, its people, its rot. But it couldn't survive without Bhumika, who held the mask-keepers and highborn and merchants and common folk together with a fragile weft of favors and loyalties, bribes and responsibilities. Priya wasn't fit for that kind of work.

"You will not be able to feign a highborn's diplomacy, never mind the kind of display expected of a country's ruler. I don't deny that."

"A teacher, maybe," Priya suggested desperately. She couldn't believe what she was saying. "Someone to train me in decorum. Or a companion on the journey to guide me."

"There is not a single highborn familiar with the intricacies of Parijatdvipan politics that I would feel comfortable entrusting with the task of supporting you on this journey," Bhumika said. "And I can only teach you so much before you leave."

"You tried to teach me once to be a lady's maid," Priya said defeatedly. "And I failed miserably at that. It may not be worth the effort."

"Well, you surely have more incentive this time," Bhumika said. "You may learn. We will try."

Bhumika did not sound sure of their success. That was fair.

"How can you trust me not to ruin everything?"

"Who else do I have to trust but you, Pri?"

True. Awful, but true.

"I think the empress has a vested interest in keeping you alive," Bhumika went on, voice low. "She thinks she knows what you are. Your strengths, and your weaknesses. She will not expect you to be a canny little politician. She will protect you from the worst of her own courtiers. So you must be what she wants and needs you to be instead, and hope that is enough to keep you safe. We'll arrange you a suitable retinue and what lessons we can."

"Don't send a big retinue with me," Priya said, speaking slowly as she stumbled through her own thoughts, trying to make sense of them. "Don't. The Parijatdvipans...I think it's better if they underestimate us."

"Your Malini wants you for what you can do," Bhumika said

quietly. "They'll know sooner or later exactly what an elder of Ahiranya is capable of. They will see, and they will fear you."

"Not if they think we're her puppets," said Priya. "Not if they think we're in her power and need her patronage to survive. What threat is a single woman with no allies, even if she has something powerful in her?" Priya smiled wryly. "It's almost the truth, isn't it? So it won't be hard to convince anyone."

"No," Bhumika said, voice unreadable. "I suppose not."

Priya brushed her arm against Bhumika's. "I thought you'd be happy."

"Happy to see you go? No."

"Happy that you don't have to part with many soldiers," Priya said. "You need every single one you have. And I'll take care of myself just fine. Perhaps I'll ask Sima to go with me. It'll keep her from taking the waters, at least—"

"Priya."

Priya went silent then. Silent and still. The timbre of Bhumika's voice—the solemn note in it—held her fast.

"Promise me you'll survive and come home," Bhumika said.

Priya swallowed.

"How can I promise that?" They both knew how dangerous the world could be—how quickly, brutally, easily a loved one could die and leave you behind, no matter how much they yearned to stay.

"Promise me," Bhumika repeated.

Bhumika had never asked for a promise that couldn't be kept. Her eyes were shining, suspiciously damp despite the severity of her expression. And Priya could only look away from her, and swallow through the thickness of her own throat, and nod.

"I promise," Priya said. "When all this is over, I'll come home to you."

There was no point in dallying. So Priya packed her possessions and passed on what responsibilities she could.

If Ganam thought it was traitorous of her to abandon Ahiranya at a Parijatdvipan imperial's bidding, he didn't say so, and the other mask-keepers were equally quiet. She was sure they were planning something—but if what they wanted was the chance to pass through the waters again, Bhumika was ready to provide it.

I hope they're ready to dig new graves, Priya thought grimly. She'd warned Ganam. That was all she could do.

Billu packed her some hashish. "And some arrack too," he said. "Vile shit it is, but who knows when you'll need it."

"Where did you even get so much of this?" Priya asked skeptically.

"I'm a close advisor of the temple elders, aren't I? People give me things."

"Billu, if you've been accepting bribes from people—"

"You'll do what?"

"Encourage you to get better-quality items," Priya said. "That's what."

He snorted.

"I bartered for it," he admitted. "It's mine by a fair trade. And now it's yours."

"When will I have time to use all of this?"

"You're going to join an army, aren't you? It's not for you, girl. It's for making friends. You'll win over soldiers faster with drugs and liquor than you ever will with pretty words."

"Thank you," she said. "I'm not—what do you want in return?"

"Why would I want anything? It's a gift." When she repeated her thanks, he shrugged and said gruffly, "Just get yourself back swiftly. You'll be missed."

She said goodbye to Rukh next.

"You'll be back soon enough," he said resolutely.

"Ah, you won't even pretend you're going to miss me?" Priya put on a front of anger, crossing her arms. "And after all I've done for you!"

Rukh gave a sigh, and rolled his eyes. But then he hugged her. He was a terrible hugger—all sharp, growing limbs and awkwardness. But she could feel the fierceness of his affection in the way his arms tightened around her. Helplessly fond, Priya hugged him in return.

"Thank you for all you've done for me, Priya," he said. "I'll miss you."

"That's better." She patted his head, even as he grumbled and shied away. He rubbed his knuckles over his eyes, clearing his throat.

"When you come back, I'll be using a proper saber," he told her. "You wait and see, you're going to be so impressed."

"You're not at all worried I might not come back, then?" He shook his head. "Brat." She ruffled the leaves of his hair, and this time he allowed it, laughing.

"You're stronger than anyone," he said. He met her gaze, and his face turned serious. "You'll be fine."

"Are you trying to comfort me?"

He shook his head.

"You know you're strong," he said. "But maybe you need to know that everyone knows."

Everyone did think she was strong.

Everyone but Bhumika, who said she trusted her, who was letting her go, but had looked at her with strange, damp eyes and begged a promise out of her. *Come home.*

Priya put that disquiet aside and sought out Sima.

She found her in Priya's own chambers, carefully folding a sari. There was already a salwar kameez neatly packed on her cot, a sachet of dried herbs for sweetness tucked into a sleeve.

Priya touched the kameez. She was almost sure she'd worn this in the training yard and dirtied it.

"You washed my clothes?"

"Was someone else going to do it?" Sima retorted.

"I could have."

"You hardly have the time," she said. "Besides, I don't mind." Priya looked up.

"I told Bhumika," Priya said, "that I'd take you with me."

"Me?" Sima blinked at her, mouth parted. "Why?"

"Don't you want to come?"

"I . . . who else? Just me?"

"Jeevan said he could spare a few men. So them. You. And that messenger Yogesh's men."

Sima was staring at her, still holding the sari in her hands.

"Why?" Sima asked again.

Priya hesitated. She didn't know how to say the truth. That she saw how their changed positions galled Sima, at least a little. That Priya could feel the rift between them. That she didn't blame Sima for it. That it was okay to want more. And that if Priya could give it to her—give her the opportunities and dangers she craved, give her a path to move forward upon—then she would.

"It would be good to have a friend with me," Priya said instead. "If...if you want to come. It might be an adventure."

"An adventure," Sima said flatly. "It's war, Pri. It's going to be a nightmare."

"You're probably right."

"Going with you would be...Pri, you shouldn't have asked me."

"But I have," Priya said. "And I mean it. If you want to come—there's a place for you. I just can't promise it's a safe one."

For a moment, Sima was silent. Then she sighed and bowed her head.

Priya could see the new looseness in her shoulders, and the smile growing on her mouth. Then Sima straightened up and abruptly began to walk away. "You can finish your own packing," she said. "I've got my own to sort out now. Spirits, Pri, you could have given me *some* notice."

"I'm sorry!" Priya called at her back.

"No you're not!"

Priya grinned. No. She wasn't.

PARUL

The key to surviving as a servant in the imperial mahal was to go unnoticed. Invisibility was as much a skill as arranging a highborn lady's hair, or cleaning lustrous, delicately embroidered silk, or gracefully serving during banquets, as Parul did.

As a child, born to palace servants, she had been taught her mother's work: the skill of artfully pouring wine, of moving easily through a hall carrying plates laden with pearly rice and steaming sabzis. She had also been taught to be efficient but not too swift or too graceful. To do your work too ill or too well will draw attention, her mother had warned her. *And no attention is good for a girl of your standing, Parul.*

Her mother had once told her a tale of two little hares. Sisters. One that liked to race, and one that liked to burrow. The racing one was charming, beautiful, loved by many. Her beauty caught the eye of many evil creatures: snakes and birds with a taste for flesh, all of whom wanted *her* flesh. But she did not fear them. "She thought she was too fast to be caught. Too quick for any snake to strike her!" Her mother had paused—her voice faltering when she pressed on, and said, with false lightness, "But she was wrong, my dove. Learn from her example."

Parul had learned. Every year she grew older, taller, prettier—she was pragmatic enough to acknowledge her own beauty, and the problems it could cause her—and survived life in the palace more or less unscathed. She had seen every tumultuous change that had rippled through the imperial mahal: Prince Aditya's departure to become a priest of the nameless, and Prince Chandra's rise to emperor; the imperial princess's refusal to burn, and all the awful burnings of other women that had followed, and never ceased; and all through it, she had been the hare that liked to burrow. The one that survived. Hidden, careful. Watching without being watched in return.

But the aftermath of the wedding had made her careless. Queen Varsha had gifted the high-ranking female servants of the palace trinkets, thin bracelets wrought of silver, and gauzy saris to celebrate her new marriage. Parul was not a high-ranked servant, of course, but she and the others had all thoroughly enjoyed wine and arrack left over from the many nights of banquets, and the little sweets lacquered in silver sugar, and one of the old aunties from the kitchens had painted Parul's hands with henna: looping, swirling birds and flowers, and a large jasmine flower right at the center of each of Parul's wrists.

Relaxed from celebrations, and perhaps a little merrier with alcohol than she should have been, Parul allowed her wariness to slip. Instead of taking the narrow servants' corridors to the servants' dormitories, she walked along the main corridors of the mahal. It was a small pleasure, and she thought it was surely safe enough. It was late night, and the residents of the mahal were either feasting or sound asleep. She was paying no particular attention to anything—simply enjoying the warm numbness of a night's drinking and celebrating—when she heard male voices. She froze, her heart in her throat.

She was near a doorway. And through it, she could see a corridor with pillars carved with looping designs. And moonlight, too much moonlight, from ceilings that were deliberately open to the sky, letting sun and stars and rain in unimpeded.

Oh, mothers save her. She knew where she was. Only one archway door separated her from a place she never dared to go.

Once, these quarters had been the chambers laid aside for the handful of Srugani advisors who had resided permanently in the mahal, serving the empire. The corridors were built in the Srugani style, welcoming to the whims of nature, and had not been altered even though the Srugani were all long gone—banished by the emperor. The quarters belonged to the emperor's priests and his priestly warriors now, raised so high in favor that they no longer resided solely in the temple, where they rightly belonged.

Those old Srugani advisors had been well liked by the servants who tended their needs. But the priests were carefully avoided.

Especially by the mahal's serving women.

Usually she walked swiftly when she came this way, slipping by the doorway as swift as a bird in flight. But she'd dawdled today, liquor making her slow prey. And the priests were drawing closer, close enough that she could see their shadows on the ground—and her own, melding into the shade thrown by the archway of the door. If she moved, they would see her shadow move. They would know she was here.

Parul knew the price of being caught. Once, at a small feast between a few of the emperor's military leaders, a serving girl called Chaiya, two years younger than Parul, had heard them speaking of battle tactics. She'd caught the eye of one of the lords—by accident, no more—and he'd laughed and asked her lightly, mockingly, if military strategy interested her?

When that lord lost his battle, he sought Chaiya out and slit her throat. She must have been a spy, he'd proclaimed. How else could he have lost?

"If Hemanth will not tell the emperor the full truth, how can he make the right choice?" An older priest with a deep voice was speaking. "Emperor Chandra has always listened to him. Always shown great respect for our priesthood, our service. If Hemanth would only explain..."

"I love the High Priest." A younger voice. "I trust him to convince the emperor."

They were speaking of the emperor. The *emperor*. What would they do to her if they found her here?

She couldn't run. It was as if her feet were rooted to the ground.

The older priest spoke again. "Kartik," he murmured. So quiet Parul could near not hear him over the pounding of her own heart, her panicked little breaths that she was desperately trying to hold in. "Hemanth believes the emperor will see reason. But I fear..."

His voice faded. She was hopeful for a moment that they had decided to walk away from her. But Kartik's voice was crisp, clear, and far too close when he said soothingly, "We are all united in our desire to protect Parijatdvipa. But I have made sure she will live long enough."

"Have you? How?" The older priest seemed relieved.

"Don't trouble yourself." Gently said. "And if the emperor will not listen to the guidance of his priests..." A pause. The scuff of footsteps pausing; the rasp of the older priest's breath, as they both drew to a stop. "There is another path," said Kartik, finally. "Still mother-blessed."

Tentatively, "And Hemanth? He approves?"

"He loves the emperor," Kartik replied. "But he will do what is best for Parijatdvipa, in the end. I have faith in that."

By now, Parul had stopped breathing entirely. She did not understand what they'd spoken of. But she knew, if they found her, that would not matter.

She could see them now: one shorter figure and the other taller. The priest Kartik stood in the moonlight with his profile to her, his gaze on his fellow priest, focused and attentive. She decided to take a risk. What else could she do?

Carefully, she took one mere step to the side. Pressed herself to the wall, where she would be better hidden, her shadow melding into the formless dark around her.

Their conversation stilled. For a second, fear grasped her. They would find her. They would burn her.

They did not.

The two priests made their farewells. "I'll leave with the dawn," Kartik said. "Return to my own temple."

"You will be missed."

"I'll return soon enough," he replied. "I find it difficult to leave Hemanth's side for long."

A moment of utter silence. Then:

Footsteps. Drawing closer.

She did not breathe. Did not breathe. Thought of the pyres—the smell of them always in the air, the screams the wind sometimes carried. There was nowhere in the mahal where the sound could truly be avoided. She thought of her own voice joining that hollow song— thought and almost wept—

He passed by. The edge of his robe skimmed the archway of the door, then vanished as he made his way along the main corridor of the Srugani quarters. His footsteps faded. And Parul shuddered, and began to stumble along, and thanked the mothers in her head and her heart for making her pass unnoticed one more time. For making her the hare in its burrow: safe in the dark, far from the harsh and killing light of a priest's eyes.

13

MALINI

It was presented to her as the unified vision of all her council: They would seek to starve Saketa out.

"Sieging the fort would be well and good if we had a proper defense against their greatest weapon," Malini said. "Have we gained one that I am unaware of, my lords?"

"Whatever weapons the High Prince may possess," Mahesh said carefully, formally, "his people cannot survive starvation. In time, they will surrender to our greater might."

"I see." Malini allowed her skepticism to seep into her voice. "Have our supplies altered? Our rice stocks? Our fuel? Our water?"

A twitch of his jaw was her response.

He knew what point she was making: For all their superior numbers, a siege was lost by the side that starved first. Malini was an empress only by prophecy and her own proclamation. Everything she had was negotiated, borrowed or bartered from her allies. Everything those allies gave her, they gave in order to see Chandra removed from the throne.

And they were growing restless.

"The empress is correct," an official piped up, much to the obvious ire of a handful of Mahesh's favored lords, who turned and glared at him. "We do not have the supplies for an extended siege."

"That is somewhat of a problem," Khalil murmured.

"Will Dwarali send more supplies to remedy it?" This was asked by a low prince of Saketa, his expression sullen. Seated among Malini's court, Raziya's eyes narrowed.

"The Lal Qila has offered what it can," Khalil said. "But I cannot speak for the sultan."

"Then you offer nothing of consequence."

Lord Narayan laid a placating hand on the low prince's arm.

"Their water supply," another lord offered. "If it's cut off—"

"The city holds deep reservoirs," Narayan said immediately. This was not new information to Malini, nor for any of the men present, and all the more reason why a planned siege was not remotely feasible.

"Nonetheless," the lord said mulishly. "It is an option."

There was a rustle from Malini's left as Lata rose to her feet. The men fell silent as she lifted her chin and spoke, her voice clear and calm.

"I must speak against this plan," Lata said, without wavering. Despite all the eyes upon her. "As a sage, I seek knowledge. I have learned about the history of our empire. And I can assure you, my lords, that the maze fort of Saketa has never been successfully sieged. It is famously impenetrable. Armies break upon its walls. In the Age of Flowers, it even kept the yaksa at bay, shielding the High Prince and his kin. To siege the fort," she concluded, "is to choose failure and the death of many, many men."

"Empress," Mahesh said firmly, ignoring Lata. "It is a gamble. None of us deny it."

She grimly marked how he was already aligning himself with the other highborn, and not with her. More proof that he would need to be dealt with.

"The High Prince," Mahesh went on. "His fortress. I do not dispute that he possesses—weapons—that we do not." She marked, again, how he paused over the word *weapons*, with something akin to reverence. "We cannot simply leave him here at our backs. He will follow us on our journey to face your brother, and we will be crushed between two forces: Parijat's and Saketa's. Whatever can be done to weaken or starve the High Prince's forces, the better. Our own difficulties may be significant, our supplies limited, but the High Prince is hemmed in. We are not. They will tire long before we do, and then we will have them. This path, Empress, and this path alone may bring us success. I am a seasoned general. You have placed your faith in me. Do not let it falter now. I beg you."

He bowed deeply, every inch the loyal soldier.

It sounded compelling when he spoke in such a way, all fealty. But it was not the whole truth.

They are not worried only about sieging Saketa, she thought. *They want to put Aditya in my place. They're buying time.*

She knew. It was, after all, not the first time men had tried. Every skirmish lost, every time the war bit like a dog at their heels—there were highborn who sought Aditya out.

A male scion of Divyanshi should rule us, not a daughter, they said to one another, when they believed she could not hear—the fools, never countenancing that she had eyes among their cup bearers, their maids, the boys who polished their armor.

Aditya is the eldest. The true heir.

Malini's time was running short. And damn him, Mahesh was stealing what little she had left.

She made sure to not let her expression change. She knew him. He was devoted to the mothers of flame. He could yet be swayed, if he could be led to believe in her again—if she could capture the moment when she'd first proclaimed herself empress, a year ago on the road to Dwarali; if she could preserve the worshipful light that had filled his eyes, and spear it through his heart—she could keep control of him.

"Then let us wait," she said. "And see what can be done, to remind Saketa that for all their weapons, they are our prisoners."

Malini went to Aditya's tent.

She brought Swati with her, carrying a tray of food.

"Brother," she greeted him, as Swati placed the food down and swiftly departed. "I missed our normal meeting. Apologies."

"None are needed," he said. "Rao told me what has been—happening."

If you had simply looked outside your tent, you would have known without his assistance.

She did not say it. She sat, tucking her legs beneath her. Smoothed her sari down. He gave her a calm look in return.

"We need to talk," she said bluntly. "Mahesh wants to place you upon the throne. Has he approached you?"

"He tried to invite me to a war council," said Aditya. "But beyond that, no." He traced the edges of the plate, touched his fingertips to the edge of the roti, feeling its heat. "There are lords who have approached me before," he said. "But not him."

"His first loyalty has always been to you."

Aditya shook his head. "He's a man of faith. Not Chandra's brand of faith in the mothers, but his belief is no less firm." Said not with cunning, but with the steady, assured understanding a priest had of religious conviction—the way it could mold a human mind and a human heart. "And the fire has shaken his faith. Blessed magical fire—"

"*The fire was not from the mothers,*" Malini said, exasperated. At least with Aditya, she didn't have to hide that much.

"It sounds very much like the blessed fire from the Book of Mothers," he said mildly. "To one such as Mahesh, a sign from the mothers will always have greater power, greater significance, than a sign from the nameless god."

She bit down on her tongue. A light, grounding pain. What was the use arguing with him? He was not saying he believed it—only that Mahesh did.

When she was calm—calmer—she spoke again.

"And if he asks you to take your place, to lead the army, to become emperor...?"

"Ah, Malini," he said softly. "You once begged me to do the same. If I could refuse you, do you think anyone else could sway me?"

She nodded tightly, the both of them staring at each other, tense and wary.

The curtain parted.

Malini had half-risen to her feet when Rao entered. He was holding a bottle of wine; he paused when he saw Malini there.

Rao offered her a tentative smile. He wasn't still angry with her, then. That was nice to know.

"I didn't know you would be here," Rao said apologetically.

"The guards didn't tell you?"

"Only a moment ago, at the door," he said. "So I don't have an extra cup for you, Malini. I'm sorry."

"I'll drink from the bottle then," she said easily. Rao nodded.

"Eat your food," Rao said to Aditya. "You're too thin."

"You sound like an auntie," Aditya said. But there was a hint of a smile at his mouth, and he finally began to eat.

"It's good, after all, that you're here too, Malini," Rao said. "It's easier to speak to you directly, with only trustworthy company. To speak to *both* of you."

He poured the wine: one glass for himself, one for Aditya.

Malini took the bottle. She had thought, once, that she would never drink again: that her slow poisoning via tainted wine during her imprisonment would sour her on it forever. But she'd discovered a curious pleasure in enjoying something that had once been a cause of pain for her. The wine was a proper Saketan vintage, rich and smooth, warming her belly.

Rao looked between them.

"Malini..."

"I don't want to discuss politics," said Malini swiftly.

Rao's expression was only faintly frustrated.

"You'll rarely have the opportunity to do so, with me, with your brother, without watchers," he pointed out.

"You're going to tell me I have Alor's support," she said. "I know that. You'll tell me Srugna chafes at the cost of war—the supplies they send us, the unglamorous drudgery of it—but they will stand by me because the nameless and the mothers have both chosen me, and I'm better than Chandra. And you're going to tell me that I need to do something about Mahesh." She took another sip of wine. Heady. "I've been told as much before. Find me a Parijati lord who can take his place, and I'll gladly remove him."

"I was going to talk about a lot of things, wasn't I?" Rao said mildly.

"I'm not wrong," Malini told him. "You would have said it all eventually. But I don't wish for that. Right now, I would simply like a moment of peace."

"I am not sure this is as peaceful as you hoped," Aditya murmured.

No. But it was a peaceful place for Rao. And mothers knew she needed Rao to remain strong. Right now he looked fragile, as if the war had leached something from him. For all the strength of his body, the new sun-darkened deep brown of his face, his arms leanly muscled beneath their bracelets of chakrams, he was ... reduced. Pared down by the ceaseless drumbeat of battle.

"We've spoken of what we need to," she said to Aditya.

"Then we should drink and do something to pass the time," Rao said. "We could play a game of five stones, if you like."

Malini laughed. She couldn't help it.

"The children's game?" She and Alori and Narina had played it time and again as girls, throwing colored stones in batches of twos, threes, fours, fives, up in the air and catching them with the same hand. Malini had always been awful at it.

"I even have painted pebbles for it," he confided.

"Fine," she said, holding out her hand. From the corner of her eye she saw Aditya smile too, shaking his head.

She lost, of course. Soundly. But at the end of it, she felt a little more relaxed. A little more herself. A little more human.

The bodies were, by tradition, kept distant from the main camp. Bodies were polluting: a source of sickness and stench. But there were always priests attending to the corpses, preparing them for the pyre, blessing them with prayers and ointment and garlands of funerary flowers.

In the very first weeks of battle—when Malini and her followers had begun to face Chandra's forces, on the great mountainous crags of Dwarali—her followers had brought priests from their own city-states and lands. But those men had not remained for long. Priests of the mothers held great respect for the dead, but death in war was hard and ugly. She did not blame them entirely for departing.

The priests maintaining the funerary tents now were not trained in Parijat. They were the keepers of small Saketan village shrines and humble temples to the mothers. In Saketa, there was a minor sect that worshipped the mothers as one being—the faceless mother, who they claimed was all women who had burned as one, joined in a single great consciousness. Small and looked down upon by Parijat's central priesthood, the sect were not afraid of hard work, and had quickly become the bulk of the priesthood serving her army.

As she approached the tent, flanked by Lata and Swati, Malini could see two men near the entrance. They were thin, tired looking, ash-marked roughly at the forehead and chin, their knot-worked hair bound back from their faces as they shared a carafe of water between them. When they saw Malini approaching, one leapt to his feet and slipped back into the tent. The other waited.

"Empress." The priest bowed low to the ground, then straightened. He did not have the tranquil, gentle gaze the priests of the mothers had all possessed in Harsinghar. His mouth was puckered, his eyes surrounded by shadows. This close, she could see that the ash at his forehead and chin had faded with sweat.

"The man who saved me was a priest," she said. "I wish to see his body."

The priest did not argue, though he apologized profusely as he guided her into the tent. "There is little we can do about the smell," he said, voice trembling. "In this heat... Empress, you would do well to carry attar of roses with you to mask it."

In the normal course of things, the man's body would have been burned immediately after the battle that had killed him. But Malini had quietly arranged for orders to be sent to the funerary tents, and to the unlucky soldiers who guarded them, that this particular body should remain untouched until she had the opportunity to see it herself.

"When I next visit here, I will do so," she said, although she could not imagine why she would ever need to do so again. Still, he nodded, mollified.

The body lay under a white sheet. Flowers had wilted at its feet. He warned her again that it would be unpleasant, before he drew the cover back.

It was.

Swati made a small miserable retching noise and rapidly backed out of the tent. Lata averted her eyes, but remained.

Malini stepped forward.

He was young. Deep brown skin. Closed eyes. No ash on his fore-head any longer, but he had the braided hair of a priest of the mothers, and the air of tranquility, even in death.

Bracing herself, she rolled up his sleeve.

There was a tattoo on his arm, a long one that stretched as low as the knobs of his wrists. It must have hurt, to be marked so close to the bone, with a bare needle and soot and tannin to darken the scarred lines. The words were in an old Saketan script, but Malini could pick up snatches of meaning here and there.

Mothers. Flame.

Void.

"No priests remain here for long," said Malini. "This is thankless work."

"There is nothing thankless about tending to the sacred rites of the dead," the priest said swiftly. Then he blinked, graying as he remembered himself. "M-my apologies, Empress."

"No need. Where is your temple?"

"Empress?"

"Your temple," Malini repeated patiently. "You accompanied Lord Narayan here, but there is no temple on his lands. I am asking where you trained and worshipped, before you came to lay Saketa's dead to rest in my camp."

"On the land held by Prince Kunal," the priest, staring at her with the alarmed look of a prey creature under the paw of a beast. "There is a temple adjoining his mahal—the priests are Parijat-trained—"

"I'm sure that is true. But that was not your temple," Malini said.

"No, Empress. N-no." He swallowed "I was trained in a small shrine. One that served the farmers, primarily. And many merchants, who passed through."

"You were well treated there? Educated?"

He nodded.

"Show me your wrists," Malini ordered softly.

He wore a long shawl, loosely coiled over his arms and shoulders. He shoved the fabric back to bare his arms and held his wrists before him. They were shaking.

"You are tattooed, as he is," she observed. "I was sheltered in the heart of the faith, in Parijat. But I know that the priests of the faceless mother carry the names of the mothers in their flesh, so that worshippers may be free to pray to one figure alone." She raised her gaze, expectant.

"My temple," he said, stiff with terror, "where I was reared. We—it—worshipped the faceless mother. Yes, Empress."

"As did this man, I see. This man, who should not have been anywhere near the battlefield, let alone poised to save my life. He should not have died for me. But he did. And I believe you know why."

"Empress," the priest choked out.

"Tell me what you know," she said, gentle in her relentlessness.

"He was sent," the priest said. "Surely he was sent."

"By who?"

"The temple's high priest," the man whispered. "Perhaps. I was told nothing of this, Empress. I promise it."

He sounded truthful enough. That did not mean she believed him. But she nodded as if she did. Gazed into his eyes, over the corpse of a fallen priest.

"Tell me more about your high priest," said Malini, "about the temple where you were trained. I want to know everything. And in return, I will forgive you for the secrets you have kept from me, however unwittingly."

14

When he woke, he heard an old voice in his head. A turning-over-in-grave-soil voice. A voice that had been woken from rest and yearned to return to it.

I never wanted this.

But it was too late. In the deathless waters beneath the Hirana, he was being reborn.

The birth took a long time. But time had no meaning to him. Time had no meaning to the waters, either. Everything grows in its correct season. Everything of flesh or earth must be shaped and hollowed and named.

For a long time, the waters were still.

Then there was a ripple. A wet gasp.

Fingers on the bank—on wet stone. The fingers pressed down, and the stone splintered into new buds, flowers pressing through stone to meet him, as the fingers clung on and dragged. Dragged.

Arms. Shoulders. His body leveraged itself from the deathless waters. He paused to breathe, learning the new weft of his own lungs, the way air filled their emptiness and sank into him. He breathed again, and felt the workings of his nose. His mouth. The fine bones of his jaw, the strangeness of the way they moved.

The muscles of his back bunched and released. He landed flat on the ground, face to the floor. Around him the stone erupted, blooming into flowers and saplings, splinters of stone fanning like a delicate spine, bursting with the beauty of bones.

He pressed his forehead to the ground and rubbed his knuckles against his eyes. Blood, against his knuckles. Red petals against his knuckles, bruised and withering, as he brushed them away.

The bones, the muscles, the nerves of his face ached. The air hurt them. His skin knitted over them, smoothing the pain, fashioned to match the needs of this world, this fragment of the cosmos.

He rose onto his hands. Turned, crawling, back toward the water.

But no. He couldn't go back.

He could only lean forward, and look.

Brilliant blue water-light shone in his eyes. He looked at his own reflection, in the gleaming water, in the shadow of the sangam, and saw a face like a mirror: blank of feeling, reflecting nothing back at himself but his own skin, his own eyes, his own bones.

He touched a fingertip to his lip. The reflection in the water didn't move.

"Rest then," he said shakily. His skin. His skin spoke. "Rest then. I'll be here for you."

And there, in the water, his reflection closed his eyes, and vanished in a swirl of pale silver leaves.

The stone of the Hirana opened for him. The world parted easily for him. That made sense. He knew this was his country. Shaped by his own hands. His own blood. His sacrifice.

And it knew he had somewhere to be.

He walked unsteadily through a city, strange with brightness, lanterns hanging in windows and on verandas, vendors hawking in the corners.

There were statues of the yaksa set back in alcoves. He wasted a long moment staring at one of them, with eyes like an owl, and a face that was all flowers. Lotus roots for fingers.

But he was being called. So he kept on walking.

The forest also parted for him. Dark, winding trees. Undergrowth soft beneath his feet. He walked until his feet threatened to bleed, and his legs—too new to the business of life—screamed for rest.

Still, he kept on moving. She was waiting for him.

Eventually, he came to a tree. Old, old. Faces a rictus upon its surface. It smelled of life on the verge of death—too rich, too bloody, a sickening odor.

He did not want to touch it.

He stumbled toward it. Pressed his hands into the mass of it and gripped. Wrenched. *Pulled.*

The rot parted, fibrous, thick with veins. And there she was beneath it, for all the world sleeping. Hair wet with sap. Her eyes closed, lashes fanned against her cheeks. The last time he had seen her she had laughed, and pressed leaves into their little sister's skirts.

Then she had been murdered. Throat slit. Body set alight.

"Sanjana," he said.

Her eyes snapped open. She shuddered out a breath.

She touched her own face.

"Sanjana," he said again, helpless. "Fuck. You're here. You're here."

"Drawn straight from the roots and the waters," she said nonsensically, in a voice that suggested agreement. She leaned forward, and as the moon slanted over her cheek, he saw that her skin was wood, not flesh. Her teeth were the piths of fruit, sharpened to fine points.

Her nostrils flared faintly. Then the wood of her face softened and reshaped itself, and she was Sanjana again. He reached for her. He took her hands and helped her from the tree.

"Come," she said. "We need to find the others. They're waiting for us."

DHIREN

There was a lake behind Dhiren's home. Once, it had been good fishing waters, and he had kept his family fed and made money selling what remained in the local market besides. But the rot struck it five years ago, and since then the waters had become useless. He'd tried to fish there regardless, at first. Then he'd gutted his first catch and found a flower growing through it, a stem instead of a spine, thorns instead of fine bones, and given the lake up for good.

It had been too late by then. The rot showed through his skin weeks later. Then it touched his wife. His sons.

They'd all perished since. Only Dhiren remained.

He barely went anywhere anymore. Sometimes a kind boy from the family who lived closest, called Anil, visited and brought him food. When Dhiren's roof had broken during a storm, Anil had climbed up and fixed it with wood from the tree branch that had felled the roof in the first place. "It seems like a fair exchange," Anil had said. "Besides, the tree was dead anyway."

Today, the boy was trying to fix netting over Dhiren's window to keep mosquitoes out. "You get so many of them over your lake," he said.

"The rot attracts them," Dhiren told him. "Don't go near it. You must be careful. You have your whole life ahead of you."

He always said this to Anil. And Anil always grinned back at him and said he'd be careful of course. No need to worry about him.

But today Anil said nothing. He held the netting in his hand, silent, and stared out at the water.

"There's something coming," Anil whispered. "Can you feel it?"

Dhiren leveraged himself carefully to his feet. His body ached terribly, but there was something in the boy's voice that compelled him to move regardless. He looked out the window.

The water of the lake was rippling. Moving. And two people were standing beside it.

"Did you hear them come?" Dhiren asked. "I did not hear them come."

Anil shook his head.

There was something strange about both of them. They were too still. Too patient. People did not stand like that—with the calm of trees, as if they belonged to the earth and always had. The calm called him. Tugged every leaf and root embedded in his flesh.

He knew them. He knew.

"Uncle—what are you doing?" Anil asked alarmed. "Don't go out there!"

"I must," Dhiren croaked. He opened the door. Went toward them.

There was a woman rising out of the water. But she was also... not a woman. Her eyes were lidless, inhuman. Her hair was the deep fronds of plants that grew in watery darkness. She turned to look at him, her face ancient and youthful all at once, and smiled.

"Yaksa," he breathed, and fell to his aching knees. "Yaksa."

"A worshipper," she said, in a voice that was liquid deep. "And so soon. How lucky I am."

"Come with us," the woman on the shore said. She was merry, bright-eyed. Her teeth, when she smiled, were sharp. "Come with us, worshipper. We're gathering our kin. Come and welcome them."

His limbs obeyed. He stood, and followed as they walked away from the lake, back into the darkness of the forest that lay behind his home. The male yaksa—who looked human, entirely human, if not for his stillness—gazed at him with dazed eyes.

"I'm finding my family," he said hoarsely. And Dhiren nodded, because a yaksa was speaking to him, and what could he do but listen, and be thankful?

Behind him, far behind him, Anil had run out of the house. Anil was yelling his name. If Dhiren had looked back, he would have seen confusion in the boy's eyes, and fear—and a new bloom, flowering its way through the boy's jaw.

But he did not. He kept his eyes forward. He followed his gods.

16

BHUMIKA

The entire household gathered to watch Priya and Sima go. Billu pushed gifts from the kitchens into Priya's hands, then directed his attentions to Sima when she protested that she couldn't possibly carry everything. Even Kritika offered them both a respectful farewell, and promised to keep them in her prayers.

Finally, Priya took Padma from Bhumika's arms and pressed kisses against Padma's cheeks and into her curls, then swore laughingly when Padma yanked at her braid in return. "Goodbye, egg," she said. "Don't swear like me, or your mother will skin me, you understand?"

Priya raised her head and met Bhumika's eyes. Her expression grew graver. "I'll be home before you know it."

She and Priya had never been good at uncomplicated affection. And Bhumika could not bring herself to embrace Priya now, when it would feel too false, or too vulnerable—too much like an admittance that she feared she would never see her sister again.

"Keep yourself safe," Bhumika replied. She took her daughter back—and if her hand grasped Priya's for one moment, gripping her fingers tight, then that was Bhumika's own business and no one else's. "I'll see you in the sangam," Bhumika said. "Go."

Priya nodded, her eyes a little shining, a little wet—and then turned her head, and walked away. And that was the end of it. Her sister was gone.

It was no surprise that Bhumika slept badly that night. She woke the next day in the early predawn with a sense of unease. *Someone is here*, she thought. Khalida, perhaps, bringing Padma to her. But when she blinked open her eyes and sat up, no one was there. A headache clawed sharply at her skull.

She stumbled through her morning, nauseated. She managed to feed Padma, then demurred when Khalida offered to bring her something light to eat. "Kichadi perhaps," Khalida suggested. But Bhumika winced at the thought of trying to stomach anything and refused.

"Is there nothing I can do to help?"

"If you can find Kritika, tell her I'd like to speak with her in my study," Bhumika said. She wiped Padma's face clean, then smoothed back her hair. "I will see *you* later," she whispered, and brushed her lips over her daughter's forehead. Padma made a contented noise.

It was Jeevan, and not Kritika, who came to see her first. He entered with a bow. There was something cupped between his hands.

"Billu sent this for you, my lady," Jeevan said, keeping his voice low. Khalida had clearly told him Bhumika was not feeling at her best. He placed the cup in front of her. "Tulsi boiled in water," he clarified, at her questioning look. "Billu assured me it should help."

She smiled, a little wryly, and lifted the cup. It was warm, a fragrant green scent rising with the steam. "Billu thinks tulsi cures everything," she said.

"Your sister," he said, gazing over her shoulder, "is of the opinion that Billu believes hashish cures everything."

"Jeevan!" She felt her smile deepen. "I didn't know you liked to gossip. I'm shocked."

His lip twitched minutely. Then his expression smoothed out into blankness again.

"Kritika is on her way, my lady," he said. "Shall I remain?"

"No, you have enough to do. Kritika is no trouble."

Jeevan's silence was somehow both respectful and deeply skeptical. Bhumika covered her amusement by taking a sip of the tulsi infusion. The warmth was pleasant, soothing. But it did nothing to ease her headache. Perhaps Jeevan *should* have brought her hashish instead.

"If you need me," he said.

"I'll summon you," Bhumika said. "Of course."

He bowed again, and then just as swiftly as he'd arrived, he departed.

Kritika arrived soon after. She wore a pale sari, her silver-white hair bound back neatly with beads of wood.

"I'm sorry I'm late, elder," she said, seating herself across from Bhumika. "I was on the Hirana. Seeing to morning pilgrims."

Her tone implied, heavily, that Bhumika should have been seeing to pilgrims, as the only true elder left in Ahiranya. There was no point arguing with Kritika. Bhumika had learned, long ago, that there were battles not worth fighting. "I wish I could go more regularly than I do," Bhumika said. "I'm thankful for your help," she added, with as much sincerity as she could muster.

Kritika had once been a rebel against Parijatdvipan rule, and fiercely loyal to Ashok. Ever since his death she had dedicated herself to the spiritual care of Ahiranya—and to ensuring that her fellow ex-rebels would have a position of respect in the new city that was being built in the absence of the empire.

"So," Kritika said. "What need do you have of me?"

"I know you want your people to pass again through the death-less waters," said Bhumika. "If you have a select few who are willing— Kritika, I believe it is time to try."

"Of course you're finally allowing it," Kritika said. A bad start. She did not sound pleased, as Bhumika had vaguely expected she would. Instead her mouth was thin. "If I may speak freely," Kritika added.

"You may," Bhumika replied, inwardly bracing herself.

"We follow you because Ashok made a vow that he would obey you. And we still believe in him, and always shall. But you're barely clinging on," Kritika said bluntly. "The city is still in disarray. Peace is tenuous. One disastrous harvest, one full rebellion from the highborn, and you lose everything. You have had need of us to grow in strength for a long time. And you allow us our rights only now, after throwing your sister to the Parijatdvipans?" She took a deep, pointed breath. "It riles me, elder."

Perhaps there would be less disarray if any of you had the patience for the dull work of keeping a nation functional, Bhumika thought. Silently, she let the irritation form, then drift away. She sipped her tulsi water.

"The deathless waters are dangerous," Bhumika said instead, treading over an old argument with steady footsteps. "They may kill any of you. Tenuous as my power is, I cannot afford to lose anyone. It has made me rightly cautious."

"My men and women are strong."

"Strong people have been killed by the waters before," Bhumika said quietly. "As you know." When Kritika remained silent, Bhumika said, "That I offer this at all is a sign of my regard for the mask-keepers. And my desire to see us build Ahiranya together. I will be glad of powerful allies."

"Then we should *all* pass through the waters, so you may have as many powerful allies as it is possible to have."

Bhumika shook her head. The ache in her skull briefly sharpened. Forcing back a wince, she said, "For all of you to make the journey would be an unwise risk." Kritika was still frowning. "You have waited this long out of respect for me. For Ashok's memory." Mostly, she knew, for Ashok's memory. "I ask you to trust my guidance in this, too. As he would have wanted."

"I will wait," Kritika said eventually. "If anyone must wait—I'll accept it. I will ask a few of my brothers and sisters to share my patience. But not all. They have the right to become twice-born, Elder Bhumika."

Bhumika inclined her head.

"Kritika."

"Yes?"

"You need not call me 'elder,'" Bhumika said. "I have told you so before."

"I show you the respect I would have shown Ashok," Kritika said, with a stiffness that was all brittle grief.

"Ashok would never have asked you to do so," Bhumika said.

"But he did," said Kritika. "He made us all promise to serve you, Elder Bhumika. So we shall." She paused, clearly struggling with the desire to speak. Then, quite sharply, she said, "But if I or any of my fellow mask-keepers were to consider turning on you—and we would not—I would point out that you are tainted by your association with the Parijatdvipan empire: your marriage. Your child."

"Tainted," Bhumika repeated flatly.

"I would point out that our country still does not have the freedom it was promised. Someone could easily claim you are another regent in all but name: a Parijatdvipan creature ready to keep us under the empire's boot, who won't allow her fellows power. I would make it clear how easily you could be toppled. But I keep Ashok's promises for him, Elder Bhumika."

"There is no need to threaten me," Bhumika said tiredly. "I've already agreed, Kritika."

"I was not threatening you," Kritika said, sounding genuinely affronted. "If I were threatening you, I would use my sickle."

"Then you have a good reason to keep me alive and in power," Bhumika replied. She gave Kritika a grim smile as she rose to her feet. "You have no sense of the kind of weapons the highborn use." *And if you do, you wield them entirely without subtlety*, Bhumika thought.

"I know exactly what weapons the highborn use," Kritika said. "I've lived under their boot in a way you cannot comprehend, wealthy and protected as you have been, Elder. I simply believe in more honest weapons. As I believe in a more honest Ahiranya. The sooner we can rise and put the weapons the empire gave our people aside, the better. *That* is what I believe."

That evening, Bhumika reached for Priya in the sangam. The shadow of her moved through three knotted cosmic rivers; the shadow of her voice called.

Priya. Priya. Where are you?

Priya did not answer her.

"I need you to send one of your men after Priya." Those were the first words she said to Jeevan when he entered her chambers and bowed, eyes sharp with concern. She had summoned him directly to her, after the second time she reached for Priya and found no answer. Now, she was standing by the window—staring out at the growing darkness, forcing herself not to pace with anxiety. She had never reached for Priya and found nothing before. Never. "Urgently. The swiftest rider you have."

He nodded. "What message should the rider carry?" Jeevan asked.

"I merely need to know if she is well," Bhumika said. "Ask your rider to carry ink and paper so she can send me a message, if she needs to. I . . ." Bhumika touched her knuckles to her lips. *Stop. Think rationally*, she told herself. *Do not allow yourself to be driven by your own worry.* "I cannot reach her," Bhumika said eventually. "In the way we usually reach one another. I fear for her health."

There was silence behind her. She turned to look at him, and saw that Jeevan's expression had hardened. "I can send a dozen men on fast horses," he said. "More, if need be. If you wish me to go myself—"

"No." She shook her head. "No. One rider will be enough." They could not afford to weaken their own defenses. And Bhumika was not one to shy away from grim truths: Priya was strong. If she was well, one rider would be enough to confirm her safety and survival and put Bhumika's fears at ease. But if something had happened to her—something so grave that she could not even enter the sangam—then no number of soldiers would be enough to save her or fight what had harmed her. Her heart ached at the thought. She pushed the fear away, desperately. "I need you here."

He nodded his understanding. "I'll send one of my best," he vowed.

"I have every faith in you," she said.

She tried to sleep after that, but it was hard. Every time she slept she woke soon after with a jolt, worry bitter on her tongue, and her heart hammering in her chest. She had only one sister left. Only one. When dawn came she felt as wrung out as a damp cloth. But she rose to her feet. Reached again into the sangam and found—again—nothing.

Kritika had gathered a group of mask-keepers she felt were suitable to pass through the deathless waters. She had insisted there was no point in wasting time—"In truth, they should have completed the ritual during the festival of the dark of the moon," Kritika had said archly. "I remember how things once were, elder." And Bhumika had not argued.

She had spent yesterday afternoon giving instructions for flowers and fruits to be carried up to the Hirana, and for the pilgrims to be dispersed. They would be barred from the temple until this was done.

Then, more discreetly, she had located an empty of plot of land in the orchard. Those who did not survive the journey would need a suitable burial, after all.

If there was one thing Bhumika took little joy in, but understood the necessity of, it was ritual. She remembered passing through the deathless waters as a girl. The dread and determination that had filled her. The white tunic she'd worn, and the way she had brushed her own hair until it shone, and prayed with her siblings around her until the moment their elders came for them, and took them to the waters.

She had not known if she was preparing for her funeral or her rise. But she had promised herself she would not die, and held that promise close as she'd lowered herself into the water. Once, twice, thrice.

Now, she tried to cobble together something resembling the ritual of her youth. The mask-keepers were told to bathe and dress in their plainest clothes. Then, as dusk fell, they met her upon the Hirana.

A shrine room had been especially prepared. There was a plate of silver resting beneath the dozens of effigies of the yaksa. Now, she instructed the mask-keepers to lay their offerings there: coconuts hewn open, thick with flowers. Fresh fruit. A handful of polished coins. They prayed together in one cramped shrine, the scent of incense coiling through the air.

As a child, Bhumika had prayed because it was a task woven into her life as a temple daughter, as essential as breathing or eating or sleeping. Now, she prayed because it was what was expected from her as the High Elder. But she could not deny that there was comfort in the act—the familiarity of the movements and the words, the smell of sandalwood incense and the cold dark beneath her eyelids as she closed her eyes and bowed her head. It brought her childhood close. Enclosed her in smallness.

And there was her magic now, of course: the living, breathing hum of the Hirana beneath her, responding to the waters in her blood. The pulse of all Ahiranya's green, pressing its seeking fingers on her skull. Once, she had prayed and felt as if the words were a plea to nothing and no one, unheard. But now she reached for the green and felt it reach back. Even if the yaksa did not hear her, the green did.

Let some of them survive this, at least, she prayed. *Let them live.*

The Hirana had its own will, and always responded best to Priya. But Priya was not here, so it was Bhumika who listened to the Hirana—the way its surface altered beneath her feet, the ripple and shudder of stone guiding her to a new gap in the ground. A new staircase leading them down to the deathless waters.

She watched the mask-keepers slip into the still depths, and very carefully did not think of her brother.

There were three mask-keepers who died. Four who lived, in the end.

The three were buried in the orchard before dawn, in the milk-gray light that preceded true daylight. The mask-keepers had told her they wanted to dig the graves themselves—*with our own hands, to honor the dead*, they had said—but Bhumika joined them regardless, dressed in her plainest clothes, her hair bound back into a knot. She brought Billu and Rukh with her.

Ganam was ankle deep in soil when they arrived. He looked up at her. His face was shiny with sweat. If there were tears mingled in with it, she did him the kindness of not noting it.

"Elder Bhumika," he said. "You're not needed for this. We're strong enough to get the work done."

She did not point out to him that she could turn the earth over with a single breath, without lifting a hand. That would have been cruel, and her intent today was to put cruelty aside. The bodies lay near, swathed in cloth. Someone had placed flowers on them, at the throat, the stomach, the feet.

"It would be an honor to assist you," she said, and waited. After a moment he nodded, and offered her a shovel.

"I . . . if I could help," Rukh said tentatively, his voice thin. "I was. I was a rebel once."

"I thought I'd also lend a hand," Billu added, as if Bhumika had not sought him out. Had not said, *You have strength. They'll be grateful for it.*

"No need," said Ganam.

Billu grunted. Said, "I know you'd do the same for any of us."

It was well done. Ganam's guarded gaze softened.

"It's not up to me who helps or doesn't," Ganam said gruffly.

It was hard work, turning up the soil. She had never done it before with hands alone, her magic set aside. Her last living blood relative, her beloved uncle, had died by fire. Her husband had been cremated, in keeping with the customs of his own people. And Ashok had drowned in the deathless waters. His body had never returned to the surface. Sometimes she dreamt of it still, deep under the weight of the waters, chained by fronds of leaf and root, blue in the glowing half dark, cold under her reaching fingertips. But she had never truly touched it. Never covered it with cloth or flowers, or wept over it, or laid it in a grave.

Now, she dug relentlessly, no magic behind the heave of her arms. By the time the hole was deep enough, she'd sweated through her clothes. She could hear Rukh and Billu still working behind her, breath huffing out of them. They had moved on to their second grave.

When they were done, the mask-keepers began to lower the bodies into the earth. For a moment, Bhumika caught her breath. She listened to the muffled sobs from the watching, the heavy breaths from the ones carrying their friends.

Then she began to sing a prayer.

Her voice came out of her clearer and stronger than she had expected it to. Steady. Some of the mask-keepers looked at her, recognition dawning in their eyes.

Although the Ahiranyi language had long been suppressed by the empire, although their tales and their books had been erased and forbidden, the mask-keepers knew their Birch Bark Mantras. They knew the shape of prayers for the dead.

Kritika had arrived at some point during the digging. Her sari was mourning white, her face drawn with grief. She looked at Bhumika. After a moment she joined in. She knew the cadence, the words.

The bodies were lowered with care and reverence. The earth was piled back over them. Ganam wiped a hand over his forehead, leaving a streak of mud behind. Then he raised his head and looked at Bhumika once more. Around him, the other mask-keepers did the same.

There were probably things a temple elder should say in such a situation. But she could not remember how her elders had grieved whenever Bhumika's siblings had drowned or died poisoned by the deathless waters. *Had* they grieved? Death had always been such an inevitability—and proof of weakness and failure. A temple child who died had been undeserving. A temple child lost, perhaps, did not deserve to be mourned.

"You can pray too, if you wish," Bhumika offered gently.

Ganam looked at the other mask-keepers, silent communication passing between them.

"It doesn't seem our place," he said.

"You will be elders too, soon enough," Bhumika said. "People will look for you to pray and worship with them." She gestured her head lightly at the graves, covered now with soil. "They would be glad, I think. To be sung to by you. All of you."

Their voices wavered together, rising as the sun rose in the sky.

Khalida had prepared the bathing room for her without being asked, which was a relief. And Padma was covered in a layer of mysterious grime, so Bhumika took her into the bathing chamber with her.

She managed to lull Padma into stillness with the careful distraction of a story about a magical deer and oiled Padma's short curls; softened them to buttery coils as she made the noises of the various animals to keep her daughter entertained, then ran water over Padma's hair, careful to avoid her eyes.

"Now," she said, lifting Padma up. "This is what you were looking forward to, isn't it?"

She held Padma in the basin of water. Padma beamed at her.

Bhumika thought of the way water could consume you and change you and kill you—and how quietly, sweetly healing it was to hold her daughter up in a small basin and watch her splash at it with utter delight. It made Bhumika smile, in turn.

Padma slammed a hand into the water and drenched Bhumika's lowered face. For half a second, Bhumika could only blink and splutter. And then quite suddenly she was laughing, and Padma was laughing back—her little joyful mirror, always marveling at her own chaos.

It was only once Padma was dry and drowsing on Bhumika's bed that Bhumika realized her headache had returned. Bathing, pouring warm water over her limbs, had eased the pain briefly. Not long enough. She rubbed her fingers against her temples, sighing. Before she could even consider whether she wanted to try tulsi again—or something rather more effective—Khalida entered.

"My lady," Khalida said. "You need to dress." She offered Bhumika a pale salwar kameez, waiting until Bhumika was dressed before continuing. "I've arranged your meal. I..." Khalida stopped, mouth still open. She was looking at the window.

Bhumika had a sudden sense of...shifting. As if her headache had tightened like a noose and twisted the world with it. Dizzying, as if she had passed through deep waters and risen to sunlight, but the water had gathered in her lungs. Her ears were ringing.

With some effort, she followed Khalida's frozen gaze.

The flowers at the window had curled. Moved. The edges of the vines had sharpened, knife-like. The blooms had deepened to a riotous, bloody red.

It took her a moment longer to realize that the conch of warning had been sounded.

She snatched Padma up and strode from her chambers with Khalida at her side. Down, down the corridors. Out into the courtyard, by the watchtower on the walls.

"My la—elder!" The soldier was one of Jeevan's old recruits, and he stumbled between one form of address and the other. "There are—dozens, maybe hundreds of people, calling themselves pilgrims. Outside."

"There are always pilgrims," Bhumika said, firm but calm. "Explain."

"Not for you," he bit out. "They are—they're following something—someone. They are—"

The gates flew open.

No hands had forced them. No hands should have been capable of such an act. And Bhumika felt the strangeness again. Something new, choking her from within. Something coming.

Leaves. Leaves, everywhere. They were not growing through the walls—they were roiling, rising and tumbling as if caught in a great wind, pouring through the open gates, filling the air. She raised a hand to protect Padma's face but did not allow herself the same kindness. She looked through the tumult.

There were pilgrims indeed. A whole swathe of them, standing beyond the mahal's walls, visible only in glimpses between the green swirling before them and around them: an eye here, a length of hair there. A shoulder, an arm, a faceless torso. One figure stepped in front of the rest, walking slowly, steadily, toward the mahal.

Bhumika should, perhaps, have told her soldiers to prepare for a fight. Told them to gather their weapons, to form a perimeter. But those were not enemies in front of her. Not warriors. And whatever this was, it was a thing driven by magic and not men. Magic that she felt in her bones.

The figure was before her. The leaves parted and fell gently.

A familiar face stared back at her.

For a moment his mouth moved, soundless. As if he was trying to understand the shape, the shift of his own facial muscles. His face. The wholeness of it: the shape of his jaw, the cut of his hair. He looked as he had on the day he had entered the deathless waters. Entered and not come back.

"Ashok," she said. Her voice sounded distant, even as she felt her own mouth move. Her own heart hammering, faint with a nausea that threatened to swallow her.

"Bhumika," he said. He too sounded dazed. "I've found my way home."

The tension in her skull fell away.

"You died." Bhumika's voice wavered. Her whole body threatened to waver. "Priya and I. And your rebels. We waited for you. By the deathless waters. We waited." She'd stood by the water for a full night. Leaving Padma in Khalida's care. Watching the gleaming, shining blue of it and hoping, hoping even as some terrible part of her had been glad she would not have to fight him in the days and months and years of Ahiranyi rule to come. "You were gone."

"Priya isn't here," he said in reply. She wasn't sure if he intended it to be a question or a statement.

"No," Bhumika said. Lips numb. She wondered if she would swoon like some kind of soft maiden—if he had brought her to this. "You. We waited. By the waters. You *died*."

"I didn't. I didn't die." He didn't try to move closer to her. His face was strangely blank. His hands were flexing at his sides. Opening, closing. Fingers moving. "I...I do not think I died."

You did, she thought, with absolute certainty. It was not the new strangeness writhing inside her that told her. It was her own familiar gut instinct. It was the way his skin had not changed from sunlight or the lack of it. It was the leaves that surrounded him and clouded the air.

It was the absence of him in the sangam. She was breathing unsteadily, her body unable to resist the brunt of the shock roiling through it. Only Padma's weight against her skin kept her steady.

He was far too uncannily himself, a picture painted a shade too perfectly.

"I didn't come alone," he said.

Behind him, she saw pilgrims fall to their knees. Murmurs of prayers, and cries. An ecstasy of weeping.

"It was inevitable," said Ashok. "Like we were inevitable. Like—the tide."

When you have lost people, they haunt you in ways large and small. Bhumika had always known this. She dreamt often of her brother, her uncle, even of her husband—strange dreams that verged on nightmares, that woke her with salt in her eyes.

She did not dream of the temple council often. But she had not forgotten their faces.

She recognized them the moment she saw them. Four figures, standing behind Ashok.

Elder Chandni, with her familiar, gentle eyes. Elder Sendhil, his face carved in forbidding lines. And there, next to them—oh. *No.*

Two of her siblings. Sanjana, with bright eyes and laughter on her lips.

Nandi, small and wide-eyed. Still a child, and forever a child.

They walked toward her. As they walked, green things rose from the earth: buds, soft ferns, life forcing its way out of the ground.

Flowers blooming like a mantle from their shoulders and hair. Arms flecked with swirls of wood.

Bhumika could only kneel. It was not awe that took her to her knees, but a lesson carefully written into her when she was so young that it had become a part of her blood, her bones, and could not be later undone.

You show the yaksa veneration, her elders had taught her. Even an image, even an echo of them—

"Bhumika," said the yaksa with Chandni's face, smiling. Speaking in her dead elder's voice. "Our temple daughter. We have finally come home."

17

PRIYA

At first, Yogesh had struck Priya as a nervous man. But it didn't take her long to realize he was simply nervous of *her*. As they rode their horses along the winding dirt tracks and roads that led to Saketa, she saw him touching the prayer stones he wore around his neck. Each stone grasped, one by one, between his fingers as he mouthed the names of the mothers of flame to himself. As if that had the strength to ward away Priya's monstrousness.

She would have been irritated by it, normally. But she was too worried to think long on Yogesh.

"I can't reach Bhumika," she confided to Sima on the first evening.

"What do you mean?"

"I can't—you know." She made a vague gesture, trying to encompass everything the sangam was without talking about it in front of Parijatdvipan strangers. "I don't know why."

Sima gave her a wide-eyed look. She understood, just as Priya did, how serious it was that Priya could not reach Ahiranya.

"We can send one of our men back," Sima said. They didn't have many to begin with. "Karan, maybe. Or Nitin?"

They couldn't afford to make their retinue even smaller. They were already a sorry group: a mere handful of Ahiranyi soldiers, Sima in her plain sari with her bow, and Priya dressed in temple elder whites that had already seen a few too many encounters with dust.

She hadn't thought she would need another way to contact

Bhumika. She'd felt a pang when she'd left everyone behind, but she had thought it would be, in a way, just like any time she had traveled through Ahiranya to deal with the rot. Difficult, certainly, and lonely. But Bhumika would be there, waiting for her in the sangam. Waiting to advise and scold and stop Priya from doing anything impulsive that would land everyone who mattered to her in a pile of shit.

Now Priya was on her own.

"Karan," Priya said reluctantly. "We'll send him."

"I'm sure everything's fine, Pri," Sima said. "Your sister will send someone after us, too. The second she realizes she can't speak to you."

What if she doesn't send anyone? Priya thought. *What if something has happened?*

She looked at the path behind them. The dust of the road and the wizened trees, and Ahiranya already so far behind them that she could not see the Hirana at all.

"We could go back," Sima said after a moment.

Priya swallowed, conflicted.

"Let's give it a day," Priya said. "Either someone will come from Bhumika, or someone won't. And then..." She couldn't continue. Worry was pooling coldly in her belly.

"Someone will come," Sima said.

Ah, spirits, how long would it take for a fast rider to reach them from Ahiranya, when they were still on the move? *Could* a rider catch up with them? How long should Priya wait before she turned back? "A few more days," she amended, settling on vagueness. When the worry became too much to stand, well—that would make her decision for her.

Her soreness and exhaustion soon distracted her. Priya wasn't a natural rider. Jeevan had insisted on giving her a handful of lessons, alongside some guidance on handling scythe and saber. But her body ached that night when they lay down to rest, and despite her worries her sleep was deep and dreamless.

It wasn't until the morning that she realized the reason for her easy sleep.

She could not hear the green.

No sangam, and no green. The disquiet grew in her, setting roots right through her, tightening her lungs. She couldn't pretend any longer that everything was well.

Perhaps everyone in Ahiranya was safe. Perhaps Priya was the problem: her magic fading out of her as swiftly as water through a cracked pot. Perhaps she had no strength beyond Ahiranya's borders, far from the gleaming blue of the deathless waters that had given her gifts to begin with.

But that hadn't been the way of it in the Birch Bark Mantras. The elders of old had possessed power no matter where they went; had conquered the subcontinent alongside the yaksa in the Age of Flowers with that magic.

I am not an elder of old, Priya reminded herself, her stomach in knots. She held her face in her hands. *I am something new. And maybe this was a terrible mistake.*

She was ready to shake Sima awake and tell her they needed to turn back when she suddenly felt something lance through her. Something sharp and green, a dart arrowing through her blood, its hum settling in the back of her skull. She stood up sharply and scrambled out of her tent. Around her, the sleeping camp fumbled awake, the men on guard reaching instinctually for their weapons. "There's something," she said to the others. "Beyond the trees."

Immediately, her own men reached for their weapons, and the soldiers attending Yogesh drew their sabers. Priya swiftly shook her head. "Not like that," she said. "No—no enemies or bandits. Look there's no need for your swords. Give me a moment—"

"Priya," Sima said. "What—"

"I can feel something," Priya said quickly, crossing the dusty ground.

Ignoring Sima's protests and Yogesh's murmured cautions, she walked through the trees. They grew close together here, slender branches twining into arches and webs around her. The scent of leaf sap and wet earth filled her nose at first, deep and lustrous and damp, then gave way quickly to something more pungent: decay.

Rot.

She stopped. A few of the men had followed her, and now they gazed silently at the village that lay hidden between the trees, in a modest clearing.

It was clearly abandoned. The buildings were overgrown, small wood and stone houses caving in beneath the pressure of strangling roots, flowering bushes. All of the trees looked slightly wrong, in a way that Priya had grown very familiar with. Their trunks appeared almost—soft. The wood too forgiving. Where the bark had stripped or the surface splintered, the trees were the deep color of exposed flesh, marbled with the white fat.

She swallowed back nausea.

"None of you should touch it," she said to the men.

"Elder Priya," Yogesh said, clearing his throat. He sounded fairly nauseated himself. "We should not—the empress would not want anyone to be risked. The business of burning the trees can be left to the local villagers."

"What villagers?" Priya asked. "There's no one here. They're all long gone."

Yogesh's soldiers made uneasy noises. But they soon melted back, returning to the path, leaving her alone with the trees.

"I'm staying," said Sima quietly.

"Sima. It's not . . . it won't be interesting."

"Someone has to keep an eye on you." She crossed her arms.

There was no point arguing, and Priya didn't want to remain here, smelling the stink of rotting meat, any longer than she had to. As she stepped closer, the call of green and life inside her grew stronger. Her limbs felt steadier, some weakness she hadn't even been aware of seeping out of them.

Priya closed her eyes. Reached—and finally, blessedly, felt the green reaching back. She pushed herself through the green, through the sangam, through cosmic rivers and the deathless waters that ran through her blood—and grasped the rot. Froze it to stillness. It would grow no further, now.

When she returned to herself, she was gasping, lungs heaving, and Sima was holding her up. They were both leaning back against a healthy tree, still alone. It couldn't have been long, then.

"I told you that you needed someone to keep an eye on you," Sima said, voice a little shaky.

Priya managed a laugh.

"Maybe you're right," she said. "Come on. We'd better head back."

They straightened up and returned to the soldiers. Behind them, the trees had settled. Nearly alive again, the ground around them resting easy, the sweet scent of fresh grass now the only smell in the air.

"Did you know there was rot this far from home?" Sima asked, voice a whisper.

"No," Priya whispered in return. Her blood still hummed and sang distractingly, warm with relief. She wasn't broken after all.

But she didn't know why her magic had faded to begin with. And that...that worried her.

That night, lying on a mat on the ground with Sima beside her, she tried to reach for Bhumika again.

It felt like she was learning how to walk a familiar path with her eyes closed. It could be done: Her feet knew this particular soil, the way this path curved and dipped. But she'd always had her eyes to rely on before, and now she had only her skin.

She closed her—real, not metaphorical—eyes and breathed deep, slow. Deep, slow. She sank under her skin, an old and practiced motion, seeking the sangam. If she could reach Bhumika, she could at least reassure her sister that Priya was safe and sound. And she could reassure herself that everyone in Ahiranya was safe, too. Maybe then she could continue on this journey without fear for what lay behind her.

The waters opened up to her. Radiant darkness. Waves lapping around her, as stars slipped their perches to whirl at her feet.

"Priya." Bhumika was kneeling in the waters. Three rivers swirled around her. She was smiling—a fixed, even smile that looked strange on her shadow of a face. "You're finally here."

"Did I worry you? Of course I did. I'm sorry. I couldn't get here. I..." She shrugged helplessly, relief pouring through her. "Honestly, Bhumika, I'm not sure when I'll be able to get here again, so let me tell you everything I can."

She spoke of the journey—the rot—the fear in Yogesh's wary eyes, his prayer stones, his watchful men. The strangeness of feeling distant and disconnected from the power she'd possessed in Ahiranya. And Bhumika listened to all of it wordlessly, fixed and still.

"Why are you still smiling?" Priya asked, eventually. "Are you really that happy to have me gone? Weren't you worried at all? I'm going to start feeling insulted."

"I'm just pleased to see you," Bhumika said. "It's been too long. I was worried."

"Is everything alright in Hiranaprastha?" Priya asked. "Padma's fine, and—Rukh?"

Bhumika inclined her head.

"Everyone is well," she said. "Just as they should be." Bhumika reached out and touched a hand to Priya's face—the shadow of it shaping Priya's cheek. "Go back to yourself," she said. "We'll see each other again soon enough."

"We may not," Priya said urgently. "Bhumika, don't you understand? I...I'm not sure if I'll always be able to reach out. If you send a messenger it'll take weeks, but if something's important you will, won't you? If you can't reach me here, like this?"

The shadow of Bhumika's mouth—the shape of her teeth—

"Of course," Bhumika said. "I'll find you when you're needed. I promise you that. Don't worry about using your strength to call me in the sangam. Focus on what lies ahead."

"But—"

"Just do as I say, Priya," Bhumika said. Her words were gentle, but they were also an order. "Now *go*."

Priya returned to her body. Stared out at the dark, breathing unevenly now, feeling odd and unsteady, some sense of wrongness grappling at the edges of her consciousness.

Eventually, she slept.

By the time she woke in the morning, and broke her fast, and heaved herself once again onto her horse, the strangeness of it all had dissipated like nothing more than a bad dream.

The army encampment was marked by banners on the horizon, all of them the gleaming white and gold of imperial Parijatdvipa, blazing in the light of the setting sun.

Despite the fact that they had traveled weeks to get here, Yogesh insisted on stopping and making camp.

"I think we should continue," Priya said, trying to channel Bhumika's effortless command. It didn't seem to be doing her much good: the men kept on setting up camp, ignoring her. "We're almost there. The empress is waiting for us."

"It would be better to take a moment here," Yogesh said, with exquisite awkwardness, his eyes darting anywhere but to her. "Night is almost here, elder."

"All the more reason to join the empress's camp," Priya retorted.

"No, no," Yogesh said, wringing his hands. "It will give you time to prepare, elder. You look—out of sorts."

"You do smell," Sima muttered, when they were alone.

"Well, so do you!" said Priya.

"I'm not Ahiranya's representative," Sima pointed out. "You are. I'm just a maid."

"I could tell people you're my bodyguard," Priya said.

There was an incredulous silence from Sima.

"If I could emulate Elder Bhumika at all, I hope you know I'd be raising an eyebrow at you right now," Sima said. "One devastating look of judgment, that's what you'd get."

"Well, you're not just a maid. Certainly not *my* maid. Isn't that the point of this—coming here with me? You're a representative of Ahiranya." Priya shrugged. "Maybe that's enough."

"You know that isn't how things work for highborn," Sima said. "They need names for things. They like everything and everyone to have their place."

Sima was right, of course.

"Advisor," Priya said, after a beat. "We can call you my advisor."

"Advisor," Sima repeated. She sounded skeptical.

"It'll mean more to the Parijatdvipans than 'friend who helps me kill Parijati soldiers' will."

"Fine," Sima said. "Advisor it is. Now go wash yourself, Pri, and leave your advisor alone."

Priya had only just finished bathing—with a cloth and bucket, behind a hastily erected sheet, Sima on guard—when she heard hurried footsteps.

"Priya," Nitin called out. "Elder Priya," he corrected himself quickly. "You have to come. She's here. The empress is here."

Her heart gave a strange thud in her chest. From the side of the sheet, Sima turned and met her gaze, eyes wide. "I'll be there in a moment," Priya called out, and tried to make herself presentable.

Her sari was a little damp, her skin faintly shiny with water, when she emerged and drew a shawl around her shoulders to hide the worst of the damage. There was a chariot coming to a stop. Soldiers alighting from their own mounts.

The soldiers parted. A parasol was raised—beaded with darts of silver, it gleamed even as it shadowed the figure that alighted from the chariot, protecting her from the fading sunlight.

Malini.

She was not as thin as she'd once been. And her hair—always so knotted and curling, when Priya had known her—had been carefully tamed into a braided bun, bound high at her scalp. But her face was the same: the same dark gray eyes, almost black. The severe eyebrows. The fullness of her mouth, not quite shaping a smile.

"Empress," Yogesh murmured, and bowed low. His men followed his example.

Around Priya, Jeevan's men hesitated. But when Priya bowed they followed suit.

Priya raised her head. Malini was watching her.

Once, her expression would have been unreadable to Priya—a blank mask, all perfection and stillness. But she knew Malini's face now—had once watched every flicker of her eyelids, every exhale from her lips, and learned them like language.

Beneath the shadow of her parasol, Malini's dark eyes were taking in every inch of Priya's form—her damp skin, the tuck of her sari at her waist. Her trailing hair, draped over a shoulder. Priya's face. Malini was looking at nothing and no one else. Only Priya, with her mouth a little parted and her eyes a little wider than normal.

Malini had missed her, too.

"Elder Priya," said Malini. "I have come to speak with you. If we may have privacy..."

"Of course. Empress." Priya nodded at her men and Sima, who nodded in return and stepped away. Yogesh was murmuring something, shaking his head.

"There is no need for a formal record of this conversation," Malini replied.

"Empress," Yogesh protested.

Malini gave the lightest flick of her head. And Yogesh swallowed, and bowed, and stepped back to join the other men.

Priya looked at Malini. Simply looked at her. The chariot was all gilt and silver behind her. There were flowers in her hair, carved from jewels and ivory. Earth and bone.

"I am sorry to come to you so suddenly, without warning," Malini said, after a moment. "If I had warned anyone, my courtiers would have followed. And I wanted..."

Malini trailed off, but Priya knew.

"We're still watched," Priya said softly.

"I know," Malini said. "But some modicum of privacy is better than nothing."

Malini, she wanted to say. Wanted to shape that name in her mouth. She took one step forward. Just one step. But Malini shook her head, subtly, and Priya took no more.

"I wanted you to see," Malini murmured. "Before I faced you in front of all my men. I wanted you to see what I am now."

Priya found some breath inside herself. "You certainly look like an empress."

"And you—you look like an Elder of Ahiranya," said Malini.

Priya couldn't help but laugh. Almost noiseless, almost breathless, like the sound didn't want to leave her. "I look like a mess," she said.

"No. You look..."

"What?"

"More alive than I remember," Malini said softly. "I didn't think such a thing was possible. But here we are. Priya. Are you well? Happy?"

It makes me happy to see you, she almost said. But that wasn't quite right. Seeing Malini made it feel like there was something fragile in her chest. Something that could wither or flourish at a single word, a single touch. "I...I am. Are you?"

Malini smiled in response. Tight-lipped.

"That's a no, then," Priya said.

"I *am*. But. Priya…" Hesitation. "In the eyes of my men, Ahiranya is not yet free," said Malini. "Ahiranya is still subordinate. And you will be—unwelcome."

The fragile thing in Priya's chest splintered, just a little. Malini's words were a reminder that there was so much more at stake than her soft feelings for Malini, or Malini's for her. Politics and war and history all stood like a chasm between them.

"You summoned me," Priya pointed out.

"Yes," Malini said. "I did. Because I am on precarious ground. Because I need someone I can trust. And because…" She stopped, and then said, carefully, "Because you are you. To me."

Priya felt a pang. *Ah, Malini.*

"But you are going to need to trust me in turn, Priya," she went on. "You will need to do what I guide you to do, and trust that I will not harm the interests of your people. That when this ends you will have what I promised you. That I wish to give you—all that is rightly yours." A hitch in her words. A stumble. "Can you obey me?"

What was rightly Priya's?

Are you rightly mine? Can I keep you too?

"Do you ask all the kings who serve you to obey you?" Priya asked.

"Not so directly," said Malini. "With them I play the necessary games and niceties. I write pacts and bargains. I flatter and dole out power as required. But you—you are not them. And I am asking you."

"Will you believe me if I say yes?" Priya asked.

"You've placed your life in my hands before," Malini said softly. "The deals we have struck between us have always held true. I'll trust you again, as I always have, and always shall."

"Don't say such things," Priya said, voice smaller than she wished it to be.

Malini's response was silence. She stood tall, elegant and untouchable in her green sari, her flowering crown, her eyes pinning Priya through the heart.

This isn't how I thought it would be, Priya thought. She had the absurd desire to reach out and unspool Malini's hair—to trace her eyebrows, her jaw, her mouth, with a fingertip. To feel her skin—to touch her—maybe that would make Malini real. Maybe it would knot them back together again.

"I wish," Malini began. And then she caught herself—almost visibly. A slight sway of her body. A flicker of her eyelids. As if she felt it too—the urge to move closer to one another. The urge to touch. The urge to say *You're here, you're here and I'm here, at last.*

Priya swallowed, steadying herself. She pushed her shoulders back. Straightened herself, grounding her feet against the soil. If Malini could wear a mask, then so could she.

"Empress," she said. Louder, clearer, drawing the eyes and ears of the men around them. "Ahiranya is loyal to you. That has not changed."

Malini straightened too. Inclined her head.

"I am glad, Elder Priya," she said. "So glad."

Priya and Sima both worked together to make something presentable out of Priya. A salwar kameez, in the Aloran style that better suited horse travel, with the chunni knotted neatly at her hip. Priya's hair bound back in a long braid that Sima hastily wound in place using a long, deep blue tasseled paranda. By the end, Priya at least felt presentable. It would have to do.

They rode to join the army.

When they entered the camp itself, Priya tried not to allow herself to be overwhelmed by the size and sheer scale of it: the milling swathes of soldiers in their bright armor. Saketa's great maze fort, looming over everything, dark-stoned and austere. The canopied tents, the elephants, the weapons.

The waiting highborn. Their cold, watchful eyes. The way they stared as Priya rode forward on her horse, and alighted, her braid whipping behind her as she hit the soil.

Let them stare. She was a temple elder. She had more power in her bones than any of them had in their titles.

Priya walked forward. Awaiting her, beneath a canopy of gold, on a dais that clearly served as a throne, sat Malini. Empress Malini, in all her glory, legs crossed and hands upon her knees. The softness in her was all gone. What remained was hard and beautiful, as bitterly sharp as a blade.

I wanted you to see.

Malini had shown her a little of this mask: the edges that made an empress out of a woman. And here, now, was the rest of it.

Yogesh stepped forward first. In a clear voice he announced Priya, Temple Elder of Ahiranya.

"Come forward," another official announced, repeating his words in both court Dvipan and common-tongue Zaban. "And pay your respects."

You're Ahiranya's representative, Priya told herself. *Think of what Bhumika would do and try to do it. Do not make a mess of this.*

She walked forward. Bowed low. Lower even than she had before. *I am a servant of Parijatdvipa*, every inch of her body said. *I am loyal. I am here for your sake, and I will obey.*

"Welcome, Elder," Malini said. "I welcome you to Saketa."

With the light of the sun behind her, Malini looked like a stranger. And that was, Priya supposed, exactly how things were meant to be.

"Empress," she said. "It's my honor."

MALINI

"Stop," said Malini. "There is no need—or time—for us to argue about this, Mahesh."

"Empress," he said, gruff and disapproving as Swati laid out breakfast—paper-thin, crisp dosas and vibrant green and orange chutneys and painfully hot tea—and bustled swiftly away. "There is ample reason to discuss this. The highborn are all talking to one another and if you do not act—"

"Argue with me about the allocation of supplies and weaponry," Malini cut in. "Tell me what reconnaissance you've gained about the fort. But this—there is no need for this. I summoned her here. She has value to me and to our siege. That should be enough."

"It isn't the value of one woman in war that concerns me," Mahesh said. "It is the place of Ahiranya in this campaign and in your empire. We recognize that you have made peace with Ahiranya's new leaders. But no man of Parijatdvipa views the Ahiranyi without suspicion. My men call them witches. Monsters. There is not a single lord who will view that woman as his equal. Her blood, the history of her country, the magic she wields..." He exhaled, shaking his head. "You are traveling through dangerous waters," Mahesh warned her. As if she did not know that already. "There are men who will say you are being used."

And Malini had met Priya alone. Met her without highborn to watch them—with no one to judge what passed between them, and measure who held the true power: The Ahiranyi witch, or the Parijat-dvipan empress with no throne.

"The Ahiranyi were instrumental to my escape from the prison my brother Chandra arranged for me," Malini said. "That does not make me their creature."

"I was not suggesting it did," Mahesh said, sounding aggravated.

Oh, you were, thought Malini.

As much as his words galled her, he was not wrong. Priya's presence had sent ripples through the camp, whispers of discontent in its wake. There would never be any trust for the Ahiranyi in Parijatdvipa. History was too weighty. Malini had known it, even when she wrote the letter to Bhumika and Priya; even as she had placed it in Yogesh's hands.

But some risks were worth taking.

Malini sipped her tea and let her gaze wander the room. Swati was still hovering obediently in the background. Four military officials sat at a remove, writing, the scratch of ink on paper a low susurration in the air as they recorded the meeting and prepared answers to those far more pressing questions of supply allocation and weaponry, as needed. Deepa sat beside them, looking through their papers with a slight frown. She had come with her father, head bowed, trying to make herself small in the face of her father's anger.

But Malini was glad for his ire. It afforded her an opportunity.

"I will make sure Elder Priya demonstrates her loyalty to Parijat-dvipa and to my rule, as you have advised," Malini said. "As, clearly, her bow to me before everyone was not enough."

"Everyone bows to you, Empress."

"Indeed," Malini agreed. "But no temple elder of the Ahiranyi has ever bowed in worship to the mothers of flame."

There was a beat of silence. Mahesh gave her a shrewd look.

"Ah—Empress. If I may, no temple of the mothers of flame will allow an Ahiranyi priest to walk through its doors," one official said tentatively, gaze lowered. He looked uncomfortable, and was visibly forcing himself to continue. "For the—ah, elder—to affirm her loyalty to Parijatdvipa in a temple will not be possible."

"Do you not consider temples of the faceless mother to be proper temples?" Malini asked, eyebrow raised.

"They are..." The official trailed off and said helplessly, "I defer to the empress, of course."

"There is a temple of the faceless mother on Low Prince Kunal's lands, is there not?"

Another rustle of paper.

"Yes, Empress."

"Then we will go there."

"Such a temple—it is not—"

"Not ideal," Malini agreed. "Not entirely pure. But it will please the Saketan foot soldiers."

Lord Mahesh said nothing.

"I think it will suffice, Mahesh," Malini said.

"It will not be enough, Empress," Mahesh said grimly. "But if you insist on moving on to other business, we shall."

The chariot arranged for Malini's journey to the temple was large, drawn by two swift horses, with space enough inside the covered interior for both Lata and Priya. But Lata agreed easily enough to travel with Sima, leaving Priya and Malini alone. Rati, Raziya, and Deepa remained behind.

They sat. Priya kept her face slightly turned away, hands clasped in her lap. It should have looked respectful. It made Malini want to take Priya's face in her hands. Turn her head. *Look at me.*

Foolishness.

Malini waited until they were on the move, the chariot juddering around them, the highborn and soldiers accompanying them creating a clatter of wheels and hooves beyond the fabric and wrought ivory of the chariot's walls.

"I missed you," Malini murmured. It was like letting an overexerted muscle finally rest. She'd spent so long controlling herself that saying something truly honest was pure relief. "I've missed you so very much, Priya. I'm so glad you're here."

"I told you I'd come if you asked me to," Priya said immediately.

Her head was still lowered, but it turned a little at the sound of Malini's voice. Malini traced the angle of Priya's jaw with her eyes, followed the line of Priya's vision, and saw that Priya was looking at her, at the place where their clothes almost touched, their legs turned toward one another. One slight movement, and their knees would be pressed together. Would Priya's skin feel warm, even through all the cloth separating them? "And I'm so glad you have, but I also..." Priya stopped, and instead of continuing her train of thought said, "I kept your letter. The first one. Did you really read the Birch Bark Mantras for me?"

"For you, and for me," Malini said, low. "You know how I like knowledge."

"I do."

"Priya." Malini leaned forward, letting their skirts mingle, knees brush. "Why won't you look at me?"

A beat of breathless silence. Malini watched Priya's mouth curve into a smile.

"Because I want to kiss you," Priya said, voice a little rough. "And I know I can't. Not when..." She gestured at the curtain, reminding Malini of all the highborn lords beyond it.

"You probably could if you were quick," Malini teased.

Priya finally lifted her head. And there she was—those bright eyes, and those golden lashes making them brighter; that crooked nose and easy smile growing wider, that skin that had felt like warmth and silk, once, under Malini's hands.

"Is that a joke?" Priya sounded delighted. "Is the Empress of Parijat-dvipa joking with me?"

"I would like to think I'm flirting with you," Malini said, feeling her own heart lighten in response. "Or daring you, perhaps. But you may call it a joke if you like."

The smile faded from Priya's lips. But the light was still in her eyes, fierce enough that it made Malini's breath catch.

"I don't really think you want a brief kiss from me," Priya said lowly. "And that's not what I want from you either."

"Perhaps we should both stare at opposite walls," Malini muttered, and Priya laughed again.

"Perhaps," she agreed. And tilted her head against the palanquin wall, even as her gaze stayed on Malini—steady, and so very soft.

I would kiss you, Malini thought. Throat aching. *I would kiss you and kiss you.*

But that isn't why I need you here. That isn't the yielding I require from you.

Not today.

The temple had clearly prepared for their arrival, despite the short notice. There were oil lamps arrayed upon the temple's entrance steps in great winding spirals of light. The pillars were festooned in garlands of flowers, honey-sweet. Bees buzzed around them, held at bay by clouds of incense, rising from joss sticks set in pillared alcoves.

A small welcoming party of priests awaited them, bowing as Malini emerged from the palanquin. Behind her she could hear the clatter of hooves and whinny of horses, and the grating call of chariot wheels turning. She ground her teeth together. Perhaps when she returned to camp, she would inform the military officials to allocate some of their funds toward oil for those wheel spokes. Clearly they were being neglected.

She did not wait for Priya, Lata, or Sima to emerge. She knew that given half the chance, one of her lords would take it upon himself to greet the priests in her place. So she glided forward and slipped her gilded sandals from her feet; held up the edge of her sari in the crook of two curled fingers and walked up the temple stairs. The priests hurriedly bowed. One, younger than the rest, was visibly sweating.

She stopped before him.

"I must speak to your head priest," Malini said. She could hear footsteps behind her. Three pairs, their tread too light to be those of her armed men. As Priya's, Sima's, and Lata's shadows mingled with her own on the marble stairs, she said, "When we have made our offerings, tell him his empress requests a private meeting."

"Y-yes. Empress." The young priest bowed jerkily. Left them.

They were ushered into the temple, directly to the worship hall.

The marble was cool beneath her bare feet. Priests stood or kneeled along the edges of the room. There was no sound but the crackling of torches. Lata motioned to another priest, spoke to him in a low voice. No doubt discussing the money that Malini had brought as a gift of devotion to the temple.

She strode forward, Priya matching her steps. Malini let her arm gently graze against Priya's own, and felt the briefest brush of skin and warmth. She felt Priya's head turn; felt soft breath against her cheek.

"You must bow," Malini murmured. "That is all. I promise, Priya."

"I hope you know how much I do not want to do this," Priya whispered in return. Her body was taut as a bow string. She was clearly out of her element in a temple of the mothers—surrounded on all sides by the forces that had annihilated her own nation's glory.

Malini could not respond. The lords had entered behind them, and she could not risk being overheard. Instead she held her own feelings in a close, anxious fist in her chest and walked a few more steps forward to the altar. She kept her gaze fixed on the statue of the faceless mother in her graceful lengha of rich flame, a dupatta of smoke coiling around her empty face.

It was a tale her teacher had told her once, many years ago. That poor worshippers who could not afford to keep idols of all the mothers would often keep a single crude effigy in their home—faceless, smoke-veiled, intended to stand for all the mothers at once. In the generations since, Saketan commoners had begun to worship the mothers as one: the faceless mother, who was all and none of them at once, a figure who stood for all the mothers of flame who had been or who would be.

The temple's head priest approached. Ash-marked at forehead and chin, he held out flowers on a beaten copper tray. His wrists were inked—names in scrolling script that wound together in whorls and knots. "Empress," he said, lowering his eyes. "We are honored."

"It is my honor," Malini said, taking the flowers from him, and the needle-darted thread that lay by their side. "Any opportunity to venerate the mothers brings me joy."

She pressed the needle through the first flower as the priests began to pray. Began to weave a garland, the scent of roses and marigolds rich on her fingertips.

Priya walked forward.

There was a moment, a pause like the brief silence before a rising storm. And then Priya bowed, pressing her head to the ground before the mothers. Witnessed by Malini's own loyal men. She held the position for two heartbeats. Three. Four.

Good.

Then she stood once more, preparing—at the behest of the priest murmuring into her ear, Malini saw—to bow to Malini, too. A gesture of her obedience to Parijatdvipa.

Malini turned to mirror her. Without hesitation, without thought, Malini took Priya by the arm, stopping her motion. The garland was crushed between them, bruised and richly fragrant. "It is the mothers who must be venerated," Malini said. "Here, within this temple, their worship supersedes all else."

Hopefully the words were pretty and politic enough to hide the instinctual nature of her action—her desire to say *I will not shame you, not you, not like this.*

Priya nodded her head without lowering her eyes. Perhaps she understood. Perhaps.

"Empress," the temple's head priest murmured then. "Would you do me the honor of speaking to me alone?"

There was some bristling of the lords, but not much. Malini inclined her head. She turned, and bowed to the altar, and lowered the finished garland at the feet of the mothers. Then she rose to her feet. Lata followed her, a quiet chaperone.

The head priest led Malini and Lata to a study, a room with high windows and ancient manuscripts bound in silk and palm leaf stored on stone shelves. It was quiet and empty, distant enough from the worship hall that Malini could only hear the faintest strains of voices.

The priest was watching her warily. Before he could fall upon niceties—offer her a tea or sherbet, and stretch out this whole business interminably—Malini seated herself on the cushions arrayed on the floor. Lata moved to stand by the door, hands clasped before her. Lata was not barring the door—certainly not. But she was a deterrent, and a message for the high priest: The empress wishes for you to remain here.

From his silence and his stillness, Malini was sure he understood.

She waited for him to sit. After a moment, he did.

"You have heard, I'm sure, that the High Prince has allied with my brother in Harsinghar," Malini said, with no further preamble. "That soldiers from Harsinghar have carried what appears to be mother-blessed magical fire with them and have turned it upon my men. One of them, a Parijati priest, turned it directly upon me." A pause. The priest before her gave no reaction; no nod, no negating shake of his head. He merely watched her—eyes wide, unblinking, as if he were staring at a mirage, liable to flicker and fade. "I would have died when the fires fell," Malini went on. "But another man saved me. Another priest. A priest of the faceless mother. One of your own."

Silence, again.

"You should speak," Malini said. "I will not leave until we have been honest with one another."

The man's gaze flickered.

"How did you know he was one of my own?" the priest said finally.

"He had a priest's hair," Malini replied. "He wore an ash mark. But he was not Parijati, and he carried the many names of the mothers, inked into his wrists. Just as you do."

"You examined his body." The priest's voice was unreadable.

"With great respect, yes," Malini responded. "I will return him to you, if you request it of me. If you do not, he will be burned."

"It was not our intent for the man to die," the priest said slowly. "It was our intent that a message be passed to you, discreetly." A wary pause. "It is difficult for you to be approached with any subtlety, Empress."

Not so difficult if they had sent a maid, a woman. But clearly, they had not considered it.

"Well, I am here now before you. I am willing to listen. What message do you have for me?" When he paused, throat working, she gestured at the room. The emptiness, only Lata watching them. The torches flickered. "You will not have another opportunity like this again."

His throat worked. And worked.

"Emperor Chandra wishes to end your life," the priest said, each word spoken with great care. "That is no secret."

Malini inclined her head in agreement.

"As you have been taught—as you have seen—a life can possess great value. And you are a daughter of Divyanshi's line."

Malini waited.

The priest swallowed once more, and Malini thought vaguely that perhaps she should have requested refreshments after all, if only to put an end to that particular tic. In the light of the study—dim as it was—she could see that his skin was slick with sweat. The ash at his forehead was oily with it.

"My temple is small, Empress. We are not significant." *And do not wish to be*, his tone implied. "Proximity. You understand."

"Your message is from someone else," she said levelly. He nodded. "You are near the siege, but not too near. Close, but not in service to any lord." Another nod. "Then your message is from a priest of significant power," she concluded.

"There are some who would make an alliance with you, Empress. If you wished it."

"Their names?"

The priest shook his head.

"It was my understanding," Malini said, "that Chandra has the complete support of the priesthood. That he has raised you above all kings and princes of Parijatdvipa. Your powerful friend must be aware I cannot do the same, when the throne is mine. And yet a priest died for me. Help me understand."

"The priests of the mothers are not perfect allies to one another. Nor do we share a perfectly agreed-upon sense of what is right. What we share in common is a desire to *do* right. To walk a righteous path. But there are some who think Emperor Chandra... Your brother. That he is the right path. And there are others who look to you, Empress. And place their hope in you."

Fine words, but Malini was not sure she could believe that any of the priesthood would so easily set aside the power they possessed under Chandra. So she waited, allowing the priest time to sweat and feel the weight of her eyes on him, and his own words press at his lungs, his lips.

"Not all of us have gained great power under Emperor Chandra," the priest added.

A truth. But not the whole truth. The secrecy here—the sense that a game was being played that she could not see the fullness of—made her teeth ache.

"How can I trust your ally, when you give me so little?"

"Your life was saved, Empress," the priest said. "One of our own sacrificed himself."

"Which was not the intent, as you have already said. But what does your ally want from me? And what can I gain from him in return? Can you tell me this, priest?"

"What can you gain—? Ah. I have a gift for you, Empress. From the man himself."

The priest rose abruptly to his feet, turning away from her and walking over to his manuscripts.

Hidden behind his books lay a small box, polished, carved from onyx. He kneeled down and held it out to Malini like an offering.

She did not take it.

"A priest of the mothers almost destroyed my men and me," Malini said. "Can I trust this gift, priest? I am not sure."

"There is no force more righteous in all of Parijatdvipa than priests of mothers," the man said, which was not what Malini had asked.

Malini felt bitter laughter threaten. She reminded herself that she was prophesied by the nameless, that she had claimed to know the voices of the mothers of flame, that she had proclaimed that she had been chosen by them for the imperial throne. She had to believe in her power, to hold all those lies steady.

She could not think of the day her heart sisters had burned. She could not think *Your righteousness is liable to kill me, if I let it.*

"I trust your righteousness," she said instead. "I trust you are loyal to ideals that may serve to save or destroy me. But priest, I assure you: ideals that bring about the murder of the last woman of Divyanshi's line are a defiance of the will of the mothers, and the will of the nameless god. I know it. So, I ask you again, as an imperial daughter with the mothers' hands on her heart: Can I trust this gift?"

"You will not die here," the priest said. "Empress. You have my word."

Malini gestured over Lata, who held out her hands for the box in Malini's stead. The head priest handed it to her. Settled deeper onto his knees.

"If this gift pleases you," he said. "If you... if you accept that our ally is benevolent. Then I must request a gesture in return. A favor. If you promise to fulfill it, I will happily supply you his whereabouts. Where he will willingly meet you, and make a pact, if you desire it."

I could torture that information from you, Malini thought dispassionately. He was already fear-struck. A little pain, the threat of more, and he'd collapse like dampened sheaves of paper.

But that would hardly win her allies. Alas.

"Bring it here, Lata," she said.

Lata held the box forward. It was solid, and now she could see that it was made of a mixture of dark wood and onyx stone, its lid carved in swirls and whorls that formed a black rose. It had to be weighty, in Lata's hands, but she held it up steadily, with no sign of strain.

Malini touched her fingers to the latch. Opened the lid.

Inside was ash. A thick, heavy layer of it, black dust mixed with white gristle. Wood, char, bone. Malini almost recoiled, but caught herself.

"Lata."

"Yes, my lady?"

"A knife, please."

Lata drew a small dagger—previously concealed in the fold of her sari—and offered it to Malini, who took it and used the tip to move the ash, peeling its surface like skin. And ah. There.

Beneath the ash lay a bud of fire.

Lata gave a muffled gasp. Malini thought of those priests upon the walls with their arrows; those priests with their swords drawn. She pressed her own blade to the flame and watched the flame shiver. Unfurl, like a blossom meeting sunlight.

She raised the dagger and the flame writhed. It moved nothing like real fire: uncanny, winding, opening and closing like a fist. It almost looked as if it were reaching for her.

She placed the knife into the box. Closed the lid with an abrupt snap.

"What does your secret ally require in return?" Malini asked the priest.

"The priest you have imprisoned," he said. "Release him."

That was a surprise.

"He sought to end my life," said Malini. "He conspired to murder my men."

"He acted out of faith," the priest before her retorted, but gently. "You have been called a priest-killer by some," he went on, watching her carefully. Was this a warning? Advice, or a threat? She was not yet sure. "You took the lives of priests of the nameless in Srugna. I have heard the tales of your fire. Lives offered willingly," he added, as if Malini had argued with him. "But nonetheless, holy lives, stolen by your flame, your men, your guiding hand. But you have not yet harmed a priest of the mothers. To fight the men who faced you from Saketa's fortress— that is an honorable battle, and no one would judge you for it. But to kill a priest of the mothers who willingly entered your war camp, who kneeled before you—it cannot be forgiven."

Malini gave herself a moment to breathe and weigh up her options. Then she nodded.

"Your ally must have very good spies, to learn so swiftly what passes on a distant battlefield," she murmured. "He is in Parijat, is he not?"

Instead of replying, the priest returned to his shelves. Drew down a cloth bundle, which he unrolled, revealing a map of Parijat.

The answer was yes, then.

"Let me show you the way," he said. "I cannot give you his name, Empress. Even here, we call him the faceless son."

"He is a servant of the faceless mother, then? Like you?"

"Ah, empress," the man murmured, inclining his head. His face was gray. "He is not like me. That, I can assure you."

It was simple enough, on their return to the army encampment, to brush aside the concerns of her highborn. To summon Lata to her side, and call for Yogesh, and relay her orders even as she walked across the camp to her own tent, the folds of her sari rippling from the speed of her footsteps.

"You wish to . . . release him." The official's voice was tentative.

Malini simply nodded. She did not have to explain herself to him. There would be plenty of people who could—and would—demand explanations of her later. Best to save her energy.

"Record what needs to be recorded in your ledgers, and see that it's done," said Malini.

Yogesh was silent for a moment, still walking beside her.

"Is anything unclear?" Malini asked.

"Ah—Empress." He cleared his throat. "Perhaps—should I speak—to Lord Mahesh?"

"No," said Malini. "There is no need for that."

Malini waited until she was back in her own tent.

Then she opened the box.

Malini had a saber of her own, fashioned to be lighter than a man's, with a smaller grip so that it would be better suited to her strength, her hands. Its metal was shining silver, its scabbard inlaid with moonstone. Swati brought it to her, and Malini placed the tip of the weapon into the ash. Sifted through it.

The fire rose from the dagger and crawled onto the edge of her saber. Shifted and glowed, flickering and swirling just as it had on the weapons of the priestly soldiers who had turned on her army at the fortress's gates.

"Be careful, my lady," Lata said, voice tight. She stood at the edge of the tent. Not as if she planned to run, or even wished to. But as if she feared the fire rising on Malini's blade.

She was right to. Malini stared into the fire, which bloomed and withered like flowers upon a steel vine, and wondered what it would do.

Would it turn on her? Leap onto her flesh, destructive by nature, and burn her to char? She imagined, as she often had in her darkest hours, being reduced to an agony of ash. She imagined the tent burning and Lata with it.

She held the sword steady and waited. Waited.

Malini moved the fire between two blades—the saber and the

dagger—watching as it coiled between them with tendrils like fingers. She watched with careful patience as it grew thinner and weaker. Waited, again.

Using the dagger, she carved a hunk of it away from the whole, and watched it grow dimmer than the rest.

This was not how true fire worked. It was not how mothers' fire was meant to work, if the Book of Mothers was to be trusted.

She waited long enough that her arm began to tremble. Then Lata walked out of the tent and spoke softly to one of the guards, and returned with water, with food, and the task of watching Malini watch the flame.

Malini waited . . . and watched the fire begin to die. It withered as if the ash had been its roots. Its color faded, flame turning from gold to blue, to darkness.

Malini thought of the Book of Mothers—of the nature of the mothers' fire and thought, *ah*.

A gift after all.

The fire of mothers did not fade. It did not wither. It was unstoppable—a force of destruction that only faded away when the yaksa were dead. But this fire had died before her eyes.

Chandra was not blessed. Not chosen. And now Malini had proof.

She could feel a smile tugging her mouth. She let it overcome her face. Let herself laugh as the fire went out.

"Look, Lata," she said softly. "The mothers love their daughter after all."

19

BHUMIKA

The yaksa let her bow at their feet. They watched her hands shake, and the mask-keepers weep. Padma stared up at them, eyes wide, her hands fisted into Bhumika's sleeves—and that, only that, made her rise to her feet. "Khalida," she said, voice hoarse. Strange in her own throat. "Take Padma. *Khalida.*"

Khalida finally broke free from the trance that had taken her. Fumbled, and then carefully took Padma into her arms. And Bhumika stood tall, and bowed—the deep, standing bow she had once seen her temple elders use for effigies of the yaksa. She straightened and said, "Your High Elder welcomes you, yaksa." A susurration ran through the crowd of worshippers; they swayed, almost, with her words. She understood it. She could feel the enormity of this moment, too. As if a myth had taken her up, and she could only allow it to carry her. "Your High Elder welcomes you to Ahiranya. To your land and your people." She bowed again, and said, "I find myself— lost. Without words. Please." She raised her head again. "Guide me."

"Take us through the mahal," said Sendhil.

"Then take us to the Hirana," Chandni said, more gently. "We desire to see everything. To know our temple, our people. Our home."

"Yaksa," Bhumika said, bowing her head again, for lack of any idea what to do. "Please. Follow me."

The worshippers surged forward. But Nandi, the smallest of them, turned. "No farther," he said sweetly. And the earth seized and roiled, and with a cry the worshippers stumbled back.

"Learn respect," he said. And then, with a child's skipping foot-steps, he followed.

One foot in front of the other. Face calm. That was all she could do for herself. No one else had followed. The yaksa only seemed to want her. They circled her like carrion birds, surrounding her, urging her forward.

A rustle of noise, and in the blink of an eye, the yaksa with Sanjana's face was walking by her side.

"Yaksa," Bhumika said again. What else could she say? "I . . ."

"Call me Sanjana if it's easier," the yaksa said, smiling sweetly. "And call her Chandni, and call him Sendhil. And Nandi of course. You have not forgotten him, have you?"

"No," said Bhumika. "I have not."

Tinkling laughter.

"None of us mind those names."

"I should address you with respect, yaksa," Bhumika said, eyes lowered. "And my . . . you are not my temple sister."

"No," Sanjana-who-was-not-Sanjana said merrily, as if the thought of it amused her. "This is just flesh, temple daughter. Just that." She tapped her own jaw lightly. "Peel it away and there's still power beneath it."

Sanjana leaned into her.

"You carve masks of wood. The wood of our bones," she breathed. "You wear us as your crowns. It seemed fitting that we do the same."

"I am sorry," Bhumika said, grappling for solid ground. "Sorry, if my actions have caused offense. If the masks—"

"Ah, no. No." The yaksa shook her head. "No offense between us, daughter. None at all." And then she was darting away again. Behind her, the marble of the corridor had cracked—splitting open for the flowers that followed her, beautiful violet blooms with deep yellow hearts.

It was like a dream. A great and terrible dream.

Bhumika turned to Ashok, who watched her still.

"And what should I call you?" Bhumika said softly.

Ashok returned her look.

"My name," he said. "What else?"

He certainly looked human. His face was the same. His body. The expression he wore as he looked at her was all Ashok—tinged with judgment, his mouth slightly curled, his eyebrows low. But he held himself with a stiffness that made her own skin itch with unease.

"I am not a yaksa," he said. "I am . . . just me, Bhumika. Returned."

"No temple child truly dies," said the yaksa with Sendhil's face; with his earthen hands and budding things rising through his throat. "We carry you with us. We hold you inside us, as you hold us within you in turn.

"You must tell us what Ahiranya is like now," he went on. "Dear one. Our daughter. When we last walked, the city and the trees were one."

"And the forest was so much larger," Chandni said. She watched Bhumika's every move, the softness of her look marred by the way her eyes refused to blink. Bhumika could only think of the eyes of beads on dolls sewn for children: lidless, unfeeling. The *idea* of eyes, more than eyes themselves.

"You do not understand how pleasing the world is," Sendhil said, with the kind of smile she had never seen on his face in life. "How good it is to be back."

Bhumika swallowed, and forced her expression to remain blank.

"Come. Let me show you the Hirana," she said.

She told herself she would think of it as an opportunity. A *gift*. The yaksa had come back, after all. Come back, they had promised her, to restore Ahiranya's glory. "To fill the Hirana with our kind," Chandni had said. "And the mahal, and the forest. To make the world new and sweet for our people, and ourselves." Her flat eyes had shone, hard and brilliant. "Isn't that joyous, daughter?"

Joyous. Yes.

But the disquiet in her belly wouldn't settle.

The yaksa had come back wearing the faces of dead children and the people who had burned them. A cruel thing, in truth.

Why those faces? Why come wearing mortal faces at all, when the effigies in the Hirana were more flower than human, their faces root and earth and thorn, not blood or flesh? What did they want? What was newness to a yaksa—what was sweet?

In her study, Bhumika watched Kritika pace. Her own limbs felt numb. It was all she could do to sit straight and tall, and feign calm.

"We must send messages across Ahiranya," Kritika was saying enthusiastically. "We must tell everyone—ah, the miracle of it! To think that we will live in the Age of Flowers returned..."

"The new worshippers won't leave," Bhumika said.

"Let them stay," said Kritika. She was too full of energy to remain still. She still wore her mourning whites but there was a glow in her face, a light that Bhumika had not realized Ashok's death had snuffed out. "They have ample reason to be here. Let them be glad."

At the door, hand on his sword, Jeevan made no comment on this. He was looking into the distance, expression fixed.

"It's not safe to constantly have strangers surrounding us," Bhumika said evenly.

"You think anyone can harm us now that Ashok has returned? Now that the yaksa are here?" Kritika shook her head. "No, no. We're safe."

Bhumika searched for words. A court, she could manipulate. With promises and bargains, she could manage highborn, merchants, even the mask-keepers. What she could not do was manage the world they had fallen into.

She'd learn. But that would take time.

"We should not simply trust," Bhumika managed to say.

"You want us to distrust the yaksa? Our own spirits? Our country's soul?"

"No," Bhumika said swiftly. "But you know as well as I, Kritika, that the desires and goals of the yaksa are not *mortal* things," she stressed. "The Birch Bark Mantras guide me in this, as they should guide you. Our protection may not be what matters most to them. We must continue to defend ourselves. To rule ourselves."

"Those things matter to Ashok," Kritika said sharply. She turned away from Bhumika, blinking tears from her eyes, dabbing them away with the edge of her pallu. When she turned back, her expression had grown more severe, more like the canny and driven rebel Bhumika had originally known. "He has returned to us with the yaksa. If they did not love us and grieve with us, would they have brought him back?"

Perhaps Kritika was right. Bhumika lowered her head.

Thought of Nandi, breaking the earth. *Learn respect.*

"Some things don't need to be questioned," Kritika went on hotly. "Some things are miracles and must be treated as such. I will not disbelieve the yaksa. I will not turn from them. I will follow them. We will *all* follow them. Do you disagree, Elder Bhumika?"

Kritika was almost vibrating with tension.

All this time spent building bonds with the mask-keepers—all the careful maneuvering, and it had come to this—a potentially impassable rift over an impossible event.

"As an elder, how could I turn from the spirits I serve?" Bhumika said gently. "How could I not be grateful to have my brother with me once more?"

It was not agreement. But Kritika nodded regardless.

"Of course," she said. And smiled, her eyes damp again. "Elder Bhumika," she continued. "We have so much to celebrate and be glad for. Ahiranya is finally changing for the better, as we always dreamt. What a blessing it is to witness it."

"Jeevan," Bhumika said, when Kritika had left. Her voice was like paper—dry and thin. "Stay with me. I need your help. I need you to discreetly summon a close few to this room." She closed her eyes. Whom could she trust? She considered it. Name after name, each one weighed against what she knew of their loyalties. Their willingness to bend to her, and no other force.

"Billu," she said. "Rukh." She named a few others—soldiers whom she knew Jeevan trusted. Khalida, she omitted. She was with Padma now, and Bhumika would speak to her later, in the privacy of the nursery. And then, after a moment, she said, "Ganam. Bring Ganam too."

"Lady Bhumika," he said. "Are you sure?"

"I am."

When they arrived, she bid Jeevan to shut the door behind them. "Thank you for coming. And listening." She paused for a moment, then said, "I know I am naturally cautious. But to venerate the yaksa as they deserve I believe we must be...careful. To cause no offense. To treat them well."

"Everyone's elated the yaksa are back. And that Ashok's back too," Ganam added, watching her intently. "I don't think anyone is worried about offending them."

"Then everyone forgets their Birch Back Mantras," said Bhumika. "And all the things the yaksa are capable of. We are beloved to them, but we are also...very mortal. And they are not."

"I don't think Ashok's Ashok," Rukh said tentatively. He was crouched near the door. His expression was very serious, brow furrowed. Hands tight on his knees. "I...I used to watch Ashok a lot. When I was." He shrugged. "You know."

A lackey for the rebels. A sick child, with no else to rely on. "Go on," Bhumika said.

"Ashok was always very—confident, you know? Sure of himself. Arrogant."

"A leader needs to be arrogant," Ganam said.

Rukh shrugged again, as if to say it was none of his business what leaders were meant to be. "All I know is that he doesn't stand like Ashok does. Doesn't speak like him. It's like..." Rukh struggled for a moment, then said. "It's like he's got Ashok's face. But there's something else under it."

A chill ran through Bhumika.

"All I ask," she said calmly, "is that if you can watch them, and see what they do—you do so. And I will be happy to listen to anything you learn. So that I may ensure we all serve them well."

After they left, Jeevan remained. He stood at the corner of the room, a silent comfort, as she wrestled with all her childhood griefs and shapeless fears. Finally, as the sky grew darker, he said softly, "You should rest, my lady."

She nodded.

"Yes," she said. "Yes. I will."

In the morning, she thought. *In the morning I will send another message to Priya. I'll warn her not to come back. I'll beg her if I must.*

It would be pointless, of course. Priya would come if Priya wanted to come. Bhumika hadn't yet found a way to stop Priya from following the strange, fierce tides of her own whims and her own heart. But if Priya was not safe, as Bhumika feared...

She reached into the sangam again. Reached and found nothing, and returned to her own skin. She would go to her room. Try and sleep. Everything else would wait until morning.

In the morning, Bhumika woke to the sound of screaming. She scrambled out of her bed, raced across her chambers to the door, and found Khalida clutching Padma, the both of them crying, terrified.

There was a body on the ground. A rider, in Ahiranyi colors. Pale flowers were sprouting through his skin. His cut throat was a garland of ashoka blossoms and oleander, empty of blood.

The rider she'd sent to Priya. The single rider Jeevan had spared.

She did not need to see a yaksa to understand the message she had been sent. She took Khalida by the shoulder and crushed her and Padma against her own chest. As if she could protect them from this. As if she had any power in this strange new world at all.

Priya was beyond her reach now.

PRIYA

Priya and her people had been given an abysmal location to set up their camp—on the edge of the grounds, far, far away from the war council tent and Malini's own grand gold-and-white abode, right where the wind cut in coldly at night and the worst of the sun beat against the canvas during the day, turning it into a sweltering oven. It was no surprise, really. No one here had any love for Ahiranyi people.

"At least we're less likely to get stabbed by other soldiers here, right, Elder Priya?" Nitin had offered helpfully, and Priya had glared at him until he'd scuttled off to sort out bedding or food, or something else that was needful.

Long after she left the temple to the faceless mother and the scent should have faded from her skin, Priya's hands smelled of flowers. Every time the fragrance reached her nose, she remembered Malini's hands on her arm, and the garland caught between their bodies. Remembered the strange, heady feeling of standing like Malini's equal, staring into her fierce eyes with the shadow of the statue of the faceless mother fanned over both of them.

She remembered how she had bowed to the mothers of flame.

That memory was like a vein of rot—something ugly threading its roots through the golden sweetness of Malini's eyes and hands on her.

Priya had done what was politically needful. She was no Bhumika, and no Malini, but she understood that sometimes unpleasant things had to be done for the sake of a greater goal. She had ruled and she had killed. *Bowing* was hardly the most difficult thing she'd done.

And yet...she'd betrayed something in herself by doing it. It was the old temple elders and her siblings who'd made her. It was Ahiranya that had shaped her into what she was. The mothers of flame were not hers to worship. If anything, they were hers to hate.

But Malini had asked, and Priya had...not said no.

Did I bow for the sake of Ahiranya, or for Malini? Priya asked herself. It wasn't a question she could answer. She wasn't sure she wanted to.

Priya stole one moment for herself—reaching and seeking in the sangam, searching for her sister in the rivers. But no matter how she called, Bhumika refused to answer, and Priya returned to her skin ill at ease, and a little angry. What was Bhumika *doing*?

She distracted herself by combing out her hair, then carefully binding it in place with darts of wood. She was already wearing a white salwar kameez—her best, one of the few nice things she had carefully carried with her, wrapped in muslin to keep it from getting dirty or moth-bitten until she had a chance to wear it with highborn company.

"Do you need to me to do your hair?" Sima asked, slipping into the tent.

Priya dropped one of her pins. Paused. "Maybe," she said.

"Oh, Pri, here. Let me."

Sima gathered up Priya's hair and began to put the staves of wood in place.

"I've been listening to the gossip," Sima said, her voice low so they wouldn't be overheard. Only Nitin and a few other Ahiranyi soldiers were around, so Priya wasn't sure who could possibly hear, but it always paid to be careful. "There's doubt among the highborn over whether the empress should be empress. They think the fire's a sign. The maids who were willing to speak to me—they said most of the common soldiers aren't so sure." One of the darts slid into place, poking Priya's scalp in the process. She winced, and Sima adjusted it. "Sorry. Anyway, the highborn think they're being subtle."

"But they're not?"

"Not at all," Sima snorted. "I can see why your empress was worried enough to drag you here."

But what can I actually do? Priya thought. Be an emissary for Ahiranya? Certainly. Moon over Malini? She could do that as easily as breathing. But if Malini wanted more from her…

Priya thought of how her powers had guttered on the journey here, and worry gnawed at her all over again.

She reminded herself that she could feel the green now. The sangam was waiting for her, waiting for her to reach out. But what use was it if Bhumika wouldn't answer her?

She forced away her unease and turned to Sima. "Let me do yours now," she said, taking Sima's long braid in her hands. "And then we should probably go or we'll be late, and who knows how insulted those highborn women will be?"

Lata, Malini's sage, had come to personally request Priya's presence at a meeting of "the empress's closest companions." Lata had looked like no sage Priya had ever seen before, her sari a glorious deep green silk, her braided hair severe but her bangles a refined beaten gold. She looked like a highborn woman, but from her serious bearing and the ink on her fingers, it was clear she was more of an advisor. And from the way the guards bowed their heads, deferring to her, a *senior* advisor.

"If you were a man, Elder Priya, you would have been required to meet the highborn men who counsel the empress," Lata had said. "But as you are not, you must meet with the wives and daughters who attend on Empress Malini."

"Must?" Priya had asked.

"Must," Lata had stated firmly.

Now, Sima and Priya left the sweltering heat of the tent and met the guard Lata had sent to guide them. They walked toward the main camp, where the tents for the other highborn stood. They passed Saketan liegemen practicing with their blade whips out in a training circle cordoned off with rope; one Srugani soldier sleeping with his mace propped at his side; and a handful of cooks carrying vats of oil and sacks of rice, who gave Priya and Sima distrustful looks as they passed. The army encampment was carefully delineated into segments by city-state and liege loyalty, but the overall atmosphere was still one of pure chaos. Priya was a little dizzied by it. She'd never seen so many people in one place, and she'd spent nearly her entire life in the most populated part of Ahiranya.

Still, she was fairly certain she'd managed to affect a look of serene calm by the time she and Sima reached their destination.

The tent they were led to was large. When the guard announced them, they entered, and were greeted by a pleasantly cool interior, faintly perfumed with rosewater and incense. There were bowls of water laid out to keep the air fresh, and a single maid desultorily waving about a horsehair fan over an older woman who was dozing on a floor cushion. Two younger noblewomen were playing a game of chaturanga, which they set carefully aside when Priya and Sima entered.

Malini was not present. Neither was Lata.

Perfect.

The younger noblewomen stood and nodded to Priya. She returned the gesture.

"Elder Priya," said one—a tall woman in a deep blue salwar kameez. "It is a pleasure to finally meet you." She didn't even sound as if she were entirely lying. "I am Lady Raziya, of the Lal Qila. This is Lady Deepa."

Deepa dipped her head and gave a small-voiced explanation of her origins.

Priya had a vague sense, once introductions were done, that they should have bowed to her and she should only have nodded in return. She was the leader of a nation, after all, as ridiculous as that thought still felt. They were the wife of the lord of a fort and the daughter of the general of the imperial army. Though powerful, they were not her equals. She'd learned enough of the cutthroat business of status and political hierarchies in the past year, watching Bhumika deftly manage Ahiranya's highborn, to recognize the disparities in their status.

But ah, what did it matter if they insulted her in this? What could she rightly do about it? She was still Ahiranyi, and they were still empire. She didn't know how to cut down a highborn woman with words anyway, not the way Bhumika would have been able to do. So she just smiled.

"This is my advisor Sima," she said, and Sima sketched out a rather abrupt bow. "Should we sit?"

"Of course," Raziya said graciously, and they all sat down as the maid lowered her fan and began to arrange refreshments and trays of sweets.

They exchanged pleasantries. Comments on weather. On travel. Deepa spoke haltingly about her family—her sisters and her mother, away from the political troubles in Parijat, safe in a family manse in Alor—then fell silent. Raziya spoke of her own home—of Dwarali's snows and mountains, and her gladness to be traveling alongside the empress herself.

"I have long claimed to fear no fight, Elder Priya," Lady Raziya said. "But the last battle the empress faced was unlike any I have seen before. I was injured, though you can see I am now well." She gestured at her skull, then lowered her hand lightly. "The battle filled me with a certainty that the empress must have stronger allies around her. Allies like you." There was a challenge in her pale eyes and her smile. "Can you demonstrate your strength to us, Elder Priya? It would gladden us all, I think, to know how you will defend our empress."

Bhumika would have known how to handle this situation. But Priya...well, she could only be more of what she was. And what she was good at being was—herself. And all the problems that entailed. She settled on downing her wine in one smooth slide. Then, when her mouth still burned pleasantly, and the alcohol hadn't quite yet warmed her blood, she said, "I'm afraid I can only use my gifts at the empress's bidding. It is a promise I have made to her, you see. To only act as she desires me to."

Sima, who was sipping at her own wine, made a curious choking noise into her cup.

"A small demonstration of skill would surely cause no harm," said Raziya.

"Oh no," Priya said. "I couldn't possibly. I know the reputation of my people." She gave Raziya and Deepa a tight smile of her own. "I must act at the empress's bidding or not at all."

"You need not do anything, Elder Priya," Deepa said, in that same small voice. "If you do not wish to. We are only curious. I have read much of Ahiranya, and I would like very much to learn more."

"Maybe in the future, if the empress allows it," Priya said. *Or if we meet a battle where Malini needs my help, or she weaves some other complex plot that requires me.* That thought shouldn't have been as fond as it felt, in her own skull. "Although I cannot show you my skills, Lady Raziya, my advisor is an able archer," Priya said cheerfully. "And I'm sure she'd be happy to demonstrate."

"An archer? Goodness," said Lady Raziya, eyebrows raising. "Well, that is a skill highly valued where I come from. I would be glad to match my arrows against your advisor's if she is willing."

"She absolutely is," said Priya firmly.

"I am going to kill you for this," Sima muttered a little while later, as they stood in a Dwarali practice yard, curious horsemen watching as Raziya strung her bow. A few maids had gathered to the side, and a group of Dwarali women were milling about. They carried bows of their own, and one of them had set herself the task of setting up the target. "Or shave off your eyebrows. Something unpleasant, you wait and see."

"Think of it this way. You never would have done this as a maidservant."

"Both eyebrows. And your hair," hissed Sima, before she took up the bow one of Raziya's guards was helpfully holding out to her.

Priya moved to stand in the shade with Deepa. A few men began to make surreptitious bets.

The target was the strangest contraption Priya had seen in a long time. In Ahiranya, Jeevan trained people with a simple painted plank of wood. But this, Raziya announced, was a Dwarali artifice, used for archery games: a fish carved from gold, hollow at the eyes, hung precariously from a high pole. The guardswoman who'd raised it up knocked the pole with her foot, and the fish began to twist wildly.

"If we were playing as Dwarali archers do," Raziya said to Sima, "we would judge where to shoot only looking at the reflection of the target in a basin of water, laid on the ground. But we won't go so far for a simple game."

Sima looked at the fish dubiously.

"So I win if I knock it from the pole?"

"Hitting it is considered enough," Raziya said, drawing her bow and nocking the arrow. "The eye is ideal. Let me demonstrate."

The arrow flew from her bow, striking the eye of the twisting golden fish, sending it spinning wildly in the opposite direction. There were cheers from the watching crowd. The other Dwarali women, though expressionless, were palpably smug.

Sima squared her shoulders like a woman going to her death, grasped her bow, and stepped forward.

There was no way this was going to end well. Priya was absolutely going to lose her eyebrows.

"Where is Lata now?" Priya asked, turning to Deepa. Deepa startled, as if she hadn't expected to be spoken to, then went still. "She was the one who summoned us here, and I haven't seen even a glimpse of her."

"Oh, with the empress, I expect," Deepa said, darting a quick look at Priya. "They have meetings all day. Usually we attend alongside her, but sometimes we have responsibilities to our own people."

"Was I your responsibility today?" Priya asked. Deepa gave her an almost alarmed look, and Priya grinned at her. "I'm sorry," she said. "I'm not highborn, Lady Deepa, and I'm an outsider here. I don't know how best to talk. Am I too blunt?"

Sima's first shot had missed. Benevolently, Raziya allowed her to try again and this time there was some mild applause as Sima's arrow took a glancing blow off the fish's torso.

"No, Elder Priya," Deepa said, when the clapping had faded. "Only—it is different. Interesting. To hear someone speak as you do. I will grow used to it, I am sure. You will need to be patient with me."

"Sahar," Raziya called, and one of the Dwarali women walked forward. "What do you think?" Lady Raziya asked. "She has some talent, doesn't she?"

"Mm," Sahar said, which was not exactly agreement. She gave Sima a critical look. "Have you used a bow in battle before?"

"Yes," Sima said steadily.

"Have you injured anyone?"

"I killed a man."

"Did he walk into your arrow?"

"Don't insult me," Sima said, but she was smiling. "I'm not *that* bad."

"No, not so bad," Sahar agreed. She turned to Lady Raziya. "My lady," she said. "I'm happy to give our guest a lesson, if that is your will." She looked in Priya's direction and said, a glimmer of amusement in her voice, "You're welcome to join in too, Lady Deepa."

Deepa squeaked out a refusal that sounded almost like *I'd accidentally shoot myself in the foot.* Priya bit back a laugh and watched the archery lesson begin.

"Your advisor has some skill," Lady Raziya observed, approaching Priya once Sima had departed. "But she is still—raw. Not yet fully trained. I think, perhaps, the bow is a new skill to her."

"We've all had to learn new skills in Ahiranya."

"I imagine so," Lady Raziya said. "When you are a people who serve another people, your options are narrowed. You are never quite given the tools to rise. And when you do rise, why—it is hard to build a palace from subpar stone, with the help of half-trained masons."

"As you say," Priya murmured.

"But perhaps you are building something quite different." A pause, as Raziya looked her over, her gaze thoughtful. "I will see your skill one day, Elder Priya. I look forward to it."

Before Priya could respond—and spirits knew what she would have said to that—she heard a yell from somewhere beyond the practice yard. It sounded like Sima's voice.

Without another thought, she turned and ran.

There was Sima, surrounded by a ring of Saketan soldiers. One was holding a sword whip out to her by the hilt. Sima was grim-faced, refusing to take it. As Priya strode closer, she began to hear what the man was saying to her.

"...fight a Dwarali, but you won't test your skills against us?"

So they'd been watching, then.

"I don't know the sword whip," Sima said steadily. "You want to test your arrows against me, fine. We'll see who wins."

"I saw you *lose*."

"I was no match for Lady Raziya," said Sima, in the tone she used on all the guards at the mahal in Hiranaprastha, when they irritated her. "But I think I can take you."

The soldier grabbed Sima by the wrist.

In that instant, the fight was inevitable.

Bhumika no doubt would have disagreed. Priya could practically hear her sister's exasperated voice in her head. *Of course the Parijat-dvipans want conflict, Priya. But you don't have to give it to them.*

The man was muttering something, too low and viperous for Priya to make out the words.

"My lord," Sima was saying, voice firm and loud enough to carry. "Please control yourself. This is not an appropriate way to talk about my mistress *or* my people."

"Our land's cursed by your blight," the soldier was ranting. "And you want me to be polite? No, the others may be too cowardly to say anything, but we don't want you here. You Ahiranyi, you ruin everything you touch."

"Then stop touching me," Sima said, wrenching her hand back. He didn't let go.

And before Priya could do anything, Sima was lifting her left hand and punching him square in the nose.

There was a crunch, and blood, and the man holding Sima yelled and raised his whip.

"*Stop*," Priya shouted. The ground rumbled beneath her. She didn't care if they felt it. Let them. "Is this how you treat advisors from other lands, soldier?" She shouldered her way through the circle of men. "What would your commander say about this?"

The soldier dropped Sima's hand. She darted away from him, moving to stand at Priya's side.

Priya took a deliberate step forward.

The man was resisting the urge to step back. She could see it in the stiffness of his shoulders; the sudden twitch of his feet. But he stayed where he was.

"You want a match with a sword whip, then I'll happily face you," Priya said. "I can show you how I've treated Emperor Chandra's men, if you like. I'd be delighted to give you a practical demonstration." Her fingers twitched at her sides. If her damnable magic failed her, she would gladly take one of those sword whips and garrote the man with it. She knew she could do it.

"No one is using any kind of whip against anyone else," Sima said. "Elder," she added, nudging her arm against Priya's. "There's no more need to defend me. I'm sure this soldier has seen sense."

"Lower your weapon, idiot," one of the other men muttered.

And the soldier did. Good.

Then he spat in Priya's face.

"Fuck," Sima said feelingly.

Once, Priya would have taken that casual violence without a word; would have lowered her eyes and gritted her own teeth and tucked the hurt and rage away to be unseen, to rot and gather dust inside herself. She would have done nothing. She would have wished, only wished, that she could show him what she truly was.

She didn't have to wish anymore.

The soil surged open like a wave. Something made of roots deeply buried—something sharpened to a blade by Priya's fury—surged up. The man screamed and danced back, dropping his whip. Yells filled the air.

Priya very calmly closed the earth back up. She turned, meeting Sima's gaze, as one of the Saketan soldiers grabbed her by the arm. Sima's eyes were wide, her face pale. Behind her, Deepa had emerged from the tent, mouth open in shock.

Don't worry, Priya wanted to say. *What can these men possibly do to me?* But she couldn't. She was being dragged away, and Sima was left alone, watching her go.

MALINI

The camp had been growing more restless by the day as the siege stretched on, so it was no surprise to Malini when one of her guards announced that Low Prince Ashutosh wished to speak with her urgently. She had expected some kind of conflict to break out sooner rather than later. She resisted the urge to sigh.

"I will hold audience later," Malini told the guard, as one of the military officials arrayed around her hurriedly gathered up the maps he'd been presenting to her. The war council tent was full of administrators, the rustle of paper, the oily musk of ink. "Tell him I will have ample time for him then."

"He has company, my lady," the guard told her. "The Ahiranyi— the woman—he has her."

"*Has* her?" Malini repeated, and the man nodded, knuckling some sweat from his brow.

Hearing the impatient noise of voices beyond the tent's walls, the clang of armor, Malini decided not to ask for further details.

"Let him in, then," she said.

Prince Ashutosh strode in. Bowed. Behind him, four of his liegemen entered, with Priya between them, cuffed at the wrists. She didn't look afraid, but she did not look entirely at ease either. She bowed along with the liegemen, and when they straightened she met Malini's eyes for one brief moment before looking away.

"Prince Ashutosh," Malini said, deciding to forgo any pleasantries. "Please explain why you're bringing my invited ally to me in chains."

Ashutosh's face was grim. "This Ahiranyi," he said, "attacked three of my liegemen. I demand that she be punished."

"I see," said Malini. She paused for a moment. "Nonetheless, low prince, I see no need for her to be bound."

"There is plenty of reason, Empress," Ashutosh said, a sullen set to his mouth, anger in his eyes.

Priya in contrast stood calm as anything, between the low prince's liegemen. The cuffs on her wrists looked weighty, but overlarge, which was no surprise. They had, no doubt, been designed to hold a grown man captive. And Priya, for all the strength of her, was slight. When Malini met her eyes, Priya's mouth quirked up, ever so slightly. Not enough to be called a smile.

They both knew she could have broken those manacles if she had wanted to. But here she was, awaiting Malini's judgment, respecting Malini's authority. Malini supposed that was generous of her.

"Are any of your men dead?" Malini asked Prince Ashutosh.

"No, Empress."

"Injured?"

"Some cuts," Ashutosh said grudgingly. "Some bruising."

Interesting. If Priya had wanted them dead, they would have been dead.

"Do you deny attacking the prince's men, Elder Priya?"

"No, Empress."

"What offense did they commit to attract your ire?"

"Disrespect," Priya replied crisply. She inclined her head. "Empress."

"Disrespect can take many forms," Malini said. "Tell me more."

"They did nothing to warrant the treatment she inflicted," Ashutosh cut in before Priya's mouth could even part. "Empress, it is not the wounds she inflicted that make me demand justice. It is the *manner* in which they were inflicted. By magic. Unnatural witchcraft. You have made an alliance with a monster."

There was an intake of breath from one of the officials. The faintest rustle of movement, as they shifted uneasily and went still.

"The Ahiranyi leadership have professed and demonstrated their loyalty to me," Malini said calmly. "All their gifts and their magic are wielded in the empire's service. The Ahiranyi elders serve me."

"We do not forget the Age of Flowers, Empress. We know what they are." His voice was sharp. "We Saketans remember, as all Parijat-dvipans do, what the Ahiranyi did to our people. Will you allow the Ahiranyi to crush us now, as they did before? Do you forget it was your ancestor who sacrificed herself to save us all?"

"Your men are not dead," Malini said. *What foolishness.* Was she witnessing anger, impetuous and unvarnished, or had this Saketan prince chosen this moment, of all moments, to test her political loyalties? "Your men are barely harmed. You will have justice, Prince Ashutosh, I assure you."

"I will take any punishment without complaint," Priya said, head held high. Ashutosh and Malini had been speaking court Dvipan, the shared language of the highest of highborn, but Priya spoke now in common-tongue Zaban, in the lilting accent of the Ahiranyi, deliberately and clearly. With her braid unraveling, and her feet squarely planted against the tent's scuffed fabric base, she did not look like a highborn—did not look like the men around her, or their wives or their daughters. She did not look like a maidservant either.

"Her life," Prince Ashutosh said. "I want her life. She used witchcraft, Empress. Her kind have no place in the empire."

Malini nearly laughed. Who was he to request the death of a ruler of another land? He would never have asked it if the ruler in question had been of Dwarali or Alor. But he had asked it of Ahiranya.

And it was because of the very history between Ahiranya and the empire that she could not throw his request aside entirely. How irritating.

"Elder Priya is an ally of Parijatdvipa," Malini said, with implacable calm; with the iron will that was her right, as empress, throne or no throne. "I will not waste the lives of my allies, when they may yet be the death of my enemies." And no one, surely, could deny Priya's value. Priya was, as she had always been, unfathomably valuable, a thing full of possibility. *Useful.* "But you are correct," Malini acknowledged. "There must be redress from Ahiranya. There must, after all, be justice among equals."

A look flickered across Ashutosh's face. He had not expected Priya to be called his equal.

There was a flurry of movement from the military officials who surrounded her; the rising shuffle of pages, and mingled voices rising. An array of punishments was suggested. Beating. Exposure to the elements. Forfeiture of lands.

Deepa entered the tent. Head bowed, she looked at no one as she bowed and then made her way to Malini's side. Her message was a whisper, quickly murmured—and then she was bowing and slipping away again.

"Public caning would be acceptable," Ashutosh said grudgingly, when it became clear no one would allow him to have the execution he desired. There was a ripple of agreement from his attendant liegemen.

Priya said nothing. Her expression was the kind of calm that settles on waters before a storm.

By the mothers, Malini would not give a woman to these men and have her caned before them. Her mouth was full of a bitterness that was like poison. She would not give *Priya* to these men. She would sacrifice a great deal, do a great deal, but not this.

"It is my understanding, from the tracts that govern justice in wartime, that a highborn lord would first, as a courtesy, have his punishment decided by a superior from his own country. Elder Priya," Malini said. "Who has the right, in your entourage?"

"No one, Empress," said Priya. "I am the most powerful representative of Ahiranya here. The only person who stands higher than me is the High Elder Bhumika, and she remains in Ahiranya."

"Then such courtesy cannot be extended to you," Malini said. She tried not to look into Priya's eyes. She looked over her head instead, at the men watching the both of them. "But I believe the punishment meted out to a highborn ruler is usually financial in nature, rather than physically inflicted. Is that not so?" Malini asked, turning her gaze on one of her officials. He stammered something incoherent, wetted his lips, then nodded.

"Financial redress has not been codified into law, Empress, and is not—ah—in line with *tradition*, but it is—a choice often made. In the past."

That sounded very much like tradition to Malini, but there was little point in arguing semantics.

"Prince Ashutosh," she said instead.

"Yes, Empress?"

"Only you can decide what would provide you redress." It was a risk, a gamble, but better this way. Better, to place the choice in his hands rather than allow her loyalties to be laid out openly before her council. "But a trade may be worth your consideration."

"There is only one thing Ahiranya trades in," one of the soldiers muttered. There was a snicker from one of the other men; a twitch of lips, here and there, among their watchers.

Ashutosh did not reprimand them.

"Prince Ashutosh," Malini said, in rebuke.

"My men only speak truth, Empress," he replied.

How stupid. Whatever he believed—whatever any one of them believed—they had seen how Malini's face had lit up when Priya had first arrived and kneeled, right there in the golden sun-burnt dirt of their war camp. Malini had felt the light sweeping into her face: the tug of her own lips wanting to form a smile, the joyful breathlessness of her lungs. How could he have seen her react so, and then say this?

Another test, perhaps. Of course it was a test.

Again, the thought came to her, uselessly, that if she were Emperor Aditya, and someone had spoken in such a manner about Rao, why— she could have had them killed, and no man in the circle surrounding her would have murmured a word of protest. When would she have the power to do as she willed—to grind laughing, spiteful men under her heel, and walk on steady ground?

Would such a time ever come?

"Prince Ashutosh," Malini said. "A number of your men suffer from the rot."

He swallowed, face pinched. He was insulted, perhaps, to have this taint on his loyal liegemen aired before an audience of his peers. Or he had not known that *she* knew. "Yes, Empress."

"Are they still camped with us?"

She knew the answer, of course. But he nodded jerkily and said, "Yes, Empress," once more. Then: "I do not abandon my men. Many of them have trained alongside me since we were mere boys."

"Elder Priya possesses the ability to save mortal lives from the rot," said Malini. "Men, and land. That is what Ahiranya trades, in my service. If your men require services of another kind, they may wish to consider what offense they may cause their empress, to speak so before her." A pause. Then, when she judged that the weight of it had crushed at least a little of the spiteful spirit from the sweating liegemen, who had bowed their heads and could not seem to meet her eyes, she said, "Out of respect for the loss my fellow highborn has suffered, I will allow him to choose the form of redress he prefers: caning, or the survival of his men. The decision lies with you, Prince Ashutosh."

All eyes turned on the prince, then.

She knew what he would say even before he opened his mouth.

"Their lives," he bit out.

"Elder Priya will save their lives, then," Malini agreed. "That will be redress enough, and the end of this. Yes?"

Priya bowed her head in acknowledgment. Ashutosh did the same, his shoulders stiff, his expression even stiffer. Whether he had learned anything from this would remain to be seen.

"One last matter, Prince Ashutosh," Malini said. He paused and waited. "I have been informed that one of your men began the matter. Have him whipped. He should not have attempted to begin a diplomatic incident. I'm sure you agree."

"Empress," Ashutosh said, face shuttered.

"Well, then," said Malini. "Elder Priya will attend upon your men tomorrow. Remove her chains, and you may go."

With the air of scolded children, the liegemen removed the manacles and stepped away, following their prince in bowing and swiftly exiting the tent. Priya remained.

"Elder," said Malini.

Priya raised her head. "Yes, Empress?"

"I hope this will not happen again," Malini said.

"You have my vow, Empress," she said. "It will not."

RAO

There was a single, makeshift shrine to the nameless god in the entire army camp. It was Rao's men that carried it whenever the army moved, and Rao's men that erected it whenever the army made camp. All it consisted of was a single water basin for communing with the nameless, a plinth—lopsided now, from being dropped during an unexpected ambush—and a thin tent of pale blue cloth, graying from long exposure to ash and dust and merciless sunlight. It was no monastery garden. But Rao's men made do.

Rao himself visited it rarely. But today he walked in, ducking low beneath the entrance of the tent. Inside, the air was musty. The tent was empty. He closed his eyes briefly in relief, and settled himself on the ground.

He started by kneeling but soon ended up sprawled, arms on his knees, head bowed. His men wouldn't be impressed if they walked in and found him like this, he knew. But no one else would be foolish enough to pray in midday heat. Just Rao.

The curtain rustled. So much for being the only foolish one.

"I've never seen you in here before," Lata said, from the entrance.

"I . . . never expected to see you here at all," Rao replied, turning to look at her. "Have you become a worshipper of the nameless?"

"I'm still a sage," she said. "Still devoted to all knowledge, as always."

"There's no knowledge to be found in here," he said. "No books. No other sages to argue with."

"What I would give," Lata said wistfully, "to argue with another sage again." She let the curtain fall and stepped inside. "There *is* knowledge in here." She gestured at the basin of water, which was oddly still. Waiting for a devotee to gaze into it, and seek the truth of the nameless. "But I didn't come for books or the nameless. I came for you." She sat down beside him.

"And what do you need from me?" he asked. "Preparation for a war council, maybe? Or are there answers you need me to pry out of one of my highborn fellows? I know how they can be."

"No," she said. "Nothing like that. You seem sad."

He laughed, soundlessly. "Lata," he said. "How could I not be sad?"

"Sad and lost, entirely adrift," she told him.

"You're not making me feel any better," he said.

"Nothing can be fixed if it goes unacknowledged," she said, lecturing in the way sages—or perhaps just Lata—liked to do. "Are you here looking for a path forward, Rao? A light at the end of the tunnel?"

"I'm still looking for the tunnel," he said. Here, with only Lata next to him, it felt easier to admit the truth to himself: His future looked like endless space. Empty. "What do you suggest I do?"

"You could ask the nameless," she suggested. "The water is right there."

"I pray with Aditya," he said. "And it calms me. But truthfully... when I'm alone, Lata, I'm not sure I can feel the nameless anymore. I don't know if my god has a purpose for me any longer. Maybe... maybe when I gave my name to the empress, it was fulfilled."

"If you don't know the will of the nameless anymore, you should ask one of his priests. And helpfully..."

"Lata," he said. Meaning, *Aditya has enough burdens.*

"Isn't that what priests do? Guide?" She shrugged, and touched a hand gently to his cheek. Then she rose to her feet. "Think on it, Rao. You already look at him like he holds stars in his hands," she said. "If he has the light you seek..."

"Lata."

"Think on it," she repeated, and left the tent.

Think on it. How could he not? He stared forward at nothing and thought of it. Going to Aditya's tent. Looking into that familiar face. Saying, *Give me a purpose, Aditya. Give me a path. Tell me what the nameless wants from me now.*

Tell me what you want from me.

He exhaled and lay back against the ground, a hand over his eyes.

"Next time," he muttered. "Just get me drunk first, Lata. That's all I ask."

PRIYA

As punishments went, it was...almost pleasant, like slipping back into her own skin. She'd done exactly this more times than she could count, in her year as a temple elder: washed her hands clean in salt water, to purify them. Entered a tent lined with cots for the sick. Sat down beside a man with rot whorling his hands and lining his face in scars of sap.

"I don't want or need the help of an Ahiranyi witch whore," one of the men snapped. At least this one hadn't spit on her.

"'Witch whore' is a bit of a mouthful," she said, baring her teeth at him in a grin. "I prefer 'temple elder' or 'Elder Priya.' You can pick."

"Your preferences don't interest me."

"Fine, fine," Priya said. Held out her hand. "If my lord would give me his palm, so I can heal him, as I've said I would?"

"I don't trust you," he said.

"You don't need to," Priya said. "You just need to give me your hand."

"So you can infect me with your dark magic? No, I—"

"Enough," said another man. He was older, lichen ringing his throat. His voice was forbidding. "You do what the woman tells you now, there's a boy."

"But, Romesh—"

"Prince Ashutosh gave his orders," he said. "We obey."

With great reluctance, the belligerent man held out his hand.

"Thank you," Priya said, with obviously false grace, and reached for her gifts.

The men were all quieter, after the first was done. There was nothing particularly awe-inspiring about her work with the rot. She couldn't erase it; only break it. Only stop it from progressing. But she'd learned, over the last months, that those with the rot always felt *something* when its trajectory was halted. A kind of release. Air moving more easily in their lungs—hope worming its way into the places the rot would have filled, in time.

The man with lichen offered his arm obediently enough, though he refused to look at her.

"I heard you're a friend of the prince," said Priya.

"I grew up alongside the prince," Romesh said gruffly. "We all did. He takes good care of us. Treats us like family."

She thought of telling him about Sima, and Rukh and Billu—about the mask-keepers. How the hierarchy between them all, once so clear-cut, had become muddled. How they were a family of a kind, too.

But ah, she was no good at winning people over with words. And why would he care, anyway? She didn't have Bhumika's clever care with people, or Malini's silver tongue. She just had her callused hands. Her magic. Her gift with the rot. And that was enough, usually. That was enough to be proud of.

"I would have done this without punishment," she said, settling on a simpler truth. It seemed important that at least one of these men knew that, even if they had not asked. Even if they ignored her, or willfully forgot, or simply decided that she was a liar. "If someone had asked—I would have done it."

He drew back his hand. Rolled down his sleeve, a wary look in his eyes.

"There are many rumors about what your people can do," he said. "A good thing like stopping the rot...I wouldn't have believed it. Knowing what your kind are, who would?"

Priya opened her mouth to respond.

There was yelling, beyond the tent. The sudden wailing of conches, calling men to war. The man's eyes widened, startled, and Priya smiled grimly, even as her heart gave a sudden thud in her chest. Whatever was happening beyond the walls of the tent, it couldn't be good.

"They've opened the gates!"

Priya was met with chaos the minute she stepped out of the sick tent. Men were running back and forth, dragging on their armor, yelling orders.

She stood for a moment, feeling the sting of the air on her face, the sharp scent of smoke, coiling through the camp.

"Where are you going?" A Saketan soldier grabbed her by the arm. He wore birds on his sash. One of Ashutosh's men, then. "There's no place for you in the battle," he barked. And Priya gave him an incredulous look, and said, "After I just saved your own people, you think there's no place—?"

"Stay back," he ordered again, then grabbed his weapons and stormed off.

Well. Fine, then.

She hurried back toward the Ahiranyi encampment.

Priya and Sima had been sleeping with a partition up to keep them separate from the soldiers, but it was a far cry from the relative luxuries of home, and a world away from the way the highborn of this army lived. Even the sickroom tent Priya had just vacated had been better appointed, deep in the Saketan section of the camp, which was green, well shaded, and vast enough to hold a branch of the army made up of innumerable highborn lords and not more than a few low princes.

But it had one benefit: It overlooked the fortress.

There was a sea of men pouring out of the fortress, so thick that it reminded Priya of ants heaving out of an anthill doused in boiling water.

Some of them were on fire.

The sight made her dizzy.

She heard footsteps behind her. Turned, and saw Sima running toward her, followed by Jeevan's men.

"Priya!" Her voice was high with relief. "Priya, I was going to look for you, but they wouldn't let me."

"I'm glad you didn't," Priya said. Jeevan's men—the pitiful group she'd brought with her—clutched their weapons, clearly unsure of what to do.

"Elder," Nitin said grimly. "They—the Parijatdvipans—weren't expecting a sieged fortress to open its gates and pour out men. They don't know how to respond."

"You can tell all of that simply by looking at them?" Priya asked, impressed.

"I heard someone yelling as he ran past," he said, which made significantly more sense.

"What," another soldier said, faltering. "What should we do?"

"I'm not sure what we *can* do," Priya said, pitching her voice loud enough so that all the men could hear her, despite the tumult of noise. "I've been told armies usually have plans and strategies and this one certainly has some damn big elephants and we have—what, a few scythes and sabers? Me?" She gestured at herself helplessly. "We stay here and we wait and we see what happens, all right? You keep watch," she ordered, gesturing at the outcrop of rocks. The man nodded and went where she'd told him to.

It only took a moment for her to realize her error. A split second for the yell of the man on the outcrop to ring out, and for her to turn.

Her own tent had a good view of the fortress city, but it was also *exposed* to it.

Fire shouldn't have been able to move like that. But of course, the fire here wasn't normal fire. She knew that.

Priya did not even have time to curse before a dozen arrows, tips aflame, cut through the air, right at them.

"Run!" she yelled at Sima. "Run, run away now!"

"Priya—"

"I can protect myself! You know that!"

She saw the fire hit one of her men, then two—saw Nitin fall.

Fire rippled through the air, leaping off arrows—not falling as it should have, as nature demanded, but *flying* with all a predatory bird's deadly grace.

She raised the earth—trying to smother the flames with heavy soil. But the flames burst through it violently.

She only had a moment to fling herself to the side, but the surprise made her slower. Clumsier.

The fire caught her at the waist. Set her clothes alight. She dropped to the ground, rolling, but it burrowed into her skin with nails, with teeth. It was like an animal, a beast—something cruel and sentient, eating its way through her.

It reached for her magic and *grasped*.

Her strength flickered. She tried to draw on her magic and felt it flutter within her, choked by fire. A stuttering fear ricocheted through her.

Her magic. Her magic was wrong.

The *fire* was stopping her magic. Something about the fire was obliterating it—

"Sima," she gasped out. Tried to look around, wild. But her vision was wavering.

She could see the gates being closed on the fort again. Clever: one ferocious attack, cutting a bloody swathe through Malini's army, then a retreat to where they couldn't be reached. Devastating.

"Sima," she gasped out again. And Sima was there, reaching for her. Dragging her to her feet—

She woke in the sangam.

Bhumika was before her—had heard Priya, perhaps, crying out as the fire hit her. Bhumika's eyes were molten.

"You fainted," she said.

Priya sat up.

"I don't faint."

"That isn't true. You did. You're here."

"I was in—a battle. An unexpected battle and..." Priya scrambled, touching her fingertips to her side. She hissed.

There was a wound. Sap poured from it, strange and unreal in the sangam.

Bhumika tutted.

"That's not good," she said.

"I would have thought you'd be more worried about me," said Priya.

"I am worried," said Bhumika. But her face remained eerily calm, her voice devoid of feeling.

Something wasn't right.

Priya was in the sangam but her body was not shadow, and neither was Bhumika's. And that was—different. Wrong, perhaps.

She bit her tongue and looked down at her side again.

"The fire caught me," she whispered. "Fire of the mothers, they called it. Should I—am I hurt?"

A sigh from Bhumika. The water rippled. As it rippled, it sang.

"I can't fix everything for you," said Bhumika. "Not when you're so far. Not always. But this I can put right."

"You...can't," said Priya. "You can't do that. We don't have the gift for that."

Bhumika frowned. "You should talk to me with more respect."

Her sister grabbed her arm.

Flowers clambered up her side: small, virulently white and pink and red, the colors of viscera. They curled around the wound. Began to burrow into it.

There was no pain. Perhaps there should have been pain.

"Still," Bhumika said, when Priya tried to flinch away. "Stay still."

"Bhumika," she said helplessly. "Bhumika, what's wrong with you?"

"Oh, Priya," she said in response. Her eyes gleamed. Marigold bright. "Nothing. Nothing at all."

One breath. Another.

Priya's eyes opened. She could see the sky above her. Brilliant blue, scarred with smoke. There were still people shouting. It couldn't have been long since the attack. And below it all, Sima, leaning over her.

"Get up," Sima was saying, and Priya blinked at her.

"Is anyone here...?"

"Just us," said Sima. "I dragged you behind a tent. Look, we were lucky—this one isn't even on fire."

Sima hoisted her up.

"Our guards...?"

"Some are—alive. I think," Sima said curtly. There was something grieving and frightened under her hard expression. "Maybe they were taken to a sickroom. Maybe they've run home."

"Don't think they have," Priya said, forcing the words out through her own pain. Sweat dripped into her eyes.

"No?"

"They don't know the way back to Ahiranya. They'll be around somewhere."

Sima laughed wildly. "You have a point."

She leaned in closer.

"The burn healed up while you were unconscious," Sima said, keeping her voice small. It took Priya a moment to realize that she was worried about being overheard. "It... it *flowered*, and you were growing things. Through your skin. And then the flowers were gone and it healed. Just like that."

"Flowered," Priya echoed, dazed. But Sima was still talking, blinking back tears.

"I thought it had killed you, Pri. You don't know how you looked. For a moment. A moment..."

Priya swallowed, and clutched Sima's hand.

"It could have killed me," Priya said. "I was lucky."

"Lucky how?"

Priya didn't know how to explain Bhumika. Those eyes gleaming gold. The flowers pouring over her, seeping into the burn. So she settled on saying, "Bhumika helped me somehow."

"*Ah.* That's good."

"It was—temple elder magic. But I can't. Can't rely on it again." A deep thrill of wrongness was working through her.

If the fire could kill her magic? Well. The fire could kill Ahiranya, too.

24

DEEPA

When the conches sounded and the fires struck again, Deepa was far from the danger. Not as far as she would have liked, of course—not home with her mother and sisters, with the comfort of her books and not a single rheumy-eyed war elephant in sight—but still in relative safety.

In her father's tent, she crouched on her knees, and placed her head on her own knees, and struggled to breathe. She could smell smoke. She couldn't run. What good would it be to run? And she was being foolish. If the fire came, she would burn, and if it didn't, then curling up on the floor would make no difference either way.

She forced herself to straighten. Wiped any stray tears from her eyes. Sat herself down—and yelped like a scalded cat when the tent flap was flung open, and a figure entered.

"Calm yourself, Lady Deepa," said Lata. She looked as stern as she always did when Deepa was in her company. "Wipe your face."

"I—I was trying. I'll do it now," she corrected hastily, when Lata gave her a look. She dabbed her eyes with the edge of her pallu. "Do you need me for something?" she asked.

Deepa had taken her responsibility of assisting Lata very seriously. She carried stacks of books and paper after her, checked her ledgers, and wrote correspondence on her behalf. Lata was exacting, and never seemed to rest. The only time Deepa had seen the sage smile had been when Prince Rao came to speak with her. Lata had actually *teased* him. Deepa had never seen anything like it.

She wondered, sometimes, if the sage loved him. How tragic if she did—a prince would surely have no place in his life for a wife who was a sage with no highborn blood in her.

It was hard to think of Lata as a romantic figure when she was looking at Deepa as she was now. Lata's jaw was tight, her brow furrowed. "Lady Deepa," she said. Then stopped. She crossed the room and sat down next to her. "It's time."

"Time for what?" Deepa asked stupidly.

"Your father," Lata said, "has failed in his duties. He ordered that the fort be sieged, against my better judgment, and the judgment of the empress. And now men are dying. You can hear it, can't you?"

Lata went silent, and in the silence, Deepa heard the hiss of the flames—smelled the smoke of them again, all anew, on the air. "Yes," she said, voice small. "I can."

Lata nodded.

"Your father cannot remain the general of the empress's army. But your family need not suffer. Plainly, you have a choice to make, Lady Deepa: your father, or the empress?"

Deepa felt suddenly dizzy.

She thought of all the secret things she had told the empress about her father. All the things she had heard said in his tent. Everything she had read when she rifled through his correspondence.

"I made my choice a long time ago," Deepa said, with more steadiness than she'd known she was capable of. "I made a promise to the empress. I wasn't planning to break it."

"I know," said Lata. "But choices so large must be made and remade over and over again. That's how paths are carved, Lady Deepa. That is how you decide your future."

Deepa nodded. She thought of her mother and sisters, and thought, finally, of herself. Of the life she wanted and had never been offered. Of being something more than invisible, something better than not good enough. Of taking something for herself.

"I'm loyal to the empress," she said. "I'll always be loyal to the empress. Tell me what I need to do."

25

ASHOK

He had thought that eventually it would stop feeling as if he were trapped in a strange dream, his skin hollowed out and uneasy over his bones, his consciousness tripping numbly through it all: the arrival at the mahal. Reuniting with Bhumika. Seeing her face—the look upon it—as if through water. Everything distorted. There were things he was meant to feel. And yet somehow, he could not.

He'd felt things very strongly, once.

Kritika had wept when they were finally alone. Gazed at him, and whispered his name with reverence, and said, "The others won't believe it. They won't, they won't. You're back."

Was he?

"The yaksa," he managed to say.

But Kritika was nodding and smiling through her tears. "They brought you back. They took so many of us, but *you*." She'd grasped his hands. Her skin, soft, paper and pulp to the carved bone and flesh of his own limbs. "You, you are a gift."

She told him his rebels had survived. Ruled Ahiranya, under the purview of Bhumika, who was thrice-born and Priya—

Priya, who had lived too. A distant feeling ran through him. It felt...golden.

He met his rebels—who named themselves mask-keepers, now.

Tried to smile where it was appropriate to smile. Tried to remember what it meant to be human.

He'd been under the water for so long. It wouldn't come easily.

He found that the orchard was a good place to be alone.

He liked to lie down, among the trees. There was one that called to him particularly: a great, strong thing that reminded him of the tree that had birthed the first yaksa he'd found.

The longer he lay under it, the more it changed. Wood, softening with rot. He plucked one of the ripe fruits from the tree. Opened it curiously, almost absently. It had the marbled quality of fat.

He heard a voice.

The yaksa he'd drawn from the tree—the yaksa who had called him, drawn him to her—was calling again. He turned, and there she was, gliding toward him. She brought the child yaksa with her. He was quiet, his eyes gleaming like fish scales.

"Should I still call you Ashok?" she asked, when she was near enough to speak.

"It is my name, yaksa," he said, bowing his head.

"You need not venerate me," she said with a smile. "Not you."

Not you. It reverberated through him. It meant something.

Not you.

"Yaksa," he said. Hesitated. He did not know what he had meant to say.

"Don't you know my name?" she asked him. She cocked her head. There was a faint rustling noise. A snapping of wood, a noise green with sap.

"No," he said.

"You called me Sanjana, when you first drew me out of the earth," she replied. "And you call me that still. I thought it was a kind of game for you, at first. You always liked to play at being human. There was always a...softness, to you." The look she gave him was thoughtful. "But perhaps not."

She was watching him curiously.

"You are not as you should be," she said.

"Something is wrong with me," he whispered in return.

She approached him then. Took his face in her hands. Her skin was like wood—all grain, rich with the scent of sandalwood.

"Don't worry," she said, dabbing her fingertips over his cheek and then his jaw with the lightest of touches—as if the feel of his skin fascinated her and repelled her in equal measure. "You won't feel like this forever.

"Let me tell you a tale," she said, cupping his face now, turning it just so. The perfect angle for their eyes to meet. "A tale mortal children know, I think. Once there was a being who swam in the cosmic rivers where all universes meet. She was a creature of those rivers. Later, humans would only be able to envisage her as a fish."

"Mani Ara," he murmured. He remembered the Birch Bark Mantras. Remembered the stories he was taught as a boy, and taught his little sister in turn.

"Yes, good," she said, sounding pleased. "The first yaksa who found the shore of a world. And the world was green and loud and so alive. She crept onto its shore, and she tasted it. The green. The life. And it was beautiful, you understand? So she decided she would enter it and become of that world."

"I know this," he said. Not to boast, not to stop her, but to say— *What is it that I don't know? Why do you stare at me like I am a child, Sanjana-who-is-not-Sanjana?*

"Deciding is easy," Sanjana said. "But to do it is—was—harder. Oh, you can touch the sangam from this world. You can dream it and envision it and worm your way into it through your gods and your griefs. But to cross from one to the other with all your flesh—to breathe with it, move with it, be within it—that takes magic." Her eyes gleamed, like coins, like the silt gold of a riverbed. "That takes sacrifice. So Mani Ara sacrificed."

This, he didn't know. It was not part of the tale Ashok had ever been told, temple-raised though he'd once been.

"What did she sacrifice?" he asked.

"What all the yaksa did, in the end," Nandi piped up. His voice was like a hollow reed—like something carved out for wind and music. "Rootlessness. We bound ourselves to this world. To its soil.

To its green. We tried to make a home of it. But there were people who rejected what the yaksa offered. And they made a sacrifice of their own. In fire. And the yaksa burned. They burned, and it hurt, and they wanted to run, but they could not flee from this world. They'd sacrificed that strength, and the path was gone. They could only sink into their roots. Into the rivers they'd bled for their priests. The trees that grew from their own agony-charred bones."

The deathless waters. The trees of sacred wood. The forest that twisted time strangely, and the bones that hung from trees. All this. All this—

"We still want this world," Sanjana said into the silence. "And we were willing to sacrifice more of ourselves to belong. We became things of green, once, giving up our rootlessness for soil. Now we have to become... things of flesh." She tilted her own face, side to side, like a child showing off a new toy or costume. "A fair exchange," she murmured. "The humans who worship us hollowed themselves—sacrificed their humanity—for power. And now we wear their flesh and their bones and their hearts like garb.

"You are in a costume, brother," she said kindly. "You wear it cinched tight, because that was always your way..."

"Stop," he choked out. Wrenched away from her hand. Where she'd touched him, his face burned. He pressed his own fingertips to it, feeling nothing but his own skin—warm, faintly marked with stubble.

He thought again, of the weary voice in his mind when he'd woken from death. Tired. Old. *I never wanted this.* And it was true, absolutely true. He did not want this. What Sanjana was offering him.

He clutched his own hands, one over the other. Holding something *in*.

"Play your game, then," she said, after a moment. She sounded faintly amused. "I will be excited, I think, to see what you do. But not all the others will be. Try and remember that, if nothing else."

She turned, beginning to walk away. He watched the shape of her shoulders. Watched as Nandi trailed after her, ferns sprouting where his feet had pressed the soil. He thought of shells—of wearing a skin, an echo. He thought of Priya. And Bhumika.

"My sisters," he managed to say.

Sanjana paused. Turned, and took in the look in his face, and shook her head.

"You worry for them? How like you. How sweet." She smiled. "Don't worry. They're beloved. Necessary. But not *us*. The dead we wear are shells. Carapaces. But your sisters are soil seeded with flowers. They bloom into something new."

"The rot—"

"Shh," she murmured. Tender. "The whole world is ours to hollow, *Ashok*. And ours to grow into—to wear and remold. Rot isn't a good name for it. Call it new life. Call it blooming, if you like." She shrugged, and lightly began to walk away again. "You'll remember eventually," she told him.

"It kills people," he called out after her.

"Just people," she agreed, in an airy voice. "But not us."

He didn't really need to sleep. So at night he walked the mahal in darkness.

Rivers. Sacrifice. Cosmos to green, green to flesh. The story rattled strange through his skull. Contemplating it too closely made him feel sick; made him feel as if his mind were filling with water formed of knowledge and poison, steadily drowning his own thoughts out.

But there was no escaping those waters. He walked, and walked, and felt the pulse of the whole of Ahiranya around him, like a fist grasping his lungs. He could feel the rot-riven—the people, the fields. He could feel Bhumika, and somewhere, like a pulse of starlight, too far to touch, Priya. He felt more than any mortal man should have felt.

A scuff of heavy footsteps on the floor. A sudden silence.

"Ashok," a voice said. Male and low, relief shot through it. "I'm so glad you're back," Ganam said, approaching. "Can I walk with you?"

Ashok nodded jerkily. And Ganam came to his side. He was carrying a scythe at his back. He was perhaps on night guard duty.

"I couldn't believe it when you returned," Ganam said. "Couldn't believe my eyes. But there you were. And the magic in me—it went wild." He thumped a hand against his chest for emphasis. "I'd never felt the like of it. You've been missed, Ashok."

Wherever Ashok had been, he had missed no one.

"Elder Bhumika and Elder Priya, they've been doing their best," Ganam was saying. "A good job. You'll be glad to know that."

Ah, this made him feel more like himself.

"Better than I would have done?"

An infinitesimal pause. Then Ganam said, haltingly, "No. It's different. Frustrating. Slower. Not bad, but…" A huff of breath, head lowering, though his eyes never truly left Ashok's face. "I miss how decisive you were, my friend. Even if our goal of a free Ahiranya was distant, we never stopped moving. Now there's too much stillness. Now there's just fighting and fighting, and we don't even know what freedom should look like anymore." He took a step closer. "Ashok, what do you want of us? What are we meant to do?"

Careful words. Cunning words, under a cover of artless friendship. Ganam had never been a good liar.

Ashok felt his sister's hand in this.

"I don't know," he said, suddenly exhausted. "I don't know what I want."

He took a step away. Stopped and turned and said, "It may be best if you leave me be. For the rest of the night."

Silence.

"Of course," Ganam said finally. "But if you ever want to talk again, you'll find me, won't you?"

I never will, Ashok thought. But he nodded all the same.

26

MALINI

"Father." Deepa's voice from beyond the tent walls was pitched high enough that it could be heard even through the drumlike billow of the canvas in the fire-feeding winds. "Please. You must see her."

"Her men must see her, not I," Mahesh replied. His voice was gruffer than ever, made hoarse by smoke. Malini did not need to see him in the flesh to know he wore ash residue on his hair and his armor, or that his face was set into grim lines that ran from his jaw to his furrowed brow. "Bid her to emerge, and I'll accompany her to the war council."

"Would you have them see her weep?" Deepa asked. Malini was impressed by the waver in her voice. She sounded convincingly over-wrought. "Please. Father, I don't know what else to do. I told you—all the women are afraid. If you could only advise the empress to be calm, perhaps...oh, that would surely help."

"There is no time for this," he said impatiently.

"I'm sorry, Father."

Heavy footsteps followed her words. Mahesh drew the curtain back and strode into the tent. He began to bow, then paused midmovement when he caught sight of Malini, who was quite clearly not weeping. Dry-eyed, seated neatly upon the floor cushions, she met his gaze and said, "Lord Mahesh."

Her voice seemed to remind him of himself. He finished his bow, then straightened to his full height. "Empress," he replied.

"I respected your guidance and did not leave the safety of my tent when I heard battle begin," she remarked mildly, as Deepa entered the tent behind her father and silently drew the curtain shut. "Your daughter kindly kept me company."

Mahesh did not turn to face his daughter, but his gaze did flicker to and fro, taking in the empty expanse of the tent. Deepa had spoken to him of *women*, but only the three of them were present. Malini had made sure of that.

"Now that you have no need to calm me, Lord Mahesh," she said, "do you wish to advise me on the state of our forces? How many men did the fire kill this time?"

"The dead and wounded are still being counted, Empress."

She nodded, acknowledging his words.

"A great number, then," she said. "As Lata warned when you insisted upon the siege. Perhaps you remember."

He watched as Malini rose to her feet; as she mirrored him, standing tall and sure, with her shoulders back and her head high.

"Did we decimate the High Prince's forces in return?" Malini asked, already knowing what answer she would receive.

He shook his head, the lines of tension at his forehead growing deeper.

"They retreated swiftly behind their walls," he replied. "They used the layers of defense the fort possesses to their advantage. One strike at us, and they were gone."

One strike. And so many of her men dead, for the sake of Mahesh's beliefs, and Malini's own designs. She would regret none of it. She could not allow herself such tenderness.

"I believed they could be contained," he said. "The fortress was surrounded from all sides—watched by a constant arrangement of cavalry and archers. They should have withered within the walls." He clenched his jaw, seeking control of his emotions or his words.

She watched patiently, waiting to see how he would splinter.

"The fort must possess hidden exits. The maze fort is known for its impenetrability. But it must be more—complex—than any of us knew. And the fire." He stopped. Then said, with a roughness that was almost pleading, "I have fought many sieges, Empress. This was the right choice. We could not have known this would come to pass."

"It was not the right choice, Lord Mahesh." Her voice was sharp. "It was the wrong choice. And it was not *our* choice. It was your own. You chose this path, despite my concern, despite my sage's cautions. Every lord and prince of Parijatdvipa in my army heard you claim this path as your own, and they will know that the deaths of their men are your responsibility."

Cruel words. But she had shaped them to be so.

"You acted to exert your own power," she said deliberately. "To prove yourself wiser than me, and greater. You have been whittling at my power, Lord Mahesh. Did you think I failed to mark your slights against me?"

"Empress," Mahesh said. "I have nothing but respect for you."

"I knew you did not slight me from a lack of respect," she said. "I know the unnatural fire from the fort shook your faith in me. I know you simply sought to pry me gently from my throne, and set Aditya in my place." He said nothing. "You can admit it," she said. "Or not, as you wish. I am already sure."

He did not argue, or beg, or even fall into anger. He merely stood before her with the battle's ash on him and continued to say nothing at all. She allowed the silence to stretch unimpeded. Then she nodded, accepting his wordlessness as the choice it was.

"I did not ask your daughter to summon you here simply so that I could berate you," she said finally. "I asked you here out of courtesy. By this evening you will no longer be the general of my army. For the sake of your honorable service to me and to the empire, I have chosen to warn you of your coming disgrace, so you may prepare yourself. But I cannot save you from what may be said by others, and what may be guessed." She gentled her voice. "I could have given you no warning. I could simply have humiliated you, stripping you of your titles before all your fellow lords. But I have chosen not to, for the sake of that bond that lies between us. You have led my men, and I do not discount that."

"Empress." Mahesh's voice broke from him, sudden and jagged. "You *cannot*."

"I can," Malini said calmly, even as something sweetly dark coiled in her chest. Power was a pleasure with many forms. To see a powerful man—a man who had betrayed her—brought low was one of its headiest. She did not let it touch her face or her voice. She was like ice. "I am Empress of Parijatdvipa."

"As long as Prince Aditya lives," Mahesh said swiftly, "there will be those who believe he must be the one on the throne. And now I have seen mothers' fire—Empress. Princess Malini. They are not wrong to believe it. *I* am not wrong to believe it."

"Do you, who loves my brother, counsel me to murder him, then? To end his life?"

"No," he said, recoiling. "I counsel you to trust what the mothers have told you through their fire and accept that a male scion of Divyanshi must take the throne."

"You will see, tomorrow, that you should have kept your faith in me." She let her tone grow gentler still. Pitying.

She wanted to tell him that she was disappointed; that he had spent a year in her company and yet he clearly knew nothing of her. He had followed her for the prophecy she had garbed herself in, then immediately sought to abandon her when the gold shell of it had cracked. He had failed to take the opportunity his closeness to her had offered to actually learn her worth.

But it did not matter if he knew her. She knew him.

"I am not Chandra," she said. "Your family will not suffer for your crimes. I admire your daughter's intelligence, her wisdom. She is a credit to your family."

Did he understand what was unsaid—that Deepa had proved herself an ally to Malini? That she had betrayed him, raising herself even as his downfall came for him? From the way he looked at his daughter as she walked forward, her own expression calm, Malini thought perhaps he did.

"Will I be exiled?" There was a deep exhaustion in his voice. And perhaps a fury, too. "Or will my throat be slit in the night?"

"Father," Deepa said. He looked away from her.

"I am disgraced," he said. "I am a traitor, in your eyes. Do not treat me cruelly, Empress. Tell me my fate."

"Your daughter has spoken for you," Malini replied. "And her love for you moved me. You will not be killed." She paused, as if considering her words. Then: "There is an opportunity to serve Parijatdvipa. To save us all. This evening, before the council...I would ask you to listen. And consider your future. It would be a chance to serve Parijatdvipa with your whole heart and soul and earn back my respect. I encourage you to take it."

After his departure, Malini's court gathered around her once more. All of them wore grim expressions, but Lata's was the most serious of all. She strode straight to Malini, close enough that her words would not be overheard.

"Empress," Lata murmured. "I've found her."

Relief coursed through Malini. "Where is she?" she breathed. She looked toward the entrance of the tent. Began to rise to her feet.

Priya entered, and froze as their gazes met. She was whole and alive, and Malini was walking to her, reaching for her before her good sense could stop her.

"Empress," Priya said swiftly. She sketched a bow, and Malini stopped—hand upraised, not yet touching. Priya raised her head. "Empress," she said again, softer now. "I'm well."

"Elder Priya," Malini said, remembering herself. She took a step back. Another. Lowered herself into her seat. She was surprised by the steadiness of her own voice. "I was told your encampment burned."

"We lost a few men," Priya said, nodding. "But not all, and well—not ourselves." She gestured at Sima, who had slipped into the tent behind her. Sima looked more than a little gray, though her expression was resolute. Her face was speckled with motes of ash. "We're unharmed."

"I am glad of it," Malini said. "I would never want any of my women to be hurt."

Priya looked into her eyes and smiled. The ash had streaked across her face like misapplied kajal. Her hair was wild darkness all around her shoulders, unspooled. *You are like ink*, Malini thought helplessly. *Ink, and all I want is to make poetry of you.* "Your women feel the same of you, Empress," she said.

"Empress," Lata said, clearing her throat. "The council are waiting."

Yes. The council. Malini forced herself to stop looking at Priya. Dragging her gaze away, she turned her attention to the other women around her.

"A show of unity," she said. "You will all come with me, and...I must ask you for a favor. An act of trust."

"Ask us," Raziya said, unflinching. "And we'll do whatever is needful."

"Don't show fear," she said. "Trust me, and be brave. That's all I ask."

The lords and princes were indeed waiting for her, but they were not an organized and silent audience. Men kept coming and going, striding from where nervous groups of archers and soldiers had been placed to watch the fort's walls for new attacks. Every time the tent was entered by a new official, still clad in armor and heavy boots, the smoke of the battlefield was carried in. Soon the air was awash with char.

They all still bowed when Malini and her women entered; when she made her way to her dais. She rose, but did not kneel down upon the cushions to signal the start of the council. Instead, she stood and waited as the women settled behind her in a watchful crescent. Waited, as the men straightened from their bows, then shifted with confused unease and then, finally, fell silent. She saw Mahesh among them. Rao. And there, at the edge of the tent, in all his priestly colors, her brother Aditya.

"My lords," she said finally. "I know many of you believe—and fear—that Chandra is blessed by the mothers. That the unnatural fire that has killed so many of our men is a sign that he is chosen, and I am not." A pause, as she watched guilty eyes slide away from her own. "But his fire is false. A lie. And I will prove it to you."

Behind her, Lata rose and carried over the box carved from black stone.

"This was bravely obtained from the battlefield," Malini lied. There was no need to mention the role of the temple of the faceless mother. This kind of gathering required a simpler story—something compelling, something their shaken faith could easily cling to. "Unnatural fire, caught in ash and contained." She opened the lid of the box, revealing the ash inside—and the beating heart of flame that lay twisting within it.

Someone flinched. A few men scrambled back, and she saw at least one figure slip out of the tent. But the majority remained still. She could not see the women behind her—Raziya or Lata, or Deepa or even Priya—but she was sure they were unmoved and unafraid. Just as she had asked them to be.

She calmly drew her own saber and touched it to the fire.

"There is no need to be afraid, my lords," she said. "The fire will not hurt you."

She had already watched a fragment of this fire gutter and die upon her blade. Now she took what remained, a small and weakened thing, a flickering, writhing, obviously unnatural thing, with only the barest strength left within it. In the faint breeze moving through the tent it bristled, coiling like a serpent.

"My lords, you are wise in scripture. Your ancestors were present when the mothers of flame burned for us all. So you will know, as I know, that the fire of the mothers was relentless. It did not falter. It did not dwindle. It climbed onto swords and arrows, and turned upon the yaksa until all our enemies were dead. Only then did it perish."

She held the fire up before her, the saber steady in her hands, allowing them to look at the flame: its smallness. The way it wavered, already diminishing before their eyes.

"This fire must be carried in the ashes," she said. "It moves, yes, with strange power—but it does not move as mothers' fire did, with holy intent." She spoke confidently. There were no priests here to disagree with her, after all. Only Aditya, who served the nameless, and would not. "And the fire dies," she went on. She drew her sword in a sharp arc—and watched the last vestiges of the flame sputter away into nothing. "This fire is not the fire of the mothers," she said. "Whatever Chandra has created, it is a falsehood. A shadow at best."

Silence. Then, a roar of noise from the highborn, as the last wisps of smoke curled away from her saber, leaving the blade bare and gleaming.

She did not meet Mahesh's eyes but oh, she wanted to. She wanted to.

"I will never disobey the messages of the mothers," announced Malini. "Through the nameless, they gave me my crown. If this fire had been the mothers' fire, my lords, I would have obeyed their will and bowed my head to the rightful emperor. But I know what I am to the mothers. I know the mothers." A pause. "That has never," she said with emphasis, "been in doubt. The throne is mine, by the faceless and the nameless and by the mothers alike. I hope that eases your doubts in me. I can understand your fears today, my lords. But I will not be so understanding again."

The men were still speaking, talking to one another or trying to gain her attention. But Malini simply kneeled at her seat. Lifted a hand and quelled them once more to silence.

It was time to return to the business of war.

"The maze fort cannot be sieged," she said. "Despite Lord Mahesh's belief in this path, the inhabitants of the fort cannot be contained. They have been clever enough to use both their fortress and the short-term strength of their false fire to their advantage. There will be brief, savage attacks on us in the future, of that I have no doubt. And the longer we remain here, the fewer our number will become."

I have trusted in the guidance of Lord Mahesh," she went on. "And he has served me wisely. But his failure is a message from the mothers, and one I cannot ignore." She saw Mahesh's chin dip forward. The subtlest indication of shame. "We cannot remain here. We must continue to Parijat, and to the capital Harsinghar itself, and overthrow the false emperor."

"Empress." Lord Prakash was the one who spoke, then. "If I may."

"I would be glad of your counsel, Lord Prakash," she replied.

"Though the fire is not mothers' fire, it is still a great danger," he said. "Many of our men are dead. If we leave this enemy behind us, I am certain we will be crushed between the High Prince's forces and the false emperor's, as Lord Mahesh feared when he recommended the siege." A murmur of agreement from the listening lords. "It is my belief, Empress, that the battle here must be fought. The High Prince's forces must be restrained. But how it may be done…" He shook his head. "That, I do not know, Empress," he said heavily.

"We will go to Parijat," said Malini. "Because we must. Because it is time." *Because I have the blessings of the mothers, and I command it*, Malini did not say, but she knew the men understood all the same. "But some of our forces must remain here to keep the High Prince pinned."

"Do you expect this battle to be won, Empress? Or do you ask your loyal men for a sacrifice of their own faithful warriors upon Saketa's pyre?" This was asked by Khalil, who had a thoughtful expression on his face.

"I desire the former, but am prepared for the latter," Malini said, with an incline of her head. "We have seen the High Prince's strength. I ask for someone willing to take a risk on behalf of our campaign, to hold the High Prince's forces at bay long enough for the war itself to be won, and Chandra dethroned."

"Give the task to your Ahiranyi," Ashutosh snapped, even as Narayan frowned, placing a placating hand on his arm that was swiftly shrugged off.

Malini could almost *feel* Priya behind her. The shift of her body. The scent of the smoke still on her beloved skin, her hair.

"You were provided justice, Prince Ashutosh," Malini said, barely managing to keep the frost of her irritation from her voice. "And I require a full force of soldiers: infantry, horses. Weapons. These are not things Ahiranya's representative can provide. I require a willing noble, ready to act on behalf of his empire."

Malini looked across the tent, at all the highborn who had vowed to serve her. She did not gaze directly at Mahesh. He would do what was needful for his honor, and for Parijatdvipa. It was merely Malini's duty to give him the opportunity.

"Will none of you make this sacrifice?" She raised her head high. "Will no one step forward and do what is needful to protect Parijat-dvipa from Chandra's rule?"

An uneasy rustle of movement. Silence.

"I will do it."

Mahesh's head turned, eyes wide. From the back of the tent, from a fall of shadow, Aditya stepped forward.

He was still in his priestly blues. His hair was loose—a sheet of black against his back. He did not look like a warrior. He did not look like a prince.

He bowed low. The bow of a supplicant before an emperor. Then he straightened once more, looking at her with his dark, steady eyes, his expression so very calm.

Malini was not calm. She held herself still and stared down at him, her heart hammering. She had not planned this. Oh, her fool brother. *Fool.*

"I will need men," he said. "And an able general to guide me."

"Prince Aditya," Mahesh said swiftly. "I will serve you. In this, as in all things."

Malini pressed her hands so hard upon her knees that she could feel her nails cut grooves into her flesh. She did not want this.

Aditya. Ah, brother, what are you doing? Why this, why now?

"Brother," she said. He looked at her. "Prince Aditya," she went on, forcing her voice steady. "Is this truly your wish?"

"Yes," he said. "Empress, it is."

No one would know how hard it was for her to remain impassive. To nod as if she condoned this, *desired* this.

"If I am to be without the guidance of Lord Mahesh, then I must seek a new general for my army," she said. This, at least, was part of her plan. "In honor of the trust held between our nations, from this moment, I will have a council of generals. A representative drawn from every nation that made vows to Divyanshi, and has now made vows to me."

The highborn looked shocked, almost stupefied, but Malini could not be sure if it was Aditya's rash decision or her own declaration that had silenced them. She pressed on.

"Lord Narayan, who stood by me in Srugna," she announced. "Will you accept the position of Saketan general of my army?"

"Perhaps," he said cautiously. "A low prince—"

"I would have you," Malini cut in calmly. *I would avoid that nest of vipers entirely*, she did not say. *Better raising a lord than one prince against the rest.* "Will you take the honor?"

"Empress," Narayan said, bowing low. "Yes. I accept."

Lord Prakash of Srugna accepted easily. Lord Khalil, with the faintest, knowing smile.

"Prince Rao," she said finally. "Who prophesied me. Will you be my general, on behalf of Alor?"

"Empress," he said stiffly. His face was bleached of color. He was not looking at Aditya; *not* looking so fixedly, and with such determination, that she knew Aditya was all he could think of. "Of course."

The noise among the men had not abated, only risen. And Malini...

Malini turned her head and peered sidelong at Priya. She could not help herself.

She could not offer Priya the position of a general of her army. She did not offer, and Priya did not ask.

Their eyes met. The noise of the highborn arguing faded like mist.

Priya raised a hand to her chest; a fist, curled against her heart.

If Malini touched her own fingertips to the needle-flower on a chain at her throat—if she looked at Priya and felt helplessly thankful, grateful that she was here—then that was no one's business but her own.

RAO

"This is madness," Rao said, keeping his voice low. They were alone in Aditya's tent, but only barely, and it would not do for him to be caught yelling at Aditya. "You can't lead an army. Not here, not in the middle of this."

"I was meant to rule an empire, once," Aditya replied. "This will surely be much simpler."

"Simpler," Rao repeated. "Simpler? Aditya, have you seen the power the High Prince's forces wield?"

"I have."

"Then how can you possibly—Aditya. *Aditya.*" Rao knew how he sounded; wild, helpless, swaying on the spot to resist the urge to pace. Aditya's own stillness made him feel restless, angrier than he had any right to be. "The magic they have—their defenses—their willingness to die—I've never seen the like of it. Even the most seasoned general would fear it. Lord Mahesh fears it. You can't face it. You're a priest; remember how you held the bow when the monastery burned? You couldn't act. You—"

"Will you stay with me, then, Rao?" Aditya asked, cutting through Rao's frenzy of words. He stood before Rao half-clad in armor, his long hair unbound over his shoulders, shawl of blue still draped over his right arm. Not quite prince. Not quite priest. "If you fear I don't have the stomach for the battle I've chosen, will you stay here and fight beside me?"

Rao stopped pacing.

"Are...are you asking me to?" Rao asked. "Are you asking me to fight for you?"

"No," Aditya said, so very calm. "I am asking you what you plan to do."

"I—I cannot," Rao said. "Aditya. You know that."

"Then you will have to trust me," Aditya said simply. He shrugged the shawl from his arm. Began to fold it with care before placing it upon his sleeping mat. "You have to trust I am obeying the will of the nameless. In this, as in all things I do."

A memory skittered through Rao's mind. Prem's skin, whorled with rot. The shawl knotted at his throat.

Rao swallowed, and swallowed again.

"Muscles long unused atrophy," said Rao, finally. "And Aditya—it's been a long, long time since you've held a sword with any intent to use it. Or led men to war. Aditya...what are you *doing*?"

"Putting on my training garb," Aditya said, drawing on a tunic. "If you want to see that my proficiency with a sword is still intact..."

"I don't want to spar."

"Don't you?"

There was a ghost of a smile on Aditya's usually passive face. Not a priestly smile—all compassion and knowing and soft edges—but something a little more barbed. As if all that had passed before the war council had woken some part of the old Aditya up.

"I'll beat you," Rao said, after a beat of fumbling silence.

"With a saber? I don't think so. With your daggers, perhaps. But in this, I have the advantage."

"Atrophy," Rao said again. "You're not as you once were."

For a second, Aditya held his gaze. Then he turned to the exit.

"Come," he said, striding out. "I'll prove it to you."

"I don't want an audience," said Rao, instead of saying *You shouldn't be doing this*. That kind of sentence never went down well.

"Then we'll go somewhere quiet." A pause. "Do you know somewhere quiet?"

The area of land they walked to—that Rao led them to—had been cordoned off from the rest by walls of tents. It was private enough for training away from prying eyes, and was often used for exactly that purpose. Rao grasped one of the sabers used for practice. It was clean and oiled, its edge sharp—soldiers were punished for allowing blades to dull—but its weight was unfamiliar in Rao's hand. He *was* more comfortable with his daggers. And when he used a saber, it was usually one of his own, crafted for his own hand. He hefted the borrowed weapon, adjusting to the feel of it.

Aditya was also reaching for a training blade.

"What are you doing?" Rao asked.

"Ensuring we have a fair fight," Aditya replied.

"You're not my equal in battle any longer, Aditya," said Rao. "Use your own saber. It won't be enough for you to win."

Something flashed in Aditya's eyes. Maybe some of his old pride resurfacing. Maybe joy in the face of a challenge. Either way, the sight of it made Rao feel giddy.

"We'll both use shields," Aditya said, determined.

Rao nodded sharply. Picked up one of the small shields and strapped it to his left hand. Aditya did the same.

They moved to the center of the cordoned space. And Rao... hesitated.

He didn't know how to begin attacking Aditya. When they were boys, they'd sparred all the time under the watchful eyes of their mentors and sages. So often that Rao had known every move Aditya would make, just by the motion of his hand on the sword, the look on his face.

He didn't know how Aditya fought anymore. Aditya stood before him, feet planted solidly to the ground, with his saber square before him and his shield raised. He gave Rao a steady look. Waiting.

"You expect me to make the first move?" Rao asked. He moved into a lighter stance, ready for movement—better suited for dagger fighting, he knew. But he couldn't change his nature. "This is your chance to prove your strength—won't you take it?"

Aditya's eyes narrowed.

"Fine," he said. And punched forward with his shield.

Those small shields were strong, and studded with metal—Rao

had been given a bloody nose by one more than a few times during his training. He ducked his head and brought his blade forward in a sweeping arc that Aditya met with his own. There was a clang of impact that jarred all the way down Rao's arm, and he let it shove him backward—and brought his saber up in one straight arc toward Aditya's chest. Aditya blocked that too.

"You're being gentle with me," Aditya said. "I know you can do better, Rao."

"But can *you*?" Rao asked. He straightened, and lunged forward again, aiming for the throat. Aditya moved like he'd always moved, swiftly and elegantly parrying Rao's strike. "A shield to the face, your blade stopping my own—won't you even *try* and hurt me?"

Aditya met his eyes. Smiled, challenge in the curl of his mouth. "No," he said.

"You bastard," Rao said, forgetting himself—forgetting they weren't still the boys they'd been, the friends they'd been. "You're really going to prove yourself by making me do all the work?"

"I told you to stop being gentle," Aditya replied, and this time, Rao swept forward, blade high, aiming for Aditya's head, above the eye line. A dangerous move that left his entire torso exposed for a blow, but effective. *Especially* against an opponent that refused to try to strike him.

It was a taunt. A challenge. *Will you really not fight me even now, Aditya?* But Aditya took it in his stride, lunging to the side and knocking Rao off-balance with the hilt of his saber. Rao released a punch of breath as he stumbled back—lunged forward—

Aditya dropped his sword.

"Fuck." Rao couldn't slow his momentum, but he could avoid skewering Aditya through. He flung his arm wide and slammed straight into Aditya, the two of them falling roughly back onto the ground. Flailing, Rao couldn't get a proper grip on his sword, and couldn't remove his shield to get his left hand under him so he could heave his body off Aditya's. He felt like an idiot.

He tried to roll to the side. Aditya slung his shield-strapped arm over Rao's shoulder, pinning him.

"You can't fight me by not fighting me," Rao panted.

"Can't I?"

"It's not honorable. And if there's one thing you value—"

Aditya's other hand shot up. Rao's grip had loosened on the saber, and Aditya's hand grasping Rao's arm knocked it clean away, out of reach. Aditya kept his hand around Rao's wrist—so tight that Rao could feel the creak of his own wrist bones, a sharp pain that jolted all the way down his arm, all the way through him. Rao tried to jerk away, and Aditya wrenched him back down against him.

"My honor," Aditya said, through harsh breaths, eyes bright, "is the honor of a priest. Not defined by my old teachers or by the rules of righteous war. My honor will hold me here, in Saketa, as long as the voice of the nameless guides me," said Aditya. "As long as my heart bids me to stay, I will stay, and I will *fight*."

Rao thought, through a haze of heat he couldn't quite understand, of Lata's words when she'd found him in the tent shrine to the nameless god.

If he has the light you seek . . .

"Aditya," he said softly. "Let go of my wrist."

Aditya stared up at him. Whatever he saw in Rao's face made him nod, once. Release him.

Rao turned his hand back and forth, easing the pain in his hand. Then he curled his fingers into a fist and punched the side of Aditya's head.

Aditya gave a yelp that made Rao holler with laughter, and then Aditya was grappling with him in return, the two of them kicking like children. "If you—try and fight the High Prince like this—" Rao managed between laughs.

Aditya shoved him back against the ground. Clambered up onto his knees.

"At least he won't expect it," said Aditya. "Get up, Rao. Look at you. Did I hurt you?"

Rao was bruised and his knuckles were bleeding. It was the best he'd felt in months.

"Not much," he said. "I can cope."

"As you can see, I can still hold a saber," Aditya said, wiping the sweat from his face.

"You can," Rao agreed. He was filthy. Before he joined the rest of the war council, he'd have to quickly bathe and change. He was a general now, after all. His appearance mattered more than it ever had.

"You didn't have to punch me, though."

"I really did," Rao said mildly. "I had to check that you remembered real battle tactics."

Aditya snorted out a laugh.

"Does that allay one of your fears?" Aditya asked.

Not the fears Rao truly needed allayed. Not the fear that Aditya wouldn't survive this war. But the fear that everything of his old friend—his crown prince, who'd grown up beside him, who'd laughed with him, drunk wine with him—was gone? *That* fear had vanished.

"In a way," he said.

Aditya held out his hand. Rao clasped it, letting Aditya guide him fully back onto his feet. Aditya took him by the shoulder. Held him where he was, so they were still close to one another, breathing hard, smiling.

"Protect the empress, Rao," Aditya said. He did not say *my sister*, as Rao had expected he would, and there was suddenly a guarded look in his eyes, folding the joy back.

"I will," said Rao. "As I always have."

They left the training ground together. Rao hesitated. Unsure of what to say, now that they had argued and fought, and found some tentative echo of their old, deep friendship. He murmured something to Aditya—some wish for good luck or good health, something approximating an acceptable goodbye—and began to walk away.

"Rao," Aditya called out. "I dreamt of you."

"What did you dream?" Rao asked.

"A dream from the nameless god, I think."

"Surely you know, priest," Rao said, but there was nothing cutting in his voice. Only curiosity.

Aditya hesitated.

"I saw your eyes, shining like stars."

"Stars?"

Aditya nodded.

"What had happened, to make them shine?"

"I don't know," Aditya said. "But Rao—perhaps one day we'll meet again, on the other side of this war, and you will be able to tell me."

BHUMIKA

The yaksa loved being upon the Hirana. And the Hirana loved them in turn. Its walls shone, lustrous with leaves and flowers that grew in profusion through new fractures in the stone. The effigies of the yaksa gleamed with vines and soft blooms. Sendhil liked to tend to them. He took great satisfaction in gazing at them, as vegetation unfurled gently around them. Once, he said to Bhumika, "They'll all return soon. All of them."

She looked at the statues. Innumerable yaksa, she thought distantly. One for every village, family, tree, flower.

"I look forward to the day," Bhumika said in return.

More than the Hirana, the yaksa loved worship. An endless stream of people rose up the Hirana with their offerings, and bowed their heads, weeping and awed before the yaksa. No guards stopped them, any longer, from milling at the Hirana's base. No guards dared, and Bhumika would not ask them to do so. The worshippers begged for good fortune. They begged for a better Ahiranya. And so very many of them begged to have the rot on their bodies cured.

A woman bowed before Chandni now. She, Sendhil, Sanjana, and Nandi sat upon the triveni in a semicircle, expressions mild, curious. Bhumika stood behind them with Ashok at her side and a mask on her face. She watched.

"Please, ancient one," the woman whispered, trembling. There were deep violet flowers rising from the knot of her bound hair, snaking their way down the exposed line of her neck. When she raised her face, Bhumika saw a cluster of buds at the corner of her mouth. "Please, I beg you. Cure me. I will give anything I have. *Please.*"

The yaksa were still. Then suddenly, Chandni leaned forward. She touched a hand to the woman's cheek.

"What offering have you brought us?"

"Food," the woman said tremulously. "All the food I have. I...I have nothing else."

"Worship us, and I promise the greenness in you will grow no larger," Chandni murmured, gazing at the woman. Beneath her fingers, the woman flinched, then went still. "See?" said Chandni. "You feel it. What you call rot won't grow. You will live. Keep your food, small one, and live on."

"Th-thank you," the woman said. Teary. "Thank you."

She prostrated again, and again. Rose to her feet, and bowed her head once more.

"And when you have a child," Chandni said, a gentle smile curving her mouth. "Bring them to us. Let us see if they are worthy of rising to our temple. That is the only offering I demand of you."

Bhumika could not control what she felt—the horror that poured through her in a wave. She wondered if the yaksa could feel it; if they could taste the salt of her fear, the frantic thrum of her heartbeat, the nausea rising in her stomach.

After the woman had stumbled away, still whimpering her thanks, Bhumika said, "Priya used to do something similar." At her side, Ashok gave her a look. Hungry, yearning. She didn't look at him in return. "She would halt the rot inside people. In plants. It was no cure, but it was survival." She paused. Then said, "Is that what you have done?"

"Such curiosity," Sanjana said, delighted. And Chandni replied, saying, "Yes, daughter. Your kin's gifts are from us, after all. As are your own."

Bhumika clasped her hands in front of her, seeking calm. Forcing it into her voice as she said, "I wish you had allowed me to summon her home."

"She cannot come home," Sendhil said. "Not yet."

She lives, Bhumika thought, relief rushing through so fiercely that she feared she might crumple, then and there. *She lives, she lives.*

"We want no one to leave Ahiranya," Nandi said. "And we want no one to come. So no one shall."

No one to leave. No one to come. Relief gave way to swift creeping horror. She thought of the merchants who regularly crossed the border. The Ahiranyi who traded regularly with neighboring cities.

"No one shall," she repeated faintly. "I understand."

"Bhumika," Ashok murmured at her side. She forced her hands to relax, and the tension in her shoulders to ease. Behind her mask, she closed her eyes and did not answer him. "Bhumika," he said again.

A new group of worshippers entered, and he fell silent. But his eyes stayed on her.

There had been no Srugani or Aloran merchants for weeks. She had thought they were too frightened to come, or simply too wise. When she had considered them, it had only been to wonder how the world beyond Ahiranya was reacting to the news of the yaksa's return. Did they fear the rise of a second Age of Flowers? Were they already rallying weapons and soldiers, working together to try to obliterate Ahiranya's power once more? She could not ruminate on the question. She had so much to worry about in her own home, her own temple.

But she had her answer now, regardless.

No one knew the yaksa lived. No one had passed the borders alive to tell the tale.

She stood in the mahal's rose garden, with her crown mask pressed to her face, and reached into the green. Far, far—through thorn and soil, through roots, to the borders of her kingdom. Tangled as she'd been with attending on the yaksa, she had not looked. Not *seen*.

She took off the mask. Her hands shook.

"Jeevan," she called out, voice thin. He stood at the edge of the gardens, waiting for her. Whatever look he saw on her face made him stride swiftly toward her, his usually impassive face softened with concern, dark eyebrows furrowed.

"My lady?"

"I have an order," she managed. She touched the back of her hand to her cheek. It came away wet. No matter. "The borders. Close them. If anyone—Ahiranyi or outsider—attempts to leave, make your men turn them back. Tell your men it is their *only* responsibility. Tell them this task is a matter of life or death." She turned the mask over in her hands. Stared at the varnished wood, the glow of it under sunlight. "The yaksa," she went on, "do not want anyone to know they live once more. And they will not ask anyone to stay in Ahiranya, or politely request that no one leaves. They will kill them. Like the rider you sent, left at my door. They..."

He touched his knuckles to her hand. His hand was so much larger than her own, flecked with scars. She quietened and looked up at him.

"It will be done," he said.

"Careful," she said in return. "The mask *will* burn you."

"I am not afraid, my lady," he said solemnly.

"Foolish," she said. "I will simply have to protect you, then." She folded the mask into her pallu. He lowered his hand, and stepped back. "Go now," she said.

He hesitated.

"Don't remain alone," he said. "My lady, go to your daughter."

She shook her head.

"I will go to my work," she replied. "But thank you, Jeevan. I..." She swallowed. She did not like to be vulnerable. "Thank you," she said again.

Ganam met her in the corridors later; sidled casually up to her and said, "Rukh and I are going to train," he told her. "During the midday rest. If you want to see his progress..."

"I'll come to the practice yard," Bhumika said.

When she arrived, after settling Padma for her nap, the two rebels were sparring, scythe blades sparking in the hot sun. She watched for a moment, from the shade. Then, when they both paused, she said to Rukh, "You're improving."

"Thank you, elder," Rukh said, panting. He wiped sweat from his brow. Hooked the scythe against his hip. The movement was almost beginning to look practiced. "Ganam, can I...?"

"Go on," he said. To Bhumika he said, "I'll keep watch. You talk."

Rukh told her the way the yaksa vanished, sometimes. Into the orchard, only returning when all the trees were twisted and strange. Out toward the forest. Even into the Hirana. "Melting the wall away," he said. "Opening a corridor and walking through it. I guess they're going to the deathless waters?"

"If you witnessed that, then you are taking too many risks, Rukh," Bhumika said sharply. "I asked for your assistance. I don't require you to put yourself in danger of death, you understand?"

"They don't notice me," said Rukh. "They never do."

"They may be pretending not to notice you," Bhumika said. Talking to Rukh always reminded her of talking to Priya when they were both only girls—an act of trying to direct wild, aimless energy to a useful purpose, without giving the fire of her more fuel. But Rukh was gentler by nature, which was a relief. He took to direction and praise like a plant thirsting for light and water. "But you've done well," Bhumika said, and as she'd expected, he brightened. Smiled at her.

But his smile quickly dimmed. "The one who looks like a little boy," he said. "He's—he doesn't know I'm watching, but..."

"But?"

"He always wants to be around other children." Hesitation. "I don't want to scare you, elder," Rukh said. "But he thinks Padma's interesting. He likes following when Khalida takes her outside."

Bhumika's insides went cold. She thought of Padma sleeping against her chest; the warm weight of her, the softness of her curls, the rise and fall of her breaths. She abruptly wanted to be with her daughter again, desperately.

"Thank you for telling me, Rukh," she said.

He looked at her and nodded resolutely.

"I'll try and find something better," he vowed. "Something more useful."

"I told you," Bhumika said. "You need to take care. No foolish risks. Promise me."

He nodded again, quickly this time. Then, as if they'd never spoken, he and Ganam resumed their sparring.

*   *   *

Passivity had never suited Bhumika.

No one was coming to save her from the strange circumstances she had found herself in. She would have to find her own solution.

One afternoon, when the day was still blisteringly hot, she called for a palanquin. She wore her temple whites as she often did. But she also wore her gold: her nath and earrings, her bracelets and a necklace, as she always did when she dealt with highborn. This had to have the appearance of a political journey. She adorned herself for the lie.

There was nothing strange about her needing to meet with one of her highborn in their own haveli. She assured herself the yaksa would not remark on it. What care did they have, after all, for mortal politics? And if they did remark she would bow her head and give some pretty explanation and that would, she hoped, be the end of it.

Jeevan met her with the palanquin and a handful of soldiers to carry it. They made their way across the city swiftly, despite the stifling heat.

In the pink lantern district, where there had once been nothing but pleasure houses, was a library. Nestled between rows of lantern-strung buildings, it was a modest building with pale walls and narrow windows, its interior pleasantly cool, and filled with the noise of rustling paper, distant strains of song and laughter from the pleasure houses, and the hum of voices reciting the Birch Bark Mantras.

Ever since she and Priya had taken over leadership of Ahiranya, Bhumika had made a point of investing in the arts in a way she had never been able to do as the regent's wife. Even when there had been precious little coin to spare, she had arranged for a library to be built, where sages and poets could study, and share their work, and keep their creations safely stored.

Under Parijatdvipan rule, it was the scholars and artists who had kept the memory of Ahiranyi faith and culture alive. The Birch Bark Mantras had survived in their recitations—in handwritten copies, hidden by household after household. Bhumika understood very well that to build a new Ahiranya would require strong foundations. A nation could not survive without food—but it could not survive without a soul either.

Kritika may have believed the Hirana was where the soul of Ahiranya lay. But in Bhumika's eyes, it was here.

Bhumika emerged from her palanquin before the library's steps. Jeevan offered his hand and she took it. He clasped it carefully, his palm warm and callused around her own. With the daylight behind him, veiling his face, he was reduced to his harshest angles—his strong jaw and that pronounced blade of a nose. But she could feel the softness of his gaze on her, just as palpably as she could feel the gentle guidance of his hand. Ever since the day in the rose garden he had been more careful with her. She straightened, and clasped his hand tighter in return. *I'm well*, she tried to say, with her eyes, her touch. His head lowered, and after a moment, he released her.

They walked together into the interior of the library. A woman met them near the entrance, with a bow and a smile.

"Elder," she said. "Welcome. How can we help you today?"

"Have you been well, Amina?" Bhumika asked.

"I have. Though my hands do ache." A rueful laugh. "I've been copying poems all morning."

Amina had survived, when a dozen other scribes and maidservants had been murdered for crimes against the empire. Now, she was a scribe herself, hair tonsured, fingers ink-stained.

"I would love to see them," Bhumika replied. "Though perhaps not today." She stepped deeper into the library; the dim interior was pleasant, after the heat of the day. "I need to see your collection of ancient texts."

"Of course," Amina said, without batting an eye. "Let me guide you."

There were few ancient tomes of faith left in Ahiranya. The Birch Bark Mantras had survived largely by word of mouth and memory. And what had once been carefully preserved on the Hirana, etched into stone and stored on inked leaf scrolls, had been burned along with Bhumika's temple siblings. But here, carefully wrapped and stored away, were texts of worship and theory and philosophy, salvaged from shops and hiding places in the oldest households and sages' personal collections. Some had even been preserved, to Bhumika's surprise, by priests of the mothers.

"Jeevan," Amina said, once Bhumika was settled at a table, surrounded by scrolls and books so fragile they near seemed to decay from contact with the air. "If you want to say hello to the others, they'll be glad to see you."

Jeevan inclined his head in mute thanks, and Amina departed.

"You've been here without me?" Bhumika asked, surprised.

If she had not known Jeevan so well, she would have missed how his jaw twitched a little, at that. He was embarrassed.

"I am not a scholar," he said.

"I meant no judgment," Bhumika said honestly. "My apologies, Jeevan."

"No need, my lady." He swallowed, then said, "I like tales. Like hearing them. The scribes like sharing them."

"You are allowed to have interests," she said quietly. "And you are allowed to have friends." She looked down at the scroll before her. The writing was archaic; the ink blurred into smears by years of humidity. Reading through all of this would be painstaking work. "You may go and see them, if you like," she said. "I'll spare you this."

Jeevan was briefly quiet. Then he came to kneel at the table across from her. "No, my lady," he said. "I'll stay and help."

They worked silently for a long time. Long enough that the sun's rays slanted and dimmed, as the afternoon settled in.

"There is one scribe," he said, "who has collected tales for children. He told me once about a mongoose and a snake that I will *not* be reciting to Padma." He frowned, so disapproving that it made her want to laugh. "But there are other, kinder stories."

"I am sure Padma would love to hear tales from you," Bhumika said. Jeevan turned to look at her, startled, and she smiled, the first true smile she'd worn in what felt like weeks. He blinked at her. "She may even like the tale of the mongoose and snake. Fables for children are often horrific, I've found," Bhumika added, as she opened another book. "And children never see the horror in them as we do."

"Lady Bhumika," Jeevan said.

"Mm?"

"What do you hope to find here?"

She reached for a new tome. Opened it.

"Any information about the yaksa I can use to understand them, and to protect our own interests," she said. "But truthfully, I expect I will find nothing. Sometimes it is necessary to act and plan, simply to know you're still capable of it," she said. "To assure yourself you are still fighting, even if your circumstances do not alter."

She opened a new scroll. Paused.

An image was laid out before her.

The shape of a body, run through with roots. It was not a yaksa. Or at least, she was fairly sure it was not. It looked far too human; a mortal bound to something grander than itself—bound by roots old and deep, stretching gold and green and red through it and beyond it, drifting into deeper waters.

Something was teasing at the corners of her memory. Something she had seen—something she had *known*.

If my elders lived, she thought, running her thumb over the hues of paint, disquiet thrumming in her blood, *what would they tell me about this image? What knowledge died with them that could save me now?*

She took the scroll with her when they departed.

That evening something touched her mind in the sangam. A call. A song.

It beckoned her, and she walked across the corridor on legs that did not obey her. That carried her from her own room to the nursery where her child slept. As if she had heard Padma cry. But she had not. There was only silence, and the susurration of leaves, and a tug beneath Bhumika's breastbone, winding, winding.

And there, in her child's room—

"I thought you would come," Chandni said. The moonlight was a spill over her shoulders. In its light, the darkness of her hair was a river—the slick, dark growth of fronds beneath water. "I called for you. The sangam carries echoes so sweetly."

Padma was awake in Nandi's arms, but she was silent. Staring up at the yaksa that held her with wide, dark eyes.

There was ice in Bhumika's veins.

"You have been resisting us," Nandi said, in that child's voice of his. Rocking Padma lightly, as if she were a much smaller baby. "Fighting us in your heart. Seeking out our secrets."

"I...I am a temple elder. It is my duty to learn," Bhumika managed. "To rule."

"If you have questions you must come to us. You must learn to trust," Chandni said, touching her fingertip to Bhumika's lower lip. Her fingertip was far too soft. Like fruit overripened. "You must trust us. With your country. Your faith. Your people." A pause. "Your child."

The hand lowered.

"We will take care of her," said Chandni. "And you will trust in us."

There was nothing in Bhumika. Nothing but the way her own eyes were drawn to the empty cot, to her baby in Nandi's arms; nothing but the desire to move forward, and grasp Padma, and run and run. It was an animal, awful desire as all her cleverness, her control, her strength crumpled inside her leaving nothing but agony. *No.*

"Yaksa," Bhumika managed. "Elder Chandni. Please. I will do—whatever you require. Only. Not this."

The yaksa who was not Chandni gave a sad smile and shook her head.

"Your little one will remain in our care for now."

A choked noise from the corner of the room, and Bhumika realized Khalida had been there all along. Trembling with terror, even as she bowed.

"I am only a maid," Khalida said, in the smallest voice Bhumika had ever heard her use. "Yaksa, immortal one, please—allow me to attend to the child."

"No," Chandni said softly. "No. That would be unwise."

She turned back to Nandi, and he placed Padma back in her cot. There were vines winding in steadily through the windows.

"Both of you go," she said. "And perhaps you will see her tomorrow."

Bhumika could not move.

"There is no need to fear, Elder Bhumika," said Chandni. "The yaksa have raised many a child before. Whole temple councils were reared by our hands. Rest well, and trust in us."

Bhumika lowered her head.

"Yaksa," she said, heart howling. "As you say."

She was bound. This was better than a knife at the throat. They had her—her own gods—by the heart. And it was too late, far too late, for anything to be done to stop it.

GANAM

Ganam had never thought he'd end up being a spy for the widow of the regent of Ahiranya. But that was life, he supposed. Unpredictable. You could spend most of it fighting to see your country free, and actually live to see the day come to pass. And then, by chance, you could also live to see your gods return, and the man you used to follow rise from the dead, and learn that the world you'd dreamed of was just more of the same. Rot, and tyrants, and keeping your eyes open for danger. So it goes.

He made his way toward Elder Bhumika's study. He'd left Rukh behind in the practice yard, staring up at the night sky, counting the stars. "I know Elder Bhumika told you to keep an eye on the yaksa," Ganam had said. "But you need to be careful, boy."

"I told her I would be," said Rukh. "I mean, I told her I *am*."

"Then you lied both times." Ganam sighed. Put a hand on Rukh's head. "There's no handling you without Priya here," he told him. "Just wait until she gets back. She'll beat some sense into you."

He'd speak to Elder Bhumika. He rehearsed what he'd say in his head. *Send the boy away. Get him some work in another household. Or at that library of yours. Anywhere he can't get into trouble.*

Leave him here, and he'll find it sooner or later.

There was a lantern lit in the study. He could see the light through the door, which was open a sliver. But there were noises from inside, muffled, and if she was talking to some highborn he didn't want to interfere.

He peered in.

At first, he thought he was seeing something he really didn't want to see. Jeevan kneeling, and Bhumika bent forward, like they were about to embrace—or kiss. But then he saw that Bhumika's hand was tight on Jeevan's arm, and her shoulders were shaking. She was shaking so hard, so hard, and Jeevan was whispering to her, "My lady, Lady Bhumika. Breathe with me. Breathe…"

She gave a hitched sob.

"I can't," she said. The heartbreak in her voice made the hairs on Ganam's neck rise. "I can't. Jeevan. My baby. My girl. My little girl…"

Jeevan was pressing a hand to Bhumika's hair as she sagged forward; as sadness racked her.

He couldn't be here for this. This wasn't his to see.

But—fuck. Padma. What had had happened to her?

He stumbled back, cold wrapping itself around his body. Quietly. As quiet as he could be. Went numbly down the corridors, searching until he finally found Khalida weeping in the kitchens with Billu, saying her mistress had sent her away. She told him all she knew.

Mothers torn from their children. Love being used like a weapon. Ganam had joined a rebellion to save his country from this. And here it was.

So it went. That was life. More of the same, in an endless, grinding cycle. But he felt the same anger hardening inside him that he'd felt years ago, when he'd vowed to risk his life for a better world.

He wasn't going to allow this.

"We'll get her back, Khalida," he promised her. "We'll get the little one safe. You wait and see. That's my promise. No matter how long it takes, we'll see it done."

30

ASHOK

Only Kritika was seated with Ashok on the Hirana today. There were no yaksa. Simply the two of them, to act as temple elders and wait for worshippers to heave themselves up the steps of the mountain.

When the final pilgrim left, Kritika departed, and Ashok slowly moved to his feet. He breathed in the cold air around him—the night's chill had already begun to settle in around the Hirana—and turned.

Ganam stood near the dangerous edge of the triveni, where it was open to the sky and the sheer cliff face surrounding the Hirana. But he didn't look afraid. Ostensibly he was Ashok's guard, but his hands were clasped behind him, weaponless. His expression was grave.

"There are going to be more tomorrow," he said. "And more worshippers the day after that. The rot's growing worse. Spreading faster than fire." His gaze flickered over Ashok, in a way that was somehow both dismissive and respectful. "Something's changed for the worse in Ahiranya," Ganam went on, as if he couldn't help himself. "And no one knows what. Strange, isn't it."

The rot growing worse. The yaksa returned, and the rot spreading great, creeping fingers across Ahiranya. And Ashok himself returning to life. All of it was a sign of—something. He didn't want to examine it. Didn't want to consider what it meant.

But instead of playing at the business of rest—of lying awake in a bed, listening to distant waters and the creaking slumber of something or someone else inside him—he walked through the mahal. Listened to the leaves whisper to him, the flowers turn to him.

There was a woman walking along the corridor ahead of him. She froze when she saw him. Then she moved out of his path murmuring a worshipful word or two. But her pause had given her guilt away, and as he drew nearer to her, he realized how close she was to rooms marked by Chandni's silver night-blooming flowers. A forbidding mark.

She'd been to see the child. Bhumika's child. He was sure of it.

The maid was trembling, her head lowered, but her pallu, drawn respectfully over her face, did not conceal the turn of her mouth. The anger. She loathed him for who he served. Loathed him for what the yaksa had already done.

"Go," he said. She was still there. Frozen, like a hare under a hawk's eyes. "I saw nothing," he told her, stressing the "nothing," giving her a hard look. "Woman, use your good sense and go before I change my mind. You will not enjoy it if I do."

She made a noise that was part squeak, part assent. She managed to scramble a brief bow, then ran away as quickly as her legs could carry her.

He watched her shadow on the marble. The flicker and fade of it, in the lantern light from the sconces on the walls.

Ashok made his way to the orchard. It was no longer peaceful. One by one, each tree had turned to rot.

Nothing and no one would be born here, he knew. It wasn't yet time.

But he watched the trees and thought of waters, deep and old. Waters that hollowed children out and gave them power. Cosmic waters where universes met, and the roots that held all things bound to both of them. The rot was fed by magical waters. The yaksa came from those waters. And Ashok...

He could feel every plant surrounding them. He knew—and did not know how he knew—that they were an extension of him as they were an extension of... others. Through them and through his own skin he reached for Bhumika. Felt for her. Considering.

A flash of an image lanced through his mind: a mortal body. Tendrils of blue and green fading into blood red, grasping its throat, its wrist. Its mind and heart. Bhumika's fingertips against paper, tracing words that blurred like smeared ink in his mind's eye.

The memory ran into him like water into well—it drifted into all that he was, consumed, as much part of him as everything else that lay within him.

Roots, he thought, in a voice that wasn't his own. Old. A creaking, lightning-struck wood of a void. *We're all bound together. We fed the world and the people those waters, and now they carry us within them. And just as we consume them, they may drink in return—*

There was something. Something on the edge of his memory and his consciousness. Something so large it threatened to obliterate his fragile self. He...

A rustle in the leaves behind him.

He turned.

Nandi stood there. He looked as serene as ever, the moonlight glancing strangely off his eyes, the rows of teeth in his mouth when he parted his lips. "I found someone watching you," he said. And shoved someone forward.

The boy gave a yelp as he fell. He was maybe ten, eleven years. If Nandi had been mortal, he would never have been able to hold him. The boy was all limbs, with rot bristling on him. He rose swiftly to his feet but did not attempt to run. Wise of him. Ashok would have stopped him, and he would not have made it pleasant.

"I'm sorry for disturbing you," the boy said stiffly.

"You're not as afraid of me as you used to be," Ashok observed, dusting the dirt from his own tunic. "And not as full of admiration, either."

The boy watched him with guarded, wary eyes.

"You remember me," the boy said.

"I do, Rukh," Ashok said pleasantly, baring his teeth in a smile. He leaned back against the tree. "You've been a fool, boy. As you always are."

"I..." The boy's voice faltered. "I did not think you thought of me enough to—to think me a fool."

"I have the measure of you. It didn't take long in my first life, and hasn't in this one either. You're the same." He gave Rukh a sidelong look. "The yaksa know you've been watching them. You're a good spy. But not good enough."

"Everyone watches them," the boy said thinly. "We're...we're admiring them. Worshipping."

"How did I send you to spy on my sister when you're so bad at lying?" Ashok marveled. He took a step closer. The rot on the boy felt strange. The rot...

"My sister froze it in you, didn't she? Choked it to stillness."

Rukh didn't move. Didn't even seem to breathe, as he watched Ashok, who watched him in return.

"How was it done?" The boy was silent. How had he forced words from throats, before his death? "Tell me or I'll do something," said Ashok. "Break your arm, maybe."

Apparently that was a realistic threat, because Rukh said, "I don't know how she did it. However the yaksa do it, I suppose."

Ashok held out a hand. Palm up, fingers slightly curled. Beckoning. "Come here," he said. "I want to feel it for myself."

Ashok had always known how to scent fear—how to use it to coax loyalty or obedience or cowering surrender from an enemy. He'd made plenty of grown men snivel and beg before ending their lives. And this one was only a boy—guarded and stiff, staring somewhere over his shoulder. He could be manipulated.

He wouldn't run.

"I wish you could see the way the roots grow from you," Ashok murmured. He took a step forward. "Boy. Give me your hand."

Rukh didn't move, so Ashok reached out.

He took Rukh's rigid, unwilling hand into his own. Turned the palm over and then back, then raised the entire limb up to the light.

He felt the magic winding through the boy's body. Yaksa magic.

"I could rip this from you," he said. "I could set you free. But our magic is bound up in you, and I don't know what would be left behind."

"Taking it out would kill me," Rukh said, in a voice that only wavered a little. "Priya told me so."

"Do you think I'll kill you?"

"What could I do to stop you?"

Ashok snorted. "So much bravado, from such a small creature." He tightened his grip. "Nothing," he said. "There is nothing you can do."

Rukh made an animal noise, and tried to pull free. Ashok's hand tightened an increment further.

"No," Ashok said.

"If. If you're going to. I just want it to be quick." His voice was shaky, but his expression was defiant.

"No," Ashok said softly. "No. I won't hurt you any further. She'd never forgive it."

She. Priya. Somehow that still mattered to him.

"Everything has a price," he said. "Everything demands sacrifice. I had to be sure. You understand that, don't you?"

Rukh stared at him, blank and uncomprehending. And Ashok reached out with magic. Reached into him.

Priya had withered the bonds between Rukh and the magic within him. But Ashok did more.

The rot comes from the waters, the old voice in his heart said. *The waters fill mortals with magic.*

The waters fill them with us. Our gifts. Our knowledge.

When waters ebb, they leave their mark behind. The memory of water. The hollow.

When waters leave, they demand their price.

He reached for the magic within Rukh. Poured more into him—more knowledge, more strength, more flowering rot, more of the cosmic rivers that had changed them both. Watched the leaves rise along the boy's spine—heard the boy cry out—

Ripped him free from the waters. Left him hollow.

A sound of agony escaped Rukh's lips. He fought, trying to escape Ashok's grip. Then sagged. Down to his knees.

Ashok kneeled with him.

"Look at me, boy," he said. "Wake up."

He repeated himself. Once, twice. Finally, Rukh's eyes opened. Slowly, painfully.

"Tell me what you learned, when I dragged you under," Ashok demanded. "Tell me what you saw. What do you remember? *Do* you remember?"

Rukh squeezed his eyes shut.

"I know who you really are," Rukh said tightly. "I know—so much—"

"Because I showed you," Ashok said savagely. His pulse was beating behind his eyes. *Tell me who I am*, he wanted to beg. *Tell me.* "Do you remember my sister's name? No, not Lady Bhumika," Ashok said, when Rukh's gaze flickered, confused. "My other sister. Do you remember how you came to meet her? Do you remember how you came to trust her enough to betray me and leave my rebels behind?"

Silence. Panicked silence. That was answer enough.

"How does it feel, not remembering? How does it feel, now that the waters have stolen her from you, and left a tale of my secrets in their place?"

Rukh said nothing. He was breathing shallowly, too fast, his face sallow. If he'd recovered himself well enough to fear what had happened to him, then Ashok considered that a good sign.

"Thank you," Ashok said. Placed a hand on Rukh's forehead. "Rest now."

He let everything fall back into place. The waters poured through Rukh once more, and he was back where he belonged, in the grip of the yaksa, where Ashok could feel the presence of the rot in him. Back in himself.

31

MALINI

There were too many people demanding Malini's attention—a cacophony of noise, her court women and highborn men and officials all thronging around her. Eventually, she left the council tent entirely. As she walked through the press, Malini searched the crowd with her eyes. When she found Priya she caught her gaze. Held out a beckoning hand to her. "Elder Priya," she said. "Please accompany me."

Priya didn't hesitate. She matched Malini's footsteps, shadowing her back to the tent.

Lata moved to stand by Malini's other side. Malini turned to her and said, in a low voice, "Ensure I have a moment. Alone."

She did not say *with Priya*. But Lata looked carefully between Malini and Priya, comprehension in her eyes, and said, "There are going to be many people who want to speak to you directly, Empress."

"Tell them they will have to wait," Malini replied.

"*You* may want to speak to them," said Lata.

"Later."

"Empress," Priya said. "If you're needed here..."

Malini didn't let her finish. She grasped Priya's wrist—one firm press of her nails to skin—and drew Priya into the tent behind her. The curtain fell shut behind them.

Inside, the tent was empty.

Malini turned on her heel. She didn't look to the curtain, or listen to the sounds beyond the canvas. She trusted Lata to do as she asked.

Instead, she cupped Priya's face in her hands, feeling the unhurt wholeness of the face under her hands, meeting the warmth of her lovely
brown eyes. "Are you really well?" she demanded. "Priya, be truthful
with me."

"What does it mean to be well when there's a war going on? I'm
well enough, Malini. I...some of my men were lost. Men I knew.
I lived with them in Ahiranya. Our tent burned. All my things are
gone. I..." She swore, and Malini felt the movement of her jaw, the
shift of those delicate bones under skin. "I brought hashish, you know.
And wine. And I have no idea if any of it survived. I suppose it doesn't
matter."

"Lata will find you a new place to sleep," Malini said. "And we'll
make sure you're reunited with any of your men that survived, I promise you."

"What if I stay here with you?" Priya asked. She gave Malini a
watery smile, a teasing edge to her smoke-strained voice. "Just like I did
when we were Ahiranya, and I was your very own maidservant? I could
sleep on the floor. You wouldn't even notice me."

"Priya," Malini said, a tug of desperate fondness beneath her breastbone. "I always noticed you." A beat. She brushed the dark hair back
from Priya's face, not wanting to release her, wanting to touch her just a
little more. "You're not a maidservant anymore, elder."

"No," Priya said. "Not yours. Not anyone's."

"Priya..." She hesitated, thinking of Priya's pride, and the war
council, and the hand curled against Priya's chest. She knew the answer
to her question, and yet she wanted to ask it. Wanted the reassurance
of words from Priya's own lips. "Does it offend you that I did not name
you my general?"

That drew a laugh out of Priya.

"What would I do with being a Parijatdvipan general? Ahiranya
doesn't belong to your empire. No—I'm better off as I am. Besides, it
seems dangerous work, being one of your creatures." Her smiled deepened, wicked. "It was an amazing thing," she said, voice low, "watching
you in there with those men. You spin beautiful webs. Even when I can
only see the edges of them, I have to admire them."

Malini never told all her plans and machinations to anyone. She had grown less open, she knew; had hardened her heart and closed the doors upon it, so she would never let anyone truly know her.

She could not risk being hurt. Could not risk giving anyone the strength to betray her.

But Priya had saved her life time and time again. Priya had let Malini hold a knife to her. Had kissed her beneath a waterfall, and *seen* her utterly, all the things in her that were cruel and vicious and broken, and cared for her, regardless.

"I'll tell you anything you like," Malini said, letting the tenderness she felt seep into her voice. "Just ask, and it's yours."

Priya gazed back at her. Her lips parted slightly, a temptation, an invitation.

"Empress." A call from the entrance. Lata's voice, pitched loud. In the space of a breath, Malini's hands lowered and Priya turned her face away. "Prince Rao is here."

"I'll meet him outside," Malini said. Then she looked at Priya again. "Priya, I..."

Priya shook her head. "I'll go and find Sima. And you..." She paused, and touched a hand to her own cheek, where Malini's fingers had been. Then she let her hand drop. "You have work to do. I'll leave you to it."

Malini met Rao under the respectable cover of an outdoor parasol, which offered a modicum of shade, but kept them exposed to watching eyes. He looked different. He'd put aside the clothing he'd worn earlier, and was in a simple tunic and dhoti. His hair was damp. He must have washed.

In the distance, behind his back, the land around the High Prince's fort was still glowing, burning with flame, a light limning him.

"Stand with me for a moment," Malini said, after Rao had bowed. He joined her under the large parasol.

"I consider Elder Priya part of my inner court," Malini said, speaking of her women. "But I also need her in the battles ahead. And I would like her to face them with you." She trusted Rao—and therefore his men—more than she did anyone else. "What do you think of her?"

"I remember the first time I met her," said Rao. "She was—blunt. Difficult." A pause. "I liked her."

"Of course you did," Malini said. Affection bled into her voice. "You don't like simpering, quiet women, do you, Rao?"

His jaw twitched.

"If you accuse me of harboring some kind of—interest—I won't be pleased."

Malini bit down on her own tongue to stop herself from laughing at that. When she spoke, her voice was suspiciously choked, but there was no helping it.

"Ah no, I'm certainly not trying to imply anything, Rao. I'm sure your intentions are entirely pure."

Rao nodded. He looked a little flushed.

"She won't be bothered by anyone when she travels with me," he said.

"I'm sure she won't."

"I'll treat her as I would any highborn leader."

"I expected no less."

"But there may be rumors," he cautioned. "I can do nothing to stop that."

"There will be rumors no matter which contingent she accompanies. There will be rumors if she travels alone. At least with you, Rao, I know there is no risk of any further incidents that may require my—intervention."

Rao made a hum of acknowledgment.

"Why did you summon her here?" Rao asked. There was curiosity in his voice, but also something very like exasperation. "It's going to cause you nothing but trouble."

"Chandra has his fire," Malini said, after a moment. "And I have her. She won't be an expected weapon. No matter what Chandra may believe he knows of Ahiranya, he has not seen her wield her gifts as I have. She gives me an advantage I sorely need."

There were two truths inside Malini's heart. It was the colder one she spoke.

But the other was this. *Because I need her. Because she saw me once, for everything I was and could be, and wanted me anyway. And she sees me and wants me still, over the chasm that should make enemies of us. And yet it does not. Cannot.* It was a truth like a wound, like a fragile heart exposed, and it frightened and awed her in equal measure.

Rao nodded. From the way he looked away, staring across the camp at the soldiers packing away weaponry and tents, he did not believe her, but had decided there was no worth in arguing.

"What would you have done if Lord Mahesh had not volunteered to remain behind?" Rao kept his voice low so that his words wouldn't be overheard. "Did you plan for this? For Mahesh and Aditya both to remain and risk their lives?"

"I planned for Mahesh," Malini admitted easily, without shame. "But Aditya? No, that surprised me as much as it did you. He has never offered to fight before. Why would I expect that to change?"

"It didn't surprise me," Rao said. "The minute you spoke of it, I knew...I *feared* I knew what he would do. And Malini, please. You must have known Aditya would volunteer. It was like a trap perfectly woven for him. A hopeless task, a service that could break him—how could he resist?"

A doubt struck her, painful as a blow. Her breath hitched. Priya had spoken so admiringly of her webs. Had Malini woven this one without realizing it?

No, she told herself fiercely. *No, I love my brother. I would not. I did not.*

"I do not think about Aditya," Malini snapped. "Why would I? If I thought of him—really thought of him and what he does, what he represents—I would have to kill him. I would have to make it appear accidental. It would need to be something less obvious than leaving him *here.*" She gestured at the distant, glowing fort, angry.

"Can you see why I doubt you?" Rao asked. "Why I think this could be a trap arranged for him?"

"You would never have thought this of me when you knew me as a girl," Malini said, trying not to feel hurt. "Never."

"I didn't know you then," Rao said heavily, "as I know you now."

You were not so spellbound by love for my brother then, Malini thought. *And not so led astray.*

But she would not speak of things he could not see.

"I'm not his keeper," said Malini. Though in another world, another time, he would have been hers.

"If you truly didn't plan for this..." Rao paused, exhaling. "You could have refused him. Given the task to someone else. You still could."

"I could have," she said. "I could have belittled him. Refused him and shamed him. Would that have been the act of a kind sister?"

"Don't mock him, please," Rao said, jaw tight.

"I am not mocking him, or you," Malini said evenly, forcing herself to be calm. "I am telling you he is still his own man, able to make his own choices."

What she would not—could not—say to Rao was this:

She felt relieved. Horribly relieved and unburdened, and guilty for feeling so. She was glad she would not carry the danger of him with her to Harsinghar; that she would not always have to think of him hiding in a dark room, meditating and praying, and waiting for a different future to come for him, while *she* waited for men to rally around him and slit her throat.

She had not tried to kill him. She had done him a greater service than any other sibling vying for a throne would have done, when she allowed him to live. She owed him no more than she'd given.

He had given her a gift, her brother.

"Will you remain here with him?" Malini asked.

"Are you asking me to, Empress?"

"None of that," Malini said softly. "There's no one listening to us now."

Rao huffed out a sigh. Then said, "Malini."

"Yes."

"Would you allow me to remain with him if I asked?"

She could hear the vulnerability in his voice—like a fracture in glass. She kept her eyes off him, offered him that small mercy as she said, "I have named you a general of my army. If you want Alor to have a voice in the battle ahead..."

"One of my own brothers, perhaps," he said quietly, as if he knew there was no point in suggesting it, but had to try regardless. "If I send a missive to Alor. To my father, one of them will perhaps come."

"There's no time." *As you well know,* she thought. "And I need your men. I need you."

"Then I won't ask," Rao said.

Silence fell between them, and Malini couldn't stop herself from turning away from him—from pacing, her whole body alive with a panicked, jittery feeling that she couldn't contain. So he didn't want to stay with her, help her—what did it matter?

"Malini," he said, finally.

"Don't," she said in return. "Mahesh will be trustworthy support for Aditya." *As he was not for me.* "He will be someone Aditya can rely on. Take peace in that."

"I will," he said. "As I take peace in knowing you'll see this war won before he is harmed."

Strange, she thought, how compliments from his lips so often sounded like despair. As if he looked at her every success—every battle won, every highborn enemy circumvented, and felt *fear.* Sometimes—often—she wanted to pry that fear apart and see its working. She wanted to ask him: *You, who named me and gave me the opportunity to seize my crown. What do you fear? Is it me and my choices? Is it what will become of me? Or what will become of men like you?*

"I'm going to see Aditya," she said, instead. "Is he well?"

"We sparred. It was..." He stopped and shook his head minutely. "He's well." There was something in his voice. Something that was not for her.

He gave her a look, and she smiled at him. She knew him. It was worth reminding him, now and again, just how well she understood him.

He cleared his throat. "I'll leave you to it," he said. "I think it won't be long before we're ready to move."

After Rao's departure, Malini summoned a guard.

"Is the fort still silent?"

"Yes, Empress."

"Good," she said. "Take me to Prince Aditya."

Aditya's usually sparse tent was full, for once, of the kind of chaos Malini had grown used to in her own space: maps of Saketa and detailed sketches of the flowering maze of Saketa's fortress. Military officials, imparting information at rapid speed—the intended formations of troops, the supplies that would remain here or travel with Malini's larger force of men. She was surprised Mahesh was not here already, bowing and kissing at Aditya's feet.

An unkind thought. She allowed herself the joy of it.

"Brother," Malini said. The room fell silent.

She looked at the watching officials. "Leave us," she said, and they departed swiftly—paper, ink, ledgers all left in their wake. In the midst of it all, Aditya looked at her with an air of utter calm. Aditya was in mussed robes, sweat-stained. He wore his blade at his side.

He looked so much like his old self—like the crown prince brother she had grown up with—that it made her heart ache with affection. And that angered her in a way she could not make sense of.

"I have a gift for you," she said.

She had stopped at her own tent to collect it—had ignored Lata's questions, and Swati's timid offers of tea or sherbet—and picked up the onyx box, and carried it with her. It was heavy in her hands. Aditya took it from her, a faint frown on his brow. Opened it.

"Ash," he said cautiously.

"This contained so-called mothers' fire," said Malini. "You saw what I told the men. It was the truth. But this..." She pushed the box forward. "This is my assurance to you that it truly wasn't the fire of the mothers. That it is not impossible to defeat."

Aditya nodded. Passive, waiting for her to speak.

"I am going to defeat Chandra," Malini said. "I will move on Parijat as swiftly as I can. I have great strength behind me, and the mothers, and the nameless also. I will defeat him. You need only survive until then, and then the full might of the Parijatdvipan empire will support you."

"I've already elected to stay," he said, laying the box over his knees. "I am not afraid of death."

"You should be," Malini said swiftly. "A man who fears death fights to survive. And the longer you fight, the better for all of us, so if you will not survive for yourself, survive for all of us. For me."

"I will fight with all that I have," Aditya replied.

"You have been told what our forces can spare here," said Malini. "But if there is anything you need…"

"No." Aditya shook his head. "Sister, I'll do well enough."

"Well enough," she repeated. "This is battle."

"I know," he said. "I was trained for battle."

"Then you must do more than *well enough*. You must do everything. Did you spar with Rao? Was that enough to win his confidence? It is not enough for me, Aditya. Now I know war, I beg you to remember your old self, and go to battle as him. Not as the priest who could not bring himself to light an arrow."

"You're angry I'm not as I once was," Aditya observed.

"I'm not angry with you."

"You are," he said. "You can barely bring yourself to visit me. And when you do, sister, you look through me—seeking the man I no longer am. You are not alone in that. You are not the only one who misses him." Did he mean that he missed himself? Or that Rao did? She did not ask.

"But you should not be angry," he went on, keeping his eyes steady on her own. "Because if I became that man again—that rightful heir to the throne of our empire—you would lose everything you have gained. Your army. Your waiting crown. For all your strength and ambition and will, you know as I do, how easily men are swayed by what they think they know."

Malini said nothing.

"Will you ask me to give up this task?" Aditya said, into the silence. "To travel with you and fight like a prince of Parijatdvipa at your side, knowing all the risk it brings to you?"

She could well imagine it: Aditya at her side in battle, wreathed in glory on a white horse. Aditya racing his chariot into battle, every inch the noble crown prince. Every inch the man her highborn lords would want to see on the throne.

He was a danger. Mahesh had soundly proved that. And yet. And yet...

She said nothing, and nothing again. There was, after all, nothing to be said.

He smiled, his eyes sad but knowing.

"No," he said. "You won't ask. You're glad I'll remain here. So don't berate me, sister, for choosing a path that protects you. From Saketa, and an army at your back, and from—me."

"I did not ask for you to sacrifice for my sake," Malini said in a low voice.

"An act of love does not require asking," said Aditya. "But I promise you. I act for the nameless, as I do all things. It's my god's voice that guides me to remain here. I will remain. And who knows," he said. "Perhaps I shall survive this war. Perhaps fate will see fit to release me."

"And then? What of you then?"

"I'll find a new monastery to take me in," he said. "I'll live out my days there. I will go to Alor itself, and seek the heart of the faith. A life of peace." His smile deepened, a soft, wistful thing. "Your crown is your own, Malini. Sister. I will never seek to take it from you."

She could not speak to him any longer. She'd hoped for...well. She did not know what she had hoped for, and that was her error. She did not want the return of her brother as he'd once been, and yet some part of her did. Or...no.

She wanted her brother as he had never been. A brother who had seen how she had been hurt and had shielded her when she had been unable to shield herself. She wanted a love from him he'd never been able to give and never could, because it was a love she had needed long ago.

She did not want him to die. There was no possibility, in death. Only an end.

She turned to go. But she paused at the exit of the tent. If she could not put that tangle of love and anger and resentment into words, she could at least tell him this.

"After your monastery burned," she began. "After, I dreamt of Alori and Narina. They told me I would kill both my brothers. And they forgave me. But I have never planned to harm you." She paused. "Your existence has been a thorn in my side. But I have not ever wanted to hurt you. I did nothing to guide you to this point, Aditya. I did not ask you to remain here in Saketa or tell you to volunteer for this. I have held no blade to your throat. And I have made no prisoner of you. I know what imprisonment is." Her voice wavered, then—fury and hurt giving it a fine edge. "I love you, brother. Though, perhaps, it would be easier if I did not."

A silence. Then, Aditya's voice behind her. "Safe travels, Malini."

"Safe siege, Aditya," she said in return.

CHANDRA

The news arrived during the deep quiet of the night, when Chandra was bedding his wife. One of his guards interrupted reluctantly, bowing and keeping his eyes resolutely lowered, for all that a painted screen and heavy curtains of silk protected Chandra and his new wife's modesty.

"Messengers bring news of the war, Emperor," the guard said. "News of your sister."

He emerged from his bed and listened to the messenger, through the screen, as his servants dressed him: a turban of stiff brocade, pinned in place with a moonstone the size of a child's fist; a necklace of prayer stones, each stone wrought from gold and silver intertwined, and carved with the name of a mother of flame. An achkan in white silk, and a dhoti of pale gold.

His father, he remembered, had never dressed so formally and lavishly in his own bedroom. The advisors allowed in his inner chambers often saw him more at ease, in simple cotton and silks, rich and subtle. Chandra had always despised that informality. It was the place of the emperor to be more than the men who had vowed to serve him: in nature, in purpose. In clothing. Ever since his rise to the throne he had made a point of not following his father's lackluster example.

He was glad of his choice now. The armor of it reminded him of who he was; of the life that the mothers had ensured for him, the crown his righteousness and purpose had granted him. His armor allowed him to rein in his own fury, when the messenger stammered through his news, gathered from Chandra's own spies, and soldiers at outposts, and a loyal priest who had fled Saketa and imprisonment in Malini's camp to bring Chandra dire tidings.

His sister still lived. His sister still ruled her horde of traitors and dishonorable vow breakers. His sister had not been killed by his holy fire. The High Prince's fort lay under siege. The High Prince would not have the easy victory Chandra had promised him.

Even when blessed fire had been sent to kill her—even when her followers should have finally turned on her and recognized Chandra's true and only claim to power—his sister had survived. His sister still led her fool men.

His sister was coming to Parijat.

He ordered one guard to summon Hemanth, and dismissed the rest. In the silence that followed, he strode over to his balcony, pushing aside the gauze that kept insects at bay, and stepped out into the cool night air.

From here, he could see the same vista his father once had, and all the emperors that came before them: the vastness of the mahal itself, with smaller manses nestled within it, and dozens of intimate court-yards full of needle-flower and jasmine, growing in lush profusion. The gardens of his mother, now nothing but blackness and the faint puls-ing glow of dying embers, starlight in soil beneath him. The mahal's walls, a gleaming length of white. And the city of Harsinghar beyond it, its white marble and sandstone both golden and blue-tinged beneath the light of the moon. He stared out fixedly, unblinking, until his eyes burned from the gentle nighttime wind, and the sting of ash it carried.

There were no winds without ash. Not in his mahal.

The guard returned.

"Join me on the balcony, priest," Chandra called. After a moment, Hemanth did. "You have had ill news," the High Priest said cautiously.

"Have you heard?" Chandra said. "No. Of course you have not. My sister is coming home, priest. You have your wish after all."

"My wish," Hemanth said, "is for your well-being. And Parijat-dvipa's. As it always has been." He drew closer and placed himself next to Chandra on the edge of the balcony. Chandra could feel Hemanth's eyes on him, could feel their concern. "She comes with an army?"

"Yes." Chandra ground his teeth. It made his jaw ache, pulsing with his tension, his anger. "All those fools who want more than they deserve. Don't they understand their place? Their *purpose* in the world Divyanshi built for them? Don't answer me." He gave a laugh, bitter and frayed. "I know they do not. Or they would bow to me, *serve* me, and be glad."

Hemanth was silent for a long moment. Then he said, comfortingly, "Be glad that she is coming here. Consider it a sign. The mothers are sending her where she must be, so that she may finally fulfill her duty to you, and to us all."

If the mothers were truly acting in my favor, Chandra thought, *then they would have killed her at the High Prince's fort. They would have ensured that the blessed fire razed her entire army.*

He felt instantly ashamed of the thought. The mothers were not at fault. Nor was Chandra. No, it was his sister—her monstrous choices, her utter refusal to accept her fate. His sister was a curse. She always had been.

"Emperor," Hemanth said, his voice breaking the quiet that had settled over them both. "What will you do? Will you greet her? Speak with her?"

"I would rather drive a dagger through her heart," said Chandra. "I would rather shoot her with an arrow through the leg, and watch her slowly bleed to death. I would rather strangle her with my own bare hands."

"She has caused you great pain," Hemanth said compassionately.

Chandra's eyes closed. He nodded. Yes. She had. He was glad Hemanth understood; glad that the High Priest had always seen the heart in him that lay under his rage, his unyielding desire for a better world, for better people.

"You know I will request this of you again," Hemanth said, placing a kindly hand on Chandra's arm. "Please, Emperor. Think of the power of her willing death."

"Think of the power I already have," Chandra retorted.

"Do not hold yourself back from greatness," Hemanth said. "Do not hold Parijatdvipa back from greatness. I know you have the capacity to help her willingly and gladly meet her own fate."

But do I have the will to see her meet it? Chandra thought. He was not sure he did. He was not sure she deserved it.

"You are a good man, Chandra," Hemanth said, finally using Chandra's name—a thing he did only rarely, in moments when he wanted to speak to Chandra with great intimacy, tenderness. "The best of men. Guide her. Teach her what she must be. Let your priests help you." He pressed on. "The mothers have sent her to you. Listen to them."

Chandra hated his sister. *Hated* her. Had he not said enough? Was he not the emperor? This was his decision, as the chosen of the mothers of flame. No one else's. Not even the High Priest's.

He turned his face away from Hemanth.

"Emperor," Hemanth said, voice soft. "Please. Will you not hear me?"

Chandra said nothing.

"I have been reluctant to speak of this, Emperor," said Hemanth, when Chandra refused to answer. "But there may be a greater danger to Parijatdvipa than the weapons of mortal men alone."

Chandra laughed abruptly, the noise forcing its way through his teeth. "Men are enough trouble."

"Emperor," he said. Sighed. "The hour is late, and your heart is troubled. Come to the temple tomorrow. We will pray together, you and I. A new supply of flowers will be brought to my priests. We will make a garland for Divyanshi together. I will put aside the finest roses and marigolds for you. And then we will speak. And I will tell you what . . . what *fears* my priests have brought to me."

"If you are simply going to attempt to convince me again of my sister's fate, there's no need," Chandra said. Half tiredness, half warning. "I understand your perspective. And you have made clear to me that you believe wholeheartedly in me. That you will follow my will."

"As a priest, as *your* priest, it is my duty to tell you all I can to guide you, to light the path before you," Hemanth said, with the chiding care of a father. "Tomorrow, Emperor. Then do with the information what you will."

The High Priest departed.

Chandra returned to his chamber.

His wife was standing by the edge of the bed, still adjusting the pleats of her sari. Her hair was loose over her shoulder. He watched her small fingers tuck the fabric into place; watched the line of concentration etched into her brow. She slowed, when she saw him looking, and gave him a nervous glance from under her lashes. She was timid, his wife. Her flinching obedience irritated him, but he could tolerate it. She was pretty enough, and did not complain or attempt to manipulate when she was called to his bed. She fulfilled her role. What more could he reasonably ask of her? Showing her his irritation, by word or violence, would be as satisfying as breaking the wing of a drab-feathered songbird.

And yet, right at that moment, the thought of breaking something beyond repair sounded very pleasant indeed. He thought of the bones of her wrists, and lower arms. He watched her delicate fingers work, then go still.

He banished his thoughts, and his anger. He wouldn't hurt her. That wasn't the kind of man he was.

"Go," he said to her abruptly. "Leave me."

She gave him a quick look. Then lowered her gaze and said, "Sleep well, husband," and swiftly departed.

He did not sleep after that. He summoned his military officials, who arrived tired-eyed and disheveled but obediently set to work discussing what must be done next. In the vast hall of the imperial mahal, where his priests and priestly warriors kept a pit of blessed fire—*mothers' fire*—burning, his loyal officials and lords advised him.

Once, this hall had been full of lords and princes and kings from across Parijatdvipa: Alorans, Srugani, Saketans, Dwarali. All of them full of hubris. All of them, leading the empire—and his father—astray. Now nearly all the faces before him were Parijati. The Parijatdvipans from other city-states who remained were clever enough to recognize their correct place: in service to him, in obedience to him. They knew better than to consider themselves his equal.

He had thought, briefly, of adding Prince Kunal to that number. The man would bow, he knew; lower his head, show obedience. But there was something about the High Prince's son that he did not trust—a kind of flinty, hunted anger in the man's eyes that told him Prince Kunal did not deserve the privilege of belonging to Chandra's inner circle.

Besides, Prince Kunal's loyalty was contingent on the success of his father against Malini; on the protection of the flames Chandra had gifted him. The power. On the lifeline, too, that Chandra had extended: food from Parijat, from its safe and fertile fields, untouched by the blight that had ruined both Ahiranya and Saketa. Contingent loyalty did not interest Chandra. He wanted men of faith. He wanted men who placed their faith in *him*.

The High Priest had taught Chandra that the mothers of flame loved him; that they spoke to him above all else, guiding him toward his fate. And he heard a loving whisper of them—in the arch and flicker of the pit of fire, which bloomed blue for a moment, against feathers of gold—as an old and seasoned lord explained to Chandra, in a gruff but respectful tone, that the princess would surely not follow the vast main road to Harsinghar.

"Her forces are depleted, Emperor," he said, as two priestly warriors quietly entered the room with a cask—opened it, and lowered more magical flame into the pit, which flared and brightened. "She will use caution. If your loyal men locate her, destroy her forces en route..."

"The High Prince's forces will attack her own from behind," said another lord. "He will not simply allow the traitor princess to march on Parijat—"

"His fort remains under siege," a quiet voice interrupted. A military advisor. "He cannot follow easily, or immediately."

Chandra listened as they debated, his priestly warriors now arrayed around him. One leaned forward. Said, in a low voice, "Lord Sushant wishes to speak with you, emperor. In privacy."

"He can wait," Chandra said dismissively.

"Emperor," the man said. "He insists that he cannot. He was greatly distressed."

"Fine," Chandra snapped. "Continue," he told his advisors, who had paused when he raised his voice. "I'll return in a moment."

If Sushant had summoned him on a fool's errand, he'd simply have the man's throat cut. That was a fitting price, surely, for wasting an emperor's time.

Sushant was from an ancient Parijati family that lost its glory and wealth long ago. It was Chandra who had raised him and his kin up; who had granted him the wealth of executed traitor highborn and allowed him access to the inner court. Sushant was, as a result, an adoring and faultlessly loyal follower, who had brought his lifetime of experience tending to the family rural estate to the task of overseeing Parijat's agriculture.

Despite the coolness of the dawn air, he was sweating, his mustache visibly damp. He bowed deeply when Chandra approached, then raised his head. "Emperor," he said. "Thank you for agreeing to meet me alone."

"You must think yourself valuable to me, Sushant," Chandra said, voice low, "to demand my time in this manner, as if I am *your* servant."

Sushant bowed hurriedly. "Forgive me, forgive me," he babbled. "But my men—farmers on a nearby estate—you must *see* . . ."

The lord opened a sack that lay at his feet. Drew it wide open. And Chandra looked within—and abruptly recoiled.

"What," he said sharply, "is that?"

Sushant's hands trembled as he drew the sack abruptly shut.

"Rot, emperor," he said. "The rot from Ahiranya, the rot that blights Saketa—it is in Parijat. I . . . I do not know how far it has spread."

A greater danger to Parijatdvipa than mortal men alone, Hemanth had said. And here it was before him. Rot in his own fields. His own country.

He felt abruptly sick. This was not meant to happen to Parijat. Not the land of the mothers. Not the land blessed by his rule.

"And what must I do?" he asked.

"E-Emperor," Sushant said. "I . . . I do not know. I do not know."

"Come with me," he said roughly.

He returned to his advisors. They bowed as he entered. Waited until he gave them permission to rise.

"Speak," he said sharply. One of them flinched visibly. "Tell me what you've planned."

"We believe she may cross the Veri river," said one of his advisors. "There is a ford. If we meet her there, we may be able to thin her forces."

"Thin," Chandra repeated. "I do not want her forces thinned. I want them destroyed. Do you understand?"

Silence from his advisors. They did not seem to want to look at him.

Somehow this was his sister's fault. Somehow the curse of her had cursed his land in turn. She did not deserve to burn. She did not deserve to rise. She only deserved pain. Only deserved nothing. To *be* nothing.

"Emperor," said Sushant. All eyes turned on him. "My people are from the land surrounding the Veri. And I . . . I may be able to suggest a way to meet her. And defeat her."

Sushant began to speak. And Chandra—pain a lance behind his eyes and through his heart—listened with clenched fists. He wished he could place his hands around his sister's throat. The sick fear that had coursed through him at the sight of the rot-riven crops had alchemized into a rage so encompassing that his only choice was to unleash it.

It was what his sister deserved.

Tomorrow, he would let Hemanth talk to him. He would let Hemanth tell him of the rot in Parijat—for surely, that was what the High Priest wanted to speak of.

And then he would trust the knowledge the mothers had surely placed directly in his heart.

I am the answer, not my sister.

Never my sister.

He would send his men to the Veri. All the men he could afford. And he would crush her. Obliterate her.

She did not deserve to burn—to *rise*. No, the only thing Malini deserved was to die.

Chandra went to the temple long after dawn. He went, and saw Hemanth approach, smiling, to greet him.

He watched as Hemanth's smile faded at the sight of Chandra's face. "Emperor," he said.

"High Priest," Chandra said in response. "Tell me what threat faces me beyond *mortal men*. Tell me what you've been hiding from me."

Chandra flung the sack to the ground. Rot-riven flowers tumbled out, the stench of flesh and decay filling the air.

The High Priest did not flinch back. He looked at the flowers, then raised his face to meet Chandra's eyes. He looked like he had always known this would come.

"Ah, Emperor," he said sorrowfully. "This is not even the smallest part of what I fear."

BHUMIKA

The sickroom was tense. Dark. There was no noise but the rasp of breath; one small body laboring over air, and Ganam matching the cadence of it. In, out. In, out. As if he were keeping them both going by sheer determination alone.

"Ganam," Bhumika said. She entered the room quietly.

"Kritika's just been." That was Ganam's low voice. "She doesn't know what to think. She doesn't want to admit it to me, but I know her. I saw it in her face."

"How is he?" Bhumika asked. She was not far from the bed now. There was a blanket over Rukh's body, but he'd managed to kick it aside, or it had been shifted, and Bhumika could see one bare foot; one thin ankle, vulnerable, limned green.

"He's sick," Ganam said in a low voice. He was sitting by Rukh's bed. "He said Ashok—did something to him. Before he stopped talking again."

Rukh was unconscious. There were new veins of green at his throat. The rot had spread further upon it; reached its tendrils through his blood, his organs. Priya would be heartbroken.

Bhumika touched her fingertips to that ankle. The boy didn't even twitch. But he was warm, still. And the realization brought a lump to Bhumika's throat.

Rukh. Her daughter. Her *daughter*.

The fear was constant inside her. The vise of it was only tightening, with every single thing the yaksa did.

"I'll return," she said softly. Ganam said nothing as she departed, his eyes still fixed on Rukh.

She didn't seek out Ashok. She didn't have to. Everywhere she went she felt him like a shadow. And sure enough, when she walked into the orchard—beneath canopies of leaves laden with strangeness, the rot that watched her with the yaksa's terrible sentience—he followed her.

Ashok found her with her palm against a great tree that was split through the trunk by a fleshy wound. She didn't want to look at him.

"What did you do to him?" Bhumika asked. "Ashok, what did you do to Rukh?"

"He's still alive?"

"Yes, he's still alive." She turned. "Were you trying to kill him?"

Ashok said nothing, nothing, and Bhumika wanted to scream. But she did not. It wasn't her way. She drew her strength around her and looked at him—simply looked at the strangely distant, lost expression on his face. The way the earth had grown new things at his feet—flowers, buds—grasping him with green hands.

"The brother I remember was often cruel," Bhumika said levelly. "Often a fool."

"I was never a fool." He sounded offended.

"Often," Bhumika repeated, stressing the word with all the anger in her, even as she felt a rush of thankfulness that he was still in there—still sharp, still difficult, still unwilling to bend to her over even the smallest things. "But he never destroyed needlessly. He always convinced himself there was need for the cruelty he inflicted. He excused himself. So what is your excuse, Ashok? What were you trying to do?"

"I was not trying to hurt him," Ashok said distantly. "I gave him a gift."

"What gift?"

"Ask him what he knows," said Ashok. "I gave him wisdom."

"He's a *child*."

"The yaksa have always understood the value of children," Ashok replied, and Bhumika did not flinch. Did not think of her daughter. He did not even seem to realize the barb had landed. He was still talking, all swift, stumbling words. "They hollow everything," Ashok said. "They hollow the world. The trees, the plants, the people. They don't know what they're doing, Bhumika. They're ripping everything apart—changing everything—so that they may survive and win."

"What are they?" Not the spirits she'd worshipped, surely. Not this. "Ashok. What are you?"

"I don't know," he said. He sounded bewildered. She had never heard him sound like that, and it made her stomach lurch. *You are not my brother. This is not my brother.*

"You are my brother," she said firmly. "You are. But what else?" Her hands tightened on his arms. "You must tell me. They have Ahiranya. They have Padma as hostage and they want Priya. Or want to *do* something to Priya. I know they do. So for her sake, if not Padma's, if not my own—"

"I am a mask." His voice was desperate. "I am a mask. I am not Ashok at all, even if I believe I am. Even if I wish to be."

She tried to find her equilibrium. Her control. She did not want to feel like the girl she'd once been, beholden to her elders, small and obedient to the will of others. She resented the change in her circumstances wholly. She could barely breathe through it.

"This can't go on," she said. And her voice was thin, but carried in it all her conviction. "Ashok, if you are yourself—even a shadow of what you once were—will you truly harm your own for no purpose, not even the glorious future you once hungered for? Will you allow the rot to take Ahiranya wholly?"

"Bhumika."

It was not Ashok who spoke.

She whirled.

"He can't help you," said the yaksa who looked like Chandni. Today, she was wearing Chandni's mien only lightly. Her skin was the pearl of shell. "But we are yours, as you are ours, Elder Bhumika. If you have questions or fears, let me ease them."

Breathe in. Out. Bhumika forced herself not to flinch—to lower her gaze in respect and speak.

"I have been foolish," said Bhumika. "I should never have distrusted you. But it is... frightening, to face what you worship. You must forgive your temple daughter's weakness."

Chandni's silence was almost a threat.

"Tell me, daughter," she said eventually, "what you fear."

"The rot," Bhumika said. Wishing her voice were not so weak. Wishing it would not waver. "It grows worse. Our people will die."

"We are trying to make a future," said the yaksa, her eyes glowing bright. "We gave up so much to be here. Why then, shouldn't we reshape the world? Make room for ourselves, make it in our image? We are flesh and flower alike. Why shouldn't you be, too?"

Those words could not have struck Bhumika harder than they did here, in what had once been her husband's prized orchard.

"The elders once welcomed us," the yaksa Chandni crooned, as if she were singing, the vines undulating around them as lulling as waves. "The first of your kind let us in. They did it so sweetly, so easily. They were glad to have us. Glad to serve us.

"Perhaps you did not know what we were, when you entered the waters. Perhaps the ones who raised you did not know. But you let us in all the same." Her hand against Bhumika's cheek. "You are bound to us. We carved a place out inside of you and made it our home. You are no more a creature of this world than we are."

Bhumika wanted to scream. Her skin crawled with revulsion. But she remained still, allowing the touch on her face.

"And what is our purpose?" Bhumika asked. "You must understand, yaksa, as children we were taught that our purpose was to venerate you. Encourage your worship and remember you for the glory you gave Ahiranya—and for the sacrifice of your deaths. But you are here now, and I think perhaps you seek more than worship from me."

"Worship never goes amiss," the yaksa said lightly, smiling with Chandni's mouth, with Chandni's eyes that crinkled up at the corners. "But no, it is not worship we seek from you. You have the same purpose your ancient elders had, when we first came to the shores of your world and made them into more than the mortals they were." The yaksa leaned closer. "War, Elder Bhumika. A brilliance of war, so large that it sweeps all of Parijatdvipa into our waiting arms."

"You're reshaping the world," Bhumika said, keeping her voice deferential. "It will all fall to you eventually. What need is there for war that may cost you worshippers?" *Or end your time on this world, as it did in the Age of Flowers?* Bhumika thought.

She knew better than to say it. You do not confront a powerful man with his failures. And for all they were spirits, gods, they wielded power with a very human cruelty indeed.

"Necessity," the yaksa said simply. Bhumika thought she would say no more, but then the yaksa sighed, a sound like the susurration of leaves, and said, "There are natural laws that must be obeyed."

Natural laws. That meant nothing. The yaksa was hiding something from her. She could feel it.

She nodded. "I understand, yaksa," she lied.

Bhumika knew the pain of being conquered. She knew what it felt like to have your history, your culture, your pride erased by increments.

She had thought, all this past year, that she and Priya and the mask-keepers had been rebuilding. Bit by bit, returning Ahiranya back to itself. But the country they had been building—sewn together by fragile threads—was no more than a shroud for an old beast.

She had a duty to protect the people of this land. She had always tried to do so, in small ways and large. But ah, she was so tired, and nothing made her wearier than the horror that seeped through her as the yaksa before her smiled and smiled, as if she had learned smiling from a tale.

"What do you need from me? How may I serve?"

"A feast," Chandni said. "Your yaksa desire a feast to celebrate our return, that all the highborn of our land must attend."

Bhumika inclined her head. Her stomach a stone.

"A feast," she repeated. "It will be done."

SWATI

There was no rest on the journey toward Parijat, not for Swati. Every time the empress's tent was disassembled or assembled, she had to supervise the packing or unpacking of all the empress's possessions: her beautiful saris, her jewels, her weapons, her books and inks and the paper she valued so much. If any of it went astray it would be Swati's fault, so Swati did not allow anyone else to interfere with her work.

As the empress's tent was erected in a grove not far from Parijat itself—only a day's journey left, at most—Swati was mending the embroidery on the map of Parijatdvipa, neatly working in knots and markings to mimic the villages and fields they had passed. Swati worked to untangle a thread with care, tongue between her teeth. Hours might have passed, or only minutes, when she felt fingertips on her shoulder. She startled and dropped her bone needle with a sharp exhale of surprise.

"I'm sorry," said a voice. The accent took a moment to place. Dwarali. Then Swati looked up, and realized it was one of Lady Raziya's archers who had interrupted her. "Come with me?" the woman asked. "There's something you will like, I think."

"I have work," Swati said, even though the map was nearly done.

"Will your lady need her map tonight?" The woman snorted delicately. "No. So come."

Swati followed, largely out of curiosity. The archer guided her to a space behind Lady Deepa's tent, where a group of women stood. She saw Lady Raziya's other guards. A few soldiers, slouching, holding bows over their shoulders. And a handful of maids and the few high-born women of Empress Malini's retinue, all of them picking up bows of their own, staring at the wooden targets set in the distance.

"Come closer!" Sahar shouted. She was one of Lady Raziya's women, an archer and charioteer, and quite frightening for it. "Pick up a bow!"

Some of the women shuffled closer. Swati tentatively joined them.

"Lady Raziya asked me to train the women of the court, and the women of the camp," Sahar said, looking them over. "If you want to learn, you're welcome to. And if you don't..." She shrugged. "Go. I'll be demonstrating, and then we will teach any of you that want to try." She gestured at the men and the other guardswomen. One of the men waved, and his fellow soldier kicked him in the foot, rolling his eyes.

Swati wrung her hands together. Took a small step back.

"Where are you going?" the woman who had found her asked.

"There are many soldiers here," Swati said, lowering her eyes in a show of humbleness. As she did so, she cast a glance around. The many booted feet of Lady Raziya's guardswomen, the delicate sandals of some of the highborn women. The feet of the woman beside her, in narrow boots beneath a dark salwar kameez. She looked up, and met the eyes of the Ahiranyi advisor, Sima.

Swati had not known what to think of the Ahiranyi when they first arrived. But she'd always had a vague sense that the Ahiranyi were *lesser*. Not truly Parijatdvipan, because of what their ancestors had done, and the gods they believed in. But the temple elders of Parijat were her mistress's allies, so she had been respectful. When she'd heard men muttering about witches, she'd simply done her best to ignore it.

Sima was giving her a questioning look. "If you don't want to shoot, I can take you back to the empress's tent," Sima said.

Was it safe, Swati wondered, to talk alone with an Ahiranyi woman? Could she curse Swati just by looking at her?

Perhaps some would claim it wasn't safe. But Sima had shot at a golden fish with Lady Raziya, and shared barbs with Sahar, a woman Swati greatly admired for doing all the things Swati would never dare to do in a thousand years. Killing, for one; drinking a whole glass of arrack in one swig, for another. So Swati stayed where she was and admitted, "I feel shy. And I don't believe I would be very good at it." Why, oh why, had the archer dragged her over?

"Here," said Sima. "I'll show you some the basics myself." She smiled, her cheek dimpling. "I'm a kinder teacher than Sahar, I promise you. I used to help teach the children back in Ahiranya."

"Oh, I..." Swati hesitated.

"You don't have to," Sima said, in that lilting Ahiranyi voice of hers. "But when you're in war, sometimes knowing you have some power, even if it's fragile, even if it's nothing against what's coming... It helps."

Swati raised her head properly, and looked at the tents. The war camp. The women around her, and their determined faces, and Sahar nocking her bow, expression intent even as she explained loudly what she was doing, and why.

Swati took a deep breath, and said, "Yes. I'd like that too."

35

MALINI

Her army had reached the very edge of Parijat. They could go no farther without making a decision.

The army generals met at dawn. The wind was blowing fiercely—strong enough that the map had to be weighed down with stones. Priya—not a general, and not simply one of Malini's inner court either—stood behind Malini with her hands clasped at her back, letting the wind whip about her loose hair without a care. If anyone wanted to question her presence, they knew better than to say so. The fact that she was here at all was a mark of her favor in the empress's eyes.

Rao leaned over the map, swiftly laying out the options that remained for them, now that they were closing in on Parijat, with the weight of the High Prince's army behind them and an unknowable number of Chandra's men ahead of them, their own forces split and depleted.

"Two possible routes," Rao stated. "One takes us through farmland, near the main road, straight to Harsinghar—"

"Absolutely not," said Narayan, frowning. "I traveled that route many a time to pay homage to the emperor. The number of outposts and watchtowers alone will ensure we fight from dawn to dusk."

"We have all traveled that route," Prince Ashutosh said sharply, clearly unwilling to allow a subordinate Saketan noble to have the final word. "We know this already."

Narayan nodded graciously.

"You'll be less familiar with the second route," Rao said, and gestured to the lines of the Veri river—no more than a stitch of blue on cloth—to illustrate his point. "The Veri provides water to Harsinghar. To follow it is a swift route, but—difficult. The ground is bad. Crossing isn't straightforward."

"Can it be dammed? Can the city be starved out?" This was asked by a keen-eyed man in the Dwarali retinue.

"Depriving the city of water is not under consideration," Malini said firmly.

"As the empress says," Rao agreed. "And I have been told by our shared military officials—and by the Srugani officers in particular," he added, with a nod of respect to Lord Prakash, "that the river would not be easily blockaded. It is . . . very, very vast, and strong."

"No good for horses," muttered Khalil.

"Nonetheless, we will have to cross it," Prakash said decisively. "Swift travel is of the greatest importance."

"If we are spotted or face Chandra's men there," Khalil said, jabbing a fingertip to the map with uncharacteristic ferocity, "we'll be dead. I have good men. Good cavalry. But on shallow waters, Chandra's forces will have the upper hand."

They were very likely to be spotted. Malini knew that.

An army could not be moved with any subtlety. Oh, she could certainly travel with a smaller contingent: some archers, the best of her siege weaponry, the swiftest horses Khalil could spare. That would, perhaps, allow her to go undetected by Chandra's spies as she followed the river. Perhaps. But she could not take the city of Harsinghar without a full horse-and-elephant cavalry—without plenty of foot soldiers and archers to barrage the city's walls and face her brother's men.

But if they avoided the river—traveled a direct path to Harsinghar . . .

Well, Narayan had been right enough.

She did not touch the map, as Khalil had. She let her eyes trace it instead, and mark the truth for her and her alone. If they crossed the river, they would shave days off of their journey. Weeks, even, if the water was not too high and the ford was unguarded.

The ford would not be unguarded. But there was an opportunity inherent in that, too.

"There is another crossing," said Malini.

The men looked at her.

"There must be another crossing," she corrected. "Shallower waters or a bridge. There are two villages, further along the Veri, beyond the ford. Both trade in crops and in fish." Malini leaned over the map. The men stepped back, allowing her to touch a finger to the place where the villages lay. They were marked on the map by nothing but two knots of thread. Swati had knotted those in herself, on Malini's guidance, after she had found those villages in the records carried by her officials and realized she had her answer. "In many ways, they consider themselves one village. They share a name. But they lie on opposite sides of the Veri." She raised her head. "To travel across the ford without access to horses—access I am sure they lack—would take them far too long. There is a crossing."

Many of the men looked puzzled. But Khalil's eyes brightened.

"I think, Lord Khalil, you understand my intent," Malini said.

Lord Khalil picked up one of the stones holding down the map.

"You believe if your brother's army comes for you, it will come here," he said, placing the stone on one side of the river. "At the ford, where the crossing is easiest, and where their superior numbers and fire may attack us directly. In such a scenario, they would win." He pressed a finger to the other side of the ford, where Malini's army would stand— where Malini's army would surely be defeated.

"But you intend to send a contingent of your army toward a crossing that your brother's men are unlikely to be aware of. You intend them to cross unnoticed, send them toward the flank of your brother's army, unseen, unexpected, and then…" He touched a fingertip to the cloth behind the stone; drew both fingers together, neatly folding the cloth around the stone. "A pincer," he said. "Chandra's army crushed in the grip of our own. We have used similar methods, when facing the Jagatay at Dwarali's borders." Khalil's mouth faintly upticked into a smile.

"Indeed," said Malini. She knew. It was the tactics used in

Dwarali—relayed to her, over feasts, in the first weeks of her campaign against her brother—that had influenced her decision.

She had thought, at first, that Chandra intended to use something similar to trap Malini's forces: the High Prince's men pinning her army from one side, and his from the other. But he had not, it seemed, left the safety and fortification of Harsinghar. Pitiful.

That did not mean there would be no Parijati warriors lying in wait on the journey, of course. This was Chandra's territory. He knew it. He knew, as she knew, every route, every path, every inch of high ground that would give him the advantage over her.

But Chandra would not have thought of the villages, linked by a shared name, and the opportunity they offered. Chandra had never had to look for home and power in the smallest things, in the dregs that were barely worth marking by eye, by record, by map, by memory.

"It would be a risky path," another lord murmured. "If there's no crossing to be found."

"If there is no crossing, we may fail," Malini acknowledged. "If Chandra has forces prepared and waiting, blocking both sides of the ford, we may fail. There is always a possibility. You are seasoned warriors. I cannot, and will not, lie to you. But my lords, I have the will of the mothers on my side. I have the best of Parijatdvipa's royalty on my side. Fate is on our side. We will *not* fail."

They continued their journey—days and nights of desperately swift travel, lumbering across Parijat, through fields and villages, past watchful villagers. Night fell, and though they were close enough to the Veri to hear the rumble of its waters, they took advantage of defensible terrain—high ground, ringed by trees—to set up camp and rest.

A scouting party relayed to Malini and her council exactly what Malini had expected to hear: There was an armed force watching the ford. Smaller than what would surely have faced them on the main road to Harsinghar, but still nothing to be scoffed at.

Her gambit would have to work.

While Malini waited for her tent to be erected, she met with Lady Raziya under the star-flecked sky. Malini was wrapped tightly in a shawl, but Raziya was dressed only lightly, too used to Dwarali cold to be disturbed by Parijat's mild nighttime cool.

"My husband and I will accompany you to the ford," Lady Raziya said, by way of greeting.

"I will gladly face what comes next with you at my side," said Malini. "You and your archers."

"Do you have faith that my guardswomen will protect you? Die for you, if need be?" Raziya's gaze was fixed on Malini, assessing. "Because if you do not, Empress, you must train your own. You must have people you can trust."

"I trust *you*," Malini said. She did not say *not wholly, not completely*. But wasn't it enough that she had learned to admire and rely upon Raziya's strength, just as she relied on Lata's clever mind, or Rao's faith, or the small, flickering light of Deepa's ambition? "I am grateful for the friendship you've given me."

Raziya nodded.

"When your throne is won," she said, "I look forward to seeing the vows that formed our friendship fulfilled."

Later, in her tent, Malini went through her evening rituals, preparing for bed, forcing her racing mind to calm.

When all was complete, she sat on her bed and waited in the darkness.

She heard Priya's voice long before she heard a single footstep.

"Sima's gone somewhere with Lady Raziya's women again." Voice pitched low. Now, Malini could hear Priya's footsteps, each one a scuff of noise against the tent floor, marking her path. "No one saw me come here."

"You're very good at being invisible when you choose to be," Malini said, fondness bleeding into her voice.

Priya kneeled by Malini's cot. The light was so muted here that Malini could barely see her. But she was keenly aware of the presence of Priya beside her: the dark shadow of her hair; the breadth of her shoulders; one strong, callused hand, pressed to her bedding, fingers curled.

"You asked me here for a reason, Malini," Priya said. "Aren't you going to use me?"

A breathless feeling moved through Malini—a bloom that was all heat. Priya must have seen it in her face, because Priya's breath hitched. She heard the rasp of cloth as Priya uncurled her fingers and pressed her hand flat to the bed, fingers outstretched.

Malini wondered if Priya's skin was flushed. If she leaned forward and pressed her hand to Priya's cheek, she would know. She wanted to reach out. Her own hands ached sweetly with the urge.

"You're asking about the battle ahead," Malini managed to say.

A pause. Then Priya exhaled. Almost another laugh, but not quite.

"Yes," she said. "Why not."

"Come and sit next to me, then, and we'll talk."

Malini moved to the side so that Priya could sit on the bedding beside her; so Malini could lean forward and reach in the dark for the supplies she always kept at her bedside: oil lantern, wick, flint for a flame. A ledger full of cramped writing.

"You have your flaws," Malini said, trying to remember herself. "There are things you're not...the best suited for. The politics. The games." The very things that exhausted Malini too, for all that they were her strength—her version of war, that never seemed to cease. "I knew that when I asked you to come. But I thought it worth the risk. I needed an ally I could trust, and I needed an ally stronger than any other. I still do."

"You have so many allies, Malini," Priya said quietly. "I'm no better than any of them."

You're the only one who has everything. All my trust. Surely you know it.

"False modesty doesn't suit you, Priya. And you must know my allies are..." She stopped. "I've always known that one ill wind could send them scattering. And what happened in Saketa—the fire—was very ill indeed. It will grow worse from here. We cannot avoid battle before reaching Harsinghar. And when we reach Harsinghar, *if* we reach Harsinghar..." Malini exhaled. "You've grown stronger, haven't you? Magically?"

Priya said nothing.

"I saw what you could do in Ahiranya, before you had your full gifts," Malini went on. "You don't need to pretend." She'd heard of what had happened to Chandra's soldiers when they'd attempted forays into Ahiranya, too. The thorns gouging them open. The nooses of vine. "When Chandra sends his forces against us, my own army will suffer great losses. We're not at full strength. He's splintered us in two, cleaving us between Saketa and Parijat." And how bitter that was: the knowledge that Chandra had done something *right*. "We'll be further splintered when we cross the Veri. But, Priya, you are a weapon he cannot defend against. He will not expect you because no one who serves me—no matter what they claim—understands what you're capable of. So I would like to keep you in reserve. To have you ready for Harsinghar. But if the worst happens upon the Veri—if our gambit fails—will you use all your strength to save my army? Will you do it as my ally?"

Ally. As if that encompassed even the half of it. But Malini could not ask for this on the basis of whatever lay between them: a handful of furious kisses, a knife against a heart, a broken flower around a throat, a yearning that never truly seemed to abate.

There was something unreadable in Priya's face. Something guarded. After a moment, she inclined her head. Yes.

"I'm stronger in Ahiranya," Priya said quietly. A confession. "I'm—all my power—is bound up in the land there. But yes. I'm still stronger than you remember. Even here, far from home."

"Should you be telling me your weaknesses, Priya?"

"Don't you know most of them? Haven't you done your best to learn them?" Priya said immediately. When Malini stiffened—and surely Priya felt it, as close as they were sitting—Priya muttered a curse. "I'm sorry," she said awkwardly. "That sounded harsher than I meant it to. Ah, spirits, Malini. I don't know what to do anymore—"

"Don't you know most of mine?"

Priya blinked at her.

"What?"

"My weaknesses, Priya. Don't you know them, too? Just as I know yours?"

Priya looked at her and looked at her, and somehow the looking had drawn them closer together. Malini could feel Priya's breath, a ghost of a kiss on her skin.

"Yes," Priya said slowly. "I used to."

"You still do." Why did those words feel like a plea? Malini forced herself to lean back, straighten her spine. "Am I forgiven, Priya?"

"Forgiven for what?"

Malini said nothing. She was not sure what she wanted forgiveness for the most: for demanding that Priya come here, leaving behind the home she wished to defend. For not yet fulfilling her vow to set Ahiranya free. For everything that had happened since Priya's arrival in Saketa. For things she had done, and things she was yet to do. There would be things, surely, that she would do that would hurt Priya. That was the nature of her.

"Malini," said Priya.

She felt Priya's knuckles brush her cheek. One hand, then the other. And Malini wanted to sink into it: the feel of Priya's skin against her. Priya, unfurling her hands and pressing her palms to Malini's jaw. But she could only hold herself tense, frozen in Priya's hands, because if she yielded, she would do so entirely, and she didn't know if she would cling to Priya and weep, or kiss her until they had no breath left between them. The uncertainty frightened her.

"I forgive you for summoning me to your battle," murmured Priya. "I forgive you for wanting my power and wanting to use me and then—not. I forgive you for the day you *do* use me. And I want to remind you that I don't fear being your weapon. I know you."

"You know one of my faces."

"Yes. The one that's under my hands now," said Priya. "The real one."

Priya didn't hate her then. How foolish, how terrible, that Malini had come to the point where it mattered to her so very much that Priya did not hate her. That on some level, in some way, Priya's heart was still hers.

She could have reached out, then. Could have said *Stay*. Could have turned her head and kissed Priya's palm. Her fingertips. Drawn her close and then down, down onto the bed.

"Go with Rao, in the morning," she murmured instead. "Go with him and find the crossing. That's what I ask of you."

"Yes, Malini," Priya said, and it sounded like *Yes, Empress* too in a way that made something dark and wanting burn in her blood. There was a smile in Priya's voice as she rose to her feet; as she slipped away as quietly as she had arrived, her footsteps as much a whisper as her voice. "Whatever you say."

36

PRIYA

Priya and Sima traveled together in the juddering chariot along the edge of the Veri, which roiled and glimmered in the rising sunlight. Priya made a point of ignoring Low Prince Ashutosh, who was riding ahead alongside Prince Rao.

It was Rao who went to the village by the riverside and paid a woman to show them the way to the crossing. As she guided them, she looked back nervously every few footsteps. Priya couldn't blame her.

The crossing she led them to was not quite a ford—not shallow enough to be easily passable by horse or foot—but was a curve in the river where the water was broken, slowed, and softened by small islets emerging from the waves like the vertebrae of a great spine. There were boats on the shore—light contraptions with oars, but properly made, with enough space and strength to carry across a horse at a time, or a handful of men, or some of their heavier weaponry if they balanced it with care.

Priya, glad to be free of the chariot, moved to stand at the edge of the water. It was dark even here, frothing as it rocked against the bank. Sima came to stand beside her; knocked her shoulder lightly against Priya's. "The owl head over there looks like he's going to cause trouble again," she muttered.

The owl head in question was Ashutosh, striding over to Rao's side.

"If one of us moves closer, we should be able to hear them," said Sima.

"Are you curious?"

"Of course I am," said Sima. "Aren't you?"

Of course she was. But Priya had to bite back a laugh at the thought of her and Sima inconspicuously shuffling toward the two men. Their days of being invisible were long gone, unfortunately.

"Let's just approach them," Priya said. "I need to speak to the good Low Prince anyway."

"Alor is known for its rivers," Rao was saying with barely feigned patience.

Ashutosh snorted. "Forgive me, Prince Rao," he said, in the kind of voice that suggested he was about to say something that might in fact be unforgivable, but didn't much care. "You're barely familiar with Alor anymore, never mind its rivers. Raised in the imperial mahal as you were, who can blame you? Whereas *my* estates are surrounded by lakes. My men are trained for this. We will go first and secure the opposite bank. Your men will follow."

"And what does Lord Narayan think of this plan?" Rao asked.

"Narayan does not outrank me," Ashutosh said sharply.

"He's the empress's Saketan general," Priya said. She couldn't help but enjoy the glare Ashutosh turned on her, even as he bowed his head stiffly in a gesture of respect, which she returned with a smile. "I'm sure he'd like to help."

"Shall I call him here, my lords?" Sima chirped.

"That would be helpful, thank you," Rao said with a nod, and Sima turned and left. "Low prince," he went on, once again meeting Ashutosh's gaze. "If you are willing to take the risk of forging ahead before my men, we are grateful."

"It's no risk," Ashutosh said. "My men are well trained. And you, elder," he said, turning his attention abruptly on Priya. "What will you be contributing to our efforts?"

"I am here under Prince Rao's protection," Priya said, knowing he'd interpret that as *nothing*. "Are your men recovering well, my lord?"

Ashutosh's throat worked. "Yes," he bit out. "They'll be joining me in the crossing."

"I am glad to hear it."

He gave her one more nod. Said, gruffly, "Prince Rao." Then he stalked off.

Rao was watching her. Priya met his eyes, feeling oddly defiant.

"Prince Rao," she said. "Is something amiss?"

He shook his head slowly.

"You're friends with Malini," he said, voice lowered.

Friends. Was there special emphasis on that word? She wasn't sure, but she nodded. "Of a kind."

He hummed in acknowledgment. "You're not very like her," he said. "That's all. You're very—forthright."

Oh, I am like her, thought Priya, even as she said nothing, even as she stared at the opposite bank—at the spindles of distant trees, and the lush fronds dipping into the eddying water. *I just wear my anger on the outside.*

The water was definitely less turbulent here—one of Ashutosh's men had dived in and confirmed there was no hidden undertow to concern them. One small islet, barely large enough for a handful of men but covered with vine-draped trees, acted as a natural resting point and a place where they could conceal themselves. If they moved slowly, with care, they'd be able to cross more or less invisibly.

Priya stood by the water's edge for a long moment, feeling the humming song of the green around her, the weight and motion of the water against the riverbed and the things that grew from it. She began to reach out subtly to reshape the world around them. But the water here didn't have the stillness of the Ahiranya marshland, or the strange magic of the deathless waters it was—it was powerful, full of energy and its own will, and trying to shift it made her head pound.

Priya left Rao with Narayan, who had arrived with a throng of archers. They waited, watchful, as Ashutosh and his men stripped off the weightiest parts of their armor, tying the metal into oilskin sacking. They waded into the water until they were chest deep, dragging the boats full of supplies in deeper after themselves. Priya was reluctantly impressed to see that Ashutosh was as willing to enter the water as any of his men.

As they moved farther into the current, Priya crouched by the edge

of the water. She let her breathing go slow and deep—not deep enough
for her to slip into the sangam, but far enough for her to stretch the limbs
of her magic. It took her an embarrassingly long time for her power to
drift across—to feel the weft of living things growing from the silt of
the riverbed, and the tangled fringe of plants breathing on the shoreline.

To feel what was waiting on the opposite bank.

Oh. Oh, *shit*.

She jerked up and stumbled over nothing. Over her own feet.

"Sima," she said. Gripped Sima's arm. "You need to get back. Find
somewhere to hide."

"Why?" Sima's eyes were dark with concern. "Pri, what's happened?"

"There are men waiting," she managed. She forced herself to let go
of Sima. Turned. "Hide, please."

"Priya, wait!"

But Priya couldn't wait. She ran to Rao and Narayan, forcing her
way through the throng of men surrounding them. "There are enemies
waiting to ambush us on the opposite bank!"

Rao gaped at her.

"What?"

"There are—"

"I heard you," Rao said. "Show me."

She swung an arm wildly out, and Rao crouched a little, following
the line of her finger. Behind him, Narayan was murmuring to the
men, directing them to draw their arrows, to ready their shields and
line the bank, and signal to Low Prince Ashutosh, if they could. Just in
case. Just in case.

"I see nothing," said Rao.

And perhaps he couldn't. Perhaps there was nothing visible, there,
to the naked mortal eye. But Priya could feel the soft grass crushed
beneath the boots; the shift of their feet just slightly beyond the reach
of her strength.

"Look again," she said. This time she watched him.

She saw the moment his eyes widened. His expression went suddenly tight. Priya didn't have to know him particularly well to read
that look as panic.

"Signal them back," he bit out. "Narayan. Signal Prince Ashutosh—"

"He's too far already," Narayan said. He was dragging off his armor, clumsy with panic. "I will follow him, tell him—"

"Don't be foolish," Priya said, shocked to hear her own voice—to feel her lips move. "Your men need you here. Light a torch, set a fire, draw their attention."

Narayan shook his head. Rao said, "We can't risk drawing attention from the enemies across the water if we haven't yet."

"But you have," Priya said. The distant thud of feet. Dozens. Hundreds? They were *waiting*. "Rao—Prince Rao—you have. Get them back here now."

But it was too late. Priya was still speaking, mouth moving, when she raised her head and saw the arrows flying through the sky.

A hush. The arrows met the water with a crash.

She felt Rao grip her roughly by the arm, forcing her behind him as if he could protect her—as if she needed protecting—and shit, where was Sima? She'd told Sima to hide, but had she? Had she got far enough away?

In the water, she saw the figures of men and horses sink through a haze of arrows and blood, their screams cut short.

There was another volley of arrows, so thick the air was black with them. The water churned, frothy with blood. Around her, the Alorans and Saketans who'd grabbed shields on Narayan's orders raised them to the sky. She heard a scream. She turned—and saw that it was Narayan, with an arrow through the thigh. She took Rao's arm and pulled him down. "Stay low," she said. "You know this, you must stop shielding me!"

"Priya!" Sima's voice. Sima dropped to her knees beside them— and dropped a heavy shield with a clang. Rao muttered something that might have been a curse or might have been thanks, and dragged it up in front of the three of them. He braced it with his arm, and Sima did the same, the two of them holding it up between them.

Priya looked around as she heard a bitten-off noise of pain. An Aloran and a Saketan soldier were shielding Narayan between them, as a third hastily tore at Narayan's trouser leg, seeking out the arrow shaft.

With some effort, Priya dragged her gaze away from the blood.

"I told you to hide," Priya managed.

"I did," Sima said. She was trembling but every inch of her coiled with tension, her arm flexed to keep the shield up. But she met Priya's eyes steadily. "And then. I came back."

There was a thud in the soil behind her—a clang as wood met metal, and Rao and Sima jerked back from the force of the arrow meeting the shield.

Malini had told her to use her gifts if the situation became hopeless. And this did seem—somewhat hopeless, didn't it? Oh, they were in the shit.

"Prince Rao," Priya said urgently. Next to her, Sima was breathing harshly through bared teeth. Priya pressed a hand to Sima's spine. Reminding her she had a spine. Reminding her to breathe. "Prince Rao. Rao. Listen to me—"

"Don't wade in after them," yelled one of the Aloran men, so loud that it drew Rao's attention away and made Priya's own voice falter. There were Saketan soldiers who had still been on the bank desperately trying to go deeper into the water, to reach the bodies of their fellows.

One of the Saketan men, up to his knees in the river, turned back. "They're not all dead! We can't leave them! Please!" His voice cracked on the last word.

Concentrate, Priya told herself harshly.

"Prince Rao, listen to me. They don't have mothers' fire," Priya said through gritted teeth; they didn't have *time* for this. Loud enough for Rao to hear her, and turn his head again. "False fire, magic fire— *whatever* it was they used at the High Prince's fort, they don't have it here or they'd be using it against us now."

"No doubt Chandra is saving the fire for the defense of Harsinghar itself," Rao said. He was not panicked any longer. He was flushed with the knife-sharp focus of a body in danger. "He clearly doesn't require it to murder us all here. We need to retreat."

"But we must cross the water if we want any chance of success," Narayan groaned out, as one of the soldiers clumsily bandaged up his leg. He tried to bat the man away. Sweat dripped from his hair. "If we do not cross, they will turn on the empress, massacre her forces—"

"We've lost any possibility of surprising them. The gambit's failed," Rao said.

"It has *not* failed," Priya said. Her words startled the men, who turned to stare at her with panicked, suspicious eyes. "They know we're here. We can't pincer them. But—but they believe we can't cross," she went on, not allowing her voice to waver or her confidence to falter. And why should it falter? She was about to hand them the key to their own success. She had to believe that. "They'll soon turn all their might on the empress's forces at the ford. They won't expect an enemy at their back."

"Because they have no enemy at their back," Rao said. "Their enemy lies dead in the water. *We* lie dead in the water."

"Ashutosh's men lie dead," Priya corrected, knowing she was brutal in her honesty. "Not all of us." She swallowed. Soldiered on, despite the sounds of dying and screaming. "Draw back, my lords, as if you're retreating. Draw back and let them think this crossing is lost to us. Let those men of Emperor Chandra's turn all their attention on the empress and then—then I'll get you across."

"Priya," Sima said in a low voice. Her face was gray. *"Pri."*

"You said you don't know everything I can do," Priya told Rao. "But *I* know what I can do. And your empress knows, or she wouldn't have summoned me. Let me do what I'm here for."

A few warriors obeyed the summons to retreat, making their way back to the shore. Some stayed in the water. Bleeding, or unconscious, or unwilling to leave the wounded or dead behind.

Narayan had been carried away by a handful of men. But Priya waited, beneath the cover of the shield, Sima and Rao beside her. Rao held the shield steady, expression grim.

"They're moving their archers forward again," he said quietly.

"They don't think we're retreating?" Priya asked, cursing inwardly. They were dragging back so obviously. If not for Priya—for the foolish plan she was holding fast to—this *would* be a true retreat.

"No, they believe it." His voice was tight. "But they can afford to leave a force of archers here. I assume their forces are extensive enough at the ford that they think they can defeat the empress without a handful more arrows."

Well, they were wrong. They had to be wrong, or this battle was already lost.

Another whistling thud of arrows. A horribly strangled shout from the water. Priya didn't even let herself wince this time. The men were withdrawing behind her in a jangle of armor and hooves and the unsteady creak of chariot wheels.

Priya tensed her muscles, rising to a half crouch.

"Guide Sima back to safety," she said. "Please."

Rao gave her a jerky nod.

"I'd rather go with you," Sima said. She was still shaking, still terrified—but there was a fierceness in her eyes that blazed.

"Sima—"

"As your advisor," she said deliberately, "and your fellow Ahiranyi, as your *friend*, I would rather be your protector. I'd rather carry a shield to keep you safe than—than simply leave you, running like a coward."

Priya shook her head.

"I won't risk you here."

"That isn't your choice to make."

"I will accompany you also," Rao said.

"You have men to lead," Priya said.

"That is one of my responsibilities," he said. "But what I must do is make sure this battle is won, Elder Priya—and I will play any role required of me. If you must live long enough to do what Malini requires of you, for this fight to end in our favor, then I'll do all I can to defend you."

She focused on the lessons of her childhood. Hollow out weakness. Move forward.

She would not allow Sima or Rao to die.

Ah, spirits, she could not watch Sima die.

So she'd leave her weaknesses—leave *them*—behind.

"The three of us will be more noticeable to them," she said, gesturing roughly at the opposite bank, "than I'll be on my own. And you'll just get in my way. So you'll both move back, or I'll make you move back. Understand?"

Priya was not sure how seriously Rao took that threat, but Sima's mouth thinned. "Priya," she said. "Please."

"There are going to be other battles," Priya said. "Sima. When this ends—when we win. Later, there are going to be other fights where it's not going to be about . . . about what I can do. And I promise when they come, you'll be by my side."

They held each other's gazes. One beat. Then Sima exhaled, her grip on the shield loosening.

"Fine," she said. "Fine, Pri. I'm going to hold you to that."

"When you move," Rao said. "We will move."

He meant, of course, that he and Sima would wait to see if she made it to the water unharmed, before they left her back undefended. But she couldn't argue any longer. She turned her focus inward.

Slow, deep breaths. Guiding her back into her own magic.

She kept breathing as she crawled from behind the shield and made her way toward the water. She moved with painful slowness—back bent, ready to throw herself flat to the ground, as she tried to be an uninteresting target. She was unarmed, small and dirtied, her hair unraveling. She was nothing and no one of consequence.

She reached the water. The arrows didn't find her.

She hoped Sima and Rao were leaving now, retreating as she had asked them to. But she couldn't look back.

Feet in, first. The water was cold, dark with blood. Someone was floating facedown near her. Fingertips skimmed the edge of her tunic as it billowed when she waded deeper.

She kept on moving. The bodies of Lord Ashutosh's men lay around her, the water barely buoying them up.

She could let herself sink now. Could reach for her magic. Could try—

Not yet, some instinct inside her said. It had a sibilant voice—rich, slithering, coiling through her blood and softening the panicked fire in it. *Not quite yet.*

It was hard to swim, weighed down as she was, shoving rafts and bodies and weaponry out of her way. But she was at the curve of one of the islets now. And there—there was Lord Ashutosh, turning his head and groaning, blood in his mouth but alive. He would have been submerged, if not for one of his men holding him up. The soldier was struggling, his left arm wounded.

She swore, half under her breath, and grasped Ashutosh under one arm. He blinked at her.

"Get out of here, you unnatural witch," he groaned.

"I'm trying to get us all out of here," she hissed, her mind working frantically. First, to get Ashutosh and his men from the water. Then, to deal with the archers. Could she do both? Was that even possible?

She looked back at the bank. Too far. It couldn't be done.

"You," she said to the soldier. "Romesh. How badly are you hurt?"

He shook his head, even though she could see the blood matting his sleeve. "I won't leave him," he said stubbornly.

"I'm not asking you to. Do you have the strength to drag him out of the water?" Priya asked, gesturing at the island with her chin.

"I've been trying," he said. "But every time we move the damn arrows—"

As if on cue, there was a whistling noise. Priya ducked her head reflexively. The arrows, thankfully, landed nowhere near them.

"I see," she managed. Water sloshed coldly over her; her fingers were pruning, her body trying to shiver for warmth. "I'm going to need you to try again."

"We'll be hit," he said flatly.

"I need you to do it," she said.

"I won't die because of your fool orders—"

"Don't try right now," she said hurriedly. "In a moment, I'm going to do something. When I do, drag him up here and you'll stand a chance."

He gave a choked, incredulous laugh.

"And what are you going to do? Murder them with your yelling? Stupid woman."

Priya ground her teeth together. As insults went, it wasn't her favorite. At least *unnatural witch* implied she had a certain level of skill and ability, even if she wasn't being lauded for it.

"I saved your life, didn't I?" She bared her teeth into a smile; sank deeper into the water, drifting carefully away from him. "I can do anything."

The last time she'd been in water as tainted as this and drawn on her gifts, she'd fallen into a dead faint. But she couldn't think of that. She couldn't allow doubt to creep in. She was in the thick of a massacre now, after all—on the brink of the collapse of all Malini's efforts, Malini's war. And if Priya had a part to play, then by the soil and sky, she was going to play it to the hilt.

She sucked in a breath. Shallower than she would have liked, as Emperor Chandra's Parijatdvipan archers in imperial white and gold drew their bows once more.

She sank beneath the water as the arrows began to rain, and she let her magic free.

The water wasn't in her grip. The silt beneath her feet—mud and fine rocks, the tiny bones of fish—wasn't rich in plant life either, curse it. But she could feel enough: algae, a faint shimmer of green. The roots of things that grew abundant along the river bank. And older roots, deeper roots, of the trees upon the islets that had once been islands, and of trees long dead, their husks still winding beneath the river bed.

She reached. And *pulled*.

The magic writhed.

It didn't want to obey her. She was asking so much from the soil, the roots, the earth.

This was not Ahiranya, where the green sang and moved with her easily. She was far from home, weaker and weakened. But she was also stubborn, just like she always had been, and she was not going to give up now. She reached deeper, and held on harder, throwing all her strength behind that movement of magic calling magic, of her soul reaching out, and the green reaching back.

Her head ached—it felt as if her skull were splitting, too tight for the power unfurling inside it, splitting through her with roots as vicious as teeth, gnawing her flesh open. *Stop*, everything in her screamed. *Stop, this is too much, too fast, too far.*

Her strength wasn't enough. The water was too heavy. The green too small. And for all that she'd been healed—that Bhumika had healed her—Priya could feel the echo of the false fire like a scar through her lungs. Breathing around it was hard. It made her magic fracture, twist.

She reached harder. Grasped the strength of the world around her. *Obey me*, she told the green. *I am a temple elder, I am thrice-born. I won my power by strength and sacrifice, and you will yield to me. You will.*

You will!

A pause. And a moment when the pain in her skull sharpened to a knife—and then the green yielded to it. An animal pinned, throat bared.

It was hers now.

Come to me.

Everything she could touch with her power breathed and struggled and rose with her call.

The earth shuddered. Shuddered again. The pain in her skull grew and grew, and through it, she forced her eyes open in the murky water and saw, through the shifting gloom, the shape of the silt breaking in two. Of roots rising up, reaching. Felt it, as the water moved, displaced by the violence of the ground beneath it. She stretched a hand before herself and drew the soil toward her own body.

Even through the water she heard the cries of shock and horror on both sides of the river as the green banks crumpled inward, responding to her. The water was clouding with dirt and blood, growing darker and darker as the water roiled and the earth churned, and the river began to collapse, pulled inexorably into her orbit. The water was hers. The earth was hers.

The tightness of her skull shattered, so swift it was like a blow, leaving her gasping—mouth open against the water, her nerves fraying with an agony so fierce it left her numb—and the darkness rushed over her.

Silence.

She knew she was in the sangam even before her eyes opened. She was lying on the convergence of waters—lying with her arms spread out and her shadow of a body floating, and gentle hands carding through her hair, gathering the weight of it together, then letting it flow free again. Those had to be her sister's hands. When she tilted her head, water lapping against her forehead, she saw it was indeed Bhumika leaning over her.

"You've used too much of your strength, little sister," Bhumika said. Her voice had a sweetness like sugarcane. She was all warm brown skin, dark hair, smiling mouth. No part of her was made of shadow. "In a moment, your flesh will need to breathe. And then you will drown."

Above Priya—above the shape of Bhumika's face—Priya could see stars blooming. She forced her mouth to open.

"I don't want to drown," she managed.

"No one does."

"That isn't what I'm here for."

Bhumika's hands moved from Priya's hair to cup her face.

"What are you here for?" Bhumika asked curiously, keeping Priya's face above water. As if, by keeping it above water here, she could do the same in the world of flesh. "What are you trying to do?"

"Use my power," Priya said. "Win this battle. That's what I want to do. Turn the river against them. In Ahiranya I could do it. I know I could."

"You're not in Ahiranya," said Bhumika. "You're on land that hasn't known the touch of the yaksa in far too long. And you're still weakened, Priya. You've made an error."

Fond, chiding words. And yet . . .

"Bhumika," Priya said. "Aren't you—angry with me? Sad that I'll die?" She looked up not at the stars this time, but into Bhumika's eyes. "You don't seem like yourself."

"I can give you what you want," Bhumika said calmly, eyes almost luminous. "You can have your strength. You can turn the waters with your mortal hands. All of that can be yours, if you want it as much as you think you do." Bhumika's hand curled tighter around Priya's face, fanning her jaw, the nails sharp points of contact. "But every time you come to me, the bond between us grows stronger. Every part of you becomes more mine, and every part of me is consumed in turn. We're changing and shifting together, sapling. And it is sweet. I don't deny the sweetness. But you should know I'll demand something in return, for the privilege of power, and the privilege of having me."

Sapling.

A cascade of memory swept over her like drowning waters: the yaksa with a mouth of thorns; the yaksa kissing her; a yaksa's nails cutting her cheek open; Priya's own hands carving open her own chest and offering all of herself, all that she had left, all that remained of her heart—

"Yaksa," she breathed. "Why do you wear my sister's face?"

"I don't want you to speak to your sister," the yaksa said simply. Smiling with Bhumika's mouth, or something that resembled Bhumika's mouth. Even as Priya watched, the teeth grew too pearly, too sharp, the lips as bruised and curled as petals. "I want you to speak to me."

All this time. The first time she reached Bhumika in the sangam. The moment when she'd almost turned back to Ahiranya, and then seen Bhumika and changed her mind—all this time—

Dread pooled in her stomach and worked its way through her, turning her blood to ice. Bhumika. Had she spoken to Bhumika at all, in truth, since she had left Ahiranya? What had happened to her sister—to everyone she'd left behind? The horror stroked fingers up along her spine. Lies upon lies. Could she believe anything she had seen in the sangam? Could she trust herself, if she couldn't even recognize that her sister was not her sister?

Priya tried to move, tried to rise—and felt the yaksa's grip tighten further.

"You want to win? You want to kill those who stand against you?" The yaksa was smiling, smiling, luminous in the haze of starlight. "Then we must work together. Your flesh, my strength."

"My flesh," Priya repeated.

"Your flesh," the yaksa agreed sweetly. Her nail traced Priya's cheek. A hot shadow of pain followed it. "My strength."

"Last time, when I thought you were..." Priya paused, gathering her words. *When I thought you were my sister. When I thought you were as human as I am. When I did not know you were a yaksa, with all that entails.* "My body went—strange. I went strange. I thought it was my own weakness."

"Not weakness," the yaksa murmured. "Little bud. Tell me. What is worship?"

"Hollowing," Priya whispered.

"And what is power?"

Priya said nothing to this. Power could be so many things. When she thought of it, she thought of Bhumika, tiredly working to hold all the shards of Ahiranya together; of Malini walking on a knife-edge. Taking Priya's power to bolster her own. And Priya... letting her.

"I don't know," she said, feeling unutterably small in the yaksa's hands.

"Sapling," the yaksa said tenderly. "You are an elder. You must know that power is a magic like any other. It demands sacrifice."

Sacrifice.

The waters swirled around them and the yaksa's face continued to change: flesh to wood, hair to vines, the eyelids lush with lichen.

"If I say no?" Priya asked. "Will you let me drown?"

"Ah." The yaksa's fingernail traced her jaw again. Possessive. "No. Death isn't so bad, sapling. I'd keep you even then. A fine skin, you'd make—a fine shell with good bones. But no. I want you as you are, living. But this battle will be lost, and many will die if you refuse me." The yaksa leaned in closer, its hair a cloak around them. Vine and darkness. "I do not care if mortals die," said the yaksa. "Not these mortals. But you do."

She didn't care about that damn Ashutosh, or Romesh, or any of the other soldiers, even if she didn't want them dead. Didn't care. But.

She thought of Sima and of Malini. Of Lady Raziya and Prince Rao, and said, "What does it mean? What price must my flesh pay, when I'm already hollow for you?"

"You gave something away that is mine," said the yaksa. There was a reverberation: a great drumbeat that made the entirety of the sangam rock, and Priya's own shadow form fracture into wisps that drew together again with a shocking snap as the yaksa snarled and held her skull still. "You have no more time, little one. But you must get it back for me. Promise."

A promise to a yaksa. A vow that couldn't be broken.

Priya couldn't feel her racing heart or tight lungs, but she felt fear—the kind of fear that doesn't need a body to give it shape. She thought of hollowness and magic; she thought of Sima on the bank of the river, waiting for her; of Malini, staring at her with want that was deeper than deathless waters; of the real water that surrounded her, heavy and thick with blood, and the people caught inside it.

Distantly she felt her body calling her home.

"I will," she said. It felt like a mistake, even as she said it. And yet, it was also the only choice she could make. The only one. "I vow it. Yaksa."

The yaksa's eyes glowed, a brilliant vermilion. Hands pressed Priya beneath the three rivers of the sangam. She breathed in, one terrible breath that hollowed her lungs with cosmic waters, and she was full, whole, changed. She was—

—rearing up out of the Veri. She spat water. Bared her teeth in a howling laugh and threw up her hands, taking the silt beneath up with her.

She felt the water rising with the earth; felt it as Romesh scrambled up onto the island, sweating and bleeding, Prince Ashutosh in his arms. Felt it, as the tree above them split and unfurled and wound itself into a new shape. A shield, a carapace.

She felt it as the waters parted around her, and the roots she'd drawn up from the earth shaped a high bridge—open now, a path that Rao and Narayan's men could take directly to the flank of Chandra's waiting forces. They could do exactly what she'd promised. Malini would not fall.

But the water—she could not hold every mote of it steady forever. So she did the only thing she could. She let it go, and sent it where it would do the most good to her.

She saw everything in pieces:

The men on the opposite bank collapsing, snared by the ground around them.

The water roiling toward them, faster and faster, all of its weight driven by nature and by her unnatural hand.

The water hitting the bank with a roar, a beast swallowing them whole as wind whipped her hair and her magic howled through her, fiery thorns in her blood, her bones.

She heard. Screams.

The yaksa's voice, a croon that rose in her skull like a song, drawing them out:

Good, sapling. Good. Just so.

Good, Priya thought nonsensically in turn. *Good. It's done.*

And then she let her eyes close, and her body fell once more.

37

MALINI

Across the ford, in a gleaming expanse of sunlight, stood Chandra's army.

"They have more men than we thought," Prakash said in a grim voice. In the chariot beside her own, he stared out at the army with a set, determined look on his face. "This must surely be the bulk of Chandra's forces. But..."

"He isn't there," Malini said, answering Prakash's unasked question. "I can see no sign of his chariot. His banner."

"He may not wish to be conspicuous," suggested Prakash.

"Oh no. My brother always wishes to be noticed. If he were here, we would know. Clearly, he refuses to face me in open battle." She felt the derision in her own voice like venom. "How little he thinks of his own kin, and the men who stand against him."

She watched the movement of distant flags on their staffs, white and gold just like her own. Imperial versus imperial. But where her army was made up of Parijati and Srugani and Dwarali, dressed conspicuously in their own colors with their own weaponry to hand, Chandra's forces were Parijati through and through.

Why had he sent so many men? Did he truly have a large enough army to hold Harsinghar without them?

It wouldn't matter, of course, if these men defeated Malini's right here, at the Veri, where their superior numbers would decimate her own.

"We hold here," she said. "We offer to negotiate." The longer they bided their time, the longer it would be before they would have to fight, and the longer Rao and the Saketan forces would have to cross the river and attack Chandra's forces from behind. She would lose plenty of men—she was aware that her strategy made that an inevitability—but keeping the count of her own dead as low as possible was a worthy endeavor.

"Of course," said Prakash. He opened his mouth to speak further.

A sudden cry cut through the air. And then another. Next to her, Raziya leaned forward, eyes narrowing, "Empress." Raziya said it sharply. She raised one hand, pointing. "Look."

Malini tightened her hands on the edge of the war chariot's walls and turned her head.

The Veri was a curving river, but so flat that it was like a silver scar across the landscape. The curve of the river, where Priya and the others were crossing, was half-hidden by the dips and swells of the landscape—well suited for the ambush that they hoped to carry out. But Malini still saw what came next. It was impossible to miss: Farther along the Veri—in the direction Rao and Ashutosh's forces had traveled at the fire light of dawn—streaming black shadows were falling in an arc across the water. They could have been birds: They moved gracefully enough.

But they were not birds. They were arrows, a huge swathe of them, released by archers in Chandra's service.

Rao, thought Malini, numbly. *Priya.*

Oh, how much of a fool she'd been to allow two of the people most precious to her to fight without her, so she could not even witness their deaths. Had they entered the water? Were they crossing, or being warned back? More arrows fell and she clenched her hands so tightly that she could feel the bite of the chariot's edge into her palms, the sweat rising up on her skin. She'd been such a fool.

There were cries of jubilation from across the water, and the sound of weapons being readied, armor jangling, elephants lowing as their reins were pulled to draw them forward. There would be no negotiation. Chandra's forces had known what Malini's gambit would be—or guessed it a possibility—and they had prepared for it.

They needed only to face her now on the ford—no enemy at their back, and a depleted enemy before them—and their numbers would eventually overwhelm her own.

More arrows fell.

The beat of hooves, as Khalil rode over to her, flanked by two of his men.

"Blood in the water," one of the Dwarali managed, panting almost as hard as his horse. "They—I couldn't get closer, but I saw—soldiers in the water—"

Prakash released an oath.

"Were all our forces in the river?" Malini asked, her voice hollow.

"I—I don't think so." Then he swallowed and blinked and said, "No, Empress. I don't know how many were out of the water and safe, I couldn't see, but—"

"You've done well," Khalil said roughly. "Go join the rest of the cavalry now. Prepare yourself."

As the rider departed, Khalil turned his attention on Malini.

"Well, Empress," he said. "We'll need to plan fast. How many men are you willing to lose here?"

"We cannot retreat," Prakash said. "They will . . . they will chase us, Lord Khalil. We would die hunted, like animals."

"If the empress survives, there is always hope that battles will be won in the future," said Khalil. His eyes were fixed on Malini's own—reading her, judging her. But waiting for her response. "Besides, my lord—Dwarali has the fastest horses. I'd be willing to take the risk."

"If you say the word," Raziya said in a low voice, "we will guide you to safety as swiftly as we can." Her own women on their horses, in their gleaming armor, were listening. Waiting.

There was no time to strategize or think the path ahead through carefully and logically. And yet Malini saw it all—saw it even as she stood on her chariot, and heard conches sound, and heard the noise of animals and dying men and the hiss and clang of weaponry, all of it the rich warning of an oncoming storm of war—the paths that lay before her.

Defeat, slow and inevitable, if she ran.

Defeated, fast and fierce, if she remained.

Unless.

She thought of Priya's strength—the steadiness and power of her. She touched her knuckles to the black flower bound by a chain to her throat—the black flower made from her own pain by Priya's hands. She breathed.

"We're showing a lack of trust," she said. "There are still men alive at the village crossing. And they are going to make it across."

"They've been slaughtered," said Prakash. "Trapped—"

"Not all of them," she said. Metal on her tongue—blood, terror. Whatever her body was trying to tell her, she couldn't allow herself to feel it. "Lives have been lost, but there are plenty of soldiers still alive. When they cross, we will move, and crush Chandra's forces, just as we planned."

"Even if they cross—and they *cannot*—their appearance will be no surprise, Empress." Prakash's voice was oddly subdued, his face grim. "Without surprise, we cannot win. Your brother's forces know we're attempting to surround them, they will not leave themselves unprotected—"

"My brother's forces know that they have rained arrows down on my soldiers, and that my soldiers are dead, or wounded, or trapped on the bank," Malini said. "My brother's forces believe, as you do, that the rest of our warriors left on the shore cannot cross. That the only strength I have is what is visible to them right now: the men that surround me. Your men. Let us use their belief against them and fight them with all our strength. Keep their focus on us, so they do not see the enemy they believe they have defeated coming at their backs, until it is too late."

Silence.

"Empress," Prakash said awkwardly, just as Khalil said bluntly, "You're relying on an impossible hope."

"I know the worth and strength of my men."

Prakash exhaled shakily. "We would be choosing death."

"You have no swift Dwarali steeds, Lord Prakash," she replied bluntly. "Nor do my Parijati soldiers. I may live—and Lord Khalil's men may live, and his wife may yet live, and her women also—but there is no choice for you but death in flight or death in battle. If you will not trust me, then trust this, at least. And make your choice."

No time. No time. But Chandra's soldiers hadn't yet crossed the ford—were preparing their archers, as Malini's own arrayed themselves along the bank. The guardswomen were drawing shields, preparing to defend the chariot where Raziya and Malini stood. So she had long enough to watch Prakash's expression crumble, then grow resolute; for his shoulders to straighten and for him to say, "I will trust in your choice, then. Empress."

"General," she said in turn. Inclined her head. "And you, my Dwarali general?"

Khalil was silent, his eyes hooded, thoughtful. He looked, not at Malini, but at the woman next to her. He gave a nod.

Whatever had passed between them was enough.

"As you said, Empress," he said finally. "I and my wife can flee. As can you. And your hope seems false." A quirk of his mouth, mirthless. "As a man who has used this very gambit, I know you've failed."

"Lord Khalil," she said. "I have long considered you one of my strongest allies. You have come this far. You waited against all hope for Aditya to rise to his fate in Srugna. You have accompanied me, every step of the way, as I have striven to meet my own. And my fate—my purpose—has not failed me yet. Will you be my ally here now, too? Will you trust in my fate?"

"I am no worshipper of the nameless, to place my hands in prophecy," he said.

"But you are a worshipper of the mothers, and *I* am their hands," she replied.

"I have long thought," he said eventually, "that loyal allies must receive loyal rewards."

"An empress fulfills all her debts, Lord Khalil," she replied, hoping the look on her face, the weight of her words, mirrored his own. "But an empress must gain her throne in order to give her words the weight of action."

"I will hold you to that, Empress." He tugged the reins of his mount; turned. "I'll prepare the cavalry. We'll throw all our might at them, and see what comes of it. Apart from too many dead horses." He patted his own mount's neck. "Survive, Empress."

"I will," she promised, with utter surety. She had no room for doubt. Either the miracle she'd asked Priya for would manifest, or Malini would soon be dead. And the dead had no capacity for regret anyway.

"Lord Prakash," Malini said, when the orders had been given. "Neither of us are great warriors, fit for wielding weapons in battle, I think."

He inclined his head in agreement.

"But I will be glad to stand beside you and shape this battle together," she went on. "I will be honored to have your guidance, as my elder, and to hear the wisdom my father once placed great trust in."

Some of the wariness, the flint her harsh words had brought out in him, softened. She saw it in his eyes.

"And I will be honored to guide you," he replied.

On one side of the ford stood Chandra's army. Archers and riders; chariots gleaming and flags flying, all imperial white and gold. On Malini's side of the ford stood her foot soldiers; her archers, higher up the bank, poised and ready to fire. Her Dwarali horsemen, holding their mounts still. Waiting for her orders.

She raised a hand. A conch was sounded.

Both sides moved forward like two clashing waves. Foot soldiers racing forward—Chandra's army outfitted with sabers, her own with maces and whips and daggers and swords, and then nothing but bodies crashing into one another—and arrows flying thick and dark from both sides of the water.

Her Dwarali riders surged forward with a cry, white mounts racing into the gleaming water.

And Malini stood tall in her chariot, bearing witness. She breathed through the scent of blood and water, as the water's edge turned to a froth of unending mud under hundreds of feet and hooves.

One thing was in her favor: Chandra's men clearly had less familiarity with the fighting styles of Srugna or Dwarali. They were struck down by maces—skulls abruptly reduced to meat, bones broken through their armor. Arrows caught them with brutal speed, Dwarali soldiers crouching on the backs of their steeds with their bows drawn for attack. As Khalil had told her, Dwarali horses were not used to warfare on water, no matter how shallow, but their riders were confident, holding them steady.

They're not seasoned, Malini observed, watching her brother's Parijatdvipan soldiers with a critical eye. They were clearly well trained. They fought fiercely. But there was an edge of cruelty and cleverness to a battle-hardened man—to her own men—that these did not have.

Slowly she began to realize that these were men reared and trained in the imperial city of Harsinghar or surrounding Parijati estates. They should have been Harsinghar's last line of defense, not the first.

What are you doing, Chandra? Malini thought, frustration and dread worming through her—she could not understand his scheme, his intent.

And then abruptly, she stopped thinking of Chandra entirely.

Malini felt the rattle of her chariot around her—gold and steel and gilded wood trembling. The horse reared uneasily, barely calmed by the charioteer's practiced hand. She steadied herself, widening her stance, and Raziya grasped her shoulder tightly—remembering, perhaps, the chariot that fell when they first faced Chandra's fire outside the High Prince's fort. Then together they looked to the Veri, to the distance, where the arrows had fallen.

At first, Malini saw nothing.

And then, the water was rising. Not like any natural wave that Malini had ever seen but like a wall, a shield. It was bright, huge. A shining mirror, reflecting death.

It fell with a roar, crashing onto the far bank, moving with terrible fury, into the flank of Chandra's army.

Too far. They were too far to see everything in perfect detail, but the explosive howl of the water was undeniable; the sheer size of the wave, and the power with which it swept over the bank. It swept over people, dark shapes running, running—then abruptly swallowed them. Malini's mind could barely comprehend it. She was frozen. Her men around her were frozen.

A noise split the air—almost inhuman, a wail of grief and horror from one of Chandra's men.

All the men in the distance were dead.

All those people, she thought. *All of them, gone. If I had blinked, I would not even have seen them die.*

Joy bloomed out of horror, suddenly, fiercely.

Ah, Priya, she thought. *Priya, you did it.*

The wave settled.

In its place, something grew out of the water, a bridge, vast and strong, a thread binding the two banks together.

Only then did the water grow entirely calm. She watched for a moment as her Aloran and Saketan forces crossed the bridge where there had been no bridge in a sudden press of bodies, shouting in triumph.

She wanted to yell with them, wanted to scream a kind of vicious triumph out. But she hadn't won yet.

She turned her focus on Chandra's army.

There was a kind of impossible, awful forward motion to an army in battle that could not be easily halted, only slowed. Chandra's men could not simply turn back and fight the enemies at their flank—Rao's men. The Saketan soldiers. Chandra's men had faltered, were wavering, frightened by the strangeness of the water, just as her own people had been frightened by the unnatural fire at Saketa.

At the maze fort, fate had turned against her. But today it was in her favor, and it was all thanks to Priya's presence. All Malini needed to do was let the tide carry her.

She raised her saber in the air and finally let out the cry bottled inside her—a thin, wild thing, like a bird of prey taking flight above a wounded hare. The sunlight caught the edges of her saber, giving the polished blade a hue like bright fire.

"For Parijatdvipa!" she yelled. "For the mothers! For your empress!"

She heard the answering cries around her, a noise that swelled and swelled, already triumphant, drowning her enemies in its song.

RAO

The water *roared*.

There was noise, crushing weight, and then—the noise of the water faded. Rao was on the ground, smeared in earth, gasping for air. The ground had sunk around him, as if the riverbed had swallowed it back into itself, churned it into silt. He got his hands under himself. Dragged himself back to his feet, wild energy roaring through him.

He saw the bridge.

He stared at it, eyes wide, wondering if he'd finally gone mad. Then Sima's hand was on his arm. Sima's voice, as if through a thick fog, demanding he move. "She's done her part!" Sima was yelling. Her eyes were wet. *"Now do yours!"*

That snapped him back into his skin. He yelled for Narayan. Called to his men to run, to ride, and the cry was taken up as they surged as one toward the strange bridge that covered the expanse of the water.

Rao swung into an empty chariot and took up the reins. "Sima," he said. "Get up here. I'll be your charioteer. You shoot."

She stared at him. Wiped an arm over her eyes and clambered up. The chariot jerked, and then the horse was guiding them swiftly over the bridge, over the water. And Sima was raising her bow, and nocking an arrow, and they were crashing into the flank of the Parijatdvipan army in a wave of motion.

Chandra's forces were crushed between Rao's half of the army and Malini's. Behind them stood Aloran and Saketan soldiers, garbed in their turbans and liegemarks. Before them were Parijati gleaming in their white armor, Srugani and Dwarali cavalry. They had nowhere to turn.

There was no clear ending to it. Only a moment when he was guiding the horse as Sima grimly shot a man through the chest. And then, as if darkness had descended and lifted abruptly in his mind, he found himself stumbling from his chariot.

There were bodies everywhere: men's screams and groans as they died, and carrion birds already wheeling hopefully overhead. But it was over. It had ended. And nameless bless them, they had not lost. They had not lost.

Prince Ashutosh had survived, to Rao's surprise. Ashutosh's men were huddled around him, watching as he was attended to by one of the camp physicians. He was gray-faced, lips mottled with cold, but when he saw Rao he gave a jerky bow of his head. Rao returned it, a strange shadow of relief blooming in his chest. He did not like Ashutosh, exactly—but he had been sure the man would die, the moment the arrows fell on the river. His survival was a small miracle.

Priya's miracle, Rao reminded himself. He couldn't entirely let himself recall the sight of her in the churning water, glassy waves rising up around her, unearthed roots spiraling above her. It made him feel as if he'd been unmoored from his skin. He breathed around the panic of it—the sense of wrongness and elation, all entangled together and impossible for him to unknot—and turned toward the ford.

He remembered the vision of the nameless that Aditya had shown him, long ago in the lacquer gardens. The way it had filled his skull with strangeness and terror. This was...possibly worse. He felt small and helpless in the face of it; painfully conscious of his mortal body and mortal bones.

He forced himself to concentrate on what was around him: the mud beneath his feet. The corpses strewn around him.

Sima, ahead of him.

Sima was striding onward without pause. It was only when she started wading into the water that he realized anything was amiss.

There was a soldier yelling at her from the bank, trying to call her back. She was submerged to the chest: Rao could only see the shape of her shoulders, the snaking line of her braid, as she waded forward through the corpses. Rao stepped to the water's edge and cupped a hand to his mouth to make his voice carry. "You don't want to be out there!" Rao called. "Please, come back to the shore."

Sima turned her head.

"No," she said, her teeth chattering. "You come in here."

"Lady Sima."

"I told you I'm not a lady!" Her voice was wild. "My lord. Prince Rao. I need—I can't. Don't you see?" A tumble of words, pouring out of her. "Priya never came back. Priya is somewhere out here and I—I need to find her."

"Sima—"

"Help me or don't," she said, and turned again, wading determinedly deeper.

Rao stripped down to his tunic and trousers, all padding and armor thrown to the ground. Then he jumped into the water after her. It was cold, fetid. He bit his tongue and waded deeper, following the figure of Sima ahead of him. He caught up with her fast. Splashed the water beside her with his hand, in a gesture that felt childish, but also better than attempting to touch her when she was trembling with barely leashed panic.

"Go back to solid ground," he entreated. "Sima, I'll find her. I promise you." Seeing doubt in her eyes, he added, "If I don't, the empress will skin me. I'm not risking that."

"I'm a strong swimmer," she said. "I..."

"I'll find her," he told her. "Please."

For a moment it looked as if Sima would argue. Then, still shaking, she nodded.

"Thank you," Rao said to her.

He waited until she'd made her way back to the bank, then swam deeper. Above him the bridge of roots arched, vast and intricately knotted, light breaking through its small perforations in bright diamonds between the shadows it threw on the water below. He called out Priya's name and heard his own voice fade into smallness, swallowed by the lapping of the water against bodies, against the struts of the great bridge.

"Prince Rao!" A yell from behind him. "My lord, wait!"

He turned and saw one of Ashutosh's men following him. The man was clearly wounded, his shoulder bandaged, blood bleeding faintly through the cloth.

"Get out of the water," Rao called back. "You'll get your wound infected."

"I spoke to the Ahiranyi girl," he said, gesturing at Sima, who was standing on the bank, with oilcloth wrapped tightly around her. "I know where the other one is. Or was."

"Show me," Rao demanded.

He led Rao to where the islet had been. Now there was nothing. The soldier pointed a hand to where exactly he'd last seen Priya, wincing as he pulled his shoulder, and said, "She protected us here. With that unnatural magic of hers." The man's mouth curled into a sneer, but it seemed more like a reflex than any true expression of disgust. Then the look faded and he hesitated momentarily, before wetting his lips and carrying on. "I saw her collapse into the water. Right—there. And I didn't see her come back up. Whatever . . . whatever she was, my lord, she deserves a decent funeral."

"You think she's dead," Rao said, strangely numb.

"Of course, my lord. How could she not be?"

How, indeed. Any right-thinking man would know that no mortal could survive after collapsing into water. No human could survive airless, weighed down by a river. Why had Rao not considered that—not even ruminated over the possibility of Priya's death?

Perhaps the hope that burned in him, despite all logic, was the result of a mind overfevered by battle. But Rao did not think so. Sometimes, a belief or instinct was a gift from the nameless. And this *felt* true: Priya was not yet dead. Not yet.

"What's your name?" Rao asked the soldier.

"Romesh, my lord."

"Wait here for me, Romesh." Rao gestured at the islet, then began to swim in the direction Romesh had pointed.

Through the water he could see fronds of things that should not have been growing there: feathery leaves so green they were almost lit from the inside; flowers the rose-rust hue of blood, and then the fading white of teeth. *Rot*, he thought at first. And then: *Priya*.

She lay beneath him in the water. Face visible, hair loose around her. Eyes closed.

He reached for her immediately, hands closing over nothing as if she were a mirage—an illusion of light, a trickery of the water. He didn't allow himself to think. Only sucked a deep breath, and dived down, the light shining through the water onto the both of them. He reached for her—

Her eyes snapped open. Black, fathomless in the dark, two points swallowing all the light around them.

She reached back.

For a moment he was entirely unmoored from his body, panicked, unable to move—and then he was...weightless. He felt as if he could breathe—or as if he did not need to breathe, as if his lungs were not struggling for air, as if he were more and less than flesh.

Worlds were revolving around them, great stars imploding and darkening into nothing as they hung suspended in darkness that rippled and lived. He felt as if a priest of the nameless had guided him into a vision and left him there; abandoned him to the maelstrom of the nameless's voice.

A coming. An inevitable coming.

Priya's eyes were not her own. She was holding him by the hand, mouthing words he couldn't read or hear, great peals of song breaking like waves against his ears. He struggled against her, trying to pull away—and then remembered himself, and reached for her instead. He was taking her back. He had made a promise. And if he did not—if he did not—

(What would Malini do, if he did not?)

Priya, he mouthed in return. Searched for his voice. Clawed it from his throat. "Priya. Whatever this is—please. *Stop* this."

She blinked. Shuddered out a breath.

And then abruptly, it was over.

Lungs heaving. Body screaming for air. Priya a dead weight in his arms. He moved her into the hold of one arm and kicked his feet against the silt, propelling them both upward. Dragged her up, up, out of the water and heaved a ragged breath. He turned her face to the side, trying to feel for the flutter of her breath one-handed. He wrenched open her jaw, trying to clear her mouth of water with his clumsy fingers. And ah, there it was—the faintest rush of air from her mouth.

It was only then that he saw the flowers. They'd tumbled from her lips—small, half-opened buds, viciously golden. There were petals threaded through her hair. When she blinked, he saw fine spiderwebs of green beneath her eyelids.

He flinched. Almost let her go. Thank the nameless, he managed to resist the impulse.

He couldn't let anyone see her like this. He needed to get her to Malini. "Romesh!"

"My lord?" Romesh yelled back from the island. "You have her? You have her!"

"She isn't dead," Rao replied. "But she isn't—decent. I need Sima, the other Ahiranyi woman. Get her a boat if you can and get her to come and meet me out here. No one else. Tell her to bring an oilcloth with her."

"I can help—"

"No," Rao said roughly. And then, with care: "You're wounded. Your prince won't thank me if you sicken. Besides, I have a care for Elder Priya's honor, you understand?"

Romesh headed to the bank with no further complaint.

Rao held Priya and waited. Waited, and did not think of Prem's death. Did not think of the wood whorls on his skin, or of his laughter, or of the way grief had carved Rao's chest open and left it unfilled.

"Stay with me, Priya," he said, somewhat ineffectually, as she breathed and bled flowers, her hair swirling in the water. "What would your people do without you?"

He didn't know how long he held her there, feeling the contraction of her ribs as she breathed, before a small makeshift boat made its way across the water, Sima clumsily directing it. Rao braced his feet against the riverbed; hefted Priya up, bending over her.

"What would Malini do without you?" he whispered, and straightened.

"Cover her up," he said roughly to Sima, as she reached out for Priya. Her eyes widened at the sight of her friend, but she said nothing; only firmed her jaw and helped Rao get Priya onto the boat. She wiped the flowers carefully away. Placed the oilcloth carefully over Priya's body, as Priya's eyes fluttered again.

"Hush," Sima said firmly. "No sound out of you, Pri. That's an order. We're getting you back to land."

Priya's mouth moved, soundless. Then her eyes closed again.

Rao stayed in the water, directing the raft with his body. Sima held Priya steady.

"Will you tell anyone?" Sima asked abruptly. "My lord. Will you?"

"Elder Priya is an important ally to Empress Malini," he said slowly. "And the empress wouldn't want anyone to know."

For a long moment there was nothing but the slap of water against the sides of the boat as he heaved it forward. Then, in a low voice, Sima said, "Thank you."

He kept his eyes on the bank. Almost there.

"There's no thanks needed," he said to her.

When they landed, he didn't wait for any of the soldiers to come and assist him. He lifted Priya up himself. "I need a horse," he barked out.

One of his men came forward with a saddled mare. With the soldier's help, and Sima's, he mounted and held Priya in front of him. Difficult as balancing her weight was, he'd be able to carry her.

"Sima—"

"I'll make my own way." She was trembling again, the bravery leaving her cold as it ebbed out of her. But he trusted the look on her face—the sheer stubborn determination in it. "Go, my lord."

He went.

Malini was no longer on the corpse-strewn battlefield but safely in the camp. Much to Rao's relief, she was not in her tent but outside it, surrounded by her guard. Lord Prakash was kneeling before her, bowing his head. When he raised it, speaking words Rao couldn't hear, there was a look of sheer emotion on his face—pure, marveling wonder.

Above her, on the tent itself, her flags were raised, the imperial Parijatdvipan white and gold painfully bright in the glare of the sun. He forced the horse to a stop. Thought of shouting out for Malini, then thought better of it. Calling undue attention seemed—unwise.

But Malini had already seen them. She turned her head. Her eyes widened, and then her face stilled, falling into a mask of calm as she made her swift way toward Rao. There was soil and blood all over the hem of her sari; dusty wind had whipped her hair askew even in its braid, faint curls haloing her face.

"Priya," she said. It was not a question—but there was something in her voice Rao had never heard, a sheer cliff edge of feeling, and Rao hurried to reply.

"She's alive, Empress."

"Summon a physician," Malini said evenly to the guard who had followed after her.

"No need," Rao said, meeting Malini's eyes and hoping she would read the warning in them. "She needs—rest, Empress. No more than that."

Malini gestured at the guard, and he went still.

"Bring her into my tent, Prince Rao," said Malini. She turned. "Lord Prakash, I will speak to you later. My apologies."

Lord Prakash bowed his head. If he thought anything of what he'd seen, Rao could not tell, and had no time to analyze his expression. All he cared about was sliding from his horse, lifting up Priya's weight, and carrying her to the tent. One of Malini's guards opened the way. She told them to wait outside.

Inside, Lata was speaking to Swati, directing her to help gather more supplies for the sickroom. When Lata saw them she clapped a hand abruptly over Swati's eyes. Swati squeaked in alarm.

"Don't worry, Swati," she said. Her gaze flicked from Rao, to Priya, then to Malini. "Empress?"

"Water," Malini said, crossing the room, smoothing down the blanket on her own cot. "Bring food, too. Swati—you won't be needed.

Only you, Lata." Without checking to see if she'd be obeyed, she went on. "Rao, lay her here."

He laid her down, all the river-soaked weight of her, as Lata ushered Swati swiftly out.

"You wrapped her like a corpse," said Malini. She crossed her arms, but not before Rao saw the way her fingers were trembling.

"She's covered in—flowers," Rao said roughly, only stumbling a little over the sheer absurdity of it. The river, crashing over men. Roots forcing themselves from silt, building a bridge. A vision. Priya bleeding *flowers*. "I had to hide it."

Muddy water stained the divan as he removed the oilcloth, drawing it back. Malini's hands hovered, not touching, as she drank in the sight of the Ahiranyi woman: the dust of green at her eyes, the petals still bruising her mouth; the snarl of them in her wet hair.

"Thank you, Rao," she said. "I'm sure you have a great deal to attend to."

He knew a dismissal when he heard one.

"Take care, Malini," he said softly. A caution.

She said nothing.

The last thing he saw before he closed the tent flap behind him was Malini touching Priya's cheek—four fingertips, tenderly pressing into the softness of it, her eyes fierce and fathomless.

MALINI

"I've told Swati to keep her distance," Lata murmured, voice low. She placed a steaming pot down and two bowls. Lifted the lid, releasing some of the steam. It was kichadi, cooked slow to a yellow, creamy thickness, likely taken from the communal pot shared by the entire camp. "She's boiling bandages for the physicians. I'll make sure the other women don't come either."

"Good," Malini said. She should have looked up at Lata—read things unsaid in her face. But she could not.

Priya was so quiet. She'd wiped some of the river murk from Priya's skin with a cloth, but her hair was still snarled and wet, leaving blotches of water on the pillow. Her eyes were closed; her gold lashes darkened to the same brown as her skin. There were gashes on her arms, and on her collarbone. They were bleeding petals.

"Your generals are looking for you," Lata said quietly.

She'd spoken to Prakash already. But oh, what a strange conversation that had been. Once he had realized the battle was truly over, he had followed her and bowed to her. *Apologized*, for all the times he had allowed her strength and her rule to be tested without interfering. "I did not treat you as what you are," he said. "Chosen of the mothers. Prophesized by the nameless. *Empress*. I will never falter again."

Usually, that confession would have brought her no end of joy.

But not now.

"Rao should distract them," Malini said.

"Shall I tell him so?"

"Please, Lata."

Malini couldn't stay away long. She knew that. They had to keep moving. They had to take advantage of this win and make their way toward Harsinghar before news of the defeat reached Chandra and he could send more men to face her own. Her path lay before her. She could not falter now.

But Priya hadn't woken.

"Lata," Malini said. "Tell him I'll join them within the hour. Please make sure no one comes to seek me out."

Lata inclined her head. She hesitated as if she wished to speak. But then she turned and walked away, the curtain of the tent swishing behind her.

Malini had thought she would struggle to stay still; struggle to keep her body unmoving. The battle felt like it was still racing through her, every roar, every shout, the hiss of every saber withdrawn. The slick, raw noise of cleaved meat.

But Priya's stillness had stilled her in turn. Malini had faced her brother's army. She had watched a river turn and a bridge grow out of nothing. Priya had saved her, as Priya always saved her.

She thought of the time they had been alone together in Ahiranya's forest. The way Priya had bled and almost died. The way they had lain next to each other by a pool of clear water, mouths bruised from kissing, and spoken of knowing each other. Of the monster Malini would have to become, for the sake of power.

Malini carefully plucked the flowers away from Priya's arms. Then she lowered her face to the crook of Priya's elbow and closed her eyes. She could smell the river—algae and soil and salt.

She felt a hand in her hair. Trembling.

Malini raised her head sharply up. Priya's eyes were open and watching her. The whites were run through with darts of green, like veins of discoloration through gemstones.

"Malini," Priya whispered. "Are you here?"

"I am," Malini confirmed. She resisted the urge to press her fingertips to Priya's cheek, or the palm of her hand to Priya's forehead—to feel for fever, or simply touch. "Have you been hallucinating?"

"I've been traveling," Priya said, which sounded like a *yes*. "I'm not myself. I think—I think you can probably tell." A laugh left her then, a laugh that was half a sob. She smiled, and the smile fell immediately from her mouth, as if her flesh refused to carry it. "What happened?"

"You drowned a swathe of my brother's men," Malini said. Hushed. She wanted to run her fingers through Priya's hair—smooth it down, pluck the green from it until it was pure and dark again. "Saved my soldiers. Allowed us to win the battle." This time she couldn't help but touch, resting her hand against Priya's own. The skin was water-chilled. "You've saved me once again."

"That's what you summoned me for, isn't it? My magic. Me saving you," Priya said. "I did it. My duty."

Malini stared at her silently. She hadn't been prepared to feel guilt. She had no use for it. But there it was, coiling up in her chest, filling her lungs so there was no room in them for air.

"It's okay," Priya said with a laugh that was all wild, sharp edges. "I wanted to do it."

Priya sat up suddenly, drawing her hand free from Malini's. She moved to stand, legs shaky under her. Buds bloomed under the soles of her feet as she took one stumbling step, then another. Malini rose swiftly in alarm.

"What are you doing?"

"Losing myself," Priya gasped out, which meant nothing to Malini at all. "Every time I go further—I become more her—not myself. She said."

"Who said?"

Priya shook her head.

"*Priya.*"

"I need to. I." A shaky exhale. Priya took another step. "My skin. I look as if I have rot. *Shit.*"

"You can stop this," Malini said. "Make it go away."

"Can I?"

"Of course you can," Malini replied, trying to pour all her conviction into her voice. "Don't look at me in that way," Malini went on, when Priya gave her a look that was unmistakable even through the flush of green in Priya's eyes, the dull light of the tent. "I may not understand the depth of your magic, Priya, but I've seen you control it before."

"What if I can't? What I'm stuck like this? What if I'm not human enough anymore?"

"We can argue about this with you lying down," Malini said. "You're going to fall."

"I threw a river," Priya laughed. "Threw it—and you think I'm going to fall over?"

"Yes."

Priya froze, limbs trembling.

She bit off a curse as she fell.

Malini managed to catch her, leaning her back against one of the tent poles. And Priya lolled back in her arms, smiling, weeping flowers from her skin.

"I told myself I wasn't doing it just for you," she said deliriously, flowers writhing from her fingertips, her scalp. "I told myself I was doing all of this for Ahiranya—my family's sake, my country's sake, my sake—but I was lying to myself, lying, lying—"

"Priya." The name came shakily to Malini's lips.

"It was for you. Maybe all of it or maybe part of it but you, you—I can't—" A flutter of broken words, little shards of words, blooming as the roses twined from Priya's skin onto Malini's steadying hands. "I barely understand it, the way I would willingly kneel for you, anywhere, for anything. The way I would fight for you. The way I want to be at your side. Is that what love is, Malini? Is that how awful love is? Because if it is, then I love you, the way that roots love the deep and leaves love the light. It's—the way I am. And no matter how much I try to be good, to do right—I'm all flowers in your arms, for your war, for you—"

"Priya. *Priya.*" Malini pressed her face against Priya's. Felt the changing skin—the rhythm of her breath, the promise that Priya was here and alive. "I should never have asked you to come," she whispered against Priya's cheek. "I should never have let you go into battle."

"But you need me. You needed me here."

"I needed you," Malini agreed. "Need you still. But not just for your gifts. Never just for your gifts. Surely, surely you know."

"I do, I do." And their faces were turning, not quite touching, sharing breath. Creeping ferns coiled out from Priya's hair. She blinked her green-struck eyes. Strangeness, horrific strangeness, and yet somehow Malini could not bring herself to let go of her. Priya's mouth parted. Words, again. Words, always cleaving distance between them. "I think there must be a scale somewhere in your head, where you weigh out how much my gifts matter to you and how much the rest of me matters, and I think—the scale is tipped, isn't it? Listing to one side. You don't have to nod or agree or—I already know, Malini. I already know."

Malini wanted to say—*Your gifts are you and you are your gifts, I don't love you in pieces, I don't separate you into parts.* But Priya would have heard the lie in that. Malini broke everyone into parts—sifted through everyone she met for strengths and weaknesses, desires and loyalties.

"Do you hate me for it?" Malini asked, framing Priya's face with her hands. "Are you angry that I don't love as you do?"

Priya laughed. A breathless sound, oddly sweet.

"Were you afraid I'd die?" Priya asked.

She took hold of Priya's hair. Heavy, dark hair, slippery as silk, riven with things flowering. Malini moved her fingers through it. She pressed her lips against Priya's neck, feeling the heat of her skin, the warmth of it. She smelled of—sweat, salt, and rain-washed soil. It should have been unpleasant, too human and too strange all at once. But Malini could do nothing but press her teeth to the tendons of Priya's throat, and breathe her in, and think with helpless hunger, *I want to taste her, taste all of her, hold her in my mouth. I want, I want, I want.*

Priya made a hitched noise—half surprise, half something else. Her head tipped back. Her fingertips traced Malini's jaw, trembling.

"As if a simple battle could kill you," Malini whispered against her skin.

She did not want to love Priya the way Priya loved her—that devotion, that terrifying gravity that took a person to their knees.

But some things were not in her control.

"If I truly feared that battle could kill you, I would never have held back my army until you drowned Chandra's at their flank," she said. "If I truly feared that you could die, I wouldn't have trusted you to rise from the water and destroy them. But I trusted you. I would trust you again. As I trust you now, to find your way back to your human skin.

"You may think you break yourself on loving me," Malini whispered. "That it makes you bow and makes you—you serve." A hitch, a stumble. She pressed on, still curved, her head against Priya's throat. "But you cannot be broken by my demands. You cannot even be broken by your own. I could try and break you a thousand times, with all my weapons, with knowledge of your every weakness, and still I—"

A hand tightened on Malini's jaw.

"Try," said Priya.

Malini raised her head and looked into Priya's eyes.

"Try and break me," Priya said. "If I'm—I'm so much, if you think I'm so much more than any other person, then—then bring me back down to just skin. Make me human. Try and break me. *Try.*"

Malini did not need to be asked again. She tangled her fingers in Priya's hair, dragging her head further back, kissing her way down Priya's throat. Her pulse, her tendons, the salt of sweat; the dip and swell of her collarbone, as Malini peeled aside the river-stained collar of her tunic so that she could set her mouth on skin unmarked by the sun, skin still water cold. Priya's arms came around her—and then Priya was brushing her mouth over Malini's forehead, her hairline, her own curling hair, achingly sweet.

There was a crash of noise somewhere beyond the tent and Malini thought distantly of her responsibilities: her generals, waiting to meet her. Lata, no doubt standing stiffly outside, waiting impatiently for Malini to emerge. Her body froze.

"I guess there's no time to try right now," Priya said after a moment. "Is there?"

Malini closed her eyes. Opened them. Straightened up.

Priya was flushed, warm blood darkening her face, the petals gone, but the strangeness still lingered in her hair and her eyes. There was still a wildness about her.

"I'll remain with you until you're yourself again," Malini said. "Entirely of your own flesh, and then I'll leave you to rest. But you will have to do so without me—breaking you."

Priya laughed, the same want and embarrassment and twisting hunger that Malini felt in her own body flickering across her face. Then Priya closed her eyes and breathed, and breathed, and Malini held her steady. Waited.

She watched the leaves wither from Priya's hair. The flowers curl to dust.

In the place of flowers lay nothing but skin—lacerated and bruised from the battle, but all Priya's own. Warm brown and alive.

Priya opened her eyes. Brown, framed by lashes more gold than dark.

"Oh, Priya," Malini whispered, tracing the shadow of a bruise beneath Priya's left eye with her thumb. "Oh. Look at you."

"You're looking," Priya agreed, with nonsensical tenderness.

"You're back. You're here."

"I'm here." There was relief in her voice. As if she really hadn't known what she was capable of. "I'm here."

Malini had generals to meet, and an army to move—but there were flower petals scattered all over the ground, and Priya in her arms.

This yearning, this want, was a force like a rising tide. It couldn't be stopped. And Malini did not want to.

"Later," Malini said, a tentative hope unfurling in her chest. "We can try again."

"Later," Priya echoed. "Yes."

BHUMIKA

Jeevan found her in her own chambers, where she was pinning her earrings into place. They were weighty things and couldn't just be worn through the lobe. Strands of gold had to be affixed in her hair to keep them in place and balance out the weight of them.

Usually, she would have had a maid to help her, but today everyone in the household was preparing for the feast, and Bhumika had not wanted to rope a girl into the pointless task of getting her into her finery. So when she heard a rap at the door, she said, "Enter," and had the pleasure of watching Jeevan jerk to a stop, embarrassment flitting over his face as he caught sight of her kneeling before her mirror, her sari a spill of dark wine silk around her.

"My lady," he said, turning his face away.

"There's no need for that," she told him. "I'm almost done. What news?"

"We have Lord Chetan," Jeevan told her. "He was—difficult."

"Where did you find him?"

"In his mistress's house," Jeevan said.

Bhumika gave a hum of acknowledgment. "So he *was* hiding."

"Not just him, my lady," he said. He still wasn't looking in her direction. So Bhumika did him the service of turning back to the mirror as she tried to hook another slender golden chain through her bound, braided hair. "I found two of his allies in a nearby pleasure house."

"They do like to complain about the economy. I'm glad they're doing their part to keep it running."

She heard Jeevan snort. When she turned around once more, his face was expressionless.

"Jeevan," she said with a sigh as the chain slipped free from its pin. "Could you find a maid for me? Any will do." She gestured at her hair ruefully. "I can't hook this correctly."

His face, still so expressionless, did something...complicated. A tightening of the jaw. A lowering of the eyes. "I," he said haltingly. And then nothing more.

But she understood.

"If you don't mind," she said softly. "I'd be thankful."

He walked over to her. He grasped one of the chains. Held the hook delicately between his slender fingers and raised it to her hair. She felt him touch one of her braids, a light pressure that shimmered through her.

She saw his reflection in the mirror behind hers. Their eyes met.

"Lord Chetan," he said, after a moment.

"Yes," Bhumika said, when she found her words. "Please. Take me to him."

"I did not want to come here," Chetan said, lips almost bloodless with terror. "Lady Bhumika, why did you send your men for me? Why have you condemned me to this?"

"Do you really believe there is anywhere you can run that the yaksa cannot find you?" Bhumika asked. "They are our highest power. They live in every part of Ahiranya—in every root, every tree, every hope we have had for our past or our future. They want all our highborn present," she continued levelly. "So you will be present, Lord Chetan, for all our sakes, especially your own."

He stared at her. For the first time, she saw something in him—a perceptiveness she had not believed him capable of. Perhaps fear had briefly sharpened his mind into something of use.

"You're afraid, Lady Bhumika," he said. "I have never seen you so afraid."

She said nothing. She had no reason to be ashamed of her fear. Anyone would be a fool *not* to fear the yaksa.

"They—they are real, then?"

"They are."

"They look—mortal."

So do I, Bhumika thought. *But I am not sure that I am anymore.*

Out loud she said, "I would show them the same respect you show your yaksa idols on your shrine, Lord Chetan, if not more. They are exactly what they claim to be. No doubt they intend to prove it at the feast." She rose to her feet and signaled the nearest guard closer. "Bring Lord Chetan water. And fresh clothes, if he wishes for them." The only men's clothing fine enough for his status had belonged to her late husband, but he did not have to know that.

"Lady Bhumika."

Something in his voice made her pause. "Yes?"

"Are they—as they were in tales? As in the Birch Bark Mantras?"

"They are..." Bhumika searched for words. "All you must do," she said finally, "is show them respect and veneration. Do not think beyond that."

"If they can see into our hearts," he blurted out. "Our minds. Then they will know."

She felt an icy trickle down her spine.

"What," she said slowly, "will they know?"

He closed his eyes.

"I told you, Lady Bhumika," he said. "I told you when we last met. Your rule has not been beneficial to all of us. We are Ahiranyi through and through, all of us. But Parijatdvipa..." He paused, swallowing painfully, heavily. "We Ahiranyi, we benefited greatly under Parijati rule. And some of us have—acted. According to the interests of the nation."

A leaden feeling in her stomach. Ah, the fool. The fool.

"I do not need to know more," she said, when he moved to speak again. "No. Do not unburden yourself to me. It is far too late for that."

"Lady Bhumika—"

"Lord Chetan," she snapped, with far more anger than she had intended. "I thought I had impressed upon you the danger of turning on me. I thought you understood the danger you placed us all in."

"You are only one woman," he said thinly. "But they. What will they do?"

"You ask me for assurances?" Her voice was incredulous. "Well, I can give you none. You will have to hope they care less about mortal politics than I do."

"Will you tell them?" Chetan asked. "If they do not know—will you tell them? Will you demand justice?"

"No," she said. "I have no need to." She swept to the door, fury heavy in her. "As you said, they already know what lies in your heart. They will make their own judgments. And you must hope they judge you kindly."

Bhumika could not delay any longer. She began to walk toward the feasting hall. At her side, Jeevan was her shadow, as always.

"My lady," he said. "At the feast. I will be there."

She waited. When it became clear he did not intend to say anything more, she said, "Of course. You'll be on guard."

His boots thumped against the marble. Her own footsteps were a swish of silk. Their rhythm was discordant. "If there is trouble," he said eventually. "If you . . . if you are in danger. I will intervene. I promise you."

"Intervene with the yaksa?"

"Yes."

"A brave thought," she said. "But it would be a pointless act."

"However pointless it would be, I would try."

"I am capable of keeping myself safe," she said quietly. "And if I can't, I would be happier knowing that someone I trust remains behind, alive, to deal with the consequences."

It was like a beautiful garden in the hall, so beautiful that she could only pause for a moment and stare at it in awe. Creepers were draped from the ceiling. Flowers bloomed at the lattice windows. A bed of sweet grasses rose from the floor that had once been plain sandstone. The mahal had long been fractured, broken by war and by root and flower, but the yaksa had turned those flowers into architecture.

Then she walked forward, a steady and even glide, between the rows of laden tables, heavy with ripe fruit, rich dhals, sabzis studded with almonds; platters of rice, colored yellow and red and gold with saffron, fat raisins, and filigrees of crisp onions flecked darkly onto their surfaces.

The yaksa were kneeling at the head of the feast, all of them seated together. To their left sat the twice-born mask-keepers and Kritika. To the right sat Ashok. Next to him was a space clearly reserved for her.

The lords of Ahiranya had come in droves. Like Chetan, many of them had been dragged here, or cajoled by Jeevan's men. But some were here for faith. She could see the certainty, the worship in their eyes.

Her lateness meant that they were all far into their meals, plates piled high, half-empty glasses of liquor arrayed in front of them.

Bhumika seated and then steeled herself; forced a smile to her mouth and reached for the food. Ashok took her hand.

"No," he said, voice hushed. He wasn't looking at her. "Wait."

"Ashok...?"

"Wait," he said again. He met her eyes. "Can't you feel it? *See* it?"

Bhumika looked down at the food. Then, she understood.

The rice on the platter before her began to glisten, soften, its surface bursting. The fruit withered, puckering like flesh in cold rain. Before her eyes, the flesh split open, seeping liquid that looked and smelled entirely like blood. The scent grew stronger, and Ashok's grip tightened punishingly.

The food was quite suddenly riven with rot.

For a moment, the room went utterly still. People froze, their mouths full and open, their fingers still pressed into bowls of what had once been food.

Then someone let out a noise—a choked, horrified scream—and the silence splintered.

Men and women wrenched themselves back from the tables, screaming. Bhumika yanked her hand free from Ashok's and stood. Flower petals fell upon her hair, their skin like flesh, their smell rotten-sweet. She could do nothing, absolutely nothing.

This was not the gentle, awful arrival of the rot as Bhumika had known.

This was fast, a swift metamorphosis of flesh to flower. She saw skin rupture, plants flowering. Saw people change, twisting before her eyes as green sprouted through skin, through hair, reshaping them.

This, then, was the purpose of the feast. *This.*

At the edge of the room, she saw Jeevan watching. Terror in his face. *Don't move,* she tried to say with her own face—with the stillness of her own body. *Stay where you are. Do not try to help me, oh please, do not.*

In front of him, a woman collapsed to the ground, knocking over bowls and plates as she went. They rolled across the floor as she crawled between them, branches of wood forcing their way through her skin. In front of Bhumika, a man clutched his own face, made an awful, broken noise as his fingers sank into mossy softness.

"We trusted, once," Chandni was saying. Her voice was as clear and bright as a song. Her unblinking eyes looked over the room of screaming, writhing people with serene compassion. "That was our error. We do not trust so easily now. Still, we offer gifts."

"Bow before us," Sanjana said, smiling. "Show your worship and loyalty, and we will ease the burden of our magic a little, so that you may continue to live."

"Or do not bow," Sendhil said. "And do not worship. And our magic will consume and keep you. We will remember your faces and your skins, and carry them with us. But you will be dead." His expression was remote. "Choose."

Bhumika looked at the room full of people. *Her* people—the ones she'd sought to protect from the empire, and lead, and provide a future. She looked at the panic in their eyes. Her limbs did not want to obey her—were trembling without her say-so—but she made them do her bidding. She walked. One step. Another. Stood herself before the yaksa.

She saw Kritika, a hand to her mouth, shaking. The mask-keepers at her side were gray-faced. Ashok stared at her from his seat, his eyes wide and lost, as if he could not comprehend what was happening before him. She looked at the yaksa who wore her family's faces. She knelt and bowed her head to the floor. Her jewelry clinked. The chains in her hair felt heavy enough to pin her skull down.

"What are you doing?" Nandi asked curiously.

"I am bowing to you," she said evenly. "I am showing you my worship and my loyalty, as you asked."

"You are already our temple daughter," Sanjana said, amused. "Already hollowed. The rot cannot touch you, daughter. And we know you are ours."

Bhumika raised her head.

"As your temple elder, it is my duty to lead by example," she said levelly. "So I have. So I shall continue to do so." She bowed again.

Behind her, other highborn finally began to understand. One stumbled forward. Then another. She heard the clink of fallen cutlery. The scrape and shuffle of bodies. Around her, shadows gathered. She bowed again, and all the highborn lords of Ahiranya followed suit.

"Good," Chandni said, pearl-eyed, smiling. "Good, my dear ones. Good. You've chosen well."

PRIYA

Priya had promised Malini, *Later.*

But some promises were older. Some things were more important. Somewhere, Bhumika was beyond Priya's reach. Had been beyond Priya's reach ever since Priya set foot outside of Ahiranya. Bhumika had not tried to seek her out. Bhumika had sent her no messages. And a yaksa had stolen her face.

Priya had to go home.

She realized now, as she quietly and carefully walked through the darkness of the camp, that she should have written a letter. *I meant what I said. Everything that I am is yours.*

But my family, my sister—

You understand, don't you? Malini. I can't stay. I'm sorry.

Spirits, she hated herself already for going. Hated thinking of what Malini would feel when she discovered that Priya was gone—had left her behind without a word.

She was almost at the edge of the camp when she heard a voice.

"Pri." A whisper. "Stop."

She turned. Sima was behind her.

"How did you find me?" Priya whispered back, as Sima drew closer.

"You were sleeping in the empress's tent, so I was sleeping outside it," Sima said with a shrug. "Those guards were useless. They didn't even move when you left."

"I did dig my way out," Priya said. A small application of a knife and her gifts had done the job for her. Hopefully Malini wouldn't notice the damage to the corner of her extremely large and luxurious movable manse.

Sima sniffed. "Still." She stopped walking. Placed a hand on Priya's arm. "Where are you going?"

"Home," said Priya.

"*What?*" Her voice was shocked, gaze searching. "Why?"

Priya thought of the yaksa, and the horror of Bhumika's face changing, of realizing her sister was a mask and nothing more than a mask. Her throat felt dry. Her whole body ached from battle, and ached with heartsickness. She didn't know how to explain it.

"Bhumika," she managed to say. And then abruptly began to cry. "Oh fuck," she gasped, and put a hand over her mouth. "I'm sorry," she garbled out beneath her hand. "I'm so—so tired. That...my magic..."

"Pri! Shit, look, don't be sorry. Be quiet." Sima embraced her bone-crushingly tight. "What happened to Elder Bhumika? Is she hurt? Don't sob, someone will come and if we need to go, we don't want that." Her grip tightened another increment. "Priya," she said with dawning, angry realization. "Were you going to go without me?"

"Let me explain," Priya gasped.

"Please do."

"As soon as I stop crying—give me a minute."

She managed to make herself stop. Wiped her face with the back of her arm. And haltingly explained it all to Sima—the sangam. The yaksa. Bhumika's stolen face, and Bhumika's silence.

"Everyone at home," Sima said in a thin voice when Priya had finished. "Anything could have happened to them."

"That's why I have to go," Priya said, voice still thick with tears. "You see? Why it's not safe for anyone but me?"

Sima was silent for a long moment. She gripped Priya's shoulder tight, some dark thing flitting across her face, through her eyes. Then she said, "What if you stay? Stay here in the empress's army?"

"What?" Priya asked, shocked. "How...how can I?"

"If they're in danger, if something has happened—what can you do

alone?" Sima's expression was conflicted. But it was growing more resolute. In a determined voice, she said, "We came here because Ahiranya
needs allies. So get allies. Let's get your empress on a throne so that
if... if something awful has happened, we can... do something. Fix it."

"I have my magic," Priya said.

"Your magic almost killed you," Sima said.

"If I stay, it won't be for allies," Priya admitted, her voice all rough
from crying, from the raw feeling inside her. "That's... that's not why
I'd stay."

It would be for Malini. For this selfish, desperate thing Priya felt
that she'd confessed in all its awfulness and ugliness to Malini, lying in
her arms with flowers growing through her skin.

"You can stay for more than one thing, Pri," Sima said. "It doesn't
make you a bad person if that's true. Besides, I'm not staying just for
allies, or an army."

"No?"

"No." Sima rubbed the back of her own hand over Priya's tear-
stained cheek. Her expression was as tender. "I'm also staying for you.
Now, let's see if we can sneak as easily back into the tent as you got out."

The army was soon on the move again. This time, Priya traveled in
Malini's own chariot, wrapped in a heavy shawl that Malini carefully
tucked around her shoulders and throat herself. When Lata made a
mild comment on the arrangement—quite rightly pointing out that
the generals and their men would notice and talk—Malini simply said
that Priya had done them a great service and suffered greatly as a result.
If the generals of her army were displeased with the actions of their
empress, they were welcome to come and tell her themselves.

None of them did. And Priya endured the jolting of the carriage,
curled on her side, and traced the shape of the embroidery sewn onto
the shawl in sinewy thread. Flowers upon flowers, twined together by
flourishes of vine that wound upon themselves in whorls, knots, clearly
embroidered by a delicate and skilled hand. She could follow them
for hours, probably, and not find the place where the thread began or
ended.

Beside her, Malini was straight-backed, staring ahead, her face empty. But her hand remained on Priya's hip, heavy and sure.

There was no sign of more Parijatdvipan soldiers on the road that day. Cautiously, they made camp. Malini was required to meet with her generals. She left Priya resting in her tent. Priya lay still for at least half an hour before she accepted that she was not tired in the slightest, and her body and mind felt as whole as they were ever going to feel. She was human flesh, blood, thoughts. No more flowers were going to pour through her skin. She felt... normal.

There was nothing she could do about the disquiet that had settled in her heart. Sharp teeth. Bruised flower mouth. A yaksa holding her up in the liquid dark.

I don't want you to speak to your sister. I want you to speak to me.

The memory shuddered through her. She pushed it aside and tried to think of more real things. Things that didn't leave her blood running cold. The thud of arrows. The weight of a shield. Romesh baring his teeth, with blood in the water around him.

Not much better. But it would have to do. At least these memories kept her in her skin.

She sat up and slid from the bedding. Rising to her feet, she neatened her new sari. Tightened the braid of her hair. When she slipped from the tent, she found Sima sitting out front with the guards.

"Pri," she said, getting to her feet. "How do you feel?"

"You're not going to believe me, but I feel perfect." It was deep night, the sky black as pitch, but the camp was brightly lit with torches. Sima's assessing look was illuminated.

Priya looked across the camp, searching. Ashutosh's men were nearer than she had expected. But that made sense. Their lord was still in the medical tent, being carefully attended to now that their journey had paused. She could see Romesh. One of his arms was bound, but the wrapping was clean of blood. That was good.

Ashutosh's men were already watching her in return.

Priya started to walk toward them. Sima matched her footsteps.

"Are you sure about this?" Sima asked.

"Absolutely."

Sima huffed. It might have been amusement. "I suppose we'd better offend them together, if we're going to do it again," she said.

"We're not going to offend them," said Priya. "We're going to make friends."

"Right." Sima sounded skeptical.

They reached the men, who looked up at them from where they were seated on the ground. They were silent.

"Mind if we join you?" Priya asked, keeping her voice friendly. "I'll only take a little offense if you say no."

Her tone eased some of the tension out of them, which was interesting. Priya hadn't known she was capable of that.

"You've saved my life twice over," Romesh said. "If you want to sit and share our wine, we won't stop you."

The men shuffled over. Priya and Sima sat down. For a long moment the silence was awkward and tense. One of the men coughed and shifted uneasily.

"How are you feeling?" Sima asked Romesh. Her voice was pitched soft—she was afraid, Priya knew, of insulting him—and he blinked at her, as if surprised by that.

"My lord got me opium," he said. "So I don't feel as shit as I should, is the truth."

One of the other men snorted. "You shouldn't say 'shit' to a lady, brother."

Sima's mouth twitched. "I'm not a lady," she said.

"Lady's advisor, then." A hand clapped Romesh's head, making him swear again. "This one was raised better. Don't think ill of Saketa because of him."

"Of course not," Sima said quickly.

"We do know how to curse in Zaban just like the rest of you," Priya said dryly. "As long as you don't call *us* shit, I can promise you we won't be angry."

"You don't act like a proper highborn," Romesh said, as if he agreed. "Don't act like I expected a priest of your kind to act, either."

"What? You thought I'd be some kind of monster?" She softened her words with a grin.

"You did turn a river into a beast. Built something out of nothing." There was a challenge in his voice, but it wasn't all unease. He respected her a little, maybe. That was good.

"I did," she agreed. "But anyone can do harm if they have the right tools. Anyone can be a monster if they have a knife. I just wear mine under my skin. I just...cut differently." That she *could* cut with a real knife—expertly and cruelly—wasn't something these men needed to know.

Sima placed a heavy hand on Priya's shoulder.

"My lady's had too much to drink," Sima said, although Priya had drunk nothing. "Ignore her."

"No, no, she's making sense," one of the other liegemen piped up.

"Am I?" Priya said.

"You're a warrior, like we are." He waved his wine for emphasis.

Romesh was watching her, wary even through a haze of wine and opium. But he offered her the bottle. She took it from him and drank. She wasn't going to reject hospitality.

She settled herself more comfortably on the ground. Tucked her feet under her and said, "That's good stuff. Tell me, do you arm wrestle?"

"Every soldier knows how to arm wrestle."

"I have some arrack," said Priya. She didn't, not anymore, now that everything had burned. But she was sure she could procure some if she needed to. Malini would give her almost anything if she asked. "If I win, it's yours. If you win, I take a bottle of your wine," she said, gesturing at the carafes at the soldiers' feet.

"Arrack's filthy stuff," Romesh observed. A murmur of agreement arose from the other men. "I'm not betting good Saketan wine for that."

"How about hashish?" Priya asked.

He gave her a measuring look. "That," he said, "I'll bet some *cheap* wine for."

"That's not a fair deal."

"Take it or leave it."

"Fine, fine." Priya leaned forward, ready to steady her arm against the ground. "A little woman like me, you should be able to beat me left-handed, no problem." She grinned.

He snorted.

"What shit. I saw you throw half a river onto an army."

"I didn't use my arms for that."

"And how do I know you won't cheat?"

"You're going to have to trust my honor," she said.

"I've always thought Ahiranyi have no honor." His tone was neutral. His eyes still fixed on her own.

This was the kind of challenge she could understand.

"Test mine and we'll see," she said.

It wasn't a fair match. Priya was plenty strong, but Romesh was burlier, and he wasn't using his injured arm. Still, she put up more of a fight than he'd expected, and by the time he slammed her hand down against the ground and held it there for a strike of three, the other Saketan men had gathered around to watch.

"Hand over my prize, then," Romesh said, grinning.

"With this arm, after the beating you've given me?" Priya rubbed her arm dramatically. "Come find me tomorrow and I'll give it to you then. Unless you want to wrestle again for the arrack after all...?"

"I don't think you should," one man said in a mildly chiding tone. "You'll get an injury."

"Sima should do it, then," Priya said.

"Me?"

Priya turned and looked at her, raising an eyebrow in challenge, and Sima said, "Ah yes. Me."

"You're going to get your advisor to wrestle a bunch of men?" Romesh asked.

"Hey now, Sima is my advisor *and* my chief arm wrestler," Priya protested. "We're more like family."

"We've known each other since we were children," said Sima. "I think I can take my lady's place, just this once."

"It's a bet, then," Romesh said, after more cheery heckling from the crowd.

Priya shuffled out of the way, and Sima sat. Cleared her throat.

"Soldier, if a maid may be so bold as to give you some advice..."

"Go on," he said, putting his own arm forward.

"It's never wise," Sima said, taking his hand, "to bet on arm wrestling against an ex-laundress."

The encampment was celebrating rowdily by the time Priya meandered her way back to Malini's tent. The guards at the entrance let her in without comment.

New lanterns had been lit, filling the tent with a warm glow. And there, at the heart of it, sat Malini. She'd removed her crown of flowers, her jewels. She was in nothing but her sari, her braid snaking along her shoulder, fraying a little into curls.

Their eyes met.

"You went out," Malini said. Her voice was carefully neutral.

"I have Saketan wine." Priya slunk deeper into the tent, over canvas onto plush carpet—the monstrously expensive, hand-knotted silk thing that lay beneath Malini's bed. She could see the stains of her river-excursion marked into it: a snaking drip from one edge to the bed, a crescent of dark water-ink. She liked the sight of it, and didn't really want to consider why.

"Do you," said Malini. She was sitting at her low desk, surrounded by maps. She was alone, at least—no sign of her inner court about. She had a piece of paper laid out in front of her, inked words drying on its surface.

"Cheap Saketan wine," Priya amended. She held it up, loosely, and thought of Malini during her imprisonment—Malini forced to drink drugged wine again and again, poisoned, hallucinating. She hesitated, no words leaving her mouth, unsure if she had overstepped.

But Malini was watching her, still. Her eyes were darker than ever in the lantern light.

"You should share it with me," Malini said.

She held out a hand, and Priya crossed the floor. Placed the bottle in her waiting palm. Malini tilted the bottle back, forth.

"This is half empty."

"Sima and I drank some of it," Priya admitted. "It was only fair."

"Was it now?"

"Sima won it in a game of arm wrestling."

Malini raised an eyebrow.

"Who did she wrestle?"

"One of Prince Ashutosh's men," Priya said with a shrug. "Don't worry, they seemed impressed." Priya looked around again. The noise of the camp seemed very distant here. There was incense lit—a soft, rich fragrance of sandalwood. "Where are your people?"

"Celebrating," said Malini. "Just like you were."

"Shouldn't you be celebrating too?" Priya sat down next to her, legs sprawled in front of her. She leaned back on her elbows, nearly lying on the floor. She tilted her head back, feeling the starry warmth of the alcohol swimming through her. "You should always celebrate when you do well in battle."

"Perhaps you're right," said Malini. "But I didn't want to celebrate with them. I wanted to...reflect. And I wanted to wait." Her gaze drifted. Traced Priya's jaw. Her throat.

She opened the wine. One easy, graceful motion of her hands. "And now here you are."

"Here I am," Priya whispered back.

Malini leaned toward her. She raised the bottle, pressing the coolness of the rim against Priya's lower lip. "Will you drink?" she asked.

"I think I've had enough," Priya said softly. But she raised her own hand, tilting the bottle along with Malini, and felt the wine brush her lips—felt the sweetness of it burst on her tongue. And then they were lowering the bottle together. Letting it meet the floor. And Malini was cupping Priya's face in her palms and tilting her face up.

The kiss was—gentle. There were no words that Priya could find inside herself for it. No more than a brush of their lips; nothing more than the caress of Malini's breath on her skin, and the scent of her—smoke and salt, and sweet jasmine oil.

Malini leaned in closer and touched her fingertips to Priya's upper arm. A light touch. Almost a question. When Priya said nothing, Malini dragged her fingers down. Her fingers were still soft, unmarked by calluses from weapons or physical work, but her touch was firm. When she drew her fingers up, her nails scraped Priya's skin, leaving a slow, steady line of fire in their wake. Priya couldn't help but make a noise—a thin, wanting thing.

"Do you still want to see if I'm capable of breaking you?" Malini asked. "Do you still want me to try?"

Something hushed, almost reverent in her voice, in the shape of her mouth, the look in her eyes. It made Priya feel dizzier than any wine; made her body feel like something alchemized.

"Yes," Priya said. "Always. Yes."

Malini tilted Priya's face up herself and kissed her again; a slow, lush kiss that made Priya's mouth part; made her feel drunk with desire, more human and more present in her own flesh than she had been in so long, so long, perhaps ever.

She could taste the wine on Malini's lips now.

"Look," Malini murmured. She took Priya's hand and led her fingers to the chain around Malini's throat. Guided them along her collarbone, down the ridges of metal against the skin and bone, to the husk of a flower that lay above her breasts.

"You still wear it," Priya managed to say. It was hard to think, when Malini was so near her. Hard to think through the faint, warm haze of wine and the sight of Malini's hair escaping its braid, sweetly unraveled, Malini's throat bared.

"I do," Malini said. "It reminds me of what I survived. And what I still have to do. And of you." She curled her hand over Priya's. Strong though Priya's hand was, callused from war and work, it fit perfectly inside Malini's own. "I would not be here without you."

"Malini," Priya said quietly.

"I like carrying a piece of you with me. A little of your magic. Sometimes when I lie back to sleep I feel it pulsing like a heartbeat. I feel it like your heart against mine. The warmth of it seeps right through me." She hesitated, her thumb brushing shapes into Priya's skin. "It makes me feel human."

Priya was powerless to stop Malini encircling her wrist and drawing her hand down over soft skin, over the buttery silk of Malini's blouse, over the shape of her body through cloth—the curve of her breasts, rising and falling with her breath. The narrowness of her rib cage. The velvet of Malini's stomach. The curve of her hip, warm through the cloth of her sari.

"I am tired of wanting and not taking," Malini said. So honest and clear. It felled Priya, just a little. Made her breath catch inside her.

"Then take," Priya said. Wanted and wanted, with an ache that ran right through her. "Take, Malini. I'm here."

"Come with me to the bed," Malini whispered, and how could Priya refuse her? How could she want to?

There was hesitation in Malini: in the way she traced the lines of Priya's throat with her nails, almost grasping, circling, *holding*, but not quite; in the bruising, then carefully softened pressure of her hand at Priya's waist as she lowered her down to the bed. The punishing warmth of her mouth, then the tenderness of it, the feather-lightness of the way she kissed the corner of Priya's eye, her cheek, the shell of her ear.

You want so much, Priya thought, her heart almost bursting over it. It shouldn't have made her feel so fond. Shouldn't have made her want to smile, or laugh with joy over it, even as she felt hot all over; even as she wanted to bare her throat and her wrists for the taking, part her legs and invite Malini to take anything, everything. *You want so much, and all I want is for you to have whatever you desire.*

She didn't know if Malini had lain with anyone before. But she didn't want to ask, and she wasn't sure she truly cared. All that mattered was here and now, and the act of gently nudging Malini's face with her own, Malini's eyes meeting hers, so Priya could see nothing but the deep darkness of them, and Malini's flushed cheeks. Her swollen mouth.

"Let me show you how to break me," Priya said. She raised her hand to cup Malini's cheek; to hold her as tenderly as she always wanted, and hardly ever could. "Please. Let me."

Malini gave the barest nod. And Priya held her one moment longer, drinking the sight of her in, then began the work of gently unhooking Malini's blouse and easing it from her shoulders.

"Like this," Priya whispered, as she undid the perfect pleats of Malini's sari and brushed cloth away from Malini's skin; as she touched and kissed her way over supple flesh and sharp bones, the faint silvery tracery of marks where skin had stretched or scarred; as she bared Malini entirely, pressing her down to the bed. Malini watched her all the way, gaze never wavering.

There was a biding, hungry patience in those eyes, learning every time Priya touched her; as Priya's hair brushed her thighs and Priya nudged with her nose at the soft skin at the bend of Malini's knee. She smiled up at Malini, and Malini's dark gaze went warm in response. She reached down—touched her thumb to the curve of Priya's eyebrow.

"Will you let me in?" Priya asked softly, flushing all over even as she said it. But Malini did not blush or squirm; only held Priya's gaze as she parted her legs and pressed a hand gently, inexorably against Priya's scalp, her fingers tangling deliberately into the lengthy darkness of her hair.

"Priya," she whispered, and that almost undid Priya—almost made her fly apart, as if her own skin couldn't contain her. "Priya. Sweetheart. Show me."

She drew Priya in, and Priya went gladly.

The bed was growing rumpled beneath them already, and Priya's clothes were too heavy by far against her sweat-slick skin. And Priya had thought—maybe thought, in the quiet of a sleepless night, when she allowed herself the indulgence—that it would be sweet, the first time. Gentle. But Malini's nails were sharp against her scalp, urging her fiercely on. And Malini was watching her, devouring her with her eyes, until suddenly she was not. Suddenly Malini was gasping, her throat flushed; Malini was tilting her head back, her body arching and falling, and her hands gripping ever tighter, until Priya could feel nothing but her, and taste nothing but her, and *want* nothing but her.

"Don't stop," she commanded, and Priya did not. Didn't stop until Malini bit out a curse, and dragged Priya up, and kissed her soundly again.

"Take this off," Malini said impatiently, when their mouths parted, and Priya could only do as she was told—untangling herself from her own sari, until she was as naked as Malini. Malini sat up with her, and her hands were on Priya in an instant—heated palms against the wings of her shoulder blades, the curve of her back. Her thighs. The pleasure pooled through her like light.

"Malini," she said. Pressed her face to Malini's hair. "Malini."

"Priya."

Priya grasped Malini's hands in her own. Held those hands between their bodies. Took a breath—simply to remind herself that she *could*—and placed her wrists against Malini's palms.

Malini stilled.

"I know you, Malini," Priya said, her voice low with want. A little breathless. "I know what you want. I promise you. It's freely given."

A beat. Two. Then Malini's grasp tightened on Priya's wrists—a hold Priya could easily have broken, but had no desire to—and set her mouth to Priya's throat. This time there was no hesitation. Just teeth and lips and tongue, punishingly fierce, all devotion.

"I've learned my lesson," Malini said, low. "I know how to break you now. Let me show you."

Priya did splinter, when she felt Malini's mouth against her; when she felt those long, elegant fingers, and Malini's voice against her skin, loving and lovingly cruel by turns.

Like that, Priya. Like this. I want to hear you. There. Just like this.

Priya. My love. Like this.

Later, they lay together in the half dark. Curled together. They stayed like that for a long time, speaking about everything and nothing all at once: about Priya's new life as an elder. About all the changes Malini had seen in her own life, since becoming empress. And that was sweet, sweeter than anything. It had been so long since they'd had the gift of being so thoroughly alone together, and so tangled up in one another.

"You have a scar," said Malini finally.

"Something strange happened to me in battle," Priya admitted. "Something I didn't expect."

"That I gathered."

Priya snorted. "Yes, I thought you might have from all the..." She gestured vaguely at her own body. "You know."

"I do," Malini agreed, a smile curling her mouth. Her eyes traced Priya's face, slowly working their way lower—over her throat, her torso, her arms like a physical touch—before rising to meet Priya's gaze again.

There was nothing heated in her expression, nothing hungry—but her look had made Priya's stomach knot and her blood burn hotter all the same.

"But I don't mean that battle. I mean—in Saketa. When the fire fell," Priya managed to say.

She took Malini's hand and placed it against the curve of her hip. "Here," she said. "Can you feel the shape of it? Like a—an arrowhead."

"I can feel it," Malini said. Her thumb moved carefully over the divot of Priya's hip—over the dip of flesh against bone.

"It was—because of my magic."

"You don't need to explain your magic," Malini said carefully.

"You want to know, though," Priya pointed out.

"I have always wanted to know."

Deep breath. "It was the fire," she said. "The fire stopped me for a moment. Took away my magic."

"But you're healed," Malini murmured.

Priya shook her head. "All that matters," she said. "Is. Is if you want me in battle..."

She trailed off. Malini's fingertips were light against her mouth. Silencing her.

"I don't want to talk about battle anymore," said Malini.

"Don't you?" A smile. "Aren't you always thinking about how you'll win?"

"Priya," Malini said. Laughter in her voice. "You're here, aren't you? I've already won."

BHUMIKA

Nowhere in the mahal was safe from the eyes of the yaksa. Bhumika crossed the corridors, following the light of the moon where it broke into the halls, between the thick foliage that wound over the windows; the creepers that hung from the ceiling, as graceful as curtains of silk. She could feel every inch of them, every bit of the life within them, like an extension of herself. And the life—the pulsing, breathing force of it—watched her in turn.

In this corridor, if she was still and silent, she could hear the distant noises of the nursery. Sometimes, she stood there by the window with her eyes closed and strained to hear a single noise—a laugh or a cry, the sound of her daughter's voice. Anything at all. Sometimes, like a cruel joke, one of the yaksa deigned to allow her a glimpse of Padma through a half-open door, or down the end of the corridor, held in their arms.

Tonight, she heard footsteps. But no yaksa emerged, and no Padma. Just Kritika, dressed in white, her expression stiff. When she caught sight of Bhumika, she paused, and her expression only grew stiffer.

"Elder Bhumika," she said. "Good evening."

"Kritika," Bhumika said in return. "Are you ... better now?"

"I was never not well," Kritika said.

"The banquet—"

"I am going to the Hirana," Kritika cut in. There was something hunted and defiant in her face. She raised her head, chin up, and said, "I am going to pray alongside the yaksa. Whom I worship. And *trust*."

Bhumika stared into her face.

"Kritika," she said. "Please."

Kritika began to walk again. Quickly, as if she could outrun the banquet. The look on Bhumika's face.

"I fought for a better world, Elder Bhumika," she said determinedly. "I will not reject it. I have faith."

Bhumika said nothing to that. What could she say? She let Kritika go.

Silence fell again. She swallowed hard, against the aching lump of grief and anger in her throat, and walked onward.

She crossed the corridor and slipped from one to the next, making her way into the narrow servants' passages that adjoined the once grand hallways reserved for the nobility. She did not see Sanjana's vibrant face, or Chandni's gentle one, or the gleam of Nandi's silvery eyes. She was glad of that.

Her people were waiting for her in the kitchens. Billu was carefully stoking the fire in one of the ovens. When he saw her, he bowed his head in greeting.

"They don't care much for flame," Billu said, adding some fuel to the embers burning low in the oven. "So I thought, I'll get some work done and keep them away while I'm at it. My lady."

She nodded.

"How is Rukh?" This, she addressed to Ganam. He was standing on the edge of the circle of servants, the only mask-keeper present. The only one, frankly, that Bhumika had felt safe inviting. Khalida was sitting cross-legged on the ground behind him, her head bent as though too heavy for her neck.

"Well enough," he said, expression grim. "Doesn't remember his mother's name, sometimes. And sometimes he looks at me like he can see right through me. But he's more himself again."

She felt helpless relief run through her. Whatever her brother had done to the boy, he had not deserved it, and she was deeply glad that it was a wound he was capable of healing from.

"I tried to see Padma again," Khalida said. She sounded subdued. Haunted and tired, in a way that years of service to the regent and the tumult that had followed his death had never managed to make her be. "They wouldn't let me."

"Ah, Khalida," Bhumika breathed. Foolish tears began to build behind her eyes. "Thank you for trying," she said.

Every time Bhumika had attempted to go near her daughter, the yaksa wearing Chandni's face had found her and taken Bhumika's arm lightly, so lightly. Would her dear temple daughter show her the mahal again? Let her touch the fruit trees in the orchard—feel their strength and change them? Would Bhumika take her to the worshippers once more, so they could meet a yaksa and touch Chandni's feet, and pray to her as they so desired to? And Bhumika had said yes and yes, obediently yes, and had not seen her daughter.

"The feast," she began. Then stopped.

They stood or sat around her and watched her. Waiting for her to speak.

"You know by now what has been done to the highborn who attended the feast," Bhumika said. "The yaksa have told them they will live, if they are obedient. And if they are not, the rot will take them. And the yaksa have told *me* that they seek a war. They have told me they desire a new Age of Flowers. The highborn will now have no choice but to help them." A pause. Then, "You know they keep my daughter from me."

Khalida let out a low sob.

"I never imagined the yaksa returning," Billu said, from his place by the pots. "But if I had, I'd have thought they'd make Ahiranya better. Make the world respect us. I'd have thought they'd treat us well." He savagely poked at the flames. Firelight running fingers across his face. "Seems to me, they're no different from the empire," he said. "We've lost one tyrant and gained another."

"At least they're ours," someone said.

"Are they? No one told me when I was a boy that the yaksa I grew up praying to would like sickening people. Hurting children," Billu replied. "I would have gone and prayed to the nameless instead if they had. At least one's not likely to move in and poison the guests."

"So what do we do? Fight them? How's *that* going to end?"

"I am not asking you to raise your voices and weapons against them," Bhumika said. "Far from it."

"Are you asking us to obey them? If I wanted to serve them," Ganam said, "I'd be sitting with Kritika right now, you understand, Elder Bhumika? I wouldn't be here of all places, with people who barely like me."

"Even Kritika's not sure if she wants to worship them anymore," said a soldier.

"As Billu rightly pointed out," Bhumika said calmly, "our people have survived oppression and mistreatment before. We know we have the strength to do so if we must."

"But we shouldn't have to again," one of the maids said. Her voice trembled. "Haven't we suffered enough?"

"It isn't fair," someone else said.

More voices clamored up, rising and tripping over one another. There was a thud. Bhumika turned, and saw that Jeevan had knocked his saber pommel hard against the wall, making a noise loud enough to silence them.

"Elder Bhumika," he said. "You were saying."

"It isn't fair," Bhumika said. "And I am . . . grief-stricken. I had so many hopes for Ahiranya. As you all did. I know. But I also have faith in all of you. I have faith you will survive. I have faith you can bend to monstrous forces, and still hold pride in your hearts. And I know if the opportunity arises, you will set yourselves free."

"And you?" Ganam asked. Eyes on her, assessing. "What will you do, Elder Bhumika? Lead their wars for them?"

She would do whatever they asked of her, but *only* what they asked of her. She would weave her way around their orders, finding hairline fractures in their control, weakening their grip on Ahiranya and its people. She would do what she had always done: play at obedience, while ever sharpening her knives. Waiting for a chance. Only a chance.

The thought made her to want to wither. She understood their frustration; their hopelessness. It was hers too.

"I will remember what we are," she said. "I will keep the thought alight in my heart, like a candle. And when our lives darken, I will use it to guide me through. I will remember that we are not what is done to us. We are, and always have been, more than that." Her voice softened as they stared back at her—grief and rage and something like hope in their faces. "That is what I will do.

"We will not die bravely and needlessly," she said. "But we will not lose hope. That is what it means to be Ahiranyi, whether the yaksa know it or not. When they destroy us, somehow we will always grow anew. Have faith in that."

She felt Ashok before she saw him. The green sang and writhed in her head, a warning and a call. And there he was. Waiting for her beyond the kitchen courtyard.

"Keep the others in the kitchen," she said softly to Jeevan. "Keep them safe." He hesitated, clearly unwilling to leave her alone—but at her urging, he abruptly nodded and walked away.

The spirit wearing her brother's face wavered on his feet. Stood on the dusty ground of the yard and looked at her with her brother's sullen eyes, always displeased, always demanding more than she could give. She stared back.

"I heard you talking," he said. "To the others."

"Then you know I counseled obedience."

"There's a tale I want to tell you," he said. His voice echoed through the dark. "A child's tale. Though you won't find the whole of it in any book. Only fragments."

That did not sound like Ashok's voice.

"Tell me," she said.

"Once," he replied. "There was a yaksa. A yaksa who came after Mani Ara to this world. Like her, he made himself part of Ahiranya. He became a green thing. Flowers in him. But it was humans he loved best. He took in orphans. He raised them like his own.

"But mortals were so lonely, by nature," he said. "His kind—his yaksa kin—were bound together by the waters. Could feel each other. Could share dreams and feelings. Thoughts. Mortals had no such skill. So he decided to give it to them.

"To have magic you have to sacrifice something. He taught them that. Told them when they drank the waters, they would have to give something up. Hollow themselves to make room for it. They chose to do it. He created a temple to train them. He led them to the waters, and let them take the waters up. Those that lived were bound to the yaksa—sharing their magic, their memories, their hearts. Those that died, he kept for himself. Beloved masks." He touched a finger to his own face.

"This is not a child's tale," said Bhumika.

"A story about children," he said. "Not for them, perhaps. Though it shaped them. It shaped you."

"Why tell me this?"

"The yaksa had a secret. He never told any of his kin," said Ashok. "He hid it from them for a long time. But he loved one child dearly. More than all the rest. She loved knowledge more than any other child he had met, and he gave her a surfeit of it. He told her everything he had taught the other children—his *temple* children. And when she passed through the waters, he gave her even more. Every secret the yaksa had. But on her third journey through the waters she nearly died. She came back alive, but the waters were poisoning her. She wouldn't live, bound to them as she was. And he could not stand to see her die, even if her shadow would remain with him forever."

Bhumika listened, saying nothing. Somewhere behind her she could hear the spit and crackle of kitchen fires. The cold of the court-yard, the night, was settling in her bones.

"She could not live with the waters," he said. "So he tore her free from them."

Tore her free.

She thought of the scroll in the library. The body with roots run-ning through it. Not roots, perhaps, after all, but rivers of gold and green and red. Rivers of heart's blood. Rivers of soul and living.

"And what," Bhumika asked, throat tight, "became of her?"

"She had hollowed herself for the deathless waters," he said. "For their magic. What remained of her after was a shadow of a girl. Magic lost. Memories in fragments. She was herself, but not herself at all. She remembered everything he had taught her. Every tale. Every secret. But she did not remember who she was."

Ashok took a step closer. His movements were jerky. As if he didn't know his own limbs.

"He bound her again to the waters, in the end. He couldn't stand to see her as she was. He couldn't stand not to *feel* her, her soul in the waters with him. Bhumika, I..." Ashok's voice. Familiar, a little rough. Panic woven through it. "I heard you. And here I am, you see? I don't have long. But I have what you need. You want our people to be free. And I...I have the knowledge that will let you free them. I have *so much* knowledge inside me. Knowledge I'm afraid to touch. I am not...myself. I am..." He sucked in a breath. "You know what I am. But you, Bhumika. You're a temple daughter. You're bound to the yaksa. Bound to me."

Her not-brother looked at her. One of his eyes was mortal, gleaming with tears. The other was living wood scraped bare, green and weeping sap.

"I can give you what he gave those children," said Ashok-who-was-not-Ashok. "I can give you all the secrets of the yaksa. I can give you the tools to destroy them. And then I can set you free. All it will cost you is—"

"My self," whispered Bhumika. "My memories. Is that what you mean?"

"Yes. Only that."

"Ashok, are you utterly mad?"

"I tested the skill on Rukh. He's not thrice-born, not a temple child. But he had the waters in him, through his rot. I know it will work." His voice changed a little again; deepened, a fracture of wood rippling across his cheek. "I owe it to you, child," he said. "I made you, after all."

A groan of pain. His head tilted forward.

She could have held him. Could have raised his face with her hands and looked at him and allowed herself to fear for him, worry for him.

What is wrong with you? What has become of you?

Could have. But did not. She thought of all that the yaksa had done in that feast—the bodies sundered by striations of wood, and Ashok's lost, frightened eyes—and stood where she was, as unmoving as the oldest tree, deep-rooted, steadfast.

"Why now?" she asked instead, when he raised his head. "Why offer me a weapon *now*?"

"Because Ashok wanted a better Ahiranya," he said. "Because Ashok had a dream, a dream he died for, and this is not what he dreamt of. Because at the feast I thought I would weep with horror, and whatever is mortal in me hates what the yaksa have done. And what is yaksa in me knows what we *will* do, and fears it.

"The yaksa are not the only ones who want to shape this world." Ashok was sweating, strange pearls of sap running down his face. "We do not want a war. We know war is inevitable. Even as we have begun to return, to make the sacrifices necessary to crawl back into this world, others have been awakening too. Seeding messages in names and prophecies. Teaching mortals the secrets of sacrifice. They've written those secrets into the blood, the bone, the earth, just as we have. But we'll be stronger this time. We've given up so much more than they have. This time we'll take the world entirely. Hollow it and make it home. But we *can* be stopped. We know it and we fear it, because losing will destroy us."

"Ashok." She made her voice a whip, hard enough to crack through the glazed look in his eyes. He blinked then, looking at her, and she pressed on, trying to keep him present and with her. "Please. Talk to me. Explain. What would you have me do?"

He blinked at her with his one mortal eye. "Ashok," he repeated. "I'm not Ashok anymore. Not really. Am I?"

"You *are* still Ashok," she said, with conviction she did not feel. "You saved our sister when our siblings burned. You kept her alive. Then you gave her to me. You have died before. And you came back. Died with our siblings. Died when you let Priya go. You can come back again. You *have*."

"That wasn't death," he rasped. "You don't know what death is like. True death—it's something unlike anything else. I was picked to pieces. Scraped clean, the bones of me reassembled into something of use to them—to me."

He took a step closer to her.

"Bhumika," he forced out. "I am a yaksa. No different from the one who wears Chandni in her smile, or uses Sanjana's voice. No different, although I believe I am."

"You are still you," she said, but saw her own uncertainty mirrored in his face.

"I am only the scraps of myself. The tatters. Take this armor apart, this thin skin, and I won't be Ashok anymore. I know it. The yaksa know it. They don't know why I cling on but it makes them curious. They're waiting to see what will happen. They think it's funny. You always loved humans, they told me. And I did. Maybe I still do."

Bhumika felt the thud of her own heart, painful as a fist.

"You are a temple elder," he said. "Bound to us by choice and sacrifice. Bound by my—by *a yaksa's*—choice. We can give you so many things. We *have* given you so many things. Strength. Power. The earth and plants at your bidding. And I can give you more. I can give you knowledge, Bhumika, the kind of knowledge that could kill us in the right hands. A secret that can be forged into a weapon. Is losing yourself not worth that price?"

What capacity did she have to do anything with that kind of knowledge? What could she possibly accomplish? To know the right knife for a task was one thing—to actually be able to wield it was another matter entirely. And yet her hands shook and her voice trembled as she said, "If I take this knowledge with me, I can stop the war?"

"You can try," said Ashok. "And that is more than you can do now. You're bound. Good as chained. This is all I can offer you."

"If you know how the yaksa can be stopped—if you feel guilt—why will you not act to stop the war yourself? Why must it be me?"

"Because it's only the part of me that is Ashok that wants to," he said. "This—skin of me." He gestured, helplessly, at his own body. "And I'm not going to be here much longer, Bhumika. You must see it. I'm fraying. I cannot leave, but—but you can. For a price."

She closed her eyes, searching for calm.

"Everything demands sacrifice."

"Of course," she said. "Of course it does."

"You've forgotten. But once, beneath the waters, a yaksa offered you a blade of sacred wood. It told you to cut out your heart for it, and you did." His voice was quiet but deep. Ashok's voice but also—not quite. Not quite. "You made space for the sangam inside you. The rivers are in you, flowing through you. We can find you anywhere, because you carry the waters. We can live in you, because you carry the waters. But if you are not bound to the waters..."

"I understand," she said. Closed her eyes, one brief moment, then opened them. "A typical Ashok strategy," she said tiredly. "To risk my health and my life—and all those who rely upon me—for the slimmest chance of success."

"When I risked death, I did it for a higher cause," he said. "Our autonomy. Our freedom. Risk is not shameful."

"Shame! You talk of shame. You wanted a return to our glorious past," she said, with all the savagery she had never been able to direct at him when he was living; that he had denied her by being her enemy, then denied her by dying and leaving both her and Priya behind. "What do you think of it, now that we have it?"

"I think you're asking a ghost about wanting to resurrect ghosts, sister," he said, with a weight and quietness she'd never heard from her brother's lips. "I'm not real anymore, Bhumika," he said. "What I once wanted doesn't matter. But you are real. And the choice is yours."

"You want to give me knowledge forbidden to me," Bhumika said, closing her eyes, feeling the night press against them. She was burning inside. This was not magic, not the fire of sacred wood. This was how panic felt. This was how it felt to have the walls close in. This was how she had felt in the moments before she had passed through the death-less waters as a girl: all her choices narrowing, and the air in her lungs with them. "You want to—risk all that I am. On the vague hope that someone may be able to use the knowledge I have."

"Yes."

"And my alternative?"

"You stay here," Ashok said. "You play the coward's game, like you always have. You play nicely with your masters, as you always have."

"I stay with my *child*," said Bhumika. "I stay with the people I've promised to protect. I do not abandon them for—for vague hopes."

"Ah, Bhumika," said Ashok. "You think we'll ever give your baby back to you?"

"You think she will survive if I leave her?"

"You think she will survive if you stay?"

"You're saying this to sway me," she said tightly.

"I'm telling you what you already know. We were trained to cut out our weaknesses for a reason." He shrugged—a sound that creaked like wood in a high wind. "You created a weakness, Bhumika. Brought your weakness into the world. Every time you fail the yaksa, they'll use her against you, and they'll blame you for being foolish enough to leave her there for them to take. And one day they will destroy her. Whether by accident or design." A pause, a breath. "They've always let children die," he said. "It's what shaped us, after all. How many temple children do you think were lost to them?"

He was manipulating her. She knew. She *knew*.

And yet.

Would she do more good here, defending her home and her people? Soothing the yaksa with honeyed words and worship? Surely she would. It was the path she had always taken.

Perhaps she would come to love them again. Feel faith in them well up in her. She'd come to love her husband. The lie of it had carried through years, years. Until it had not.

But her husband had never known her heart. And the yaksa held hers in their hands. She'd given them her heart—torn it out herself. She'd made herself their creature in return for power. And they had Padma. Her child. The compass of her heart.

The walls were closing in upon her tighter, tighter.

"This opportunity won't exist for long," said Ashok.

"Because you won't."

"Yes."

She squeezed her hands into fists, hard enough that her fingers ached.

"Can you protect her when I'm gone?" Bhumika asked, and felt wretched. How could she ask this? How could she consider this? "Can you keep my little one safe? She's a child, Ashok. She deserves—"

"We deserved a great deal too," Ashok said. "They burned us anyway. The people who should have loved us."

"And you think I want to visit that kind of grief on her, too? No. Ashok. I'll do it, if you can promise me her life."

"You have no way to hold me to that promise," he said. "*I* have no way to hold me to that promise."

"You once saved our sister's life. When she was—small. When she was afraid. You carried her." She looked at him. "And the yaksa you spoke of loved children. Children like my own. Ghost or not, fading or not—you won't leave my daughter. Will you?"

He looked back at her. Something flickered over his face— something soft and wounded that reminded her of the boy he'd been before their siblings burned.

"I'll try," he said. "That. That's all I can vow."

She nodded. She couldn't thank him. She hated—she *hated*—

"Why did you have to die?" Bhumika's voice broke and ah—she hated it, how small losing all her allies had made her. Hated that her greatest strengths—her love for her own people, her love for what little family she'd cobbled together, for the possibility for a future, for her *child*—had been turned upon her. "Why did I have to be left to carry this burden alone?"

Ashok hesitated. Raised a hand, as if he would reach for her. It hovered for a moment, then, slowly, lowered.

"Because I made bad choices," said Ashok. "Because bad choices were made by the people who raised me, and the people who raised them, and the immortals who built our world. Because we are small and disposable, Bhumika, every one of us, and it was just your luck to make it longer than the rest of us."

"Of course you only admit how bad your choices were now that you're gone," Bhumika said, with a laugh that was all grief. "Of course." She forced her hands to loosen. Forced herself not to sway on her feet, or crumple. Strong roots. Deep roots, holding her fast. "When will we do it?"

"Meet me at the bower of bones," Ashok said. "Before dawn."

"Are you giving me time to say goodbye?"

"If you need it," he said. "Time to prepare."

And then he turned and walked away from her. She watched him go—the bend of his spine, the shape of him. A shell, a skin, for a yaksa she did not know.

She turned back. Jeevan stood in the doorway. He was in the shadows, far back enough that she could only see the gleam of his eyes.

"You listened to everything."

Jeevan gave one jerky nod. He said nothing.

"I've never been the impetuous one," she said. "I don't take foolish risks. I know better. I have worked so hard, Jeevan, to ensure I am strong enough to find a way through for all of us. This is not what I want."

"My lady," he said. "I will go with you."

"To the bower of bones?"

"Anywhere," he said.

Her heart ached.

"No debt you owe me demands this of you. And. My daughter..."

"I don't do it for debt," he said. Mouth firm. "I cannot protect her. Against them, I am powerless. But you. Perhaps."

She wanted to refuse him. Wanted to spare him this. But if she was going to lose herself, she could not do this alone.

She did not want to do this alone.

"Perhaps," she echoed. "Well, then. If you like, yes. You may."

43

MALINI

The temple was so large it was visible even from quite a distance. The sight of it struck an old memory in her. She knew this place: its golden sandstones, its ivory inlaid domes. Something about it felt familiar. She didn't know why.

Beneath the light of sunset, it would glow like burning embers, like the finest temples in the city of Harsinghar itself. But those temples were by necessity awe-inspiring: They served Parijat's highborn and royalty, and reflected the grandeur of the empire, the importance of the faith.

There was no reason for a temple surrounded by swathes of barren land and sparse, bedraggled copses of trees to be so ornate. As the chariot jolted forward along the dirt track, Malini raised a hand to protect her eyes from the glare of the sun and surveyed the land around them. It was not farmland as she'd first assumed, but a wasteland. The soil was largely arid and strangely jagged. Rock formations roiled like waves, fossilized in the act of breaking on a shore. Holes pitted the ground.

"This was a battleground, once," Lata murmured from her place beside her.

"I thought it a possibility. Or the site of some terrible natural disaster," Malini agreed, looking down once more at the great gouges in the earth. She thought of Priya then—her gifts, the way she could reshape the earth—and wondered with a strange feeling in her chest if the temple elders had fought here during the Age of Flowers. "You can tell from the ground alone?"

"I am not reading the soil, my lady, although I wish I had the skill to do so," Lata said, with a slightly embarrassed smile. "I recognize the temple's architecture. Look between the domes. There."

Lata raised a hand, pointing, and Malini followed her guidance. Between the domes of the temple stood a tower. It was no watchtower, no edifice made for practical use. It was thin as a blade, thin enough to cut only the faintest scar against the blue-white sky.

Ah.

Now that she had seen it, she remembered the tale. The battle that ended the Age of Flowers was preceded by a meeting of the highborn of the subcontinent's city-states. Called together, they shared their sorrows and their angers—their great fear of the yaksa, and how their land had changed under the touch of those immortal spirits.

And then the yaksa had come.

It had been a massacre. All of the most venerable of kings and princes had been killed, including Divyanshi's own highborn father. The land never recovered from the deaths, but a temple was erected there, marked with a "tower like a blade"—or so the Book of Mothers said.

Malini knew its words very, very well.

Only one priest awaited them at the entrance of the temple. He was a small figure—narrow shouldered with large eyes, sharp bones.

"My name is Mitul," the slight man said, by way of greeting, when Malini alighted from her chariot. His eyes were oddly pale—the almost-green Malini had only ever seen in the faces of Dwarali soldiers who carried blood of the Jagatay and Babure tribes that harried Parijat-dvipa's borders. "You have been eagerly awaited, Empress."

"And who awaits me?" Malini asked.

"You followed a message here," Mitul replied, eyes politely lowered. "I am sure the empress knows."

The words verged on insulting, but Malini allowed them to pass. But she could not hide her anger when Mitul shook his head and stood before the door, barring the way when Malini's followers approached: her highborn, her guards. Her women. Priya.

"All of you cannot enter," the priest said. Apparently unfazed by the armed men at Malini's back, he said, "This is a holy place."

"All temples are holy," Malini said, watching the priest with intent eyes. "And all temples, surely, welcome the highborn of Parijatdvipa."

"Only you, Empress," he said.

"I would be a great fool to enter even a holy place unprotected," Malini said evenly.

"True faith demands risk," Mitul replied.

She stood for a moment, still and silent. The men behind her were equally silent—unwilling, it seemed, to argue with a priest of the mothers.

"A maid or a guard," Malini said, after a moment. The priest shook his head.

"Faith," he repeated again. "Just as Divyanshi acted with faith, so must you, Empress."

Faith that demanded mindless acts, acts with no grounding in logic, in what could be risked and what could be gained—ah, she hated to be asked this, just as she'd hated releasing the priest at Saketa, when he had more than deserved a slow death.

But what use would it be to turn away, and not see what was being offered to her?

She turned.

"I will return within an hour," Malini said.

Lata inclined her head. Her jaw was set, her eyes watchful. Deepa looked worried but said nothing, and Raziya was frowning.

Priya's eyes were strangely distant.

"There are flowers in the temple," Priya said, in a voice quiet enough that Mitul would surely not hear it.

There were weapons, then, within the temple. There was comfort in that thought, even though Malini knew well enough that there was little anyone could do for her—not even Priya—if someone simply decided to slit her throat.

Malini ascended the steps alone, and followed the priest inside.

There was another priest waiting for her.

He waited in a room that had the look of every private prayer room Malini had seen in her life. Plain walls. One latticed window that allowed a fracture of light in. There were statues of the mothers arranged on an altar, their bodies half a man's height and wrought in silver, garlands of pale flowers at their feet. The room itself was lit by warm candlelight and perfumed by incense that was strangely fresh rather than cloying. Its scent reminded her of the wind that had reached her from the ocean, sharp with salt yet faintly sweet. And the priest himself, when he turned to look at her, was just as unremarkable as his surroundings.

He was of average height, with a mark of ash on his forehead and no ink limned onto his arms or hands, which were bare, his shawl draped only loosely at his shoulders, in deference to the heat. His hair was tied back from his face, each braid bound with thread to keep it at bay, leaving his features exposed. His face was unlined—he was, perhaps, only a few years older than her. He bowed as she approached, then rose in one fluid motion from the floor cushions where he had been seated, by all appearances meditating.

"Are you the one called the faceless son?" Malini asked.

He inclined his head. *Yes.*

"What is your name?" Malini asked.

"Kartik," he said. "You do not remember me."

"Should I?" Malini asked.

"You were a girl when I met you," he replied. His voice was deep, and inflected with an accent she did not quite recognize. Saketan, perhaps. "Many, many years ago. You came with your brother to the imperial temple. You laid flowers at the feet of the mothers and whispered to them. Made promises to them. I was only a boy then, training in faith, and swept the floors when you departed."

She could not recall the moment he spoke of, but it seemed . . . possible. Likely, even. She had gone to the imperial temple alone, from time to time, as a girl. For all that she'd had little room in her heart for faith, she had found the temple itself comforting—its silence, its relative privacy, compared with the noise and bustle of the mahal, where there were always courtiers and warriors and other highborn streaming through the corridors.

How long had he held this memory close, preserved perfectly in his mind's eye? Did he know what this one tale—this one brief insight into his past—revealed about him and his desires to her, all in one fell swoop?

I know you, his words had said. *I remember you. You matter to me.*

I want to matter to you, too.

"You are a royal priest, then," she said, mildly. Had he been one of the men who had prepared her pyre and prayed over her, and waited to see if she would choose to burn? The day she should have died was crystal clear in her memories, in some ways, and blurred in others. "And yet—the faceless son?"

"Names have power," he said. "Your Aloran prince could tell you so. You would not have come on the bidding of Kartik, who serves the High Priest loyally, but is not the High Priest. Kartik is not your brother's closest confidant and the power behind the throne. But for the faceless son, who has power in the temples that lie at the farthest reaches of the empire, who holds power among the priests who do not rise under Chandra's rule, who has men who will die for him—for him, you have come."

"I did indeed," Malini agreed. She let warmth touch her voice; let it draw him, as light draws moths. "And I am glad to be here. You cannot know how glad. I thought the priesthood stood entirely against me. I witnessed priestly warriors turn upon me, at Saketa's maze fort—priests who used the fire born of dead women to win my brother's battles for him. And it pained me. Because I am a scion of Divyanshi. Because I know the mothers set me upon this path. And the very priests of the mothers themselves, it seemed, could not see it. See *me*.

"And then I was saved," she went on, quiet weight in her words. "Saved by a priest dressed as a soldier, who worshipped not as your brethren do in Parijat itself, but as Saketans do. With no less faith, but with different effigies. With marks on their skin. And I placed my trust in his Saketan fellows—who saw me, it seemed, as I knew I should be seen: as a devoted worshipper of the mothers. As someone who wanted to save Parijatdvipa. They asked me to obey, and I obeyed. And for my piety, I was sent here, to you." She stepped closer to him. His gaze was steady and piercing, as all priests' eyes were, but that did not mean she had failed to understand him and his wants. "It can be no secret, why

I'm here. I want the support of the priests of the mothers when I take my throne. I cannot rule Parijatdvipa without you. Nor do I wish to."

"You would admit such vulnerability?" His voice was soft, almost kind. "I am a stranger to you, even if you are not one to me."

"No priest of the mothers is truly a stranger to me," Malini said in return. "I share blood with Divyanshi, the first mother of flame. I felt her voice in me when I took up the mantle of empress. If the priests of the mothers are the hands and eyes of the mothers and serve their will, then we are almost kin, you and I."

"Generous words," he said. "But you are willing to kill your kin. And kill priests, also."

"Priests of the nameless, who died willingly. Surely you will not denigrate their sacrifice by calling it murder at my hands."

He inclined his head, accepting her words.

"I am an orphan, Divyanshi's scion," he said—she noted, neatly sidestepping the question of whether to call her empress or princess in the process. "I had no one, before a temple of the faceless mother claimed me. But it was the High Priest who raised me to the position I now occupy, and he is perhaps the closest thing to a father I possess. And he supports your brother Chandra wholeheartedly."

"And yet," Malini said, "Here I stand."

"Perhaps this is a trap for you," he replied, speaking her own suspicions. "To return you to your brother's care."

She shook her head.

"I was given a gift," said Malini. "A box of stone, with a bloom of magical fire inside it."

"A good lure," he said. "One small gift of mother-blessed fire? An easy way to lull you into trust. Did you not consider that? Surely you did."

"I did."

"And you brought no guards with you? No soldiers? Such unpreparedness suggests a mind ill-suited to the throne."

"The fire itself was not the gift," Malini said, ignoring his taunt. She would not be lured into revealing what defenses—and weapons—she had easily to hand. "It was its death that was your gift to me. Priest, I held the flame on my own saber. Felt its strength and heat. And I watched it wither and fade. That is not how the fire the mothers died for—the fire that saved us from the yaksa—behaves. I know every line of the Book of Mothers. I know this with utter certainty.

"The fire of the mothers could not be quenched," she quoted. "It burned as the sun burns. It burned with blessed strength."

"It carried in it the hearts of the mothers," he continued, taking up the cadence of her words. There was—she was fairly sure—a light of approval in his eyes. "It ate and ate, burned with fury, until it swallowed all the yaksa whole, and left the people of Parijatdvipa unharmed. And with the yaksa dead, the mothers' fire departed."

"You gave me the fire as a message," Malini said, as his words died into silence. "You know, priest, that the fire my brother has created is not the fire of the mothers. You know he is not the worthy heir to Parijatdvipa that he believes he is. That the priests of the mothers have, perhaps, long believed he is. I can only assume that you want something from me that Chandra cannot give you."

His expression remained approving. He inclined his head.

"You are wise in your scripture," he murmured.

"As all Parijatdvipans should be," Malini replied. She filled her voice with conviction. "I want to serve Parijatdvipa. I want to lead Parijatdvipa, as I know the mothers desire from me. You know what I want from you and your fellows, priest. I know you want to help me. I *feel* it. But we are creatures that live in the world, flawed though it may be, and we seek to protect our own. The Parijati priesthood has gained a great deal of power under my brother's rule. Military power. Political. I understand that remaining loyal to him may be—compelling. So I must ask: What do you need from me that he cannot provide?"

He was silent. Malini took a step closer still.

"All I have done, I have done for faith," she said. "Now place your faith in me, priest. It is only fair. Only just."

He inclined his head in agreement.

"There is a war coming," the priest said.

"You don't speak of my war with Chandra," Malini murmured.

"No. Not that. Though it is the priests I have trained who serve in Chandra's battles."

Ah. That explained his rise in the ranks of royal priestly service, then, despite his Saketan heritage.

"Once, the priests who stand above me—the High Priest among them—believed that the fight for a better Ahiranya would be fought by its emperor, against disloyal highborn. Men who had forgotten their vows to the mothers. But I always knew that was not so." A pause. Then he said, "You perhaps saw things unnatural and strange in Ahiranya. Or Prince Aditya showed you visions of the nameless. Or you have seen what comes in the presence of the rot." His voice had a steady cadence, even and sure. "You know what I know. You know our ancient enemy comes. *That* is the war that lies upon the horizon. The nameless, the mothers, the faceless mother herself—they speak with the same voice. The yaksa will return. The rot heralded them. They will come, and there will be war again."

The hair on the back of her neck rose.

The yaksa.

There was a terrible sense, within her, of things slotting into place—as what she had seen in Ahiranya, and what she had seen since, reworked into new shapes in her head and heart. Rot flowering across the empire, and Priya's great magic. Rivers upended, and vines working their way through skin. Alone these things were horrors and miracles; wound together, in one garland, they were a warning. A harbinger.

"You can't be sure," she said, reflexive, unwilling to believe it. But she already knew it was true. The dread had flooded through her body and settled coldly within her.

"I am sure," he said. "If you seek Prince Aditya, he will assure you of the same. His nameless god has spoken to him as I have been spoken to. I do not doubt it. The yaksa are coming, and they will attempt to seize all of Parijatdvipa as their own once more."

Had Aditya truly known this was coming? Why hadn't he told her, *warned* her? Had he tried, all those times he has spoken of his faith and its power—and had she simply failed to heed him? She could not consider it further now; couldn't allow the memory of her priest brother to distract her from the priest who stood before her.

"You would have me lead that war," she said, even as her heart turned, even as she knew. She knew.

"I would have you *win* that war," he said. "For Parijatdvipa. For your people. I would have you win it with all the merciful strength of your great ancestor."

"You want me to agree to burn," she said. It did not shock her as much as it should have. Even as she felt numb horror work its way through her—even as her body went colder still, and the memory of smoke filled her throat—

She had known, in her heart of hearts, that fire would come for her again.

"You want me to rise to the pyre," she said.

"With willingness and with joy," he agreed. Leaned forward, a softness in his mien that soothed her when it should not have. "You have the look of Divyanshi, you know," he said.

"I have been told so," Malini said. "Many times."

"The High Priest seeks to make a world that is stronger and better—more true to the hopes and dreams of the mothers who burned for us. In Chandra, he saw the means to create that world. But he saw it in you too when you were a girl. You were good," Kartik said with absolute certainty. An intimacy in his voice that he had no right to. "Good and dutiful. The High Priest and all the venerable priests of the imperial temple impressed upon Chandra the importance of maintaining your purity of spirit, and Chandra sought to do so. He sought to make you into what you must be. A worthy symbol of Parijatdvipa's glory. Divyanshi's scion, your brother, wished for you to burn to make your purity everlasting, and Parijatdvipa's along with it. When you refused, it hurt him sorely."

"It was my right," Malini said, instead of replying with the truth in its entirety—that there had been nothing pure about the fury that had led him to see her heart sisters burned; that framing a violent hatred in the flesh of faith did not make it any less brutal or monstrous. That her hurt had been far greater, and of far more worth than whatever paltry excuse for a heart lived inside him. "If Chandra had been a true faithful of the mothers, he would have accepted my choice. He did not."

Kartik inclined his head in acknowledgment.

"He did not," he agreed. "Emperor Chandra is a man of . . . focus.

His vision is like an arrow. Now, he has begun to understand that the war for a better Parijatdvipa will not be fought against princes and kings. Or a sister in revolt. He understands this is the return of an ancient struggle. But years of belief that he will face a mortal war have...led him astray. And his mind will not be easily moved.

"You must burn," Kartik went on. "Your willing death would be an incomparable weapon against the yaksa. But your brother believes that if you will refuse him and defy him, then there are other sacrifices that will do well enough in your place."

The women he had murdered in their droves to make his weapons. The fire that burned Malini's men in turn, when it flew on strange wings from the maze fort's walls. The fire on her saber, gifted to her by Kartik's people, flickering and fading away. "He would kill you, or allow you to perish, now that he has made his false fire. But his false fire will not save us. Just as your death unwilling and stolen from you will not save us."

"You understand, then," Malini said, in a voice that was far calmer than she felt. "That I will never be willing, so long as Chandra lives and holds the throne."

"No priest has ever desired your unwilling death," he said, with tenderness that galled. "We have always respected your worth. Always sought your glad sacrifice. If this is the gift you demand for your willing service, then tell me so. That is all I ask."

"If the High Priest and the inner circle who serve Chandra do not support me wholeheartedly, then I will not burn," Malini said, into the silence that fell as his words faded, feeling her own horror only distantly. Her determination to win was stronger.

"But you would be willing," he said, "if we served you, lovingly and loyally? Divyanshi's scion, tell me: If you wear the crown and sit upon the throne—will you die for it?"

"It is the will of the mothers that brought me to war against Chandra," Malini said. "It is the priests of the mothers that brought me here. For Parijatdvipa, and for faith, I will take the throne. And I will burn to save us. That is my vow."

He smiled at her, and nodded.

"Then I will send a message to my allies in Harsinghar," he said. "And when you reach the city—when you are at the doors of the mahal—my allies will find you."

"How will you send a message swiftly enough?" Malini demanded.

"I will outpace you to Harsinghar," he said, amused. "You have an army to move. I am one man, and the lanterns in the temple spires will light my message for me, if I do not."

"What assurance..." Malini paused. Shook her head. "Faith," she said. "You will tell me my only assurance is faith."

"Just so, Divyanshi's scion," he said. "There will still be a battle ahead of you. Your men will still die. But when you are captured—and you shall be—the tide will turn in your favor. And I will tell you how."

He told her what was to come. And when he was done, she thought of the battle that awaited her. Thought of men dead, and bloodied soil, and Rao's tired eyes. Thought of Aditya, in Saketa, fighting to keep the enemy at her back at bay.

She knew that Chandra had wasted swathes of men at the battle on the Veri. But he still had his fire—and false though it was, it would still devastate her army before it died. It would still cost her the bulk of her forces—those allies she had brought along with her using nothing but the fraying promise of the myth that surrounded her, all its gilt and glory.

She was still so terribly likely to lose.

She would have to trust this man. This priest, who spoke to her as if he knew her. Called her good. Dutiful. Pure. She would, if all else failed, have to place her life in his hands. Her skin crawled, even as she held the certainty inside herself, cold and sure.

She would make her own plans, of course. She would ensure Chandra's death if she had the power to do it. If the priest betrayed her, then she would make sure she would not die helpless, all her work undone. By the mothers, and by her own vicious nature, *some* of her ambitions would outlive her.

She would need Priya's help for that.

She thought of Priya. Priya, who was a temple elder. Priya, who worshipped the yaksa, and loved her people and her flowering gods.

She felt a terrible realization slide its way between her ribs.

She could not tell Priya the truth.

She would ask Priya to fight for her, maybe die for her, on the basis of lies. To enter battle for the sake not just of the bonds between their nations but for love. For the trust she'd placed in Malini long ago, when she'd allowed Malini to hold a knife to her heart. When she'd kissed Malini in a forest and told Malini she did not have the power to hurt her.

But I do, Malini thought. Her heart hurt. She wanted to be sick.

Malini had always known in her soul what her mission would make of her. She touched her fingertips to the flower beneath her blouse—a helpless gesture. She loved Priya. The feeling was dark and deep within her, with its own steady undercurrent, always reaching for her, always dragging her under. But she needed to win this war. Needed it more than tenderness or love, needed it with a fire that burned and burned and screamed in her heart sisters' names. She needed it because her brother's blade had found her and cut the goodness from her long before she'd ever learned the shape of a gentle, encompassing love. If she had to risk Priya for her vengeance—if she had to place her in danger in order to win, and see her brother dead?

So be it.

RAO

Rao watched Priya. She was standing out in the bare sunlight, arms crossed, her head lowered as if she were lost in thought. Sima was standing next to her, worrying at the end of her own braid with her fingers. If anything, Sima looked far more agitated than Priya. But Rao had seen enough of Priya's gifts to guess that Priya somehow—*somehow*—had her attention trained on Malini, wherever she was within the temple.

"The empress has made a fast friend of that one," Prakash said. He found the heat harder than most, and had seated himself beneath a parasol with his charioteer fanning him.

Rao made a meaningless noise, and Prakash took it as encouragement, as Rao had expected he would.

"She keeps her even closer than the sage," said Prakash, referring to Lata. "She keeps her constantly at her side."

"Elder Priya was injured," Rao murmured.

"She's not injured anymore, Prince Rao," said Prakash. He dabbed at the sweat on his brow with his knuckles. "There will be men who do not appreciate her holding an Ahiranyi witch in high prestige."

"She has few women of similar status that she can talk to," Rao said in response. "When her court is properly established, things will change."

Prakash laughed.

"Instead of wedding our women for alliances, we will be sending our sisters and daughters to court as emissaries to win the empress's favor," he said, as if it were a great joke. Shook his head. "It will be a strange business, having a woman on the throne."

"Prince Rao." A clear, light voice. Rao turned and met the eyes of the priest Mitul. "Will you come with me?"

"Me?"

Mitul inclined his head.

He glanced back at the others. Everyone looked as confused as he felt. But there was nothing to be done save nod in agreement.

He climbed the sandstone steps of the temple. Followed Mitul through the archway into a column-lined corridor, and from there, through narrower and narrower corridors that seemed to lead nowhere.

"You are not taking me to the empress, I think," Rao said cautiously.

"No, Prince Rao."

"I'm not familiar with the temples of the mothers, or all the traditions of your faith," said Rao, emphasizing his Aloran accent—as if he had not been reared at the heart of the faith of the mothers of flame, alongside the imperial princes of Parijatdvipa. "What need do you have of me, a worshipper of the nameless?"

Mitul said nothing for a long moment. He guided Rao across a path next to a central garden courtyard, ushering him into a quiet room, walls carved from a pale, lustrous stone.

"I have not always been a priest of the mothers," Mitul said. "Nor has the priest the empress has come to meet. I, too, am Aloran."

Rao felt a brief sense of surprise. He had never met an Aloran priest of the mothers before. His people worshipped the nameless. But Aditya had become a priest of the nameless, leaving the mothers of flame behind; he supposed it wasn't so impossible for the reverse to happen.

Rao was not sure what reaction the priest wanted, so he simply nodded, keeping his voice attentive, curious.

"How did an Aloran come to be a priest of the mothers?" he asked.

"The nameless guides our fates," said Mitul. "And the nameless guided me to the service of the mothers. Here, I found others who shared my vision." Cryptically put, but Mitul was looking at Rao with his pale eyes. "You believe in the nameless god. And you believe in the mothers of flame."

"Of course."

"And the yaksa?"

"It is not a matter of belief," Rao replied. "The yaksa, the mothers of flame, the nameless god—all of them exist, do they not? I don't disagree with your—path. But I venerate the mothers of flame, and I worship the nameless god. That was how I was raised."

"And the yaksa?"

"I am simply glad they're gone," said Rao.

"Ah, Prince Rao," Mitul said with a faint smile. "They are not gone."

For a moment, Rao was not sure he had heard correctly.

"They are not gone," Mitul said again. His pale eyes seemed to cut through Rao before he turned, guiding Rao deeper into the room. "Let me show you the worth of this temple, and why priests of the mothers tend to it so lovingly."

Tension knotted its way through Rao's body. It was a feeling somewhere between fear and anticipation. It carried him across the room. Held him silent.

The nameless. Somehow, he was sure, the nameless god had called him here.

"The fire of the mothers burned the yaksa grievously," Mitul said, with that priestly, storytelling cadence to his voice. "But there were yaksa who, dying, laid their bodies in Ahiranya's soil. Trees grew from their corpses, or so the Ahiranyi believe. There are many who dismiss the Ahiranyi because they worshipped monsters. But their truth is no less than ours—only darker. Only crueler.

"We kept one such yaksa here," Mitul went on. "One dying yaksa, carried into this temple. One yaksa, laid in our temple's soil to perish. Its body has not survived the centuries unchanged or intact. It is no more than wood—strange, and rich with heat, but nonetheless, no more than wood." He touched his fingertips to a long box that lay on a high table. "Then, a decade ago, it began to change."

He lifted the lid. Inside it, Rao could see soil—rich, soft earth. And upon it . . .

An arm.

At first Rao had thought it was human. Nameless help him, in the course of war he had seen many a severed limb. He knew the shape of one—the absolute horror of a limb flung on a battlefield, still human and freshly alive, fingers curling, knuckles scarred, garbed in some poor soldier's broken armor.

The thing within the box *resembled* an arm: It had five fingers, curling toward a palm. A wrist with jutting bones, the shadow of veins beneath thin skin, leading to the jut of an elbow, an upper arm cut ragged. But the veins, even in the dim light, were the green of sap. The skin was not skin, but wood. If a hand had carved it—and Rao was certain no hand had—then it would have been called beautiful workmanship, eerily lifelike. Roots, white and green, emerged from the stump, sinking into the soil.

It was alive.

"The priest of the mothers reared in Parijat do not know the meaning of what lies before them," said the priest. "They see this arm and do not understand. But we who serve the mothers but also came from other branches and other faiths—we see with clearer eyes. We understand." Mitul looked at him steadily. "This," he said, "is yours, now."

He raised the box and held it forward.

Rao took a reflexive step back.

"This should be shown to the empress."

"It is yours."

"It should be hers. She must—she needs to be told of this, immediately."

"The empress already knows," said Mitul. "And if she does not, my teacher will tell her. He is wise in such matters."

"Why give this to me?" Rao demanded. "Why me, of all the men waiting beyond this temple? Why part with it at all?"

"This is no temple to the nameless, but the nameless speaks everywhere," said Mitul. "You have named and crowned your empress. You have followed her through months of endless war. And now she finally turns her face to Harsinghar and the throne. It is the nameless god's voice—and the mothers alongside it—who tell me it must be you. And you know it too, Prince Rao. You hear it in your heart." He held the box forward again once more. "You know what must be done."

Rao stared at him.

"Does the nameless not speak in your heart?" The priest's voice was kind. "Does the nameless not show you the way?"

Rao knew what his heart said. But he couldn't do what it urged him to do.

He had a duty here, on the path that lay before him, in the battle that awaited Malini at Harsinghar. If there was a voice in his heart, always tugging him away, turning his footsteps back, back, back, then he had no right to listen to it. No right to follow it.

But he held out his own hands and took the box of stone, and the yaksa's severed limb with it. It fit into his waiting hands like it belonged there.

He stepped out into the central gardens of the temple. They were no monastery gardens of the nameless, no gleaming grasses and fruit-heavy trees, no water-laden plinths for seeking visions. There were flowers, and only flowers: gently flowering jasmine blossoms, vibrant pink roses, and sunbursts of yellow oleander, lovely and poisonous. And across from him stood Malini.

Malini was standing under the cover of the temple's columns, in soft shadow. Whatever the priest had said to her had left no mark—she looked as calm as ever, the wind catching the pale folds of her sari, a few stray flower petals from the shrine caught in her hair. She was looking down at him, and as she stared and he stared back, a slight frown creased her brow.

He wondered what she could see in his face.

"I did not expect to find you here," she said. She swept forward, unhurried. The frown had settled, fixing in place. "Did you come in search of me?"

"Malini," he said. "I. No."

She said nothing. She looked at him and looked at him, with those dark eyes that were a mirror of Aditya's and Chandra's.

"I am going to Aditya," he said. The words wrenched their way out of him. "I must..." He tightened his hands against the box. He could not lie to her. He owed her this: the truth. The reason for his fractured loyalty. "The priest told me the yaksa are returning. He gave me..." He could not explain, so he simply opened the box, and she peered in. Her face went very still.

"A limb of wood," she murmured.

"A message," he said. "Proof that Aditya's visions are true. And proof to me, that I should follow my instincts. What the nameless has been telling me in my heart." He let out a shaky breath. "Malini," he said. "I. I have to go back to Aditya. I have to go back to Saketa."

"You are my Aloran general," Malini said. "If you are not here, who will lead your men?"

"My commanders are wise and able," Rao said. She would not part with his soldiers, then. He was not surprised by that. "I trust them to you. My father would support me in this."

"Would he," Malini said noncommittally. She looked at him, measuring him up. There was a new coolness in her tone when she said, "A priest spoke to me of yaksa too. Rao. Tell me truly. You believe danger is coming for us? A danger greater than even Chandra presents?"

"I do," he said.

"And you think the answer lies with Aditya? Not with me?" A strange urgency to her tone.

"I think there is something Aditya must do," he said. "I think he has a purpose. And if the crown is your purpose, then his is something else altogether. And I...I must help him find it."

"Ah, Rao," she murmured, bitterness and fondness twining together in her voice. "Always the helper."

"If that is my role in life, it isn't such a bad one," he said. "I only ask—Empress—that you give me permission to fulfill it."

"If I deny you, won't you simply slip away in the night?" Her mouth curled—not quite a smile. It was too knowing for that.

"I don't believe I would," he said, after a brief hesitation. She caught it. Of course she did.

"Then you don't really know yourself," she said. "You followed your name across the empire. You sought me out for its sake. And now you've been handed a new purpose...? You'll follow it pitilessly, no matter what demands I place on you. So I shall not place any."

He could say nothing. It was true—the kind of true that struck him through swift and brutal as an arrow.

"You may only take the bare minimum of men you need to reach Saketa safely," Malini said, after a moment.

"Thank you," he said.

"Don't thank me," she said. "You must do what you have been guided to by higher forces. And so, apparently, must I."

45

PRIYA

"No," Raziya said, voice like iron. "Empress, I cannot. My guards-women will not."

"You call me empress and still refuse me?" Malini shook her head. "Lady Raziya, I have good reason."

"Why would you refuse our protection?" Raziya demanded. "The battle to take Harsinghar will be dangerous beyond compare, Empress. Why would you send us to the back of the battlefield to fight like cowards?"

"You saw what a bloodbath took place on the Veri," said Malini.

"All the more reason to allow us to protect you!" Raziya made a sweeping gesture with her hand. "If you insist on going without the defense we can offer, at least keep Elder Priya by your side in battle."

Internally, Priya agreed. But for now, she watched with interest, keeping her silence.

Malini shook her head.

"No," she said. "I have a plan. It isn't for you to understand it now."

Raziya's eyes sharpened with irritation. "Empress," she began.

"Lady Raziya," said Malini. "When this war ends, I want your women to train my personal guard. I want guardswomen of my own. And I want to learn how to use a bow with my own two hands." Priya looked at her hands; those soft, uncallused, cruel hands. "I spoke to a priest in secrecy," Malini went on. "And now I'm telling you, if you are at my side in this war, none of that will come to pass. If you have faith in the mothers, please, ask me no more."

Raziya pursed her lips but finally relented.

The women left, and Priya remained. If anyone thought anything of it, they didn't say so—though Lady Deepa's gaze lingered on Priya, curious, before she turned her head and departed.

Malini's eyes met her own.

"Tell me the truth," Priya said simply.

"The priests *have* offered me an alliance," Malini said. "And Rao has returned to Saketa to advise my brother. I did not lie about that."

"So they'll give you their support," Priya said. "All those priests of the mothers. Just like that?"

"Yes."

"For nothing in return?" Priya pressed. She knew there was something else here that Malini hadn't spoken of yet. Raziya had rightly sensed it. They all had.

"Oh, they want something," Malini said. She went abruptly silent.

In Malini's position Priya would have paced the floor. As it was, she could barely keep still. Her body was raw, bright with feeling. She could have run, or howled, or grown a tree to splinter the soil. But instead she clutched her own knees and kept her attention on Malini, who looked as brittle as glass, and just as sharp. The conversation with the priest had clearly shaken her.

Priya waited, and eventually Malini spoke again.

"They want me to burn—willingly," Malini said.

Priya's heart gave a thud.

"Malini."

"I told them I would." She raised a hand, silencing Priya before Priya could protest, could tell her what foolishness that was. "I lied, Priya," she said. "I will never allow myself to burn. But all this—demanding I release the priest who wanted me dead, detouring to this temple, even meeting the so-called faceless son alone—all of it was a test of my willingness to bend to their orders, to do things unthinkingly and obediently. And I have done it. They have every reason to believe me, and every reason to give me their backing in return." A twist to her mouth. "They think I'll make a fine puppet. A good, pure, and righteous puppet."

"But why?" Priya asked, bewildered and horrified. "What would your burning give them?"

Malini looked into her eyes.

"Faith is strange, and powerful," she said. "Think of what was done to you for faith, by your own elders."

"Passing through the waters did give me power," Priya pointed out, even as the bitterness of that settled over her.

"And Divyanshi's burning *did* bless Parijatdvipa, as did the deaths of all the mothers," Malini said levelly. "Their belief in the value of my death is—not untrue."

"That doesn't make it any less monstrous," Priya whispered.

"No." Malini's eyes finally lowered. "No."

"I don't trust your priests," Priya said. "But then, why would I?"

"*I* don't trust my priests."

Malini swayed, and then exhaled, turning her body so that she was leaning against Priya. It startled Priya, almost, that sudden yielding— the weight of Malini against her, Malini tucking her feet close to her body, resting a hand against Priya's arm.

"They've asked me for another act of faith," Malini whispered against her skin. The warmth of her breath, the tightness of her shoulders—all of it made Priya want to curl over her, shield her, hold her like a shell around a vulnerable yolk. "When we attack Harsinghar I am going to...I am going to fight with all my strength. But if all else fails—if the fire is too much for my army...and I fear it will be... Priya, I'm going to allow myself to be captured. Taken to Chandra."

"Malini," Priya said. Heart thudding. "That..."

"I know."

"It's a trap. Surely, it's a trap."

"I know," said Malini, voice a little muffled against Priya. "But perhaps it's not."

"You're not the kind of person who takes wild risks," Priya said, helpless at the thought of it, of Malini handing herself meekly over for slaughter. "What do you even know about this priest?"

"That he has connections and power, and hungers for more," Malini murmured. "That he cannot gain more power under Chandra.

I remember the priests Chandra raised up—all Parijati by blood and rearing. This faceless son still has a Saketan inflection to his voice. He cannot hide it. That he has nonetheless risen so far shows his ambition. He fears losing his position, but he is willing to do it for the sake of that ambition. And his ideals."

"Ideals?"

"Oh, he dreams of what Chandra dreams of. A better Parijat-dvipa, reshaped by faith. But their understanding of what faith should build—that is different. 'Better' for Chandra means a world that fits him and his desires. 'Better' for a priest from Saketa...well." Priya could feel Malini's smile against her skin—the *anger* in it. "He will not find that with Chandra."

"Maybe handing you to Chandra will give him what he wouldn't get otherwise," Priya managed. "Malini, I'm no good at politics or the kind of—the *games* you have to play. But this. You cannot do this—"

"I've considered my options," said Malini. "And this is the best path. We can perhaps—perhaps—take Harsinghar and the throne. But I cannot keep it if the priests of the mothers refuse to serve me. Kartik is the key, Priya, and this is the price he demands of me."

"You should negotiate with him then. Get a more reasonable price. It's so clear you've never haggled at a market," Priya added in a mutter.

That coaxed a true, unguarded laugh out of Malini. The sound made Priya's heart ache.

"That's the problem. Faith doesn't allow for negotiation. Only—obedience."

"I'm a temple elder," said Priya. "I think I know all about faith. More than you, even. He's only human. He can be negotiated with."

There was something Priya couldn't understand about this—something driving Malini, something making her press her fingers into the fabric that covered Priya's stomach, her breath soft against Priya's shoulder. Malini had made this decision, but Priya was sure there had to be reasons beyond the ones she'd given her.

"You're not an obedient person," Priya said, instead of interrogating Malini—instead of trying to pry the real truth out of her.

"No." Malini was silent for a moment. "You're going to have to trust that I understand the priests of the mothers," she said quietly. "You're going to have to believe that I know their ways, and how to manage them."

"I know what you are," said Priya. "I know you understand people. But Malini, this kind of risk…" An exhale. "I'm going to have to have faith, am I?"

"In me? Yes."

Priya closed her eyes. "I don't think I like faith very much." Behind the closed lids of her eyes, in that brief darkness, she saw the sangam, and the yaksa, and felt an echo of fear run through her.

She pushed it away. She couldn't examine it now.

"And you, a temple elder," Malini was saying. "An expert on faith!"

"Don't throw my own words back at me, Malini."

"Then don't ask me to change my nature." There was a hint of a true smile in her voice now. It made Priya want to see her face, so Priya gave in to the impulse to touch her fingertips to Malini's cheek. She moved her hand to Malini's jaw. Urged her chin up with a light nudge of her fingers. Malini moved easily with her.

Their eyes met. If Priya had thought seeing Malini's face would give her answers—well. Malini had always been good at hiding what she felt. But there was a tenderness in her eyes, her expression so gentle it made Priya's heart hurt.

"What do you need from me?" Priya asked. "If you're going to be foolish—how can I help you?"

"Foolish," Malini repeated.

"Of course you're being foolish," said Priya. "But I can't stop you. I could try to be captured with you, I suppose, but that's not what you want, is it?"

Malini's smile faded.

"I don't want you with me when I'm taken. That battle is mine to fight. I want you to stay with the army. Khalil is canny, and Prakash is experienced. Narayan has a good sense of how to manage the rifts between the Saketan princes and lords and keep their forces whole. Between their combined might, we stand a chance of taking Harsinghar. But our chance is…slim. Chandra is prepared. He knows my army has been sorely depleted. He has the unnatural fire. But I... I have you." A pause. A breath. "If all else fails—Priya. If there is nothing else to be done, then I must ask you to act. To use what you are and help my army win." Malini held her tighter—an almost reflexive clench of her fingers on cloth. "If I die, or I'm lost—at least I'll know you won't allow my brother to hold his throne."

"You can't put so much faith in me," Priya said immediately. *I can't live up to what you think I am*, she thought. "And I told you—I showed you—the fire can hurt me—"

"There are Aloran forces that can be spared to protect," said Malini. "Or Saketan. Whatever you want, Priya. They will be arranged to defend you. A crescent of shields and archers, with whip or dagger wielders within it, to keep Chandra's forces at bay and their fire, too. As long as you can work through a barrier—"

"I can't bring down a whole city," said Priya swiftly. Her heart was hammering again. She felt almost suffocated by Malini's weight against her. She could not do what Malini wanted. She could not. "I barely survived bringing down the river. Malini..."

She trailed off. Malini was still leaning into her. It was, Priya realized, as if Malini was afraid that if she let go, Priya would vanish entirely.

"It would be," Malini said, "a last resort."

Priya exhaled through an ache in her lungs she couldn't put a name to.

How can you look at me so tenderly, and ask me to die for you?

"What would you have done if I hadn't come?" Priya asked. "What then?"

"I would have faced all my battles with everything in me," said Malini. "I would have struggled with Mahesh's faith and his loyalties. I would have watched Rao seek to turn from me, back to my brother's light, again and again. And I would have kept on fighting, Priya, for all that I want, and all that I deserve. And I would have lost." Her eyes fluttered closed. "I may lose, still. But I cannot let Chandra win. Let Aditya be forced onto the throne, if he must. Let me die. *But Chandra cannot have it.*"

The kind of power Malini was asking her to use was not power Priya had.

The kind of power she had used in the river—

It was yaksa born. Yaksa gifted. And it came with a price.

The yaksa in the sangam had wanted something from her. The yaksa had made her vow to give—something. More than she had. More than her heart.

What was left to give? What could the yaksa—who lay beyond this world, who were gone—want from Priya now, in return for the strength to win Malini's war?

And was Priya willing to give it?

"I can't believe we're having this kind of conversation like this," Priya said eventually.

"Like what?"

"With you clinging to me."

"I'm not clinging," Malini said.

"Really?"

"'Clinging' doesn't sound very dignified." Malini's voice was faintly disgruntled. Even through her fear—even through everything—Priya felt a lance of fondness.

Priya placed her hand around Malini's wrist. Maybe Malini thought Priya wanted to untangle them from each other, because her grip tightened, nails against the skin of Priya's belly, cloth scrunched tightly in her hand.

"If I can't hold on to you, then I can hold on to no one," Malini said quietly. "And here. Now. What else can I do?"

Ah. Priya swallowed.

How lonely it was, to have power. How lonely.

Priya was glad suddenly, of the home she'd left behind. The broken regent's mahal. Billu lording over his kitchens, and Khalida's glares; Ganam, grumpy and steady and sure, and even Kritika with her fanatic desire for a better world. And Rukh growing taller and stronger, more sure of himself every day, as Padma learned to kick her tiny legs and shape the shadows of words, grasping the world with her fingers like every little bit of it was wondrous to her. Maybe by the time she returned home, Padma would be walking in truth. *Speaking.* For all that she feared for her family—for Bhumika, for *all* of them—she still had the hope that something golden and true was waiting for her.

"Hold on to me, then," Priya said, and pressed her lips to Malini's eyebrow, her cheek, her jaw. Drew her down onto the bed.

It was hours later, in the dark after the candles had died, when Priya finally turned and touched her forehead to Malini's. Shared breath with her again.

"I'll do it. If it comes to it . . . I'll fight with all I have."

Malini's next exhale was a shudder. She cupped Priya's cheek. Said nothing, as Priya whispered battle plans to her like they were love stories.

"When this ends," Malini said finally, in a voice like a scrap of silk—like a fragile weft against Priya's lips, her hands. "When I am alive and I am empress. When you have everything I've vowed to you and Ahiranya . . ." Silence, as Malini cupped Priya's waist with a hand; as she stretched her fingers wide, as if she could encompass it, hold Priya and keep her. "I've dreamt of garlanding you," Malini confessed. A small, secret thing. "Flowers around your throat, and you garlanding me in turn. The two of us making our own promises to each other. I've dreamt of naming you my own. My heart. My wife."

Priya swallowed. Her heart ached, and it was like her whole self ached with it.

"That's a cruel thing to let yourself dream of," she whispered. "Isn't it?"

"It is," Malini agreed, sounding wretched and yet sweet, sweet because she was Priya's. "And yet. Women could marry women once in Ahiranya. And in my foolish dreams I can't forget that."

Priya blinked back tears. Silly of her. They were like children, weren't they? Wanting things they shouldn't, when there were bigger things than the both of them shaping the world, and those forces would wash them away without a care. There was something living in Priya's skin and her soul. There was a throne waiting in Malini's future. And yet. And yet.

She took Malini's hand from her hip and guided it up, until Malini's warm fingers were against the nape of her neck. Until Malini was drawing Priya close, and Priya's fingers were moving, tracing Malini's bare ribs, her breasts; the flower at her throat.

This is my garland. Her own fingers, pressing against the chain at Malini's neck, and the flower that lay there. Malini's hand on her skin. *And this is yours.*

Perhaps Malini understood, because she cupped the back of Priya's neck and kissed her deeply, sweetly. Traced a circle, ever so gently, against the first point of Priya's spine.

This could be the last time, Priya realized. The last time they lay next to each other in the dark. The last time they were both together and alive. The last time they kissed.

But oh, how Priya hoped it would not be.

The morning came, cold and pale, and the army readied itself for war.

Priya found Sima sitting with Lata. When Priya approached, Lata rose to her feet, giving Priya a nod of greeting before walking away.

"What were you talking about?" Priya asked.

Sima shook her head.

"It doesn't matter. What is it, Pri?"

Priya stepped forward. Kneeled down.

"Please," said Priya. "Don't follow me into the next battle. The last one was—bad."

"Terrible," Sima agreed.

"This one is going to be worse," Priya said. She'd seen the look on Malini's face—haunted, almost gutted by the knowledge that both failure and success were so very close, but failure was closer. "I...I'd feel so much better if you stayed away. Like Lady Deepa."

"I'd rather be like Lady Raziya," said Sima. "Leading my own little army around."

Sima shuffled closer to Priya.

"You made a promise to me, Pri," she added. A quiet, firm voice. "You promised I'd be by your side in the next battle. Well, it's here."

"It is."

"And I'm not letting you break that promise. You can say what you like, but I'm going with you."

"Sima," Priya murmured, helpless.

"It's my choice." Her tone brooked no argument. But Sima was watching her carefully. Waiting to see what she'd say.

"This time you're not going into battle unprotected," said Priya finally. "No snatching up shields at the last minute, all right? And your bow won't be enough. We need to get you something more. Better. You won't be able to rely on me. So. We'll have to make sure you can protect yourself. I'll get it sorted."

Sima smiled then, and nudged her arm against Priya's.

"Thank you," she said.

"No thanks needed," said Priya. "We protect each other."

On the last leg of the army's journey to Harsinghar, Priya made her way to Ashutosh. She offered Ashutosh the bow of an equal—shoulders straight, inclining her head. Surrounded by his men, he bowed in return, expression wary.

"Prince Ashutosh," Priya said. "You owe me a favor."

His eyes narrowed.

"I owe you no such thing."

"I saved your life." She smiled at him, aiming for charm and achieving...something that made his right eyebrow twitch. Obnoxiousness, maybe. "Come now, we're fellow leaders of an army, aren't we? Warriors in the service of our empress."

His nostrils flared.

"Tell me what you want," he said.

"Armor," she told him. "For my fellow Ahiranyi woman. Armor to keep her alive." A beat. "And something else," she added. "Something for the battle. If you're brave enough, and you believe your men may be willing to work with the Ahiranyi witch that saved their lives."

"Shut up about lifesaving, I beg you," he muttered. Then he said, "Speak. And don't insult the bravery of my men again."

One of Ashutosh's men that she'd healed, back in Saketa, was small. He had spare armor—a little dented but serviceable—that were given over to Priya for Sima's use.

It was Priya who helped Sima dress and bind the plates over her salwar kameez, tying severe knots into fabric and metal to hold it all in place.

"You should have gotten something for yourself, too," Sima said.

Priya shook her head.

"I carry my armor with me," she said. And there was nothing, in Ashutosh's possession, or in the possession of anyone in this army, that would protect her from the fire. The only thing that had saved her in Saketa had been the yaksa wearing Bhumika's face—the yaksa's magic within her.

She wasn't sure if she wanted it to save her again.

But she would do whatever she had to do. Today, she and Sima climbed into their own chariot. Lata watched, something dark in her eyes, her shawl drawn tight around her shoulders by her white-knuckled hands.

"Doesn't the empress need you?" Priya asked.

"The empress has already said her goodbyes to me, and to all of us," said Lata. "Including you. I tried to change her mind again. As did Lady Raziya." She met Priya's gaze. "I should have known if she would not fight with you by her side, she would not take any of us."

"You sages," Priya said with a smile. "I was always told you could see too much."

"The gift and curse of all who seek knowledge," Lata said dryly. "Perhaps I will see you again, Elder Priya." Her expression was so very grave. "I shall hope that I do. But I must admit, our situation looks somewhat dire."

Priya wanted to say something brave, or funny—wanted to laugh, and show her teeth, and tell Lata that of course she'd survive. No "perhaps" was necessary. But Priya knew better, and Lata did too.

"Perhaps," Priya agreed, instead.

Lata inclined her head and stepped back. And then the charioteer clicked his teeth, and raised the reins—and then they were on the move, the chariot racing over the ground, the rumble of an entire army surrounding them.

46

KUNAL

"This," Kunal whispered, "is how I must find out? From my sister, in secret?"

Varsha's face was drawn.

"He won't tell you, brother," she said, speaking of the emperor. "I shouldn't even know. If I hadn't heard him talking to his priest, I would know nothing either."

Saketa under siege. Hundreds of his father's loyal men dead, many of them by the very fire that Emperor Chandra had assured them would be an unbeatable weapon.

"I—I must go home," said Kunal. "Must go and protect Father. Protect Saketa. I must speak to the emperor."

"He's never going to allow you to leave," said Varsha. She was flushed, her hands restless on her lap. She looked close to tears, which he knew was a sign not of nervousness but of anger. "Perhaps he'll allow you to go once Father has done everything he's asked—once Prince Aditya is dead and Princess Malini is defeated—but I don't know. I don't know."

"If we wait, there won't be anything left of Saketa." He thought of the inhumanity of the emperor—of his sister's increasing timidity, her smallness growing more deliberate, erasing her. Of the constant smell of smoke. Of *home*. "We can go together," he said impulsively. "We can go home, Varsha. Father will protect us once we are there. What benefit is the emperor truly giving him now, after all?"

"Brother," she said, cutting through his words. "I'm already carrying his child."

A beat of silence.

"Oh," Kunal managed.

"I couldn't leave here regardless. I'm his wife. I'm his now, you understand? Father has made his bargain, and I must respect it. But if I give him a son, a future emperor of Parijatdvipa..." She kept her eyes on his. "If I win his affection and trust, if he wishes to reward me—Kunal, there's no end to what Saketa may gain."

"You think I shouldn't go and help Father," said Kunal, finally. "You think I should stay here where the emperor wants me. A—a glorified hostage, in all but name. Is that what you really think, Varsha?"

"You must do what you feel is right," she said, lowering her eyes. "You...What can I do to stop you?"

Tell your husband I'm running away, he thought. *Say a single word in front of one of those maids he has spy on you.* But no, there was no point giving her ideas, and Varsha—simple as she was—knew better than to speak of this before a single living soul who was not her brother, her kin.

He bribed his way from the mahal. Took only a handful of guards and his horse with him and absconded in the night. Traveled in the dark, by starlight. He was determined to get home. Determined to help his father.

His luck held for nearly a week.

Then he crossed paths with strangers on the road. A group of men on horseback.

"Friends," Kunal said, giving them a nod. "If you allow me to pass..."

They did not move.

"No closer, friend," said the man on the farthest horse. Like his companions, he was dressed plainly, in a simple gray tunic and dhoti. He had a pleasant, forgettable face—wide, watchful eyes. "What business do you have here?"

"Nothing that concerns you," Kunal said, raising his chin.

"It's a simple question," one of the other men grumbled.

He didn't want a fight. What he wanted was to ride as far as he could, as fast as he could, until he was back at his father's side.

"I am going home," Kunal said begrudgingly.

"Home," the stranger repeated. His gaze lingered on the green in Kunal's tunic; the hints of metal embroidery glinting in the silk.

Kunal shivered. He had thought his clothing subtle, almost invisibly dull, when he'd fled the imperial mahal. But now, under the stranger's eyes, he realized the cut of his tunic was distinctively Saketan—that his belt was shaped to carry a whip, even if he did not have one to hand. That the metal on his jacket might not have been silver or gold, but it was still a polished hue that shone like a beacon in the firelight.

"You look as if home is across the border," the stranger said.

"It is not a crime to be from Saketa," Kunal responded. "And you, I think, friend—you are far from home. Very far."

"Oh, very far," the stranger agreed. "Well, if we're both travelers, why don't we share a meal? My men and I were planning to rest. You're welcome to join us."

"A meal," he repeated. "I'd feel happier accepting if you would have your men lower their weapons."

"Your men haven't yet lowered their own," the stranger said. "So I'm afraid I can't."

"Let me pass," Kunal said again.

"You're heading for the city of Saketa," the stranger said. When Kunal said nothing, the stranger nodded to himself. "Please tell me your name."

"Sunil," Kunal said.

"I had a friend once," the stranger went on as if Kunal hadn't spoken. "He was a low prince of Saketa. I trained with him many times. And spent time in his home. Sometimes other highborn brought along their children to visit while I was there. There was never a shortage of young princes in Saketa." A pause. "I recognize your face, Prince Kunal."

Kunal should have raced away. Should have reached for his blade. But he was outnumbered, exhausted, afraid. And he could not.

"I'm afraid you're coming with me," said the stranger. He drew a chakram from his wrist. His eyes were gentle, sorrowful even as he raised it in the air. "You have my apologies," he said. "But I cannot afford to let you go."

47

CHANDRA

Chandra kept dreaming the same dream.

He stood upon a field. It was night, and the field was black beneath him, the ash smoldering, fractured with starlight. Around him were women dressed in bridal red, crowns of fire glowing on their skulls. They stretched off into the distance, so many women that he could not count them all.

"We are waiting for you," one said, wreaths of smoke gathering at her feet.

Always, it was the same: relief crashing through him. Elation. He was where he was meant to be. He knew them, and they knew him.

He went to his knees.

"Mothers," he gasped. "Mothers of flame. I am here. Tell me what you desire, and it will be done."

"Oh, Chandra," another said pityingly. "We are not the mothers. The mothers don't wait to greet you with glory. You are no one's chosen. A tale you tell yourself is not a true thing simply because you say so. Do the tides obey you? The waning of the moon? No. Then why should pitiless fate garb you in glory, simply because you believe you should be glorious?"

"You are not chosen," said another voice. Sweet, airy. He almost knew it. Had he heard it before, in the palace, from a girl walking at his sister's side? "Your mothers speak. The nameless speaks. And you close your ears."

"I *am* chosen," he said, and the ashen wind caught his voice and carried it away, leaving his mouth empty. "I am," he whispered. "My faith guides me. My faith protects me."

"Faith," one laughs. *Faith*, the rest echo. "What is there to have faith in? There is only the void, Chandra."

She loomed over him. Her crown was dripping fire like water. It poured down over her face, which was empty—nothing and everything all at once.

"We are waiting," she said. "In the void, Chandra. We are waiting for you."

The fire wound its way into his mouth. Burned, hot and vicious and agonizing, through his lungs, his belly, the viscera of him.

He woke with a howl.

One of his loyal lords advised him in the presence of the court that he should lead the fight against his sister. "You must go beyond the walls, Emperor," he urged desperately. "You did not go to the Veri. But you must defend Harsinghar. Your men need you."

"An emperor's place is in his mahal," Chandra snapped. "Not in the dirt of battle. I will not abandon my throne."

"Emperor, it would not be abandonment," the man said. "Your father led his men in battle. And his father before him—"

"Am I my father?" Chandra thundered. His vision was swimming, exhaustion and fury mingling together. "Am I an emperor who debases himself, lowers himself to the level of those who do not have Divyanshi's blood? No."

Silence. The lord bowed deep, lowering his gaze.

I will not leave my throne, Chandra thought wildly. *It is mine, by the mothers, by destiny, by blood.* There was a terrible fear in him that if he walked away from the mahal—walked from this hall, this throne, the carapace of his power—he would have nothing. He would *be* nothing.

"Get out of my sight," he said. "You do not deserve to be in my presence. Go. All of you."

The lords ran. And Chandra placed his face in his hands and wept.

He went to the temple.

Even before Hemanth had taken him under his wing, the temple had been his solace. He had never avoided worship, as Aditya had; had never smiled and allowed the words of the Book of Mothers to slide off him like water, ignoring every entreaty from the priesthood to stay and learn and know what it meant to serve Parijatdvipa. No, unlike his brother, he had read the Book of Mothers over and over to himself. He had gone willingly to worship at the imperial temple, his sister arranging garlands at the altar with his mother.

He had watched them both: The slight figure of his mother laying out flowers, and his sister's even slighter form beside her, performing piety, and thought of them burning. He'd felt something rise through him at that thought. A peace, and a rightness.

He had told his mother of it once. She had looked at him as if he were a stranger.

Hemanth had never recoiled from him. Hemanth had truly *seen* Chandra, and molded him into a man worthy of his name. He had given Chandra a faith that was simple and pure, as clear as glass: The Parijati were the mothers' chosen. Chandra had a holy bloodline, and holy purpose. The only rightful path for the empire lay in his heart and his hands.

Chandra sat in the gardens upon a bench. Beneath trees, in gentle sunlight. Lowered his head into his palms.

He heard Hemanth's approach. The gentle whisper of robes. He felt Hemanth's hand come to rest upon his forehead. Tender.

"The world," Chandra said into the silence, "is even stranger and crueler than I imagined."

The priest said nothing.

"You should have told me all your fears," Chandra said. "All the things your priests had said. You should have told me a long time ago. Why didn't you?"

"I knew," said the High Priest, as he stroked Chandra's hair, "that you would respond as you have. That you would fear the yaksa more than you have ever feared any mortal man. More than any subordinate king, claiming falsely to be your equal."

"I fear nothing," Chandra choked out, knowing it was a lie.

"You have always desired order and meaning. And I have striven to give it to you. Faith has been your armor and your guiding star. I am sorry that the sky is clouded by ill omens."

Chandra let a breath shudder out of him. At least he had Hemanth. Even Hemanth's loyalty was imperfect. But Hemanth loved him, and Chandra loved him in turn. Hemanth was better than any family Chandra had ever possessed. He could forgive this. He would.

"I'll do it," Chandra said finally. "I will tell all my men, all my warriors—capture her. Bring her to me. And then I'll...convince her." His voice choked on that word. Convince. Would he be expected to beg her? He would not.

"My emperor is wise," Hemanth said. "As I always knew."

"I dream sometimes of the women who have burned to save Parijat-dvipa," Chandra confessed. "I dream that they—they *laugh* at me. They tell me I will join them. That the mothers do not choose me." He squeezed his eyes tight, holding back furious tears. "Tell me the dreams are false."

Hemanth's hand paused upon his hair. A beat passed, and then he resumed the motion. "The dreams are false," he said.

"The mothers chose me, didn't they?" Chandra said, knowing his voice sounded like a plea and not caring. "I am the one who will defeat the yaksa, am I not? I'll fashion the empire into greatness, placing Parijat high?"

"The mothers made you," Hemanth said. "Your faith and your idealism, your vision for a better world, and the bravery with which you seek it. Be the man they made you, Chandra. Go beyond the walls. Claim your sister."

He thought of it. Going beyond the walls. His fire on a sword in his hands.

Like a knife strike, the image came to him again—the faceless burned woman. The laughter.

In the void, Chandra. We are waiting for you.

"I will send my men," he said, through the dizzying feeling running through him—a feeling like the heat of a pyre. "I will meet her before the holy fire. And I will claim my fate. As the mothers intend."

48

PRIYA

Harsinghar appeared in the distance. The army did not stop to gaze upon it, but behind the body of the charioteer, Priya could make out glimpses of white marble and golden spires. She could sense the tug of the ancient trees, with great drooping branches and roots shallow enough to feel footsteps on their surface, or the sun beating down on them.

She closed her eyes and tried to feel nothing but the green—the trees and flowers and the soft creepers wound around windows and colonnades. Every inch of it sang comfortingly. She was surrounded by weapons. She could do what Malini had asked. She could survive this.

"You should open your eyes," Sima said.

"I don't have anyone to impress here," Priya said, still reaching out for green.

"No. Pri. Look."

Priya opened her eyes.

A sea of shining white and gold filled her vision.

The Parijati army surrounded the city in a gleaming wall of sun-lit armor, vast Parijatdvipan flags on gold-and-white swathes of cloth wavering in the breeze. They were waiting.

Their sabers—held aloft before them—were alight with flame.

"It doesn't look like the emperor's willing to negotiate," Sima said.

"No." Priya's mouth felt dry. She wetted her lips with her tongue; breathed in the air, already rich with the smell of fire. "He never struck me as the type, really."

"Hold on tight," their charioteer said tersely. "I've been instructed to carry you as near to the city's walls as I can."

Priya gave a jerky nod. She brushed her knuckles against Sima's own. Said, "Keep your shield up."

"Don't worry about me," Sima said. She clutched Priya's hand for a single moment, then let it go. "Let me worry about you for once."

Priya was afraid for Sima. Afraid for herself. For all of them, really. As the chariot jolted forward, she looked out at the riders around them—almost all of them were Ashutosh's liegemen.

Conches sounded. And her foot soldiers were racing forward, the dust churning beneath their feet. She heard the clashing, roaring noise of boots and metal and—screaming. Of course there was screaming.

Her stomach was writhing. Whenever she blinked, she saw the yaksa behind her eyes.

The chariot gave a sickening lurch. The charioteer swore and veered hard to the left as men piled past them.

"Almost time," their charioteer called. There was a sheen of sweat on his face, but his mouth was set in grim determination. Priya breathed out, and lowered herself to the ground of the chariot. Sima kneeled with her, her armor creaking.

There was an unnatural pressure to the air. A heaviness, as the wind howled against flags, as horse hooves thudded against the ground, as elephants made low, chuffing noises.

"I'll make sure nothing touches you," said Sima quietly, beside her.

"I'm only worried about one thing," Priya said, voice already a little ragged—as if she were running, fast, hard—not sitting still on the floor of a chariot with Sima crouched beside her, a great shield strapped to her arm. "If the fire touches me..."

"It won't," Sima said. "I won't let it."

Priya closed her eyes. "Just you and your shield," she said. "Come on, Sima. Don't coddle me."

"Don't underestimate my strength," Sima said. "You and me, we're going to be okay. We're going to get through."

"If I don't—"

"Priya, no—"

"If I don't," Priya said more firmly. "Then I want you to be okay. Don't die for me. Whatever happens."

"You're my best friend," Sima said quietly.

"*Sima.*"

Sima squeezed her hand. "You don't have time to argue with me right now." She stood, in the shadow of their charioteer. Stared out at the raging battlefield.

"The army's getting closer," Sima said, and then Priya felt the jolt of the chariot beneath them.

Listened to the crash of metal. The screaming.

She watched as fire crossed the sky above her head like a shooting star.

She held her breath. Held it inside her, then released it. Held, released. An inhale and exhale and inhale and exhale like a wheel turning, as if she were not so much reaching for the sangam as churning its waters, frothing them into violence. She got one of her feet beneath her. A knee against the ground.

Drew her magic and held it.

Plans she'd whispered like they were loving things. Plans for battle, in the dark with Malini. Now, in the light of day, she'd have to see them through.

She hoped Ashutosh's men were are brave as he'd claimed.

Priya had arranged armor for Sima, but she'd arranged a different kind of defense for herself. Buds tucked behind her ears. Seeds sewn and folded into her chunni, her tunic.

Seeds tucked in the sleeves of the soldiers' armor. In their collars and turbans, helms and boots. Just as she'd asked, Ashutosh's men had carried her weapons on themselves. They'd been brave after all, and trusted the witch who had saved their lord's life. Good.

She reached her strength out.

The seeds and buds began to unfurl. Ready. Thorns prickled up at her sleeves—drawing drops of blood at her upper arms, her shoulders. Grounding pain.

The kind of power she would need to take the city terrified her. But until the moment came when the battle was clearly almost lost—until there was no other choice—Priya could rely on some old tricks. Breaking the earth. Throwing up roots. Sending skewers of thorn and branch to pierce and bind.

What was the earth, what was mere soil, compared to the weight of a river?

The ground cracked open, a great lightning strike gouge that spread in splinters, fanning out with the patterned grace of leaf veins. She had to look—stood, gripping the edge of the chariot as she raised her other hand before her—and aimed her strength.

Thorns and roots rose from the ground, burrowing out of the deep soil. Those roots caught legs, snared bodies. Those thorns forced their way through flesh, spearing limbs before flinging them back violently down. Bodies fell, and Sima twisted to the side, shield up, keeping them safe. Through the gaps between shield and armor and Sima's protective shadow, Priya saw thorns rise on the surface of the Saketan liegemen's armor. If they were terrified, or feared her gifts, they didn't show it. Only pressed on.

Chandra's army had sentient fire. But her plants had her own mind in them. And if they couldn't stand against flame, at least they could shoot out like arrows—cut enemy flesh. They could break a throat, a spine.

The harder Priya worked, the more fiercely Ashutosh's men fought, their whips shining against the air, the blood streaming in an arc after them.

Her vision was beginning to blur. She closed her eyes once more, and *focused*.

Fiery arrows were still falling. Priya felt one thud into the ground by the wheel to the left of her. The fire arced up, and Sima swore and shoved the shield down, trying to bar the flames even as the chariot swerved.

The chariot lurched wildly.

She could hear the screaming clash of the battle. Louder, louder.

"Are we losing?" Priya yelled.

"I have no idea!" Sima yelled back, ducking low. She drew the shield up, over them, high now. In front of them, their charioteer swore.

Distantly, she heard the wail of conches. A chorus.

The empress had been captured.

Malini, Priya thought. It was a helpless thought, like a call into the void.

A part of her truly hadn't believed Malini would allow it. But she had told Priya she would, and Malini hadn't lied to her for a long, long time.

"Take us a little closer to the city," she yelled to the charioteer, who nodded sharply.

"They've got more fire," the charioteer called, and Sima looked at Priya. Said to the charioteer, "I think we need to—avoid—"

Her words were cut off. A huge gout of fire hit the ground to the right of them, sending their chariot careening. Priya felt the hot wind lash her face.

One of Ashutosh's liegemen fell from his horse, rolling away roughly with a panicked, terrible yell. Priya squeezed her eyes shut, reaching abruptly for the green tangled into his armor. She grasped it with her magic and *dragged* him out of the path of the flames, by the earth and the green and anything she could hold in that moment, on that breath. Her eyes snapped open, firelight burning across her vision, and saw another soldier lean down from his horse and grab the man and desperately, swiftly haul him up.

They're all going to die, she thought with something like terror, and reached again—reached for all the green she could feel, pushing those men back in a wave, away from the falling flames. Crests of earth rose, like waves to give them a little shelter. *Go back*, she thought. *All the strength you have is nothing against that fire—*

There was another blast. Ringing in Priya's ears. She heard Sima scream, her voice ringing like a distant bell. Before the heat could even touch her—and it was coming, gold-glint of fire, it was coming—Priya wrenched a hand up in the air. Drew the earth over them, a dark wall, a wave, but not enough. Not enough.

The earth shuddered. She'd done too much. Already, too much, as the chariot rolled, the horses screamed.

Fell, fell, fell—

Back into cosmic waters. Back into waiting arms.

"Sapling," the yaksa whispered. "Your debt has come due."

49

RAO

The sun had faded, the sky white-gray with the falling night, when they finally stopped to rest. Prince Kunal was untied, on Rao's orders. Kunal rubbed his wrists, flexed his fingers to get the blood moving. He considered running—Rao could tell, from the back-and-forth flick of his gaze and the tension in his shoulders—but he clearly thought better of it. Rao's men were, after all, watching him in return.

Rao helped to settle the horses and start the campfire, then kneeled down in front of him. He placed food and water in front of Kunal, and watched the prince frown and lower his head.

"Drink," said Rao. "You must be thirsty. If you won't eat, at least do that." He waited. Kunal did not move. "It's only water," Rao told him then. "I'll drink first, if it'll put your mind at ease."

"I don't know what you hope to do with me," the prince rasped, still not touching the flask. "But I'm no use to you. I have nothing for you."

Not true, and surely they both knew it. There was a hunted look in Prince Kunal's eyes. The light of the campfire flickered over his face in golden scars.

"I heard of your sister's marriage," Rao said eventually. "Congratulations." He watched Kunal's mouth tighten. "Perhaps you don't want my congratulations," Rao added carefully, and watched that mouth tighten an increment further.

"I have nothing useful to tell you," Kunal said again through gritted teeth.

"Emperor Chandra is a difficult man," Rao said. "He always has been." Silence.

"I've only met you once before," Rao continued. "You won't remember it. You're a few years younger than me, I think. How old were you when your father took you to Harsinghar as a child? Five? Six?"

"Tell me your name," Prince Kunal demanded.

"Prince Rao. A son of the King of Alor."

Kunal gave a jerky laugh.

"A nameless prince," he said. "*The* nameless prince."

"Not nameless," Rao said quietly. "Everyone knows my name now. But Rao will do."

"Then Rao. Prince Rao, I beg you: Let me go. I have no army with me. You've killed the few men I had. I am no danger to you."

Rao swallowed the guilt that burned at the back of his throat. He had no reason for guilt, he knew: Prince Kunal's men had not been willing to surrender, and Rao's purpose was far too important for him to allow them to live. He had killed before, and he would kill again. That was necessary in war. It didn't stop him from feeling as he did.

"I can't allow you to return to your father," Rao said gently. "And I can't simply allow you to run off into the distance. Where would you go?"

"I have nowhere to go," said Kunal. "And that is why—that is why you have no reason to keep me."

"We're both highborn. Both royal. So I know very well that we were not raised to survive with nothing and rebuild ourselves, Prince Kunal. If I let you run, I'm condemning you. And I would rather not." *Not unless I have to*, he thought grimly. *And not without getting something of worth out of you before I do.* "I would rather make you my ally."

"You said yourself. My sister is wed to the emperor." His voice was flat. "My father is loyal to him. And I am loyal to my father."

But not, Rao noted, loyal directly to Chandra. Good.

"There are many Saketan highborn who have allied themselves to Empress Malini," Rao told him. "And many of them once fought our empress on the battlefield. There is no shame in changing your allegiance to the true heir to the Parijatdvipan crown. No shame in ensuring that you inherit your father's throne—"

A hand gripped sharply at Rao's wrist. He heard the hiss of steel as his men drew their daggers.

"You have news about my father," Kunal said. His voice was tight, eyes wide. "You have news about Saketa—the city. Tell me, please."

"I know Empress Malini's army stands against him," Rao said calmly. He did not move, did not flinch, as his men waited for his signal. He didn't think he would need to give it. "All I can tell you is that you should ally with Empress Malini. All I can tell you is that if you wish to ensure your future, that's the best path. The only path."

Kunal fell silent again. He was trembling. Slowly, his fingers unclasped from Rao's wrist. He reached for the water. Took an unsteady drink, wild and wasteful, water running down his chin. He lowered it back down.

"I'll ally with your empress," Kunal said finally. "I've seen what Emperor Chandra is. I'll do it. For—for Saketa's sake. For our future."

"Good," said Rao. "That's good. Eat now, and rest if you can. We'll be on the move again tonight." He clapped a hand lightly against Kunal's shoulder, all friendly camaraderie, then rose to his feet.

He walked to the edge of their small encampment, away from the shadow of the fire. One of his men was on guard, sharpening his daggers with a spark of steel against stone.

"He's lying," the man muttered. "My lord."

Rao gave the smallest nod.

"Go and eat," he said. "I'll keep watch."

"You haven't eaten yet, my lord."

"I'll eat later," he said.

Rao stayed where he was, staring out into the dark. He wasn't hungry. His stomach felt weighed down by what lay ahead of him, and what he would have to do.

The nameless knew how much Rao didn't want to do what was needful. But need—and the nameless—had little mercy for one man's overly tender heart.

The first thing Rao saw, on their approach to the fortress, was smoke. The sky was gray with it. He could feel it getting into his lungs. Around him, his men were hacking. Prince Kunal looked gray as the smoke and ash surrounding them. He hadn't expected this either, then.

Rao drew his shawl over his mouth and kept on moving forward.

When the bulk of Malini's army had left the ground surrounding the Saketan fortress, they had left green plains of grass behind them. Rocky ground, yes, but trees too.

Now there was nothing but blasted earth, scorched by fire.

Rao's small group were met immediately by an armed band of soldiers, bows drawn. But the bows were lowered swiftly when Rao announced himself.

They were led to the remains of the camp. A handful of tents. A straggling group of men, sparse enough that Rao knew without a doubt how close Aditya's efforts were to failure.

Chained at the wrists, his arm held by one of Rao's men, Kunal was trembling. But Rao could not think of him. He could only watch as a figure emerged from one of the tents, dressed in armor that had seen better days. Hair a little ragged, from mistreatment and too-close brushes with flame. Skin darkened by sunlight.

"Rao," Aditya called. And there was no pause, after that, for pleas-antries or bowing, for Rao to say *Prince Aditya*, and explain his reasons for being here. There was only Aditya drawing him into a crushing hug. Only Aditya murmuring against his hair, "I knew you'd come."

"Of course," Rao choked out. This was right. This was where he was meant to be. "Of course, Aditya."

Mahesh looked tired. Old in a way he simply never had before. His gaze dimmed, visibly, when he learned that Rao had not brought reinforcements.

"We won't last for much longer," Mahesh said bluntly. "You've brought us nothing, Prince Rao?"

Rao shook his head.

"The empress could spare nothing."

"Then I pray the empress takes Parijat swiftly," Mahesh said. He looked at Aditya. Then said, "We've faced battle once already today. Those priestly soldiers do not relent. Fire arrows and swords and their

TASHA SURI

bodies thrown at us—they'll do anything, as long as they think they're acting in the interests of the mothers. Another attack like that, and I fear the High Prince's men will escape our grip."

"Lord Mahesh is correct," Aditya said quietly. "We have little left to give."

"You've stopped them from leaving the fort and marching on Parijat. That counts for something. I didn't think you would manage that." When Aditya gave him a look, Rao said, "I didn't think anyone could manage that."

"It counts for less than you would think." Aditya pushed his hair back from his face. His hand left a smear of dirt and sweat in its wake. "The maze of that fort—we must infiltrate it to get to the High Prince, to end this—and, Rao, I can only send men in in small groups, and they're felled fast. And despite the cost of this war—the lives we've paid with to hold them at bay—small numbers of his men keep breaking free. Somehow. We cannot stop them." Aditya met his eyes, naked exhaustion in his face. "Their fires are dying. Whatever stock of flames they have—my sister was not wrong about that. But their water doesn't run out. Their food doesn't run out. And our own..."

Rao nodded wordlessly. Inwardly, he cursed. He should have brought supplies. But he had only made it this far, this swiftly, because he had come unencumbered. Even dragging Prince Kunal along had delayed him more than he would have liked.

Abruptly, he became aware again of the weight of the arm strapped to his back. Embarrassment rushed through him. How could he have allowed himself to forget something so important? He should have spoken to Aditya immediately, but the sight of his old friend had undone him.

"Lord Mahesh," he said. "I must speak to Prince Aditya alone. My apologies."

Mahesh nodded and departed with a swiftness that surprised Rao. But Aditya smiled, a little sadly, and said, "We rest when we can now. What is it, Rao?"

Rao took the box—strapped close to his back all through this journey—and placed it on the ground in front of Aditya.

"You once showed me a vision from the nameless," Rao said, into the silence that followed. "A coming. An inevitable coming. And here... here is the proof. The yaksa are returning. Their remains are reviving. You had the vision, Aditya. I was given this proof, but I believe... I believe it was meant for you."

He opened the box with a click. Aditya leaned forward and looked upon it.

He exhaled; a soft, worshipful noise.

Aditya's eyes near shone. Through all the grime and dirt, Rao saw priest and prince in him.

"My purpose," Aditya murmured. "I've been waiting all this time, and here it is. A war greater than any we're fighting here. A war calling me."

"What will you do," Rao said in return, voice just as soft. "Now that you know?"

Aditya lowered his head. A long silence followed, that Rao could not read.

"We win here," he said finally. "We win, knowing that the nameless has a higher purpose for us. And then we face what comes."

Rao nodded, oddly relieved. This wasn't the end. This couldn't be the end. The nameless had promised it to them.

"If you need to navigate the fort," Rao said, "then I have someone that may be useful to you. But he'll need some—convincing."

50

MALINI

Her first thought, on beholding Harsinghar, should not have been *I'm finally home.*

But it was.

Almost her entire life had been spent in Harsinghar—in its white marble and pale sandstone, its sweet-smelling flowers and streets lined with trees laden with green leaves, golden blossoms. But it was fitting that the Harsinghar she beheld now smelled of flames held upon swords.

It was fitting that she wasn't sure if today she would live and succeed, or die.

She had surrounded herself with some of the strongest warriors in her army. But the press of men around her ebbed and swelled as Chandra's forces pushed forward, forward—all their strength aimed at getting to *her.*

Men fell around her, caught in the press of boots and weapons. She heard so many voices crying out that it was like a roar. She tried not to listen to it. The wind was sharp on her face. Her back was straight, her hand clenched against the chariot's edge.

She'd been right not to allow Raziya at her side.

Her men did not know how to respond. They had expected Chandra to behave by reasonable rules of warfare—to defend his city, his *home*, before all else. But his army was pressing toward her with single-minded focus, and Malini could only hold herself steady on her chariot, as the thing jerked with the movement of the bodies around her, caught in a violent sea.

Either Malini would be captured as the priest had told her—or soon an arrow would go through her throat, or her chariot would be upended, and she would be dead.

I have Priya, she reminded herself, through the cloying haze of her own fear. What use was fear? How could she face what came next with anything less than all the bravery she had in her?

Her chariot was as carefully defended as she could have made it, ringed on all sides with soldiers and cavalry. But Chandra's men cut down the foot soldiers. They barreled forward with their horses. Sabers wreathed in flame cut a swathe through the men around her, and the smell of fire and dying struck Malini sharply, like a blow.

Raziya had spoken, sometimes, of what it took to hunt prey on Dwarali's mountains. As Malini's chariot ground to a halt within the press of bodies—as her charioteer begged the men around him to take the empress, to carry her to safety—Malini thought of that tale and did not move.

You must close in on the animal. Circle it with a dozen men, drawing in closer and closer, ensuring that it has no means of escape. If it finds a gap, it will take it, Empress. That is the way of things that want to live.

But once you have it caged, a simple net is enough to contain it. And then, the knife.

She wasn't prey, born to leap into the crush of the battle below her chariot and be felled with a horse's hoof to the skull, or a sword of fire to the chest. She would not run. She would—despite every instinct in her—have faith.

Faith was submission. Faith was obedience to a higher power, a baring of the neck to a knife, a step into absolute darkness with no light but the heart's own foolishness. She had set in motion all that she could. It was time to take one final risk.

"Cut the horses free," Malini forced out. The charioteer protested, and she said, "Do it. Now."

He grasped his saber and sliced the reins. The chariot fell still.

"*Go*," she said to the charioteer. "You. Go to—"

It was too late. Quicker than she could understand, someone swung onto the chariot, and in the next moment, a blade had sliced through the poor charioteer's neck.

The man wielding the blade dropped his weapon. Turned to her.

"Princess Malini," the stranger said; blood and ash matted to darkness on his forehead, his priestly hair loose at his shoulders. "You must come with me."

In that moment, the obedience Kartik had asked of her demanded the same thing as her pride did: to not fight or scream or panic as Chandra's soldiers closed in on her. The fire-swept wind ran over her skin, hot and cold all at once.

She removed her own saber and held it before herself.

"Take me to my brother, priest," she said. Her own voice was a stranger's in her ears. She thought, absurdly and achingly, of Rao kneeling before her on the road to Dwarali. Her voice sounded like his had, she thought. Like a hollow thing with a fate in it, a conch calling forth a war. "I'm ready."

Malini was led to a horse; lifted and carried away before she knew it.

She was dragged from a horse to a gate, and from a gate to a doorway, and from a doorway though an underground tunnel, and from there into the walls of the mahal itself, and she thought of Priya.

If all else fails and I die, she will fight my brother. And she will see him dead.

Malini had not expected to survive this long and rise so far. The fact that she still wanted to rise—the fact that she *deserved* to rise— meant nothing. If she fell, at least she would take her brother with her. At least she had found the kind of love that would break the world for her sake, and make it into something that would always wear her mark.

The corridor she was led through was dimly lit and flanked by soldiers dressed in imperial armor. They clearly recognized her—she saw contempt and respect warring on any number of faces. Some men sneered. Many lowered their eyes.

Malini looked straight ahead and went to her fate.

In the court of the imperial mahal, a fire was burning.

A pit had been prepared to contain it, lined in clay bricks. The clay was an ugly, squalid thing in comparison to the sandstone and marble of the court that surrounded it, but at first glance Malini thought someone had made an effort to beautify it. There were flowers clustered at the edges of the pit, spilling onto the floor. They were bright, marigold oranges and yellows, the flicker of the fire making them move strangely. Beyond it stood a line of priests. They were solemn faced. Waiting for her.

As she was led closer, she realized the flowers were not flowers at all, but flames. Blooming and growing and withering, with all the beauty of real blossoms.

"Sister." Malini saw a shadow across the floor. Felt a soldier's hand at her back, pressing her down.

She knelt, and looked up, and faced her brother.

He had not been on the battlefield outside his city, she was sure of that. The armor he wore was unmarked, shining, more decorative than practical. He wore prayer stones at his throat, bound with elaborate gemstones and darts of silver-gold. Threads of pearls surrounded his neck. He looked every inch the emperor.

His boots made a heavy noise against the ground as he approached her. He stopped before her. He was close enough that she had to tilt her head to meet his eyes, which were just as she remembered. A mirror of her own.

"Sister," he said. His voice was low, rumbling. "Welcome home."

She had thought often of what she would say to him when they finally met again. So many eviscerating, clever words. But now that she was here, she could only laugh soundlessly and watch his expression darken in response.

"Brother," she said. She let her gaze flicker pointedly from the soldiers behind her, to the fire, to his face. "Is this how you *welcome* your sister, Chandra? By pushing her to the floor to crouch like a dog?"

He swallowed, visibly. Already trying to control his temper.

"You are kneeling," he said, "because I am emperor. And you are my sister, my responsibility, and my subject. You kneel like a princess."

"I am not a princess," she said. "I am an empress. *The* empress. You should be kneeling to me."

To her surprise—and unease—he slowly lowered himself down to his knees, until they were almost level. She could feel the heat of his breath on her face. She forced herself not to flinch. Instead, she took him in: The exhausted circles around his eyes. The lines of tension bracketing his mouth.

"You're lying to yourself," he murmured. "You know that. You're not an empress. You are impure and broken and *worthless*. In your heart you know I'm telling the truth." He took her chin in his hands. Revulsion ran through her at his touch. He had no right to touch her. He never had. "You have one chance at redemption," he told her. "Only one. Rise to the pyre, sister. Accept your fate and the mothers will forgive." A beat. "*I* will forgive you."

"Beg me," she whispered in return. "Grovel with your face to the floor. Cry. Maybe if you're pitiful enough, I'll consider rising to the pyre." She cocked her head to the side in his grip. "Go on," she urged.

His hand on her jaw tightened brutally.

"I want to kill you so very much," he rasped.

She smiled through the pain.

"I know," she said. "It's been a long time, brother."

He released her.

Slapped her, openhanded around the face. Her ears rang. Her mouth tasted of blood.

"Emperor," the High Priest said, alarmed. "You cannot—"

"She's barely hurt," Chandra said, eyes cold. "She could take more. I could break her legs and her arms, and she could still burn. It would be no less than she deserves, wouldn't it?"

"If you want me to burn for you," she said, feeling the cut on her lip with her tongue, "this is a poor way to convince me."

He hit her again. Of course he did.

Another noise of alarm from the High Priest. She raised her head, and for a moment stars danced across her vision. Standing to the High Priest's left, she saw Kartik. His gaze was intent. Solemn. Very subtly, he offered her a tilt of his head.

"I could throw you in the fire pit now," Chandra was saying. "The fire there was born from the deaths of thousands of pure, good women. Perhaps it would purify you in turn."

"Wrong," Malini said. "Ah, Chandra. You do not see it. Perhaps your priests do. I am pure. I am pure in a way you cannot touch, a way that is inviolable. It lies in my heart. It lies in my blood, beyond the dirt of your mortal ambitions." She bared her bloodied teeth at him. "You cannot alchemize me into your glory. I will not allow it. My glory is my own."

"Your life has never been your own," Chandra said. "Your life has always belonged to Parijatdvipa. You refused to sacrifice it. I've given you the chance to reflect, and repent, and choose your rightful death. *So many chances.* And you still never learn, never change."

"Ask your priests the worth of an unwilling death," Malini said. "See what they do if you try and burn me now."

He grasped her by the hair hard, wrenching her neck.

"Just like a spoiled boy," she gasped out. Did he think he could humiliate her? Shame her? She had suffered so much worse. These petty games could not harm her any longer. "You know nothing of true cruelty, Chandra. Perhaps one day I'll teach you."

He stood abruptly and dragged her forward. Her scalp hurt. Her legs were slipping against the ground, hands chained before her. And still, she refused to be silent, her voice echoing off the walls, as the heat of the fire grew stronger. "The last time you had me here, I humiliated you," she forced out. A jolt of her hip against marble. Her knees. "I told all your highborn rulers what you are. My words are sharper than any of your swords."

"Then I will rip out your tongue before I burn you," he said furiously, spittle flying from his lips. "I will do whatever it takes for Parijatdvipa."

"Perhaps," she managed to say. Forced herself to breathe. "Perhaps you wish to. But you cannot. Only I can burn willingly. Only I can do what is needful. And I will not," she said loudly. "I will not do it unless I have my throne."

The silence was vast, impenetrable. The fire crackled. And Chandra looked down at her. The same eyes as her own. The same brows.

"Emperor Chandra," said the High Priest. His voice was distant. "I am so very sorry."

Chandra froze. A sword tip was at his throat.

"Step away from Empress Malini," said Kartik calmly. The soldier holding the sword to Chandra's throat never wavered.

Nothing. Nothing for a long moment.

The sword pressed harder. A bead of blood welled up.

"Step away," the priest repeated.

Chandra turned his gaze on the High Priest, face painfully still. His eyes were pleading.

"I have always done what was right for Parijatdvipa," he said. "I did what I was taught. What—what is this?"

The High Priest exhaled. Closed his eyes.

"Release your sister, Emperor," he said. "With regret. With love. Release her."

Chandra did.

Malini remained where she was. Hands still chained before her. Watching the look in her brother's eyes—watched the horror rupture him as his world was upended. All his life, he had worshipped staunchly. Followed the High Priest with the loyalty of a slavering dog, rabid to anyone save his master.

Now his faith had turned on him.

His own saber was taken from him. He stood, suddenly powerless despite his priestly soldiers, his men. His throne.

The High Priest was weeping.

He stepped back. Kartik stepped forward.

Kartik smiled at her, the faintest upraising of the corners of his mouth. For a moment he did not move. Only looked down at her.

One command. That was all it would take, to see Malini's life ended, or Malini locked up once more, and the priesthood in power. It was more, perhaps, than Kartik had even imagined he could achieve for himself. It was enough power to compel a sensible, cunning man to act upon his ambitions, his hungers.

She was entirely powerless. The cold knowledge of that washed over her. She allowed it to show on her face. The faintest weakness—a trembling of her hands as she looked up at him. So he needed to believe he had power over her? Well then, let him. It was not untrue.

That wouldn't be the case forever. She'd make sure of it.

She either had the measure of him, or she did not.

I will only give you what you want if I have my throne, she thought, keeping her eyes on his. *Even if I fear you—if you wish to see me burn, and the yaksa die by my fire, you must raise me up.*

His gaze flickered.

Then he bowed low to the ground. All the priests and soldiers around him followed suit.

"Empress," he said. "We welcome you to Parijatdvipa. May you lead us always to unity and greatness."

"Priest," Malini said, holding her hands before her. Smiling, as if she had known fate would carry her here all along. "Free me, and I promise greatness is exactly what you will have."

PRIYA

Water all around them. Above, below.

"Here again, sapling," the yaksa whispered, smiling, her teeth more pearl than thorn. This time the yaksa was not wearing Bhumika's face. Instead, she gazed at Priya with a mirror of her own face wrought beautiful and strange, lustrous wooden bones pressing against fragile skin, leaf-thin and glowing from within. "Here at last."

Priya gazed at it. Her thorn-and-pearl mouth, her flowering eyes.

"What do I owe you, yaksa," she said, "that I haven't given?"

"Oh my darling one," the yaksa crooned, as if Priya had delighted her. "What else? Your heart."

"I…I hollowed my heart." Priya remembered it, now that she was here. The pain. The wood of her ribs, the flowers within her. "You have it."

"Not all of it." The yaksa's mouth parted. A needle-flower bloomed between her teeth, then withered. Faded. Then she smiled. "Not all of it," she repeated.

Malini.

It was with Malini.

"I will give you a knife to carve it," the yaksa murmured. "A knife to hollow it. A knife to make you ours."

Horror ran through her.

"No, yaksa," Priya whispered. "Please. No."

"You already promised me this," said the yaksa. "You promised me your heart."

"I didn't think you meant this," Priya said, horrified, helpless. "If I had known I would never have agreed."

"I know," the yaksa said, soothing. "You have done so much for her sake, after all. I have seen it all, sapling. Left your people. Bowed before her gods. Fought her wars. Lain with her. Made promises with your dreams you cannot keep. All you needed was the flimsy excuse of a message—a vow, an alliance—and you let yourself be entirely hers. But you made a promise, and you cannot break it now."

Priya could only shake her head in mute denial.

"Did the women who burned to destroy my kin know how it would feel to die? Did they know the pain the fire would inflict upon them? No." The yaksa shook her head. Golden petals fell to the water around her; swirled and faded into darkness. "They chose their sacrifice with a warm cloak of heroism, of goodness, of virtue, draped around their foolish shoulders. They did not know how unutterable the pain of such a death is until it was too late. They chose their path unknowing, just as you chose yours—with no way back, only forward."

Does a sacrifice have the same power if you don't know what you are sacrificing? If you cut out your heart so flowers could grow, so magic could wind its roots in your yielding lungs, without understanding that you would end up here, kneeling before a thorn-mouthed god, being told you must kill what you love? Surely not. Surely the way of things couldn't be this cruel.

"I . . . I won't," Priya said. Everything in her rebelled. She thought of Malini—the reverent touch of her hands, and the shape of her smile when she was unguarded, vulnerable, lying by Priya on a bed in a spill of soft shadow. "I *won't*."

"My kin and I are the source of all your strength. You are just meat, flesh, a vessel for a higher power. That is all mortals are—and it is a blessing, a beautiful thing, but it also makes you nothing without us, nothing of consequence, nothing worthy of love. I cannot take what you refuse to give," the yaksa said, with utter merciless kindness. "I cannot turn your knife upon her. I cannot make you cut out the heart you gave her. But I can use you as the vessel you are. I can wear your skin like my own. I can murder her. Perhaps under your hands she may live. But not under mine."

A shudder worked its way through Priya—unnatural, strange, like an insect working its skittering way over skin. She lifted her shadowy hands before herself and watched the not-flesh of them split open—ashoka blossoms, blood-red and saffron, worming their way free. The yaksa inside her. The yaksa showing her exactly how much of Priya belonged not to Priya, but to the spirit she'd given herself to.

"Your loved ones are waiting for you in Ahiranya, sapling," the yaksa said. "And I do not need them as I need you. I can kill them all, and splay their entrails beautifully before you, and accept your tears as my due. That is your choice to make. You have shown time and time again that you love them less than her. You can be my weapon, empty, and lose everything. Or you can take up your knife, and act as you must."

Priya shuddered again. Quailed.

It wasn't true. She did love her people. She thought with sickening, terrified horror of Bhumika demanding that Priya return home; Padma's weight, solid and warm in her arms; Sima holding a shield up to protect her; Billu laughing, and Ganam lifting her out of the marsh, and Rukh hugging her fiercely, all sharp bones and awkward affection. They were *home*, and she could not lose them. Could not.

How do you stand against a god that lives inside you?

"Please," she whispered.

"This has always been inevitable," the yaksa told her. Priya's hands moved, as if of their own volition, to take the blade. The hilt bloomed under her hands, seeking her skin: great flowers, red as blood, gold as a rising sun. "I would always need you completely. I would always want you completely. And you'll be mine. With me, you will find wholeness."

"But not my beloved," Priya whispered. Malini. Beloved and betrayed, although she did not know it.

"Do not worry," the yaksa said, smiling, smiling. "I'll be beloved enough for you from now on."

The kiss the yaksa placed on her brow rippled through Priya.

"I am Mani Ara, sapling," said the yaksa, framing her face in hands of flowering gold. "And you are my priestess."

*　　*　　*

Priya woke beneath the earth, in a hollow she'd carved with her own magic, her own hands.

Someone was calling her name. A small voice through the dark.

"Sima," she called in return, weakly. "Are you okay?"

"I am." A pause. "I think we both are."

She heard the groan of their charioteer, with some relief.

There was a burning ache between her ribs. She shifted under the soil, moving, feeling it hollow to accommodate her.

The knife had existed in the sangam. The knife was not here in the world. The knife—

A certainty settled into Priya's bones.

She touched her own ribs. Felt her skin part, strange and unnatural, a softness that should not have been there.

She pulled the blade free. The skin closed behind it.

It was hot against her palm. She gasped raggedly, hands shaking around the blade.

"What was that?"

"Nothing," said Priya. "Nothing."

"Do you think," Sima called out, in the dark, "that the battle's been won or lost?"

Priya's hands were sticky with sap. She pressed the thorn blade into the knot of her chunni against her hip. A clumsy movement, made clumsier by the dark.

"I don't know. But there's only one way for us to find out."

She opened the soil. Clasped Sima's hand and dragged them all free, back into the light.

BHUMIKA

They went into the forest. Deep, dark trees enfolded them. The branches seemed to turn to meet her. The undergrowth rustled at her feet. Above her, the leaves were dark as lacquer, the light bleeding through them.

The last thing she had done before leaving the mahal was write a letter.

Priya,

Perhaps you're dead and gone, and I have done you the cruelty of not mourning you. But I think you live. I hope you live. And though I also hope you will never return here, I know that if you are alive, you will.

When you do, I hope you can forgive me for leaving you behind.

The bower of bones waited for them. Above them, bound into the trees with ribbons of yellow and red, the bones clicked against one another. But the bower was otherwise silent, without even the chirp of birdsong.

Ashok waited for her, standing among a riot of oleander blossoms that seemed to grow from nowhere—that twined through his hair, and wound at his feet.

"Why here?" Bhumika asked.

"It's a space for travel," he said. "From here, you can go far."

The bower was both the entrance to a path carved long ago by yaksa hands, and a grave where rot-riven animals came to die. Cursed and strange, it did feel like a fitting place for Bhumika to leave her life behind. She raised her head and stared at the bleached bones hung above them, warning the unwary that they had come to a place where no sensible person should.

"What shall I do now?" she asked.

"Kneel," Ashok said. "And then we can begin."

Jeevan was silent, as Bhumika knelt on the ground. She looked up at his face. His gaze was heavy, full of grief and unspoken things she did not want to contemplate. Not now.

"Don't fear for me," she said softly. "Jeevan."

He said nothing. Only looked at her in return.

"You think I am being self-sacrificing," Bhumika went on, straightening where she sat, so that her spine was a tall, unbroken column, her shoulders unbowed. A noble enough look, she hoped, from the outside. She did not want Jeevan to fear for her. She did not want to fear for herself.

"You *are* being self-sacrificing," said Ashok. "That's what the magic demands of you."

Jeevan lowered his eyes.

"No. Sacrifice would be remaining here and trying to carve out a measure of safety for our people. My people," she corrected. Because whatever Ashok was, he was no longer one of her own, no longer mortal and frightened, struggling against immortal strength vast enough to crush them with the faintest breath, the vaguest desire. "Sacrifice would be doing so day in, day out, even with the sure knowledge of my inevitable failure.

"The Parijatdvipans think they know what it means to sacrifice," she went on. "Grand gestures of self-destruction, they think. They glorify it. But it's not so. The slow way, fighting even when you know it may have no worth...that is sacrifice." She thought of all her people in the mahal. And thought of Padma, laughing, Bhumika's heart clutched in her perfect, tiny fists. Felt her heart turn and break, as she said, "And this? This is freedom. This is escape."

This was a foolish chance.

Ashok snorted. "Call it what you like," he said.

"I will not know what I have to mourn," she said. "Not for a long time. Perhaps forever. What greater gift can I ask for?"

And then, undoing all her own work, she turned her head away from her brother who was not her brother, and covered her face with her hands. And wept.

She heard the sound of footsteps. Jeevan's voice, as he said, "A moment. Just a moment—"

"A moment, Ashok," Bhumika agreed, voice choked. "Then I'll be ready."

More footsteps. She felt it, as Jeevan knelt before her.

"My lady," he said. She did not answer. "Bhumika," he murmured. "He's gone."

She looked at him through her fingers. His hand was held out, palm upraised. She forced the tears to stop—breathed through the simple grief that had overwhelmed her—and placed her hand against his own.

"Whatever you cannot mourn, I will mourn for you," Jeevan said quietly. "And when your work is done, I will bring you back. I vow, as long as I'm living, it will be done."

She stared at him: his severe face that concealed the gentleness that resided inside him, his straight back, and his steady gaze. Her breath caught for a moment as she looked into his eyes. She believed he believed it, and she was glad of that. That he could hope for her, even when she could not.

She leaned forward. Pressed her mouth to his.

It was the softest touch of her lips to his own. She felt the warmth of his breath; the sudden clench of his hand around her own, holding her as if he were afraid she would vanish if he let go. But he kissed her in return gently, with a tenderness that made her heart ache for what could have been, and what never would be.

She drew back.

"Thank you," she whispered.

Whatever ephemeral thing had grown between them deserved better than the kiss she had given him, kneeling in the dirt, on the verge of losing herself. But Jeevan only touched his thumb to her cheek, brushing away her tears. Then he released her hand. He stood, and stepped back, and turned his face away to stare into the woods, his face in shadow.

"Ashok," Bhumika said. Her throat dry.

She thought, perhaps, she'd feel embarrassed. But when her brother appeared and she looked at him there was no expression on his face. Nothing human, really, left in his eyes at all, to make her feel shame.

"Are you ready now?" Ashok asked.

No. No. This was madness.

"Yes," she said, and held out her hands.

He kneeled with her. He took her hands in his own.

She entered the sangam, not with the slow ease she always had, breath by measured breath, but with the awful suddenness of a blow to the skull, or a body being dragged under a river's inexorable weight. She was in her skin, and then in the space of a breath she was not.

Stars above her head, skeins and threads of them tangling and bursting light. The rivers winding around her. And as before, she could not feel Ashok. Could not see him or touch him.

That made sense, of course. She understood now.

He was not Ashok. He only wore his skin, his dreams, the dust of his memories. Only masqueraded as him. He was a yaksa—old and strange, and misled by her brother's heart.

And she had placed her life in his hands.

Beneath her, in the water, flowers bloomed up, rising through dark liquid to curl against her, where the shadow of her body met the water. A ring of yellow at her waist. Marigolds, the color of fire. Oleander, a piercing yellow, a warning and welcome, a poison.

Hands settled on her shoulders.

"Don't look." A voice from behind her. Not her brother's entirely, but something layered. Two echoes twining. "Don't look, Bhumika. I don't know what you'll see."

"I won't," she said. She looked down. There was no true sun here, no true light, and yet she felt as if she could see their shared reflection in the water. Her own form, haloed by something profuse in leaves, with the steady strength of an old tree grown twisted, made strange by ill winds. "How do we begin?"

"You've already hollowed yourself for us. You're already bound to the yaksa—by rivers, by root, by emptiness." The flowers were growing more swiftly now, more thickly. Filling the water. They were climbing her now, winding around her body, reshaping her, bloom by bloom. "We've already begun."

The last touched her mouth.

She opened her lips. And.

Knowledge poured through her.

How the yaksa had clawed their way from one world to another. Mani Ara, the first, with her thorn-sharp smile, her flowering eyes. And all the others, flowering and growing, gathering followers. The way the world changed where they walked. The way the world became their own—

(She heard a cry, distantly, in the sangam. Or felt it. Something had realized what was being done, here. Someone had turned their focus toward her and Ashok. Someone was coming.)

The knowledge poured into her. Poured and she remembered—cutting out her own heart. Hollowing herself open. This was the same and yet worse, a thousand times worse. Knowledge flowed into her, and with it an understanding of the immortal that wore her brother's skin and memories as if it were his own.

It was not a simple kind of knowledge, this. It was as ancient as the yaksa, and as complex. It was a thing that could not be stored in tomes, had never been recited by poets. It was memory: the feel of soil underfoot. The first time this yaksa had spilled blood. The world they had come from, and the world they sought to build.

The sacrifices they had made in order to come here. The dark grief in their hearts.

I know how you can die, she tried to say. *I know, I know, I know.* But the knowing had eaten its way through her, filled her hollowness to the brim.

"I need to do it before they find you," said Ashok-who-was-not-Ashok. And very suddenly, she sagged forward, back in her own flesh again. "I need to..."

He went silent as she reached up and touched his face. When she drew her hand back, she drew moss with it, thick with blood.

"It's all falling away," she said.

He stared at her. Eyes as yellow as the flowers that had consumed her.

"You have it," he said. "You have everything I know."

He touched her face in return. A mirror of her movement.

"Goodbye, Bhumika," he said.

She felt something twist. Something deep within her go silent. Dizziness overcame her.

When she next opened her eyes, she could see trees above her. She was in someone's arms.

"Where shall I take you, my lady?" the man asked. *Jeevan*, her mind whispered, and then the name turned to dust. Fled from her.

"You cannot—call me that. Anymore," she whispered. Her eyes would not stay open. But she tried. She could hear the huff of his breath. The crunch of undergrowth beneath his feet as he carried her as swiftly as he could, as if he feared the yaksa were at his heels.

"Bhumika, then," he said. "Where shall we go?"

A lake of knowledge in her head. A history with its roots cut. She licked her dry lips.

"The seeker's path," she said. "And then—Alor. Take me to Alor."

Who is Bhumika? she thought. And then nothing. Nothing.

The last thing she saw was the night sky above her.

RAO

After the work was done, they gathered.

"I hate having to trust knowledge gained through torture," Rao murmured.

"Are your fine morals troubling you, Prince Rao?"

Rao gave Mahesh a tight smile.

"Not at all," said Rao. "I'm only—concerned—that fear makes liars of people. As does pain. They'll say anything to put an end to it."

"I do not believe he was lying," Mahesh said. He had good reason to know. He had watched alongside Rao, unflinching, as Kunal was tortured. As each piece of information was pried out of him, bloody and screaming. "We have a way to access the fort. A route through its maze. We will face the High Prince and put an end to this."

Rao was not convinced. But before he could speak, Aditya did.

"We will," Aditya agreed. "And we will lead the men. Lord Mahesh and I."

"As you say," Mahesh murmured, bowing his head.

"Aditya," Rao said sharply, once Mahesh had departed. He knew how his own voice sounded. Rough. A little angry. But Aditya's eyes on him were tranquil, forgiving him—as if Rao's anger was not justified. As if this was not utter madness. "You don't send princes or generals into a fortress—not in this kind of battle."

"Who must be sent, then?"

There were politic answers that Rao could have reached for. Men with the skills for subtle warfare. Spies who could move subtly through a grand fortress city without being caught.

"Men your sister can afford to lose," he said bluntly. "Who will lead the men here if you die foolishly of an arrow to the throat?"

"We have no such men. We cannot afford to lose anyone." Aditya's voice was calm. "In this battle, the life of every soldier has value."

"Aditya, I admire your goodness, your morality, but—"

"Those are my ethics," Aditya acknowledged, cutting through Rao's words. "But I simply mean it in a practical sense. We've lost too many, Rao. You don't need to read any ledgers of rice or grain or weaponry or—or death tallies to see it."

"I've brought myself," Rao said. "That must count for something."

"You would have me risk you?" Aditya asked. "Send you to your death, and not myself?"

Rao swallowed. His heart was thudding, his body nauseated with fear for Aditya. And perhaps...perhaps also for himself.

"When my father sent me to the imperial palace as a child, he sent me to build bonds with the crown prince," Rao said. "He sent me to be yours. As a friend. As a hostage, of a kind. If I must fight for you..." Rao shrugged. "It wouldn't be so bad. It would be—right."

"You showed me the sign," said Aditya calmly. "The sign I was waiting for. A yaksa's severed arm with life breathed into it. A portent placed straight into my hands. Every dark and terrible thing the nameless showed me will come to pass. Is coming to pass, right now. And I am here, and I feel it. A knowing inside me. For once, I'm sure." He touched a fist to his breastbone. "I must fight the High Prince. I must go where the war carries me. And if this siege has a tide, Rao, a—a natural order, like a monsoon, like sunrise, like the waning of the moon— then it is guiding me to the fortress. To the end of the High Prince's defiance, and my sister's success."

"If that's your path," Rao said, "then you have to take it. But so do I." He looked at Aditya and thought of Lata's words, long ago. He thought of how, in the end, the nameless had brought Rao back here: to Aditya's side, to share Aditya's purpose. "Wherever you go," he said, "I go with you."

*   *   *

They timed their efforts to enter the fortress city not around any advice from Kunal, wrenched out of him by pain, but by using their own knowledge. Mahesh's handpicked men had watched the change of patrols on the walls and decided when it would be safest to approach.

Mahesh was a good general when he wasn't trying to sabotage the ruler he followed. Rao tried not to think of all that Mahesh could have done on behalf of Malini's cause if he had placed half as much faith in her as he did in Aditya.

Much to Rao's relief, Kunal's directions clearly hadn't all been the desperate lies of a man under duress. They found the entrance into the fortress just as Kunal had described: a perforation in the stone walls, only accessible from a ledge large enough for a man to carefully approach sidelong. Rao examined it. Murmured to Aditya, "It's low in height."

Aditya nodded in understanding. Behind him, Mahesh looked grim. Low doors were a sensible architectural feature in any building likely to be sieged: place a guard discreetly on the other side with a sharp blade to hand, and you could simply wait for your enemy to enter with their neck helpfully presented for the cut.

"You'll go first," Rao said to Kunal. He held out a hand to him.

Kunal stared back, gray-faced. He didn't move.

"No further harm will come to you," Aditya said with noble earnestness. It wasn't a promise he could keep, and from the look on Kunal's face—and the wary eyes he kept fixed on Rao—Kunal knew it.

Rao looked back steadily.

"You are our ally in this," Rao said. "And the brother of the empress herself has promised you your safety if you help us wholeheartedly. You have nothing to fear."

Unless a trap lies in wait, Rao did not say. *Unless you're attempting to trick and condemn us. Then you die with us.*

Kunal's jaw tightened. He stepped forward, ignoring Rao's hand, and slipped through the gap. Rao followed swiftly behind him, no distance between them. He felt a tug of something at his feet in the darkness—a cobweb, or vegetation growing through the ground, he didn't know—and kept on walking.

The fortress was just as much of a maze as it was famed to be. Each passage was narrow, and opened to multiple other doorways, which led to corridor upon corridor in turn. But they moved forward with confidence—following the path Kunal had set out for them, and guided them on now.

They came to a large, columned room. Doors on each side. There were no windows, but the vast space was oddly bright, so well-lit by hung lanterns that its walls were a shimmering, liquid expanse of gold.

The fear punched its way through Rao's body a second before the realization struck his conscious mind: Those lanterns did not contain normal fire. The flames were writhing, slow and unnatural, their movement making Rao's limbs stiffen with instinctual, animal wariness.

Someone swore. And behind the weight of that whisper, Rao heard a distant sound. Booted footsteps.

There was a bark of laughter behind him.

"You're trapped," Kunal said, holding his head up at what would have been a brave and noble angle, if Rao hadn't been viewing it through a haze of fury and panic. "There was a wire set in the ground at the entrance. When we unbalanced the weight upon it—my father knows. His men are coming. Either you leave here now, or you die."

"You fool," Rao said sharply. "You're willing to die with us? On the ends of our blades?"

"For Saketa's sake?" His breathing was ragged. "Y-yes."

"Saketa's sake? Saketa is burning. Riven with rot. Your low princes have turned from your father and serve Empress Malini. As they should."

"She cannot beat the emperor," Kunal said. There was something haunted in his eyes. "I've seen him. I know him."

"Not as I know him. Not as I know her," Rao said, anger in his voice.

Mahesh gestured at one of his loyal men, and in the blink of an eye the Parijati warrior had Kunal by the throat—was slamming him hard against the wall.

Mahesh looked around—one door, and the next, and the next, a full honeycomb of corridors.

"It's even more of a maze in here than we ever expected, and the bastard's made sure we're entirely lost," Mahesh said grimly. "All we can hope to do is find the High Prince by some miracle and cut the man's throat. Put an end to this."

And lose all their lives in the process. But what did their lives matter, now?

Aditya had a hand on one of the walls. He was gazing up at the stone—the way it curved toward the dome of a ceiling. Kunal, held against the wall, was still making choked, wet noises, hands flailing ineffectually.

Rao should have told the soldier to let Prince Kunal go. But he didn't. He watched Aditya instead.

He saw it when Aditya's mouth firmed. When he exhaled—pained, small. Then straightened, lowering his arms.

"The High Prince's—and Chandra's—false fire destroyed swathes of our army," Aditya murmured. He sounded as if he were lost in thought, but his eyes were sharp. "Imagine..."

He paused. There was silence, apart from the crackle of torches, the pained wheeze of Kunal's fading breath.

"I wonder," he said finally, "what true fire could do."

"True fire," Rao repeated.

"You mean fire of the mothers?" Mahesh asked. Aditya nodded. "Prince Aditya," Mahesh replied, voice heavy. "We have no such thing."

"Sometimes you can hear the voice of the nameless even without a basin of water to open the way." Aditya's voice was steady. Sure. "Sometimes the nameless speaks clearly."

"The fire is fading," said Rao, staring at the flames in their sconces.

"A magic born from an imperfect sacrifice," murmured Aditya, "will never be anything but a mimicry of what the mothers accomplished for us."

In his voice—the cadence of it, the surety, the way the men hung on his every word—Rao saw a shadow of Malini in her brother.

"Sacrifice," Aditya was saying. "A sacrifice not compelled. A sacrifice chosen."

He closed his eyes. Opened them.

"The lanterns haven't yet guttered," said Aditya.

"No," said Rao, even as the fire twisted and spat, bristling in the sconces. He did not understand. "Not yet. We should go. Now."

Aditya walked over to one of the flames. Almost close enough to touch.

"Aditya," Rao said sharply. "What are you doing?" And then Aditya turned his head, eyes wet and shining and Rao knew. He *knew*.

"You are men of Parijat," Aditya said, his voice hoarse, cracked through but strong. "You are men of Parijat and Dwarali and Alor, Srugna and Saketa. You knew when you chose to fight alongside me that this path might cost your life. But you remained for the sake of the empire. Because you believed—and still do—that it cannot be strong in my brother's hands.

"I am a priest of the nameless," said Aditya, visibly mustering up his courage. Rao tried to stride forward, but Mahesh gripped him by the arm, his fist a band of iron. "But I am also Divyanshi's blood. I remember and honor the vows your forefathers made to her. Loyalty to a Parijatdvipan throne. To a shared vision, a shared empire. And now I ask you for a new vow: I will make my sacrifice here. I will see the High Prince's rule ended. I will wrest control of the fire, and with my sacrifice, turn it against him and his soldiers. They will burn, and you will walk free, unscathed, unharmed. And you will return to my sister's side, and say I died for her. You will say Empress Malini was crowned by a willing sacrifice. A new pact between us all." He swallowed. Smiled, bright and tear-sharp. "You will honor her."

Kunal made an awful noise. And Rao trembled and shook his head. "No," he said. "Aditya. No."

But Mahesh was still holding on to him. Mahesh was speaking.

"My ancestors were there, when Divyanshi demanded our vows to serve her sons. My ancestors watched her burn. I can do no less for you, my prince. I will do no less for you." His expression was somber, and though there were no tears in his eyes, he was swallowing desperately to hold them back. He touched a fist to his chest and bowed low, dragging Rao with him.

And somehow, the men around Rao were bowing too.

"Rao, will you say goodbye to me?" Aditya asked.

Rao shook his head. No, no. But he couldn't speak.

"I'm sorry, Rao," Aditya said, and his eyes were gleaming but he was smiling, smiling like he was full of both joy and hurt too large for his body, so large the feelings had to overflow. "I know you've lost too many people. But you shouldn't think of me as lost. I've finally found what the nameless wants from me."

"It's a monstrous thing to demand a sacrifice like this from someone," Rao choked wretchedly. "Even from yourself. *Aditya*."

He managed to wrench himself free. Strode to his friend. Gripped him by the front of his tunic, drawing him close.

"What kind of god would demand this from you?" Rao wanted to yell but he couldn't; could only dig his fists into Aditya's clothes, drag him closer. "What kind of god would demand this from anyone?"

"Our god," said Aditya. Gently pushed him back. The booted footsteps were getting closer.

"You won't burn," said Rao. "It's not so simple. You have no oil—no lac—"

"The mothers will guide me."

"You can't."

"Ah, Rao," Aditya said. Soft. "I can."

The lanterns were flickering to life all around them—flame after flame. The air felt like a swelling wave—a roiling storm, boiling up, up, up.

As if they sensed Aditya. As if they were doing it for him.

"I know now," Aditya said. "Why I dreamt of you as I did. Don't forget what stars are, Rao."

Then he raised up a hand. Touched it to the flame.

It raced over his body like a falling star against the night sky. And Rao held him and felt nothing—only skin. Only his own body untouched, a sacrifice unwanted, a sacrifice unasked for.

"Prince Rao," Lord Mahesh gritted out. "We have witnessed. We have seen. Now we must survive. Come!"

"I'll stay with you," Rao said raggedly. He was crying, he realized. "Aditya, I'll stay. I won't leave you alone."

Aditya could not respond. The fire was climbing over him, darting and arcing, trailing as sweetly as flowers climbing a vine. But it burned, and burned, and Rao could smell smoke. Could see—could see Aditya's skin—

The fire turned on them with wild life. The chakrams on his arms were spinning circles of gold. And Rao saw light, light, light. A hand grasping at his back.

Then, nothing.

MALINI

With Chandra her prisoner, and the priesthood her allies, there was no need to siege Harsinghar, as Saketa's fortress city had been sieged. The gates could simply be opened.

The priests and their own warriors were accommodating. They welcomed Malini's army. Bowed their loyalty to her, before a makeshift audience. The servants—terrified at first—soon found some semblance of calm when Malini ordered that they be left unharmed. She asked for a feast to be prepared, and the mahal was soon bustling with the noise of impending celebration.

"Your brother is imprisoned in a cell," Kartik said, with great priestly calm, once the pomp and ceremony was done with. "Do you wish to be taken to him?"

"Of course," said Malini. "I would be very grateful."

Once, she'd wanted to give him a slow death. She'd wanted to see him humiliated before all his peers: before kings and princes, highborn and warriors—and her court of women, who would never have been equals in his eyes but would stand above him from now on. For so long, she had comforted herself with the vicious thought of how it would feel to rip his false sense of self, his overblown pride, to pieces.

But she'd had a taste of that victory when the priests had turned on him, and it had done nothing to slake her rage. Now, she simply wanted him gone.

Chandra had been chained, but his prison cell was sumptuous. There was a fine bed. A carafe of wine. It was far more than he deserved.

He watched her with ugly, barely banked fury as she entered the room.

"I went to my old chambers," she said casually, and gestured at her own clothing—the shining silk of her sari, the gold at her wrists and her waist. The saber clinking against her hip. "I hadn't expected them to remain untouched."

He was silent, eyes narrowed.

"I considered what must be done with you," she said. "I don't think you fear being powerless. I don't think you have ever considered how it would feel, to be small, to be helpless with a knife at your neck. You think there is natural order to the world. A *rightness*. But there is not, Chandra."

"If you kill me, your name will be tarnished," he said evenly. "Everyone will know you are the impure woman who murdered her own brother."

"Chandra," she said. "Brother. Nothing would give me greater joy than driving this sword through your body myself. I am not a strong woman; nor am I well-trained in use of a blade. I would do a poor job of it. It would, I think, take you a long time to die.

"Now *you*," she went on, filling the silence he'd left. "You know how to use a saber. I think if you are brave enough, you could run yourself through now and save yourself the indignity of the slow, unpleasant, *humiliating* death I am going to give you. Let me tell you about it."

She took a bottle from her waist chain.

The bottle was small. Its contents were dark, almost oily. She placed it on the table beside his bed with an audible clink.

"Needle-flower tincture," she said. "A dose like this would kill you. Small doses, over time, will destroy you. And there will be doses, brother. To be placed in your wine. Your meals. You will die in slow increments, your mind rotting in your skull. The poison will kill you unhurriedly, and by the time you face the kings and warriors of Parijatdvipa—by the time I drag you before the court—you will be a shadow of your old self." She leaned forward. "I will allow you your old princely finery, so that all the men who once bowed to you will be able to see how emaciated you have become. You will look a pitiable sight, I promise you, stumbling into the court in your gold and your turban, with your skin sticking to your ribs. I will ask you to plead your case, and all those men will hear you stumble over your words. They will *laugh* at you, brother. I will steal everything from you, as you tried to steal it from me."

His throat worked. He said nothing.

"I would never, in the normal course of things, condemn any being to such a fate," said Malini. "But you condemned me to it. You condemned me to public shame. You dragged me into the court to be broken and killed before all the powerful highborn men of our empire. You tried to murder me, and when I would not die at your bidding, you tried to take my mind from me. Oh, you may shake your head now. You may have convinced yourself you acted for a higher purpose, for Parijatdvipa, but you know the truth."

"You have a monstrous mind, sister," he said. His voice dripped with disgust, but there was a hunted look to his face—to the way his hands shook in their manacles, as if he could barely contain the urge to get his fingers around her throat. "If I could live my life again, I would take yours from you when you were a girl. I would spare the world your tarnish. I would tell our mother to whelp a better daughter."

"Would you kill me now, if you could?" She cocked her head, inspecting him as if he were dirt. She hoped he felt it—that he would remember being nothing but dirt in her eyes.

"The only worth you have is in your death. Even the priests see it. You are just a tool to them," he spat out, savage. "They just want to use you. Mark my words, Malini, you'll burn as I wanted, whether I am here to watch it or not. It is your purpose, your fate. It was written in the stars of your birth."

"Ah, but I'll burn for my own glory, not yours," she said, baring her teeth in a feral smile. "And I will be remembered as a mother, a goddess, and you—you will not be remembered at all."

She stepped away from him.

"You have a choice, brother," she said, kindly now. She could afford to be kind. "The needle-flower lies beside you. Do what you will."

Then she turned and left him behind. Locked the door behind her. And pressed her back against the wall. And waited.

55

CHANDRA

He stared at the vial of needle-flower. The blood was beating like a drum in his skull. He thought of running a saber through his sister's stomach. He thought of her on the pyre burning and screaming in agony, begging for mercy, and felt a despair so encompassing it was like a wave, like drowning.

He would never see her die. He could not lie to himself. Hemanth had turned from him, tears in his eyes. *With regret. With love*, he'd said.

Chandra reached for the vial and grasped it. Raised it up.

He did not want to die.

The memory of a blade at his throat lanced through him. Humiliation made him grit his teeth, the taste of blood on his tongue.

Had Hemanth ever truly loved him? When the High Priest had told him he was destined for greatness—when he had given Chandra hope and purpose—had he known that one day he would betray him?

The world was flawed, decayed, rotten. And Chandra was the only noble man left. Betrayed by all the men who should have kneeled before him. Humiliated and condemned by the sister who should have died for him.

Chandra deserved to live. He *needed* to live. Parijatdvipa would fall without him.

He clenched his hand tight around the vial. The urge to fling it against the wall and watch it shatter was a powerful thing. He wanted the paltry pleasure that destroying it would bring—the sight of glass and needle-flower smeared against the floor and walls.

His hand was shaking. His arm did not want to lift it. It felt as if he were looking at the vial from a great distance. He could not throw it. He could not drink it. He was frozen.

Wetness, miserable and weak, was streaming from his eyes. These were not his tears. This was not his heartbreak.

Hemanth, he thought. *How could you betray me?*

He thought of lowering the vial back to his bedside. He thought of trusting in the gloriousness of his own fate.

He thought again of Hemanth, and felt his own faith wither.

He thought of his sister's threats: Of slowly administered doses of needle-flower. Of wasting away. Of being jeered at and mocked by Parijatdvipa's highborn, as his mind betrayed him, and his body followed. The terror that thought instilled in him was vast. He could not breathe around it. He felt like a child again—trapped under a sea of dark emotion, entirely adrift. But now, there was no one to raise him up. No one to show him the way. There was only the fear. And the vial.

I will die as myself. I will die with my pride and my honor.

This was the brave path. The only path.

A swift death. A clean death.

Before he could dissuade himself, he quickly poured the needle-flower into his mouth with a hand that shook so wildly his grip on the vial almost slipped. Then he grasped the carafe of wine and drank deep from it, draining it too. The wine's richness washed away the taste of the needle-flower, leaving nothing in Chandra's mouth but the taste of overripe fruit and the bitterness of his own panic.

He flung the carafe hard at the wall. It collided with stone with a clang, then tumbled to the ground, rolling to the edge of his bed. He let out an awful sob, muffled by his own hand.

Mothers condemn his sister. Let her rot and writhe. He was meant to be emperor and die an old man in his bed, surrounded by his sons and heirs. She had condemned Parijatdvipa by condemning him. She had—

He.

His hands were growing numb.

His heart was pounding. Faster, and faster still. As the room began to waver, and his vision lurched, and his body slid from the bed, awkwardly hooked by the chains at his wrists, he thought, *That was not needle-flower.*

He vomited. Violently. Once, and again.

His stomach was still roiling when he heard the door open once more.

"Malini," he rasped out. Retched, again. *"Malini."*

She sat down on his bed and folded her hands on her lap.

He looked up at her. Her calm face. The light in her eyes.

Traitor, he thought. *Whore. Monster.*

He tried to claw his way up from the floor. But all he could do was grasp the hem of her sari. His hands were slick with sweat. His heart would not stop pounding faster and faster, and he could not breathe around the thrum of his own blood.

Malini made a humming noise, thoughtful. She leaned down.

"Tell me," Malini said, placing her hand over his own. He could not feel her fingers. His skin was tingling, growing leaden. "Does it hurt?"

He opened his mouth. Nothing but a rasp left it. He felt something dribble from his lips.

She nodded as if he had spoken.

His sight was beginning to go gray. He could not breathe. And the twisting nausea in his stomach was growing, gouging him from the inside out. He was being clawed open. Eviscerated.

The ground beneath him was ash, and what lived in the ash was eating through him, heat and cold and bitter, scrabbling finger bones.

Surrounding him were faceless brides, their blood-red saris brushing his writhing body. Flames leapt from their clothes to his skin as they laughed and hissed his name, watching him from beneath crowns of molten kindling and starlight.

He was burning and burning, his skin peeling from the inside, fire blistering his soft flesh, his organs. He could not run from it. The fire was him, and he was the fire, and in the void that yawned before him there was only more fire still.

Yes, it hurt. It *hurt*, and he would have paid any price to end it. Anything at all.

"Good," Malini said, from a long distance. Her voice was an echo. "I'm glad."

56

MALINI

She waited until she was sure he would not survive. His grip on her had fallen lax. He lay facedown in his own bile and sickness, his breathing no more than a wheeze, wet with his own blood.

She stared at the opposite wall, stained with a little wine. She felt curiously empty, hollow and light as air. The feeling would come for her later, she knew. Like the tide ever returned to the shore.

She stood and left the room.

There were guards at the end of a corridor. She'd commanded them to keep their distance so that she could speak to Chandra privately.

"He's resting," she said, now. "See that he isn't disturbed."

"Empress," the soldier acknowledged, bowing.

She walked away.

She went to the women's quarters of the mahal. Lata was waiting for her, expression tense and intent.

"I'm glad you're here," Lata said, which was as close to asking Malini where she had been as Lata would allow herself in the presence of strangers. Malini had no interest in answering that unsaid question.

"Chandra's wife," she said, instead. "Do you have her?"

"It was lucky," Lata said, without inflection, "that Queen Varsha's maids brought her directly to me. If she had been found by the wrong soldiers..."

"Show me to her," said Malini.

Queen Varsha. The High Prince's daughter—a thin, big-eyed thing with wild clouds of hair, oiled back into a curling braid—was huddled at the edge of a room with the two women who clearly served her. They were all weeping. She looked up, and when she saw Malini, she flinched.

Malini felt suddenly nauseated. She removed her saber and laid it aside. Entered the room.

"Please!" Varsha fell to her knees, dragging the two women down with her. She was crying. Great big miserable tears streamed down her face. "I've done no wrong, Empress. I'm a loyal daughter. I obeyed my father and wed as I was bid. Is that a crime?"

"Do you think I will harm you?" Malini asked.

This caused another bout of weeping. "Please do not," Varsha begged. "Please spare me."

"I have done you a great kindness," said Malini. "I doubt my brother was a worthy or useful husband."

"No, Empress," Varsha said tearily. "He was not a good husband at all."

Noise, from beyond the doors. Malini turned at the noise. Lata drew them open, and two soldiers strode in. One was shaking visibly, his face damp with sweat.

"Empress," he said. "The emperor—your brother—he..."

"He drank poison," the other guard said. "He must have hidden it upon his person. Empress, we offer our most sincere apologies; any punishment we must face, we will face." He prostrated himself on the floor. The other soldier followed suit. "He—he is dead."

Behind her Varsha abruptly stopped crying.

"Dead," Malini repeated. She stared at the soldiers. Dead. The world ran through her like the wail of a conch. "Are you certain of this?"

"Yes, Empress."

"By his own hand?"

"There was a vial in his room. And wine. Empress, please—*please* show us mercy."

"You are not responsible for this. Calm yourselves," Malini said.

"Summon a physician to confirm it. Call upon a priest, also. Can you be trusted to do this?"

"Yes, Empress," one said hurriedly, then the other.

"Then get up off the floor," she commanded. "And *go*."

They scrambled to their feet. Left as quickly as they had come. There were hushed noises behind Malini. Gasps of shocked breath.

She placed a hand over her eyes and felt her whole body begin to tremble, overcome. Finally relief struck her, vast and strong. He was dead. He was dead. He was dead. Part of her had believed that she had imagined it; *dreamt* it, even though she had been the one to frighten him and taunt him with the possibility of his own slow demise. Even though she had left him a poison of oleander and aconite, a poison that would burn him from the inside, and had told him it was a simple tincture of needle-flower. A soft death like sleep.

She wanted to laugh.

She did not laugh. Did not scream with the joy of it, either—the sudden lightness in her chest. The savage beauty of it.

Needle-flower indeed. What a fool he'd been to believe she would make it so easy, or half so swift.

She felt a hand on her arm. Lowered her own hand from her face and saw Lata touching her, watching her. There was concern in Lata's eyes, but knowing, too.

"What can I do for you, Empress? How can I ease your burden?" Lata asked.

"Inform my general," Malini replied. "And deal with—this." She gestured at her brother's widow. The women around them. She could not stomach being wept at any longer. "I need to be alone."

"Of course," Lata murmured.

Malini slipped out of the room. Her body felt light and leaden all at once. She did not grasp her saber again. Instead, she walked away from the women's quarters, through the grand corridors of her mahal. She walked under ceilings inlaid with glittering stones; beneath columns limned in emeralds and pearls, and over flowers embellished in traceries of gold, sunbursts of liquid light.

The soldiers—as she had suspected—had not been subtle when

they had run to inform her of Chandra's death. They had not been subtle, in the aftermath, in their search for a physician and a priest. Already, the news of Chandra's demise was spreading through the mahal. The few servants she saw lowered their eyes when she passed, or bowed. The warriors she saw—*her* warriors—lowered their heads and touched their hearts in gestures of respect. The emperor was dead. She had won them a war.

She needed no weapon. Her own tale shielded her.

She walked to her throne room. Her guards bowed to her and opened the doors. "Empress," they said.

She stepped through the doors. Heard them close behind her.

Finally alone, she looked at the room where she should have burned, the room where her heart sisters had perished. The fire was burning, still. Shadows and light played on the walls. The fragrance of needle-flower and jasmine wafted in it, honeyed, mingling with the scent of ash.

She closed her eyes and let herself feel everything: Her fear of fire. Her grief. Her rage. Her relief. The bloodied, vicious weight of her own joy.

She smiled—one smile so bright and fierce that she felt like her whole body was shining with it. She had done it. Finally, she had done it.

She had truly won.

57

PRIYA

The celebration that took place after the battle for Harsinghar was almost a frenzy. The grand gardens of the mahal had been taken over by tables of fruits and wine, of tandoor and colored rice. Sima and Priya were soon separated by the press, and for a long moment Priya stood alone, surrounded by noise and color. It made Priya wince a little, imagining what the kitchens had gone through to make such a celebration possible, in the midst of their home and city being overrun, their emperor being captured and dying by his own hand.

Lata had turned up before them briefly, a somber figure carving her way through the noise and feasting.

She'd relaxed at the sight of Priya. Just a little unraveling of the tension in her shoulders, and a smoothing of her brow, before her face went severe again. She took Priya aside. "I will tell the empress that you're safe and well. She feared for you."

"Is she...?"

"Almost unhurt," said Lata. "Triumphant. Relieved. As we all are." Her gaze softened. "The empress's other women are in the old queen's quarters now, if you want to seek them out. They'd be glad to see you well. Sima, too."

"Later," Priya managed to say. "Thank you."

Lata nodded, eyes oddly kind, and disappeared back into the chaos of the crowd.

Malini was going to be empress in truth: Parijat under her control.

Emperor Chandra dead. In a different time, in a life Priya wasn't living, she'd be elated in this moment. It meant Malini would have her throne. It meant Ahiranya would finally have its freedom from Parijatdvipa.

In a different time, she would have left Malini behind and gone home and helped build Ahiranya into something new and whole, piece by piece. Until one day, maybe, Ahiranya would be safe and secure, its fields free from rot, its temple council large enough and trustworthy enough that Bhumika could finally sleep easily at night. And then Priya would, perhaps, leave again. Would come to Harsinghar and see it in peacetime. See Malini in peacetime. And then, then—

Foolish dreams. Even more foolish hopes. None of that lay ahead of her.

There was only the yaksa. Only the ache in Priya's chest.

Only her purpose.

"You there," one highborn slurred. "Should you be here?"

"Yes," Priya said flatly.

He looked over her—her plain salwar kameez, her boots, the knotted cloth of her chunni, rumpled but bound in place at her hip. She was clearly no dancer or courtesan, and his face creased into a frown. He reached for her, one big hand trying to grip her arm, and Priya took a pointed step back. He opened his mouth.

"See here—"

"The Ahiranyi woman is allowed to be here," Ashutosh said sharply. "Leave her be." He stayed when the highborn stranger apologized and skulked away. "My men are looking for you," he said abruptly. "Something about a rematch." Then he gestured broadly at the edge of the hall and walked away.

Priya walked toward where he'd pointed. She saw Romesh and the others, flowers and vines still strewn across their armor, with carafes of wine scattered all around them. They were shouting and laughing, and Raziya's women were with them. One was rolling up her sleeve. "If a little thing like Sima can beat you," she was saying, "then what trouble are you going to give me?"

"Oh, big talk," said one of Ashutosh's men. "What are you betting to back that pride up, huh?"

"You really want to bet against an archer?" She flexed her arm pointedly, and one of the men whooped like she'd just offered to kiss him. "I'm not betting wine, sweetheart. I'm betting real money."

"I want archery lessons," said the man. "If I win, that's what I want from you."

"You'd be better letting her teach you." The Dwarali woman gestured at Sima, who was sitting with a carafe in her lap, her face glowing with joy and liquor. "She's got all the patience, don't you, Sima?"

"I'm not bad," Sima said. "But you'll have to beat me at arm wrestling too if you want me to teach you. That's only fair. And frankly, I don't see that happening."

There was some more good-natured yelling. When Priya walked over, numb inside, Romesh looked up. "Elder Priya," he said, smiling. His careworn face was...happy. "Come join us. Have a drink."

"I have your favorite, my lady," Sahar said. Waved a bottle in the air. "We can share."

A pang of grief ran through Priya like lightning. She thought of sitting there with all of them, drinking that wine, laughing with them. Thought of being embraced by all that new trust. By *friendship*. She thought of how far they'd come, all of them and how rosy the future looked, like something good could be cobbled together out of all the blood and death and sacrifices, the horrors they'd seen.

She was going to ruin it all. She had to ruin it all.

"I'd love to," she said, with false lightness. "But I need to talk to my advisor alone first." She grabbed Sima's arm, smiling. "Come on," she said. "I've got something to tell you."

"I think Romesh really likes you now," Sima mused. "He still won't offer to share a drink with me without making some kind of bargain, you know." She was looking around at the hall, a smile on her mouth. "Fuck, this is such a relief, isn't it, Pri? We're finally through. We can talk to your empress. Tell her what we need. We can go home and hopefully—"

"Remember," Priya said, suddenly mustering her courage. "How I once told you passing through the deathless waters wasn't something I wanted for you?" She watched the highborn lords laughing, jubilant;

the flicker of torchlight turning the lattices of the marble and sand-stone palace golden, liquid, alien. Watched as Sima's smile faded with disquiet.

"I remember," said Sima, voice low.

"The waters have done something to me. They've demanded a price. And I . . ." Priya's voice faltered. Her heart hurt, hurt so much she didn't know how her ribs could contain it.

"I'm going to leave this feast in a moment," Priya told Sima. "I want you to speak to Lata, if you can find her. Or Lord Raziya. Or Lord Khalil. You choose. Tell them I'm planning to betray the empire. Tell them . . . tell them I'm going to kill her. Tell them you came as soon as you realized, and they must stop me."

"Wh-what?" Sima's eyes were wide, her expression horrified.

"You heard me," Priya said wretchedly.

"I'm not letting you do that," Sima said, after one beat of silence. "You—that isn't something you want. I know it isn't. You need to *explain*, Pri. Not just talk like this—like you're not yourself."

I'm not myself, Priya thought miserably. *I'm not.*

"Something reached for me when I used my gifts in the battle," Priya said. "A yaksa spoke to me again. It said if . . . if I want all the people we love to live, I need to do what it asks. I need to do this. I'm afraid, Sima. But I have no choice." Her voice cracked. She forced it to remain low, to not draw attention. "I just need your help to control the outcome."

"Okay," Sima said, blinking rapidly like she was trying to hold back panic. "Okay. And then what? We leave?"

"No," said Priya. "You stay. You have to stay, to warn them. And then you convince them to protect you, because whatever is in Ahiranya—it's dangerous, Sima, and it doesn't love us. It doesn't love anyone."

"These Parijatdvipans will rip me apart."

"They won't," Priya said, not knowing if she believed it or if she *wanted* to believe it. "You're smart. You'll survive. And you'll have betrayed me. Maybe—maybe that will count for something."

"D-don't be stupid." Sima stumbled over her words, sounding close to tears, all her joy twisted to horror.

"Please," Priya said in a small voice. "I can't. I can't save myself. Or you. This is all I have. I have to do this for our family. For Bhumika, and Padma and Rukh and—everyone. The yaksa will kill them if I don't. I have to do this for love."

Love and love. Like two opposite points she was forever reaching for, stretching her thin. Love for Malini and love for home. Love like a future, and love like sacrifice.

"There's something wrong with Ahiranya," Priya said, as dancers swirled around them, as the wail of the sarangi filled the incense-laden air. "I can feel it. And more than that—no. It isn't important. I've spoken too much already." She looked across the crowd, at Ashutosh's men and Raziya's women playing some kind of game of dice. At Sahar throwing back her head in a laugh, and Romesh shaking his own head, but smiling. Smiling like the war was finally done, and there was nothing but better days ahead of them. "There are people here who know you. Who like you. They'll protect you if you let them."

"Priya, you can't," said Sima helplessly. "You love her—"

"It doesn't matter," Priya managed to say, forcing the words out. "And I love you too, Sima. And I'm so sorry."

Sima made a choked noise.

"Don't cry," Priya said sternly, pressing her arm harder against Sima's own. "Please. Don't."

"Fine," said Sima. "Fine. I won't. I'm trusting you. Fuck knows why." A beat. "I love you too. Oh, Pri."

Priya's chest was tight. Inside it, something burned.

"Give me half an hour," she said. "Then tell them."

There had been no sign of Empress Malini at the celebration. That had disturbed no one. Apparently, emperors past had often arrived belatedly to their own celebrations and left swiftly. It allowed their men to debauch themselves without shame, without an imperial audience.

That was all to Priya's benefit. Malini was not surrounded by eyes.

She knew where Malini would be.

She walked, and walked, and somehow no one stopped her. The corridors of the mahal were beautiful. Silk on the walls. Gemstones inlaid in the ceilings, the columns. The wind moved through the gauze curtains at the window and made them dance, soft-winged like resting birds. The moon was out. It was a beautiful night.

Against her side, the thorn knife burned.

She could feel the thrum of the trees in the garden.

She could feel the needle-flower at Malini's throat. It called to her like a song.

There were guards, of course, at the doors of the imperial courtroom. Five of them looked like priests. Priya did not have to approach them. The seeds sewn into her clothes bloomed, and vines drifted across the floor. She choked them quietly unconscious. It was a gentle business, as these things went. She was almost sure they would awaken again.

Then she walked in.

Malini was standing alone in the court. Above her on a dais was the throne: an expansive pillow of silver, backed by ivory carved into delicate flowers, flecked gold by the light. Empty, for now. Next to her stood a pit of fire, which flickered and burned strangely, the flames inside it dying down. Soon they would be nothing but sputtering embers. She turned. The firelight shone on her face, which was cold, remote. But then she clearly realized it was Priya before her, and her expression went tender, warmed by more than flame.

"Priya," she said. "It's done."

Priya walked forward. Cold marble beneath her. Malini's bright face before her. Beloved.

"I need," said Priya, "to cut the needle-flower from your throat. I need to take it from you. I'm so sorry, Malini."

MALINI

Malini had never seen such a look in Priya's eyes before.

Priya looked a little ragged. A little wild. Dirt on her clothes. Her face raised up, the gold of the mothers' fire glinting in her eyes.

"I've trusted you, Malini," Priya said. "I've trusted you so many times. I'm sorry. I'm going to need you to trust me in return."

Malini took a step toward her. Stopped.

She knew that look. She knew it because she had worn it.

It was like... like gazing into her own past. Into a dark mirror, which showed the reflection not of her face but of her own terrors.

Priya looked like a feral thing caged, desperate to get out.

Some deep, inborn instinct held Malini very still.

"Priya," she called out. Gentle. "If this is what you need from me, you have it." Slowly, she lifted the chain above her blouse. Laid the needle-flower upon it against cloth, so that it was visible to Priya's eyes. "Take it," she said.

Priya walked over to her. In her hand lay a blade—a strange thing, narrow and whittled to sharpness, more thorn than knife. But it was as sharp as any steel, severing the needle-flower neatly from the necklace that held it. Malini felt the coolness, the lightness of its absence from her throat.

"This isn't what she meant," Priya whispered. Her voice, her eyes, were hollowed out, an emotion Malini could not possibly read.

"I don't understand," said Malini.

"She said she needed it back." Priya swallowed, and met her eyes. "The yaksa."

Malini stepped back. Reflexive.

A war coming. A war, and Priya before her, spilling a secret with barbs. A yaksa. She had been speaking to a yaksa.

"Will you ask me to trust you," Malini said tightly, "now that you have spoken of yaksa? Now that you have claimed to *talk* to one?"

Priya stared at her. "No," she said. "No. Though you've asked me for more trust than that. Asked me to trust that you'll keep your vows to Ahiranya. Asked me to risk my life, my magic, everything I am—"

"You gave everything willingly."

"You still *asked*. I won't do the same to you. Because I. I..." Priya's eyes closed, and she swayed on her feet. "My power," she said. "Comes at a price. And if I had known...Malini, I wouldn't have paid it. But now I have to do this. For my family. For Ahiranya. I can't betray them."

Malini tried to move forward, around her to the door. Foolish. The marble cracked with a sound like thunder. Something wrapped tight around her feet, holding her fast by the flickering fire pit, before Priya's tired, tortured face.

"Priya." She was breathing hard suddenly. Shaking. "Priya, don't you dare betray me. Don't. Don't." *Please*, she did not say. *Please, not you.* Not you.

Priya was breathing the pained breaths of someone trying not to weep. It was ugly. It made Malini furious.

"I gave you my heart. I need to take it back," said Priya. "I need to hollow it, like everything else. Like the rest of me."

"Whatever you gave me doesn't live in that insipid flower," Malini gasped, furious that she was crying, furious at the salt on her face, the way her heart hammered as she edged back, back, fighting Priya's magical grip on her, as Priya circled her, the mothers' fire flickering palely strange in the lamps, in the pit.

"Don't say it," said Priya. "Don't."

But it was too late.

"It lives in me," Malini said. Furious. "It lives in me, and you cannot take it."

Priya shuddered. The knife moved in her hand, sharpening as if of its own volition.

"I love you," Priya choked out. "I really do. I don't want to do this."

"That doesn't make it better," Malini rasped. "Do you really think I haven't been hurt by people who love me, who claimed I gave them no choice?"

"I know you have," said Priya. "I know."

"Don't you know how I love you?" Malini asked. Those were not soft words. She threw them out like a lash. "Don't you know that I hold everyone at bay, that I cannot stand to love anyone and yet I love you utterly? Don't you understand?"

Priya took a step forward. Took hold of her. It was almost an embrace; almost like being held tenderly, and it was so cruel that Malini could not stand it. She flinched back, and Priya's grip tightened.

Malini snarled—a sound she had never, ever made—and twisted. Wrenched. Priya refused to let go of her, and they were both stumbling. Both falling. Both on the marble, the coldness of it jarring Malini's back, her skull. Priya was above her, fierce and breathing fast, eyes wet. She was beautiful and Malini wanted nothing more than to fling her away, to be free of her. She bucked, pushing at Priya with her fists, her nails. But Priya was immovable. Speaking, her voice too close, too familiar, too *much*.

"If you hold still, I—"

"No," Malini snapped, clawing at Priya's arm, yanking her braid. Grasping that soft hair in her hands, wishing she could wrench it right out. "No, no, I won't make this easy for you. Priya you fool, you fool, how dare you—"

The thorn blade met the marble at her side and Malini rolled. Grasped the edge of the pit.

"Don't," she said again. Pleaded. "Don't, Priya, don't."

"I have to," Priya snapped, in a voice that was wild. "Malini, *I have to.*"

There was wood, laid at its side, ready to be thrown on the flames. Malini grabbed a piece—unseeing, almost unthinking through the haze of her own fury and fear—and shoved it into the fire. And lifted it. And turned.

She thrust the fire at Priya, watching it arc from the blade, lash and bind itself against Priya's skin.

Priya made a noise. Clutched her neck, as light flared in the room, as the ground shook, all those strange flowers bursting and dying. Malini gritted her teeth and held the fire steady, steady. Let it burn her. Let it burn her, then. All Priya had to do was run away, and it would stop. All Priya had to do was stop trying to kill her.

And Priya leaned forward, leaned into it, said tightly, "Malini."

And there—ah. Ever so gentle. Sliding in easily through flesh, through muscle, raw against bone.

Priya had stabbed her through.

She's missed my heart, Malini thought distantly. *I hope she has missed my heart.*

The torch rolled from her nerveless hands.

"I had no choice," Priya said again.

"You did," Malini managed. She was afraid to move. The pain was finally registering: moving through her, setting new knives into her blood. "You—you did."

Her body crumpled. Priya caught her, lowering her down gently. What a mockery it was, that gentleness.

"You won't die," Priya sobbed, miserable tears falling down her cheeks. "You won't die. I didn't cut out your heart. I didn't. I only, I only…"

Her words dissolved. There was a white-edged silence, as Malini bled, and Priya scrubbed tears from her own eyes.

"It has to be enough," whispered Priya, "that I've lost you. That we're severed from one another. It has to be enough."

Priya touched her own hand over her own heart.

"It has to be," she said.

And maybe it was.

The fire twisted wildly. And there were flowers, blooming from Priya's skin. Leaves feathering through her hair. Sap, pearling at her eyes.

Priya, she thought. Priya was not human at all.

It was awful to still love her.

"I'll never forgive you," Malini choked out, through a mouth of blood, salt. "I'll never—I'll never…"

One hand, twined with white leaves, touched her face. Wiped the blood away.

"Live, then," said Priya. "Hate me. Just *live*."

There was an awful noise. The lattices, entwined with flowers, were cracking. Splintering open.

Malini felt lips against hair. The faintest brush. The wound in her chest pulsed in response. Hot, livid, living. Her vision grayed as she was lowered. But she saw Priya walk away from her. Saw the marigolds rupture the ground behind her. A trail of gold.

Saw the shadow of Priya, vanishing through the broken lattice, a hollow to the night.

59

ASHOK

Ashok returned to the mahal alone.

For good or ill, Bhumika was gone. And soon Ashok—whatever he was now, a ghost, an echo, a cloth already half frayed to dust—would be gone too. He could feel himself slipping away. It was a little, as he remembered it, like dying.

There was an ancient sentience stirring under his own. He was nothing but a boat on its waters. He walked forward slowly, on legs that felt like strangers beneath him, carrying him forward along the mahal's corridors. The green, the flowers, even the soil, turned with him. Watching him go.

There was no one in the nursery watching Bhumika's baby sleep. But Ashok could feel the flowers in their bowls of waters, the vines with their limbs wound through the lattice windows, and knew the yaksa had their eyes on her. And on him, now. But they did nothing when he leaned forward and brushed Padma's fine hair back from her face. Her eyes were screwed tight shut, her cheeks stained with salt. She'd cried herself to sleep.

Distantly, he felt a pang of emotion. It ached like a rotten tooth.

He picked her up. She didn't stir. He carried her from the room, unimpeded.

Perhaps the others were curious. Perhaps they wondered what he would do with his sister's child—his niece, in a way, even if no blood bound them. Perhaps they thought he would destroy her, as he'd almost destroyed Rukh.

He remembered the yaksa who wore Sanjana's face. Remembered the tilt of her head. *I'm curious to see what you'll do.*

Padma was light in his arms.

She was, he thought distantly, small for her age. Like Priya had been. There was no shared blood between Priya and Padma either, but Padma had the same scrunched forehead, the same way of curling her hands into fists, the same banked fury written into her flesh. She'd be formidable one day, or dangerous, if she lived long enough to grow into herself.

Bhumika would want her to live.

Did Ashok?

He had not lived long enough to know Padma or love her; to hold her in his arms and want the world for her.

So he held a different scrap of memory—Priya's small body, Priya's weight in his arms, the love and fear that had welled up in him as he'd held her close instead. He kept on walking.

The infirmary was nearly empty. Only one body lay curled on a cot, blankets thrown back. Ashok was met with a bowed spine spiked with leaves. Then the body stiffened, and turned, and Rukh looked up at him.

"Sit up," said Ashok.

Rukh did not try to run or reach for a weapon. He merely sat up in the bed as ordered, hands in tight fists.

"I'm not here to hurt you," Ashok told him. It did not sound like a lie, or feel like one, but the boy did not calm.

Last time, Ashok remembered vaguely, he'd told the boy he was going to help him. And then he had hurt him. So perhaps this was reasonable. Perhaps the boy was right to be wary.

Ashok stepped forward. Rukh's gaze flickered—from Ashok's face, down to Padma in his arms, and back up again. Ashok held Padma forward.

"Take her," he said.

"Wh-where," Rukh began. Cleared his throat, and forged on. "Where is Elder Bhumika?"

Ashok shook his head.

"Take her," he repeated.

"Elder Bhumika," the boy said again. "She—she wouldn't. Wouldn't leave. Her."

What little you know, Ashok thought savagely. Hadn't Bhumika left them all behind in the Hirana when they had been children, choosing to be a highborn girl instead of a temple daughter? Hadn't she chosen to wed the regent and carry his child, instead of fighting tooth and nail for a better world, as he had?

Bhumika had looked at him, as she'd kneeled among the trees, and told him she was being selfish. Told him she was setting herself free.

"There is no one left for the infant but you," Ashok said. "Keep her or the yaksa will keep her. Keep her, or *we* will keep her."

Rukh's hands were trembling in his lap. Ashok stared him down, until finally the boy's fingers uncurled, and he held up his arms. He took Padma. She looked bigger in his smaller arms. More human. Enough weight to pin the boy—slight and mind-wounded as he was—down.

"She's mine now," Rukh said hesitantly, as if testing the words.

"Yes," Ashok said. "Yours."

"I . . ." Another hesitation. "I don't know what that means."

"It means you keep her alive," said Ashok. "You protect her. You keep her fed and clothed. You make sure we have no reason to harm her. Or don't. But her life is in your hands, now." A pause. He watched the words sink in. "The next time I meet you or her, I will not be like this," Ashok went on. A warning. "I will not be as . . . as kind."

The boy's arms tightened. Padma stirred a little, making a noise of complaint.

You're not kind now, every inch of Rukh's body screamed. *You frighten me.*

Rukh would have to learn to hide those weaknesses, if he wanted to survive. The yaksa—*he*—would not accept weakness. But the boy would learn, or he would not, and soon it would be no concern of Ashok's. He could feel himself fading. The waters were carrying him away.

He remembered—Meena, so long ago. The shadow of her, spools of ink in the deathless waters—

He remembered Priya. Priya. He would have liked to say goodbye. But what was there to say between them? Only grief and bad blood bound them, and there was no way to leave her happily. He knew what lay ahead of her.

Priya, in his arms. Priya, with only him to rely on. And here before him now, Rukh, a foolish child clinging to an even smaller child, trying to grapple with the cruelty that had been inflicted on the both of them. Trying to survive.

There was a vicious satisfaction in knowing that nothing ended, that all griefs in the world came back over and over again, spinning like a terrible wheel. He'd thought he would be able to forge a better world once. He'd thought he could bring back all of the goodness and joy Ahiranya had lost.

That he had only managed to bring back this—his own childhood made strange, as if seen through water—seemed...fitting. It seemed fitting.

He left the boy without another word. Now that Padma was no longer in his arms, he let them hang heavily at his sides. The strength was leaching out of them. These were no longer his arms, after all, and this skin no longer fit his bones.

Sanjana was waiting for him. She was sitting under a shaft of sunlight coming in through the broken ceiling, half in shadow, half in light.

"You have betrayed yourself," she said. She sounded oddly delighted. In the light, her visible face was shaped into a smile. Elegant striations of wood shaped her mouth, her jaw, the rise of her cheek, moving liquidly as she spoke. "Turned upon yourself. Turned on *us*. Poured our secrets into the hollow gourd of a temple daughter and cut her from her roots. She'll decay and die and go to waste, and it's all your doing. Will you beg mercy?"

"You know everything," Ashok said heavily. His legs felt like dead wood beneath him. He could barely move them. "What use is begging for pity from the pitiless?"

"What does she know?"

Ashok said nothing.

"A mortal can only remember so much, I suppose," said Sanjana. "Never mind. Whatever she knows, the war ahead of us has only one outcome. What did you do with her baby?"

"It's not her child any longer."

"We took that child from our temple elder," Sanjana agreed. "But we told our temple elder she had to obey or the child would die, and she has not. By rights, we should kill it."

"As Bhumika is now—the death would cause her no sorrow. So what does it accomplish?"

"Balance."

"The child will grow," Ashok said, with a calm that wasn't his own. "The child will become stronger. She will learn to hollow out her weaknesses. And she will survive the deathless waters, thrice, and she will serve us as her mother should have. That's balance enough."

"You do not remember yourself," Sanjana said, rising. "But—curious, curious, dear heart—all the same instincts guide you, as they always have."

He could not respond. He was breathless. Fraying, fraying. He'd misplaced his lungs. She crossed the distance between them.

"You always adored them," she said, with great fondness. She touched a thumb to his chin, and beneath her touch he felt his skin writhe and change—flesh to bone, bone to wood, and then upon the wood, the pulpy softness of lichen began to grow, licking the whorls of her finger. Her smile gentled. "You raised the first temple children. You hollowed them out so tenderly. And when they died for us you mourned. Bound the echoes of them in your roots, as if you could keep them—"

"Stop," he begged. "Stop, yaksa, please."

"Shh," she hushed. Petted his face, as if he were an animal or a child to be gentled. In the wake of her touch his skin tore and remade itself, a pain that erased him.

He could not pull away from her, only make wounded noises, as the inevitable overcame him. Memories unspooling. The shape of Ashok falling away like the dust it was. Dead, dead, dead.

"I told you then: There's too much mortal weakness in you. Too much mortal, and not enough of what you truly *are*."

"Sacrifice," he managed to say. He felt as if his teeth did not fit his mouth. "It was—inevitable. To be—mortal."

"This has gone on long enough, I think," said Sanjana. "Before Mani Ara returns—ah, dear heart. You must remember yourself now. I think you must."

"I am," he told her—even though he did not want to. He was forgetting and remembering all at once. And then he could speak no more, as the waves came over him, and the tide drowned him.

And he was—

He was.

He was. Kneeling on the floor. Taller now—new, elongated bones, a longer body and graceful fingers, a drapery of leaves trailing from his skull as he raised his head to meet her hands, which reached for him. He knew her hands. Beneath the veil of flesh she wore, he knew her hands.

"Arahli," she said. Framed his face. A half name for a half him. "Arahli Ara. Do you know yourself?"

Arahli opened his eyes.

"I do," he replied.

MALINI

There was fire, and then there was nothing.

Priya was gone.

The thorn blade was still in her side. She was bleeding, red spilling between her fingers as she felt around her own chest.

I will not die. Her own voice, in her own head, was detached. Limbless, lungless, it could not feel the pain coursing through her, and it could not tremble. It was calm and it made her calmer in turn, even though the blood kept pouring, hot between her fingers. *I have won my throne. I will not die.*

Not yet.

She knew she should not remove the blade. She knew she had to seek out help. A physician. Medicine. Something to stem the blood loss and keep infection at bay.

The memory of needle-flower on her tongue rose in her, nauseating. With it mingled the image of Priya crouching over her, a burn blooming on her neck, her face miserable.

I had no choice, Priya had said.

There was always a choice.

She tried to move. Tried to crawl.

Hours or seconds passed.

Footsteps.

They were a steady rhythm against the ground. A slow heartbeat. Thump. Thump.

And there was the priest again. Kartik. Barefoot. His gaze was clear, unmarked by fear or worry. He looked at her as if he looked upon bleeding empresses every day, and there was nothing about her or her predicament that impressed or concerned him.

"You are dying, Divyanshi's scion," he said gravely. He kneeled before her, on the cold marble, blood-splattered and fractured by flowers. It was almost a bow, the way he kneeled: head gracefully lowered, one knee beneath him. "The yaksa have tried to take their due."

Memories flickered through her. His temple. His reach. The way he had spoken of the nameless. Prophecies and certainties—the price of power, and the unquestioning necessity of faith.

"You knew," she forced out.

"The nameless grants visions," he said. "Gather enough together with care, weave them with the knowledge we gained from the mothers, and you can build an image of what lies ahead, and be prepared, if you are brave, and you have faith." He raised his head and met her eyes. "You, like everyone, are but a single light dancing at the whim of cosmic forces," Kartik said pitilessly. "The yaksa were always meant to return. Your life was always forfeit. You were always walking toward the pyre. And here we are. The fire awaits you, Empress.

"You must choose to burn before you die," he said. He stroked her hair back from her forehead. "Decide it. I'll make sure it is done. I will make sure there is no pain."

She closed her eyes and let out a sob.

If you are told your whole life that your greatest worth is as a sacrifice, inevitably there must come a day when you believe it. Perhaps this was finally Malini's day. She had fought so long and so hard for power and even now—even beyond the point of success—it had been taken from her.

"Yes," she forced out. "For—for Parijatdvipa. If I must die..." Hitched breath, wet with blood. There were tears coursing down her face. "I will die for the good. I will die for my people."

"Good," he said gently. "Good. You will be remembered with love and reverence for it, Empress. I promise it."

"Help me up," she begged.

He did.

"Here," he said kindly. "I will guide you to the fire. Call my men—" His voice cut off abruptly, into a wet gurgle. His eyes widened.

She felt heat against her own face. Wet. Her own chest no longer even throbbed. It had been easy, so easy, to draw the thorn knife free, and place it in Kartik's neck.

"I have never," she said, "been a woman of faith. And you forgot one truth about me, faceless son: I have never been afraid of killing priests."

He was still staring at her in glassy-eyed shock as she dug the thorn knife deeper and finished slitting his throat.

Then she let him fall, and dropped the thorn knife beside him.

It was his faith and the faith of his priests—faith in her blood and her purpose—that had helped her claw her way to power.

She had not expected power to be like this: her body curved over the gout of a wound, her sari wet with blood. But this time, there was enough anger in her to allow her to crawl toward the court doors. To claw her way to standing.

I will survive this, she told herself. Pressed her palm against the wound. It burned unnaturally. Whatever it had done to her—whatever Priya had done to her—she would heal from it.

Then she closed her eyes and forced herself to scream.

"Help! Help! Ah, help me! *Murder!*"

There were footsteps. Running, running—and then Lord Khalil was before her, his face grim as he gathered her up. She saw Prakash approaching and Narayan, and a handful of warriors and highborn, and priests who looked upon the bloodied court and the unconscious bodies of the guards at the door in horror.

"He tried to protect me," she ground out, forcing the words through pain, tears. "The priest—Kartik—he tried to save me from—from—"

"The Ahiranyi," one man said quietly, and the words rippled away from him, carried from one mouth to the next. The Ahiranyi. The Ahiranyi. The Ahiranyi witch.

"Someone find a physician," Khalil ordered. "Now, men. Go!"

Running again. And she was being carried. It hurt. It hurt.

Her work was almost done. Almost.

"He told me that if he must die, after all he has done to protect our empire from Chandra's malice, then I must live for the good of Parijatdvipa," Malini said. She allowed herself to weep. Her tears were not evidence of weakness now, but noble tears, brave tears. "The yaksa are coming, and I must live."

"Calm yourself, Empress," Khalil said, striding faster. His tunic was wet with blood. "A physician! *Quickly!*"

I was foolish, Malini thought bitterly, as her vision began to fade, and her body waver, *to ever think I could have Priya and also have this.*

61

MALINI

She woke in pain. That was no surprise. The surprise was waking at all.

The light filtered in, muted by silk screens drawn over the lattices. Rao was largely in shadow, but ah, what a relief for him to be there at all: sitting at her side, when almost everyone else she had trusted was gone.

Her heart felt deadened: Priya. Priya. Priya. It was not a howl but a muted grief that twisted through her, throbbing dully with her wound.

Kartik had told her it would kill her. But she had seen, at the end of a thorn blade, the exact limitations of what Kartik had known.

She sat up.

"Malini," Rao said. Leaden. Then he corrected himself. "Empress. I'll call the physician."

Rao's eyes were strange, almost fathomless. For a moment, as he leaned over her, she stared into them and saw no pupils, no sclera, only blazing fire—

Then he blinked, and his eyes were his own again.

A trick of the light, surely. A trick of her grieving heart.

"Rao," she whispered. "Tell me. How long have I slept?"

An exhale.

"Weeks," he said heavily. "Weeks and weeks. Your generals have been running the city. Lady Raziya, Lady Deepa, Lata—they've spoken for you. You woke, a few times. But you don't remember."

"No," she said. "No."

She looked at him. His tired, pinched face. The tremble of his jaw.

"Tell me," she said. "You have something to tell me."

He bowed his head.

"Malini," he said. "I'm so sorry. Your brother is dead."

"I know," she said dully. "I know."

"Not Chandra," said Rao. "Not only Chandra. I . . ." He swallowed. Lowered his head. "I'm sorry."

Malini stared at him, uncomprehending.

"No," she said.

"I'm sorry."

"No." She did not want to accept. Did not want to contemplate it. Ah, by the mothers, did she really have room for more grief in her? *"No."*

Rao's eyes were red, his voice scratchy. She had never seen his face like this before. Haggard beyond his years, and full of a grief so palpable it made her whole body want to recoil, to curl in on itself as if it could ward off the pain of that look, the pain that was seeping through her own blood and bone.

"It was—fire." He stumbled. "In battle. He made. Mothers' fire. True fire. He chose it."

He was still speaking to her, but she could not hear it. Noise. Nothing but noise. She turned her face away.

"The priest," she said thinly.

"The priesthood will want to speak with you eventually," he said. "They're demanding war with Ahiranya."

Of course they were. Malini did not think it would be difficult to give them what they wanted. Ahiranya, it seemed, wanted war with them too.

"Leave me, please," she said. He was silent for a moment. "Please, Rao," she said.

She would be herself tomorrow. She would don all her lies and armor tomorrow.

He touched his fingertips against her own. The lightest, kindest touch. And then he departed.

Her chest was bandaged. It hurt to move. And still, she pressed her hands to her eyes, her mouth, and wept.

She had never cried like this, guttural, full-throated sobs with nothing sweet or soft about them, nothing that would engender pity. She was howling like a beast. She wanted to rip apart the room. Rip apart her skin. The empire was hers, Parijatdvipa was hers, a pearl in her hand. She was empress of Parijatdvipa. And it was not enough. It would never be enough.

She'd wash her heart clean with grief. Wear it down to stone. And then tomorrow, and ever after—

A true war awaited her. She intended to meet it.

RAO

The men who had been in the fortress with him—the men who had watched Aditya die—were already spinning tales.

They told everyone that they had won the fortress because of Aditya's sacrifice. The fire howled its way through the halls, the men said. It burned the High Prince and all his men and all those loyal to him to death in agony, cleansing the maze fort, leaving nothing but Prince Aditya's loyal followers behind.

Rao had no choice but to believe them. He couldn't remember any of it. Only hands on his arms, guiding him along. Only salt on his own face, as he wept. Only silence, in the aftermath, where his heart had once been.

Prince Aditya was called by the mothers, the men claimed. The flames reached for him with the mothers' own hands—firm, loving, implacable. There had been no pain for Prince Aditya. The mothers had raised him up, as no man had ever been raised.

He had named his sister empress. Just as Rao had named her empress. Prince Aditya had died for her, just as a priest in Harsinghar had died for her, protecting her from the vile yaksa that had returned—perhaps they had even died in the very same moment, two holy deaths shielding Empress Malini from harm.

None of it was a lie. None of it was true, either.

Rao had been carried partway back to Harsinghar. Slumped in a chariot, no good to anyone. The severed yaksa arm rattling in its case beside him, a constant reminder of what he'd lost.

And then, somehow, he'd found the strength to sit up. The strength to drink himself into a stupor. The strength, then, to ride on his own horse, head pounding, his body riven with misery.

A day later, he'd learned from Mahesh how—and when—Chandra had died. Once Rao understood that Malini had seized her throne before he and Aditya had sieged the maze fort, before Aditya had turned the flames on himself, sure of his own destiny, his inevitable fate...

Well, Rao drank a great deal more after that. The journey was a blank space for him—a void where grief lived, and nothing else.

He did not even dream anymore.

Alori. Prem. Aditya.

He thought of Prem grinning at him over a bottle of wine. The shawl knotted at his throat. *Remember when were boys? Remember the games we played?*

Aditya, staring at him with peaceful eyes. Ready to leave him behind.

Alori, her crown of wooden stars burning as her hair ignited, as she screamed—

In the rest of the mahal, the soldiers who had returned with them were no doubt spreading the tale of what Aditya had done, and what he had made them vow to him in turn. In days, the story would be all over the city.

Perhaps they would raise up a statue of gold for Aditya, just as they had for Rao's sister. Perhaps all his loved ones would be nothing but effigies for Rao to gaze upon, and remember what he had lost.

Once he'd seen Malini he found a corner to be alone in. A veranda overlooking the training grounds where he and Aditya had once sparred. He leaned over the edge. Pressed his head to cool marble.

"Rao."

Lata's soft voice. Of course.

He raised his head. Her face was full of compassion.

"Rao," she said. "I'm so sorry."

"Don't be," he said reflexively.

"You were with the prince when he passed," she said, eyes still sorrowful.

He nodded once, silently.

"What did you see when he burned?" Lata asked. "Forgive me. I must ask."

"Must you?"

Lata stared back at him.

"Is this a sage's curiosity, Lata? Or something else?" She'd been tending to Malini, he knew. She looked tired.

"What else would it be?" Lata asked.

"A sage's curiosity, then," he said bitterly. "Tell me. What will the sages write about Aditya's death? Will they say now that my sister should not have burned on a pyre? That *I* should have?" He turned on her, hating how he felt. But he was unable to undo it. "All of this means nothing. Nothing."

"You don't mean that," she said.

"I do. I really do." The air wavered around her. He swallowed around the dryness of his mouth. "What do you really want from me, Lata?"

A pause. Lata drew closer, standing next to him on the veranda, her hands in the sun, her body in the shade.

"The Ahiranyi woman. Priya. She left someone behind. I...I do not believe she will be safe. With anyone else."

"Sima," he said. "You mean Sima. She *left* her?"

Lata nodded silently.

"Will you protect her, Rao? You liked her, I think."

"Well enough," he said. Exhaled. "Well enough." He tightened his grip on the edge of the veranda. "I don't want to care about anyone else, Lata. I'm not built for it. I can't."

Lata was silent.

"Fine," he said eventually. "I'll do it."

Lata nodded. "Thank you," she said.

He stared out at the horizon for a moment longer. Thought of the night when he and Aditya had drunk too much wine, and Aditya had discovered his calling in a monastery of the nameless. Remembered

Aditya laughing as they stumbled drunkenly to the gardens together, naming each star for each mother of flame. Slipping into riddles and poetry.

What is a star, he thought, in Aditya's slurred, smiling voice, *but distant fire, reaching for you across worlds?*

EPILOGUE

PRIYA

Malini,

Would it have been better if I had left you answers? Written you one final letter, and folded it into your trunk, or in your bed, in the place where I slept beside you?

Would it comfort you at all to know that I wanted to love you forever? That I wanted to be yours for the rest of my life? That I chose hurting you over letting you and everyone I love die?

Maybe not. Maybe it's better like this.

Hate me, Malini. Hate me and live. I can love enough for the both of us.

She walked alone. It felt like she was crossing the world.

It would have been easier if she'd felt more animal and less human. If she hadn't felt like herself—like a heartbroken failure—when she walked until her feet burned or slept mosquito-bitten under a black night sky. But she was still Priya. Still an ex-maidservant. Still a temple daughter.

She did not know if Malini was alive or dead. But she knew flowers grew wherever she stepped. She knew the rot sang to her, sang of inevitable comings, of births, of life returning where life had been lost.

She knew that sometimes sap pearled on her skin instead of sweat. She knew she had hollowed herself out for the yaksa, and the first of them, the oldest, had named her their beloved. Their priestess.

"Mani Ara," she whispered to the night. "Will you show me your face?"

The earth rippled around her and went still.

Not yet, then, Not yet.

She ate when she remembered to eat. She walked when she remembered to walk. She reached, in the sangam, for anyone and anything and found nothing. Echoes, rippling and never reaching her. No mask-keepers. No Bhumika.

Priya had never, ever been so utterly alone.

She made it to the edges of Ahiranya. Felt it calling to her, and stood upon the edges of its green. The sangam lapped at her feet. The green called out to her, watched her. The trees bent toward her at her approach.

At the base of the Hirana, she saw someone waiting for her.

Not Bhumika. Not Rukh. Not Billu, or scowling Khalida. Not straight-backed Kritika, or Ganam with his arms crossed.

Just one stranger.

Taller than any man should be, with hair wild, all leaves of silver, gold, green. The wind caught his hair and made it fly gracefully, made it coil around his face.

His face.

"Ashok," she whispered.

He gazed at her with a solemn expression that was not quite her brother's. Like her brother's face carved beautifully from wood. Like a mask.

"Priya," he said. "Sister. Welcome home."

The story continues in . . .

BOOK THREE OF
THE BURNING KINGDOMS

ACKNOWLEDGMENTS

The Oleander Sword was a hard book for me to write, and I would never have been able to finish it without the help, guidance, and sheer kindness of a whole army of people, including my wonderful agent Laura Crockett and the whole team at Triada US. Thank you to the entire team at Orbit US and UK, especially my amazing editor Priyanka Krishnan, Hillary Sames, Ellen Wright, Angela Man, Jenni Hill, Nazia Khatun, Anna Jackson, Tim Holman, Bryn A. McDonald, Amy J. Schneider, Casey Davoren, and Lauren Panepinto. Thank you, Micah Epstein, for the stunningly gorgeous cover art. And thank you to the team at Hachette Audio, and my audiobook narrator, Shiromi Arserio.

I have definitely forgotten someone, and to that person: Thank you. I'm sorry. I will buy you apology chocolates. Just let me know what you like.

I am very lucky to have such wonderful friends. Thank you to all of you (you know who you are, I hope) for being there for me. Especially my bunker pals, and also friends in London. Love and gratitude to my family, who were very nice to me through the entire book drafting process, even though it turned me into a gremlin. Thanks, especially, to my mum. And thanks, always, to Carly. You're the best of me.

Thank you to my readers for joining me for the second book in this series. I'm so glad you're here. I hope it wasn't too traumatic.

Finally, thank you to Asami, who was a writer's cat through and through, and sat with me every night while I worked on this book. I hope you're warm and safe in the great cat basket in the sky.

CAST OF CHARACTERS

Ahiranyi

Amina—Scribe
Anil—Villager
Ashok—Rebel against Parijatdvipan rule, temple son, deceased
Bhumika—Temple elder, ruler of Ahiranya
Billu—Cook in the household of the regent of Ahiranya
Bojal—Temple elder, deceased
Chandni—Temple elder, deceased
Dhiren—Villager, rot sufferer
Ganam—Mask-keeper, once-born, ex-rebel against Parijatdvipan rule
Jeevan—Captain of the guard to the elders of Ahiranya
Karan—Ahiranyi soldier
Khalida—Maidservant to Lady Bhumika
Kritika—Mask-keeper, ex-rebel against Parijatdvipan rule
Mani Ara—Yaksa
Nandi—Temple son, deceased
Nitin—Ahiranyi soldier
Padma—Daughter of Bhumika
Priya—Temple elder, ruler of Ahiranya
Rukh—Young servant in the household of the temple elders, rot sufferer
Sanjana—Temple daughter, deceased
Sendhil—Temple elder, deceased
Sima—Priya's friend, advisor

Aloran

Alori—Princess of Alor, attendant of Princess Malini, deceased
Rao—Prince of Alor

Viraj—King of Alor
Yogesh—Military administrator

Dwarali

Khalil—Lord of the Lal Qila
Manvi—Archer, guardswoman of Lady Raziya
Raziya—Highborn lady, wife of Lord Khalil
Sahar—Archer, guardswoman of Lady Raziya

Parijati

Aditya—Ex–crown prince of Parijatdvipa; priest of the nameless
Chandra—Emperor of Parijatdvipa
Deepa—Daughter of Lord Mahesh
Divyanshi—First mother of flame, founder of Parijatdvipa, deceased
Hemanth—High Priest of the Mothers of Flame
Kartik—Priest of the Mothers of Flame; faceless son
Lata—Sage
Mahesh—Highborn lord, loyal to Prince Aditya
Mitul—Priest of the Mothers of Flame
Malini—Empress of Parijatdvipa
Narina—Noble attendant of Princess Malini, deceased
Sikander—Previous emperor of Parijatdvipa, deceased
Sushant—Highborn lord; advisor to Emperor Chandra
Vikram—Regent of Ahiranya, deceased

Saketan

Ashutosh—Low prince of Saketa
High Prince—Ruler of Saketa
Kunal—Son of the High Prince; royal heir to Saketa
Narayan—Highborn lord
Prem—Low prince of Saketa, deceased
Romesh—Liegeman to low prince Ashutosh; rot sufferer
Varsha—Daughter of the High Prince, wife of Emperor Chandra

Srugani

Prakash—Highborn lord
Rohit—Highborn lord

extras

orbit

meet the author

Photo Credit: Shekhar Bhatia

TASHA SURI is the author of the Burning Kingdoms trilogy, the Books of Ambha duology, and the YA novel *What Souls Are Made Of.* She studied English and creative writing at Warwick University and is now a cat-owning librarian in London. A love of period Bollywood films, history, and mythology led her to write South Asian–influenced fantasy. Find her on Twitter @tashadrinkstea.

Find out more about Tasha Suri and other Orbit authors by registering for the free monthly newsletter at orbitbooks.net.

if you enjoyed
THE OLEANDER SWORD

look out for

THE CITY OF DUSK
Book One of The Dark Gods

by

Tara Sim

For every realm, there is a god.
For every god, there is an heir.
For every heir, there is a price.

The Four Realms—Life, Death, Light, and Darkness—all converge
on the City of Dusk. But the gods have withdrawn their favor
from the once thriving and vibrant metropolis. And without it,
all the realms are dying.

Unwilling to stand by and watch the destruction, the four heirs to
divine power—Angelica, an elementalist with her eyes set on
the throne; Risha, a necromancer fighting to keep the peace;
Nikolas, a soldier who struggles to see the light; and Taesia,
a shadow-wielding rogue with a reckless heart—will become
reluctant allies in the quest to save their city.

But their rebellion will cost them dearly.

I

Taesia Lastrider had never considered herself a good person, nor did she have any intention of becoming one.

She was fine with that. Beyond the confines of her House's villa, she was freer to do whatever she wanted. Be whomever she wanted.

The last breath of summer's heat coiled around her as she shifted in the shadow of a market awning. Shoppers were buying melon juice and sarab, a clear Parithvian alcohol served with a pinch of orange-colored spice that cooled the body down. Jewelry on a nearby cart glittered in the sunlight, cuffs of hammered silver and brass sending spangles into her vision. Taesia blinked and retreated even farther into the shade.

It put her in view of the building she had been adamantly trying to ignore. But it was almost impossible to overlook the size of it, the swirling, conch-like design of shimmering sandstone, the length of the shadow it cast across the city of Nexus.

It was quite lovely, for a prison. But crack that pretty shell open, and all its filth would come pouring out, the discarded and condemned souls of Nexus's convicts.

Someone bumped into her as they passed by, and the shadows twitched at her fingertips. She was so jumpy it took her a moment to realize it was merely a common thieves' tactic: make someone paranoid enough to pat their trousers or their sleeves to know where to strike later.

An amateur trick. It didn't matter there were more guards than usual patrolling the marketplace; pickpockets would take any chance they could get.

At the next stall over, a man was prying open boxes with a crowbar, chatting with the vendor as they checked the wares inside. "Would've gotten here sooner if I hadn't been held at the city gates," the man with the crowbar said. "Guards were sniffing around me like the dogs they are."

"King's got 'em on alert." The vendor glanced at the nearest guards and lowered his voice. "Had an incident not too long ago. Some weird magic shit went down near the palace."

"What kinda weird magic?"

"Wasn't there myself, but sounds to me like it was necromancy. Folks say a buncha spirits came and wrecked shit."

"*Spirits?* Were the Vakaras acting up? I've heard they can kill with just a snap of their fingers."

This caught Taesia's attention like thread on a nail. It was well known throughout Vaega—as well as beyond its borders—that those who made up House Vakara, descended from the god of death, were the only ones who possessed the power of necromancy. It was also well known that once in a while, a stray spirit managed to wander from Nexus's overcrowded necropolis to cause trouble.

But the incident the two men were gossiping about had been different: a sudden influx of violent spirits converging close to the palace square, destroying buildings and harming those unfortunate enough to be in their path. People had been rightfully terrified—and confused about who to blame.

"No idea," the vendor mumbled. "But it was nasty stuff. Heard a man got his arm ripped clean off. Whole city's gonna be tighter than a clenched asshole from now on."

A tremor rolled across her body as Taesia turned back to the Gravespire. When the vendor beside her wasn't looking, she grabbed a glass of sarab and downed it in one go, wiping her mouth with the back of her wrist.

Citizens blaming the Houses for their troubles wasn't anything new. But the thought of Risha getting caught up in it made her want to punch something.

The shadows twitched again. Impatience crackled at the base of her lungs, made her roll onto the balls of her feet as if poised on the edge of something reckless.

"Follow me," a low voice whispered behind her.

She breathed a sigh of relief and waited a couple seconds before turning and following her brother through the market. Dante was dressed down today in a long, sleeveless tunic with a hood, the lean muscle of his dusky brown arms on display. A few people pretended not to stare as he stalked by. Not in recognition, but in appreciation of his features despite the hood's shadow. Or maybe they were drawn to the smooth, confident way he moved, the way Taesia never seemed to get quite right.

"Did you get the information you needed?" she whispered.

"I did. We should be—"

She nearly ran into his back when he suddenly stopped. He lifted a hand for her to stay put.

She soon saw why. A couple Greyhounds had descended on a confused vendor. They were inspecting jars from her stall, dropping what didn't interest them to the ground. The vendor flinched at the sound of breaking pottery.

Taesia cursed under her breath. Although the vendor had no horns, the bluish dark of her skin and the white tattoos on her forehead marked her as a Noctan. Perhaps a mixed-race offspring from one of the refugees. Mixed blood would explain how she could stand to be in this heat in the middle of the day; most of the night-dwellers from Noctus couldn't bear it, often getting sunsick if forced to endure it for too long.

"Please, I have no contraband," the vendor said softly. They were beginning to draw spectators eagerly searching for a distraction from the heat. "These were all fairly traded within Vaega."

"We're not looking for foreign goods," one of the guards said.

His partner waved a small pot in his direction. The guard took it, sniffed, and scowled.

"Sulfur." The single word was leveled at the vendor like an arrow. "A Conjuration ingredient."

Taesia sucked in a breath. While many were eager to call the incident last week necromancy, the Vakaras had never been shy to demonstrate their magic, and their methods didn't line up with the attack. For in the ravaged spot where the spirits had congregated, something had been left behind: a cleverly drawn circle containing a seven-pointed star and a ring of strange glyphs.

Conjuration. An occult practice that hadn't been seen in decades.

The vendor shook. "I—I didn't know! I swear, I—"

The Greyhounds didn't waste time listening to her stammer. They shackled her wrists as excited murmurs ran through the small crowd they'd gathered.

"Wouldn't have bought from her anyway," someone muttered. "Anything the Noctans touch is tainted."

"Did they say Conjuration? Isn't that demon—?"

"Shh! The Greyhounds won't hesitate to haul you off, too."

"She should have stayed in the Noctus Quarter."

Taesia curled her hand into a fist. Dante grabbed her as she took a step forward.

"Don't," he said. Not a warning, but an order.

"We're responsible for the refugees."

"They're cracking down on Conjuration materials," Dante whispered. "If you interfere, think about how it'll reflect on the House."

She didn't give two shits about that. "You're saying you're all right with this?"

"Of course I'm not. But we can't do anything about it right now."

Taesia watched the guards haul away the vendor, who was trying and failing to stifle her terrified tears. Dante didn't let Taesia go until the tension left her body. When he did, she spun to face him. "Are you sure you want to go through with this? You said it yourself: We can't have anything negatively impacting the House." She dropped her voice to a murmur. "Especially considering what the Vakaras are going through. Even if you manage to find what you need, what are you going to do with it?"

"Not summon a horde of spirits, if that's what you're concerned about."

It wasn't—not really—but there was so much about Conjuration they didn't understand, since all the old texts had been destroyed.

"You want to put a stop to these scenes, right?" Dante nodded in the direction of the vendor's abandoned stall. "To not have to worry about House politics when it comes to issues like defending the people?"

She swallowed, certain her hunger for that very thing was plain on her face. "What does that have to do with Conjuration?"

"Indulge me a little longer, and you'll see." He paused, then leaned forward and sniffed. "Have you been drinking?"

"Don't worry about it."

They walked past the beehive hum of the crowd and continued on to the edge of the market, where four children were playing with a couple of dogs. A gangly man was slumped over a counter. He watched the children with an air of someone who probably should be worried about their safety but couldn't muster up the energy.

"I don't *want* to be Thana," one of the children was complaining in a nasal voice. "Thana's scary. I want to be Deia!"

"*I'm* Deia," said another child, a tall girl with dirt smudged across her face. "I'm always Deia."

"Just because you have weak earth magic doesn't mean you can be Deia every time," mumbled a boy with Mariian black skin. Judging by the crown made of twigs and sticks resting on the tight coils of his hair, he was supposed to play the part of Nyx, god of night and shadow.

"It's not weak!" With a flick of her finger, she flung a pebble at his forehead, making him cry out.

"You can be Phos instead," said the last child, likely the Mariian boy's brother. He handed the girl who didn't want to be Thana his toy wings made of fluttering leaves, which made her brighten. "And I'll be Thana. I'll put her in a cage of bones."

Taesia smiled wryly. It was common for children to play at being gods; she herself had done it with her siblings when they were younger. That was before they'd understood only one god demanded their family's piety.

Dante rapped his knuckles on the wooden counter, making the gangly man start. "Heard you have good prices," Dante said, his cautious inflection almost making it a question.

The corner of the man's mouth twitched. "Come see for yourself."

Dante glanced at the children, the dogs barking and chasing after them when they ran. "Will they be all right on their own?"

The man shrugged and headed toward the nearest alley. They were led away from the market to a building that had seen better days, with a tarp-covered window and weeds sprouting along its base. The man eased the door open and ushered them inside. A second door on the far end of the room was open, revealing a set of stairs leading down. Taesia's nose wrinkled immediately at the smell, a bitter blend of ash and pepper.

"Ruben," the gangly man called. "Customer." He left to return to the market.

A heavyset man in shirtsleeves appeared on the stairs, wiping his hands on a handkerchief. "Hello, hello. This way, please."

Dante kept his hood up as he and Taesia descended into a basement. It might have once been a wine cellar, cramped and cool. But instead of racks of wine, the place was now stocked with sacks of herbs and roots, boxes of chalk, and jars of sulfur. There was even a display of small knives along the wall.

Dante's eyes lit up the way Taesia imagined a librarian's would at finding a rare book for their collection. He began to wade through the assortment, peering into sacks and running his hands through unknown substances. Taesia meandered toward the knives and inspected one with a serpentine blade.

The man, Ruben, cleared his throat. "Let's keep this brief, yes? No guards saw you come this way?"

"Not that I'm aware of." Dante's voice was distant, the tone he got when someone tried to interrupt him. He picked up a jar and shook it, the black specks inside rattling. "What's this?"

"That would be powdered lodestone."

"And what does it do?"

"It's a magnetized bit of mineral, known for attracting iron. Rich deposits of it along the eastern coast."

"I'll take ten grams, as well as loose chalk." Dante paused before pointing at a nearby sack. "Throw in some hellebore root as well."

Taesia grimaced. For all his intelligence and charisma, her brother wasn't particularly skilled at pretending to be something he was not. The order strung through his words might as well have painted a broadsheet across his face reading *I'm a noble, can't you tell?*

Ruben didn't seem particularly affected by it either way. Taesia obediently held the sachet of hellebore root Dante handed to her while he tucked the vial of powdered lodestone and pouch of chalk into his own pockets. Coins exchanged hands, the clink of gold loud in the cellar.

"A pleasure," Ruben said with a sickly smile.

Taesia took a much-needed deep breath once they were back on the street. "Again, are you absolutely sure about this?"

"I'll be careful." Despite Dante's light tone, she noted the divot between his brows. He was nervous.

Spotting the tip of the Gravespire rising above the buildings, Taesia thought about the Noctan who had been hauled away and swallowed.

Nexus had once prided itself on harboring people from every country, every realm, to form an eclectic microcosm of their broad universe. Now it seemed as if they were doing their best to eradicate those who *didn't belong*, whatever that meant.

She was jolted from her thoughts when someone slammed into her and sent her crashing to the ground.

"Stop her!" someone shouted.

Taesia gaped up at the face staring down at hers. The girl couldn't have been much older than her, with lustrous black skin and a cloud of dark hair. She winked and scrambled off Taesia in a flash, slipping into the startled crowd like a fish.

Dante helped her up as a few Greyhounds ran by in pursuit. Taesia stared after the girl, rubbing a sore spot on her chest.

"You all right?" Dante asked.

"Yeah, I'm—" She checked her pockets. "She stole the hellebore root!" Not an amateur thief, then.

Dante shushed her. "It's fine, I can get by without—Tae!"

She charged after the thief with a fire kindled in her chest, stoked and restless since Dante had stopped her from interfering with the guards.

Finally, some damn action.

The Greyhounds were slowed by the crowd, but Taesia easily evaded limbs and bodies. The thief hoisted herself onto the roof of a stall, so Taesia did the same. She rolled across an awning and leapt onto the next roof, which swayed dangerously under her feet.

She lifted her hand. To anyone else, the silver ring on her fourth finger bore an onyx jewel, but the illusion broke when her shadow familiar spilled from the bezel and into her palm.

"Do something for me?" she panted as she leapt the space between two stalls.

Umbra elongated, forming a snakelike head of shadow. It tilted from side to side before it nodded.

Taesia flung out her hand and Umbra shot forward in a black, inky rope. One end lashed around the thief's wrist, making her stumble. With a sharp pull on Taesia's end, the thief crashed through an awning.

Taesia jumped down. The thief groaned and staggered away from cages full of exotic birds flapping their wings and squawking at the disturbance. The vendor gawked at them as Taesia summoned Umbra back to her ring and took off after the girl.

The last thing she wanted was for rumors of a Shade tussling in the market to reach her mother.

Taesia dove into a narrow alley to try and cut the thief off at the cross street, only to be met with an arm that swung out from around the corner. It collided with her chest and Taesia fell onto her back with a grunt.

The thief stood over her, breathless and smiling. "Well! Gotta admit, this is a first. Never stole from someone like you before."

Taesia coughed. "You punched me in the tit."

"And I'd do it again."

Taesia braced herself on the ground and kicked the girl in the chest, sending her reeling backward. "Now we're almost even."

The girl wheezed around a laugh. "Suit yourself."

Taesia sprang to her feet and charged. The thief ducked and hit her in the back, dangerously close to her kidneys. Taesia caught her arm and twisted. The thief stomped on her instep, making her yelp and let go.

"Whew!" The girl's face was alive with glee despite the dirt and sweat streaked across it. "Must've stolen something you care about."

"Not really." The shadows trembled around her, ready to be called in, but she couldn't risk it. She'd already been too careless using Umbra. "Just needed to stretch my legs today."

The girl barked a laugh as they circled. Her dark eyes flitted to the alley over Taesia's shoulder before a blow caught Taesia across the backs of her knees, sending her reeling forward.

As Taesia fell, a young woman—likely the thief's partner—ran to the nearest wall and made a broad swirling motion with her arms. Both of the thieves were caught in a sudden cyclone of wind that lifted them up onto the roof.

An air elementalist.

Cheater.

"Better luck next time," the thief called with a mocking salute. Taesia gave a rude gesture in reply, and the girl laughed before she and her partner disappeared.

A moment later, Dante burst out of the alley. "Taesia, what the *fuck*—"

"She got away."

"I don't care! I told you it didn't matter." He ran a hand through his hair, hood fallen across his shoulders. "You're filthy. We can't let anyone in the villa see you like this." He pointed a stern finger at her. "Do *not* do that again."

She wasn't sure if he meant chasing after thieves or using her shadow magic out in the open. Before she could ask, he turned and began the trek home, not even bothering to see if Taesia would follow.

Like always, she did.

Follow us:

/orbitbooksUS

/orbitbooks

/orbitbooks

Join our mailing list
to receive alerts on our
latest releases and deals.

orbitbooks.net

Enter our monthly
giveaway for the chance
to win some epic prizes.

orbitloot.com